MW01132798

Devil May Care

Book #2

The Veil Series

Pippa DaCosta

ISBN: 1497305012
ISBN-13: 978-1497305014

Paperback Edition.
US Edition.
Version 1.

Chapter One

I handed my Enforcer ID card to the police officer guarding the entrance to the apartment complex. Rainwater dripped into my eyes. I swept my wet hair back from my face and winced as a camera flashed somewhere to my right. Behind me, the press jostled against the black and yellow crime scene tape. I kept my head down, my collar up, and avoided eye contact. In the last six months, I'd escaped press attention, but other Enforcers hadn't been as lucky. They'd been consigned to desk jobs as a result. Officially, Enforcers didn't exist. Neither did demons. Unofficially, there was no smoke without fire, and the public knew it.

The cop shone his flashlight over my ID, highlighting the entwined scorpion motif. He flicked the beam into my face. I flinched away too late to prevent the tight white beam from bleaching my night vision.

"Enforcer, huh." The cop sniffed. Water dripped from his cap. "Your buddy's inside." He held out the card. As I reached for it, his grip lingered. "You must be tougher than you look."

I smiled and plucked my ID from his fingers, saluting him with it before ducking under another strip of tape and walking through the gates. I felt his gaze on me and resisted the urge to give him a single finger salute over my shoulder. He wasn't the first to underestimate me and wouldn't be the last. Flipping off an officer of the law was the sort of behavior my boss had recently suggested I refrain from. Again.

Inside the apartment building, a sprinkling of uniformed cops peppered the crowd and half a dozen forensic investigators suited up in protective coveralls. I recognized the hushed ambiance of most murders scenes— quiet respect. Nothing reminds us of our mortality quite like witnessing the aftermath of death. This was my day job.

I flashed my card at the officer at the bottom of the stairs and received a disinterested nod.

"Miss Henderson..." Detective Coleman wove his way through the crowd. "I'll take you up." The briefest tick of a smile fled across his lips.

"How you doin', Detective?" I struggled to warm my own smile. It takes a lot to earn my trust, and Coleman was no exception. He had noted my frosty demeanor when we'd first met, a few months before, but he hadn't taken offense. Unlike me, he was a professional.

"I'm good, Miss Henderson," he said flatly. He jogged ahead, ash-gray jacket rippling open, revealing a glimpse of his sidearm. He was lean in the way people are when they skip meals and survive on black coffee, but what he lost in body mass, he made up for in tenacity. We passed a few of the forensic team carrying bagged and tagged items. "Detective Hill is already on scene. Have you been briefed?" Small-talk was apparently off the agenda.

He had gained a few more worry lines around his eyes since I'd last seen him. "Only in so much as there's been a murder, and you believe it to be demon related. I was... indisposed when the call came in." We paused on the steps to let some cops pass.

Coleman's fingers instinctively twisted the wedding band on his left hand. Coleman had seen more demon kills than I'd had hot dinners, and I'd lived much of my life among demons. The Boston PD's go-to guy for demon related incidents, he handled the collateral damage until the Institute bulldozed in and covered it up with misinformation and distraction tactics. Tonight though, he was twitchy as hell.

We reached the third floor and emerged into a narrow wood-paneled corridor with numbered apartments either side. I saw Ryder— my partner-handler-sometime-babysitter—standing outside an apartment, thumbs hooked into the pockets of his faded black jeans. His scuffed leather jacket glistened from the rain. His wet hair had darkened to a hazelnut color and clung to his cheeks in places. He scratched at his stubble-dashed chin and nodded at something Detective Amanda Hill said.

Hill spoke quietly with her back to me. Her hands gestured around her like pale hummingbirds. She was petite, like me, but that's where our similarities ended. Hill was red-headed with a volatile temper to boot. Ryder referred to her as Scully in private, referencing a fifteen year old TV show. Fifteen years before, I'd been yanked from the netherworld, the only world I knew, and was learning how to talk like an American teen without growling my consonants.

Coleman greeted Ryder with a broad grin and eager handshake. He acknowledged Hill with an appreciative nod.

"Detective Coleman," Ryder drawled. "How's the Missus?" He leaned a shoulder against the doorframe.

Mention of Coleman's wife had the Detective twisting his ring again. "Julia is fine. Thanks for asking." He noticed his nervous gesture and tucked his hands into his pockets. "Have you been inside?"

"Nope, been waitin' for Miss Henderson." Ryder's sharp eyes fixed on me. His eyes gave him away. He might've looked like something washed up on a beach, but his eyes sparkled with an intelligence reserved for those who cared to look deeper. "You owe me a beer," he said, referring to our 'last-on-scene-buys-the-beers' ritual. I always lost.

I shrugged. "Got held up." When the call had come in, I'd been in the midst of a *Progress Report* with our head of department, Adam Harper, a man I detested with every part of my half-blood body.

Coleman reached for the closed door. "Let's get this done. Forensics will be finishing up. There's some evidence Miss Henderson will need to examine. Ready?" He opened the door.

I could smell the blood from the hallway. The metallic odor hung in the air and set my teeth on edge. Inside, the apartment wasn't anything special: framed pastel artwork, cream walls, a few rugs scattered over painted wooden floors, and an ultra-thin TV. No photos. The window blinds were closed, possibly to keep out the prying eyes of the press. A demon killing was front page material, much to chagrin of the Institute, who continued to try and sweep these events under a burgeoning rug.

As we neared a bedroom doorway, the pungent eye-watering odor of blood, excrement, and something worse clogged my nose and lodged in my throat. Something I knew well... burned flesh. My stomach rolled.

I followed the detectives inside, and my overwhelmed senses struggled to piece together a cohesive image of the scene. Papers, pictures, fragments of broken furniture had all been tossed about the room like the aftermath of a burglary. The forensic photographer on the opposite side of the room took a picture, and the resulting flash burned the room into my memory. Coleman was talking to Ryder, saying something about excessive violence, but their voices trailed off behind the silent scream bubbling inside my head. I wasn't going to freak out. Not yet.

I moved forward and felt my boot sink into something pliable. I glanced down and realized the shriveled strips of what looked like bacon belonged to what remained of the body on the bed. My stomach flipped over again, and I gulped back excess saliva. The body on the bed had been flash-burned; beneath the blackened skin, the flesh blushed pink. Whatever had burned him or her, had done so too quickly to scorch below the surface of the skin. Nothing else in the room had been touched by fire. Nothing quite points the finger at a demon perpetrator like the roasted pork smell of charred flesh.

"We initially thought perhaps a minor explosion," Coleman explained. Hill stood bolt upright beside him, lips pinched into a thin line. "But the splatter pattern rules that out. See how the arc of blood behind the bed indicates the victim had time to struggle?"

I followed the detective's gaze up the wall and wished I hadn't. I didn't sign up for this. Come to think of it, I didn't sign up at all.

"Torture?" Ryder asked.

"In all likelihood."

I coughed, attracting a few concerned glances, and lifted a hand, indicating I was not about to empty the contents of my stomach all over a crime scene. Tentatively stepping forward, boots crushing paper and glass with each step, I approached the bed. Blood had dried to rust-red on the sheets. Papers and what looked like the pages from a book had fallen into a sticky pool of blood beside a bedside cabinet. So much blood...

I followed a dangling arm to where it hung from what remained of a shoulder. I saw the charred ghost of a tattoo and recognized it instantly as the scorpion motif on my ID card.

"He's an Enforcer?"

None of the three faces looking back at me appeared surprised.

"*She* is. Newly qualified," Ryder said. "A sleeper."

A sleeper was an Enforcer who was not yet on active duty, likely fresh out of training. My lip curled. Ryder's clinical choice of words grated on my already sensitive nerves. "Anything else you'd like to tell me, or shall I continue to stumble in the dark?"

Detective Hill coughed into her gloved hand. "Actually, we were hoping you could tell us something." Her voice pitched higher than her normal, authoritative monotone.

The forensic photographer shuffled past me, muttering an apology. The distraction allowed me to move back from the corpse and return to Ryder's side. Hill glanced at Coleman, who glanced at Ryder. They would have been comical if not for the grim circumstances.

"What?" I sensed their reluctance.

Ryder scratched his forehead. He pinched his lips closed and then met my gaze. "They want you to read something."

Here came the truth and the reason why I was here: not for my questionable talents as a newbie Enforcer, but for my unique skill when it came to 'reading' metals. Hill looked apologetic, her porcelain face cut in a frown, while Coleman wouldn't meet my eyes. I knew why. Someone had told the two detectives what I could do, and with it came the knowledge of what I was. A half-demon Enforcer didn't sit well with Coleman. On another night, I might have been able to sympathize with his short-sighted prejudice, but the evening appeared to be getting worse, and I was in no mood to pussyfoot around his feelings.

I gave them an overly eager grin. "Let's get on with it."

We filed out of the room. Hill conferred with one of the forensic team, and I tucked my hands deep inside my jacket pockets. Ryder tried to catch my eye while Coleman had decided to put as much distance between him and me as possible. So this was how it was going to be: use the half-blood for her peculiar party tricks. I should have expected it. I'd been used to it most of my life. Why should things change now?

Ryder approached just as Hill collected a large, clear garbage bag from one of the forensic team and turned toward me. Inside the bag I could make out a metal chain with links as thick as my forearm.

"You okay with this?" Ryder asked, not quite meeting my eyes.

"Sure thing." My gaze locked on the bag. Something about the chain... It tugged on buried memories. Smears of blood on the inside of the bag obscured the contents, but I couldn't shake the sensation of familiarity.

"I know you've not done this since—"

I glared at Ryder, silently daring him to mention the events of six months ago when I'd been foolish enough to read a sword and witness the metal-memory of my ex-demon-lover killing a good friend. Before Ryder could elaborate, Hill unceremoniously dumped the bag on the floor at my feet.

She straightened and flicked her hair out of her face. "Work your magic." She gestured absently and stole a few hasty steps back, as though my half-demon nature might be contagious.

It wouldn't take long, and the quicker I could get it over with, the better. I'd learned that dragging these things out didn't lessen the impact of whatever secrets lay hidden.

"Do you need anything to help with the...y'know?" Hill asked.

I ignored her and crouched down, knees cracking. I opened the seal on the bag. The smell of wet metal burned my nose and laced my throat. I turned my head away and steeled myself against a few wayward memories. Snippets from my past tugged at my carefully placed mental restraints. The chain, the blood. They meant something on a personal level, but I couldn't allow the thought to surface. Not here. My memories were dangerous territory, best kept hidden, especially in the company of others.

"I'm sorry," Hill said.

I looked up at the detective and snorted. "Sorry that you're making me do this, or sorry that I'm half demon?" She pulled back with a frown. I could have been kinder, but that would've meant admitting how afraid I was. "I'm going to have to get my blood on this for it to work..."

"Go ahead." Hill locked her arms across her chest, her face impassive. She wouldn't make the mistake of offering me insincere niceties again.

Ryder handed me a Leatherman. I used the knife to cut my finger and watched the blood swell until it dripped into the palm of my hand. *Make her bleed. Make her read...* I hissed as the memory bubbled up through my efforts to keep them all submerged in the dark pool of my subconscious. I'd not heard that little nugget for a long time. I blinked rapidly and steadied my breathing. I had a job to do, and refusing to read the chain didn't even cross my mind.

I smeared blood over my hands and held them over the bag.

"Muse..." My real name slipped from Ryder's lips as I plunged my hands into the bag and wrapped my fingers around the links.

A rush of images flooded through me, over me, and spilled into my mind. The apartment, Ryder, Hill, the dead Enforcer—all of it vanished beneath a stream of information. Unable to look away or block the torrent, I saw a face in profile, male by the set of the jaw and the solid rise of the cheekbone. Dark hair, too long, past his shoulders. Something inside my subconscious chimed alarm bells, but the image swept away before I could focus. More pictures rushed me. Calloused gray fingers tipped with razor-edged claws curled around the chain. The links rattled. I saw the victim. Her eyes bulged, and her mouth gaped. She clawed at the chain around her throat. Her killer responded by tightening it. Her face contorted, lips blue, cheeks swollen, and then he tugged the chain free, twisting her head at an unnatural angle. Those claw-tipped fingers dragged down her face, furrowing her cheek. The demon straddling her leaned in and nuzzled his taut face against hers. He breathed in her scent. His body quivered, and a moan dragged from between his lips.

You are mine, Muse. His words chewed up inside a growl, and he spat them out.

Wrenched from the vision and back into real-time, I fell back onto my arms. Ragged gasps came hard and fast. My heart drummed against my ribs. Tremors wracked me, memories of agony and shame manifesting in my muscles. A scream clawed up my throat in a bid for freedom. I couldn't control any of it. If I'd had access to my demon, she'd have come barreling forward, but she was gone. I was alone with the horror. Ryder reached for me, but I batted his hand away. If he touched me, I didn't trust myself not to lash out at him.

Before he could ask me what was wrong, I was on my feet and running. I shoved though the doorway and past Coleman, ignoring his shouts of alarm. My boots hammered on the stairs as I stumbled down them. I staggered down the last few steps, barged between some uniformed officers, and burst through the front doors into the courtyard.

Rain pattered gently against my face. The cool night air nipped at my flushed cheeks. The chill grounded my thoughts back where they belonged, in the here and now. I stumbled a few more steps and reached for the wall. My stomach dry-heaved as my body tried to rid itself of the ghastly sensations. Coughing, spluttering, I waited for the violent urge to vomit to pass.

It wasn't long before I noticed Coleman loitering in my peripheral vision. He glanced over at the gate where the press hounded any passing cop. I kept my head low and focused on subduing my tremors. The physical effects of terror would eventually subside. The same couldn't be said for the images or the memories.

"What did you see?" He moved closer. I winced at the sound of his shoes crunching on gravel. It all seemed too loud, too abrasive, too acute.

Ryder jogged into sight. "Hey." He jerked his chin at Coleman. "Back off."

Coleman swept an arm at me. "She obviously saw what happened. We need answers. The Institute is sitting on this, Ryder. I need answers before the demon who's doing this starts targeting the public."

"I know that. Charlie'll give you answers. Just give her a second." Ryder stepped into Coleman's personal space, deliberately squaring up to him. They were matched in height, but that was where the similarity ended. If it came to blows, Ryder would fight dirty, and Coleman wouldn't see it coming.

A camera flash blanched the front of the apartment complex, capturing the three of us in the midst of our heated discussion. Coleman finally backed down. He turned away from Ryder and approached the entrance. "May I remind you leeches we're in the middle of an investigation here and do not need—" The press came alive like hungry chicks squabbling in a nest.

"Is it true this is the third Enforcer killed in the last three weeks?"

"What's the victim's name?"

"Is it linked to last week's attacks?"

My labored breathing drowned out the cacophony of squawking reporters. I bowed my head. My stomach and throat worked to undermine my efforts at suppressing my gag reflex. Rainwater streamed through my hair and down my face, masking my tears. If I let them, the memories would chew me up and spit me out a shivering muttering mess. I couldn't allow them purchase. The feeling would pass, the horror would fade, and I could go back to pretending I was perfectly fine.

I sniffed and dabbed at my nose. When my hand came away, a smear of blood stood out in stark contrast against my pale skin. I quickly wiped it away and checked that Ryder hadn't seen. He hadn't. He was still scowling after Coleman. If he suspected I was unfit to continue my training, I'd soon find myself locked away like a lab rat. Again.

Ryder noticed me watching him and gave me a nod. I bobbed my head in response. He never had been one for personal chats, preferring actions to words, but he cared, and in what remained of my world, he was the only one who did.

Chapter Two

At the Stone's Throw bar, the TV chatted to itself in the corner. The jukebox hadn't worked for months, and the owner, Ben Stone, had been promising to fix the pool table just as long. Besides me and a lone guy nursing a Bud at one of the tables, the Stone's Throw was empty. The warm beer and cold atmosphere probably had something to do with the lack of customers.

"... the body of a twenty eight year old woman found on Lancer Drive this evening has been identified as Karen Jackson. Boston PD has released a statement that they are following a number of leads and do not believe the general public is in any immediate danger..."

I peered through narrowed eyes at the TV. The report flashed up an image of Coleman with his hand out as though directing traffic with the silhouettes of Ryder and myself in the background. Thankfully, we were too poorly lit to be identified. An Enforcer's biggest asset was his or her anonymity. Demons aren't stupid. They're ignorant to begin with, but if they're smart enough to cross the veil and settle here, they're intelligent enough to cover their tracks. They know the Enforcers are looking for them.

One such demon played on my mind.

You are mine, Muse.

It couldn't be him. It wasn't possible.

Ryder joined me at the bar. He hailed the bartender with a wave. "Two beers. She's buying." He jerked a thumb at me.

I gave the bartender a nod. Last one on the scene buys the beers. It had been that way since Ryder had been assigned as my mentor.

Ryder eased himself onto the stool next to me. He got comfortable, toyed with a coaster, rustled in his pockets for some gum, cursed when he couldn't find any, and then finally met my gaze. "So, lil' firecracker, you gonna tell me what the hell went down back there?"

My brief smile died. "I lost it." That was the truth—not all of it, but enough.

The bartender planted our beers in front of us. I took a drink from the bottle and wished Ryder had ordered something stronger. From experience, I knew drinking myself into a stupor wouldn't lessen the horrors, but old habits die hard. "It's not easy. The images are real. The smells, the sensations... I'm right there in the middle of it. I watched her die." He didn't need to know it went even deeper than seeing her murder. The unfiltered thrill had rippled through the demon and slithered through me. Her death had aroused him. I'd touched on glee, on physical excitement, on his unwavering sense of power and control. He wasn't concerned about being caught and hadn't cared for the woman he'd killed. She meant nothing to him, not even in death. It wasn't about her; it had been all about him. He had all the hallmarks of a sociopath—most demons do—but he'd taken it to a whole new level. At least, that's what I *knew* about him. I pushed my beer away and leaned on the bar.

Ryder took a swig of his beer and glared at the bottle as though it had all the answers. "You've seen some shit, Muse. I know you have. The Institute, they just tell me what I need to know, which is a damn sight more than you've ever said, but I ain't blind."

Ryder was the Institute's spy, my handler, put in place to report back on every word, every wrong move, every utterance I made. It was an uncomfortable fact that Ryder worked for my enemy, but then so did I. It had been so long since they'd captured me that I'd almost become accustomed to it all. Almost.

"I served. Ten years ago. Before the Institute," he said. "I've seen the same look in your eyes that I've seen in guys fresh from the killing fields."

I slid my gaze toward him. I hadn't known he was ex-military. He didn't seem the sort. Weren't they all steely-eyed hardasses? But then I'd not really been paying attention, much too caught up in my own crap to notice. Ryder could do steely-eyed, and he was definitely a badass if you happened to be of the demonic persuasion.

He met my stare, unblinking.

"I freaked," I said again, adding a shrug. I wanted to tell him. We could prop up the bar, and I'd spill my guts until dawn. When it was over, he'd look at me differently. He'd pity me, and I couldn't stomach that, not from him, or anyone. I didn't want pity. I wanted to forget.

He nodded, but the smallest twitch of an eyebrow told me he didn't believe me. We often pretended everything was fine for the sake of the necessary reports, but we both knew it was a lie. It was the same whenever Stefan's name came up—my one-time fling who'd simultaneously tried to kill me and save me. He was dead, or so the Institute wanted me to believe, and that's what Ryder reported. Also a lie. I was so sick of lies, and I couldn't seem to escape them.

"Did you get a look at the demon?" Ryder fell back on facts before things got too bleary eyed and emotional.

I teased the edges of the beer label with my nail. "Yeah, a little. He's male. Long hair, dark, almost black... His face was thin, too thin..." I tried to recall the image but it skipped just out of reach, the details frustratingly elusive. In the memory, I'd seen fragments of the demon's human vessel and also his true demon appearance. I suspected he'd arrived at the victim's apartment looking every part the mortal man. "He must have tricked her somehow. There's no way he could have entered that apartment without an invite."

"So he's a higher demon?"

I nodded. Higher demons cannot physically enter a home without an invite. Something about the chaos energies they wield blocks them. However, once they're over the threshold, the game changes. The inexperienced Enforcer made a mistake, one which had cost her her life. She should have known better. Her training would have prepared her, taught her how to weed out the demons in their human-suits. Maybe she hadn't expected one to come knocking on her door. Nobody does.

"Did you get a sense of his element?"

I shook my head. "No, it was too quick."

"The body was burned... Have we got a fire elemental here?"

I shook my head and added a shrug for good measure. He'd burned the body as a message to me. A reminder of my sins.

"Did he say or do anything that might help track him?"

I pursed my lips then looked down at my beer. "No. Nothing. I only get the moment the metal comes into contact with the victim, and talking wasn't on his mind..." *You are mine, Muse.*

Ryder considered my answers for a few seconds before he turned to face me and tried to hook me with his gaze. I wouldn't—couldn't—meet his eyes.

"Because this demon... he's killing Enforcers," he said. "Butchering them. If you know anything, you'd tell me... Right?"

I wanted to. I should. I knew that. A better woman probably would have told him everything. I'd never been a good woman. I didn't have it in me. All I could do was try to keep panic from spilling into my mind. I wanted to run. I wanted to run so damn fast and hide in the darkest corner where nobody would find me. I may not have been a good woman, but I wasn't a coward. I wouldn't run.

You are mine, Muse.

Ryder sat very still and waited for me to tell him the truth. This was my chance to come clean and admit I knew the demon who'd killed that woman. *Right now. Say it. Just say the words, and it will all be out in the open.* But the truth lodged somewhere in my mind and didn't reach my vocal cords. If I told Ryder who the demon was, he'd have no choice but to report it to the Institute, and I'd be taken off the job 'for my own safety.' I couldn't afford another stint behind bars. I needed my demon back if I was going to go after Stefan, and to get her back, I had to play the Enforcer game without fault. I didn't want to delve into my past. I couldn't face it all again. Not now. Not ever. I'd locked it all away in my head for a reason.

"I'm calling it a night." I tossed some cash on the bar and slid from the stool, avoiding Ryder's glare.

"You're gonna have to tell them sooner or later," he called after me. I zipped up my jacket as I shoved through the door. It swung shut behind me, cutting off Ryder's muffled curse.

Chapter Three

Living at the Institute was like living at a minimal security prison. Sure, I could come and go as I pleased, but everything I did was logged. Everything I ate, every book I read from the on-site library, every conversation—all of it meticulously recorded. It's why I tried to avoid checking-in unless I had to. At least the weekly medical exams had been reduced to monthly. Psych evaluations remained a weekly necessity. I had yet to convince the powers-that-be that I was mentally stable. I knew something they didn't; I hadn't ever been mentally stable, and it was unlikely I ever would be. I grew up a half-human, half-demon female on the wrong side of the veil where the strong ate the weak. I had control issues, enough emotional baggage to excite a team of psychiatrists, and—thanks to my demon half—a penchant for snap decisions driven by instinct. And that was when my demon was subdued. When she came to the party, I was as stable as a nuclear reactor on meltdown. She wasn't coming back any time soon though. Six months before, the Institute had subdued my demon. It felt like a lifetime.

My demon was half my soul. When the Institute incarcerated me, they'd locked her away by pumping me full of the drug PC34. If administered to lesser demons, those without conscious thought, it knocked them out, but if given to a half blood, like me, it overwhelmed the demon, chasing it away as though it never existed. The Institute used PC34 to control me and ensure I did exactly as they asked. It worked.

I'd considered bailing many times, but if I had any hope of getting my demon back and rescuing Stefan from the netherworld, I would need my demon. They—or more specifically Adam—had me dancing to his tune like a wind-up musical monkey.

My carbon-copy apartment at the Institute didn't have any windows. The entire Boston operation was housed in a vast warehouse complex, and few rooms had the benefit of natural light. At first, I'd hated its generic furnishing and landscape pictures, but hate and I had come to an understanding of late. Better to move on than harbor hate. Once I'd realized that, life wasn't so bad. I still had room in my heart to hate one man.

Adam Harper, Head of Operations, had been trying to reach me on my cell phone since I'd left the bar. Now that I was back at HQ, he would send one of his minions to collect me, but I liked to keep him waiting. I showered, washed the blood from my hands, and dressed in jeans and short-sleeved black tee. Scrunching my hair in front of the bathroom mirror, I noticed a dribble of blood running down my top lip. I wiped it away and dabbed at my nose. My hand came away bloody as it had at the crime scene. Okay, this wasn't normal. Snatching a few tissues, I bunched them against my nose until the bleeding stopped. *Probably stress.*

The phone rang, startling me. It would be Adam's summons. He wasn't going to stop hounding me until I'd answered his questions.

***

Adam Harper was like your best friend's father, all smiles and fake greetings, but you never really knew him. He was as cold as a slab of concrete and just as stubborn. He didn't look up when I entered his office. With his glasses pinched in his right hand, he didn't even lift his gaze to acknowledge me. I sat myself at his claw-footed desk and listened to the tick-tock of the wall clock. His office smelled of old books and leather, the sort of nostalgic scents you'd associate with libraries. It should have been comforting, but I'd always felt slightly uneasy at his desk, and it wasn't just the man. Perhaps it was the muffled quiet; I'd never liked the quiet. The netherworld was quiet, until it wasn't.

Adam continued to read the report spread in front of him. He rubbed a thumb across his lips but otherwise didn't move. Finally, he flipped the file closed and looked up.

"Muse."

"Adam." I shifted position in the large leather seat.

"Detective Coleman requires your written report on his desk within the hour."

Does he now? I drew in a deep breath and exhaled slowly. "Detective Coleman can do his own police work." I chose my words carefully; the ones in my head hadn't been nearly as polite.

"He is. A murder has been committed. The perpetrator is, in all likelihood, demon. Therefore, it is the assigned Enforcer's responsibility to assist the police department by all means available to him or her. Would you like me to remind you of your obligations? Again?"

"Sure, I've got all night. Hit me with 'em one more time."

He glared at me. "You will be a capable Enforcer, Muse—you just have to swallow your attitude."

I didn't want to be an Enforcer. I wanted my demon back. I wanted Stefan back. I wanted my damn life back. But we'd had that discussion so many times I no longer needed to say the words.

It was the middle of the night, and I'd already been hauled in front of Adam earlier in the evening before visiting the crime scene. I'd never been known for my patience, and what little I had was wearing thin. I tapped my fingers on the arm of the chair. "When were you going to tell me three Enforcers were dead?"

"When you needed to know." Adam's straight face made his answer seem perfectly reasonable. Perhaps to him, it was. At least I knew exactly where I stood with Adam: right under the sole of his shoe.

"Ryder knew."

Adam finally straightened. He slipped his glasses back on, took a few moments to consider his reply, and leaned back in his chair. "Ryder tells me you're withholding information. So I have to ask myself why that would be. You've been reasonably compliant until now. Something about this case has struck a nerve, and given Ryder's report—" He tapped the file in front of him. "I suspect it's something to do with what you read in that chain."

I looked away and admired his collection of books without really focusing on them. Ryder had told him everything. I shouldn't have been surprised or bothered by it, but I was. I made a mental note to lie more convincingly to Ryder in future. Sometimes, when you sleep with the enemy, waking up is the hardest part. It was all too easy to forget why I was there. *Play their game. Get my demon back.*

Facing Adam, I swallowed the unexpected knot of anger working its way up my throat. "I saw a demon kill a woman. He strangled her with a chain before... tearing into her."

Adam held my gaze, his soft brown eyes deceptively beguiling. He had no right to look so accommodating when I knew the sort of man he really was; the sort who sacrificed his own son in the name of science, the sort who used his daughter to entrap a Prince of Hell. I'd known demons more human than Adam Harper.

"So the demon is male. Would you like to tell me anything else about him?"

I ground my teeth. I could tell Adam exactly what I'd seen and more. If the demon turned out to be who I suspected, I knew him in the most intimate ways possible. He'd beaten me to within an inch of my life on a regular basis. You don't get much more intimate than that. I knew how he stole pleasure from the suffering of others. Pain excited him. He reveled in destroying defiance and dominating those he thought below him. If I let myself think about it, I could recall how he'd raped and beaten me until I'd fled my own conscious thoughts and withdrawn to the darkest parts of my subconscious. If I let myself remember.

My stomach tightened. I swallowed back the acrid taste of bile. *You are mine, Muse.*

"Three of my Enforcers in three weeks." Adam paused to let those words hang in the quiet around us, a quiet punctuated only by the ticking clock. "This isn't an accident. He has a source inside the Institute. I've done what I can and locked down the necessary files, but your name could well be on his list."

My real demon name wouldn't be, otherwise he'd have already found me. "I'll tell you," I said, flicking my head up, "if you give my demon back."

Adam's lips twitched. "You're not ready."

"Bullshit. I've done everything you've asked of me."

"Muse, you're too dangerous. I can't sanction the return of your demon until I'm convinced you won't tear this place down around me. You know that."

"You're an asshole." Eloquent, that's me.

My insult barely scratched him. He'd heard worse from me. "You're looking at another six months before I can even consider restoring you—"

I jerked out of the seat and slammed my hands down on the desk. "Give me my demon back, and I'll tell you what you need to know. Until then, I'm not telling you a damn thing."

He looked up at me. "People are dying, Muse."

"And I'll be one of them if you don't restore me."

Chapter Four

The workshop lights buzzed and blinked on, one by one. The carcass of a 1970s Dodge Charger occupied most of the room, although a dust-sheet protected the car's identity and dignity. A breeze gusted in through the open door behind me and rippled the sheet. Dust bellowed into the air.

Adam's words rang in my head as I hesitated in the doorway. *People are dying...* Telling the Institute about my past wouldn't save anyone, but it could get me locked up, and I couldn't afford for that to happen. The workshop looked exactly as it had the day Stefan left. Ryder hadn't attempted to clear it, and he wasn't brave enough to broach the subject with me. So it stayed a moment captured in time. A tactile memory. A sanctuary.

I stepped over the threshold and into my past. Sometimes, buildings are ripe with so much history, that memories crowd the air. Stefan's workshop felt that like that. I could almost hear his voice from the back office, that dangerous tone lifted only by his crooked smile. I ached to see that smile again, to hear his voice for real.

I pinched the sheet and flicked it back. The Charger had been stripped to bare metal. The panels were missing, and the interior had been gutted. The car was little more than a skeletal chassis. Stefan had been restoring it when he'd crossed the veil.

I ran a hand over the cold metal frame and plucked Ryder's Leatherman from my jacket pocket. A little blood would seal the link between my physical being and the memories in the metal. I reopened the cut I'd made at the crime scene and rubbed my bloody fingertips together. As soon as my fingers made contact with the chassis, a barrage of images cascaded over me. *Sunlight streamed in through the double doors. Dust motes danced in the air. Stefan lay on his back beneath the car with one leg drawn up. His loose, faded and torn blue jeans sported a few smudges of oil across the thighs. I couldn't see his torso, hidden as he was beneath the car, but I heard his voice.*

"I didn't say that. I said... I'd like to see you try." The familiarity of his voice wrapped around me like a security blanket. Nothing fazed him. He was a half-blood like me, but he'd known the truth about a half-blood's limitless power, whereas I'd had a lifetime of lies stacked atop one another, creating a mountain of self-disgust.

Ryder's image shimmered into view as he leaned against the car. His hair was longer and his eyes brighter. He teased a toothpick around his lips with his tongue then plucked it free and used it to punctuate his words. *"I could, y'know. They're ugly bastards, but they're slow. Distract it— that's where you come in—and I'd have it running back through the veil in a heartbeat, cryin' for its bitch of a mother. If it has a heartbeat. Do they have heartbeats?"*

"Two." Stefan chuckled from beneath the car. *"How you've survived this long is a mystery."*

"Professionalism..." Ryder grinned. *"Or luck."*

Stefan shoved himself out from under the car. His image wavered as he let go of the metal, but it came sharply back into focus as he leaned against the chassis. He wore a snug-fitting white tank top, torn in places, and carried himself with a relaxed fluidity that seemed at odds with his lean muscular build. I knew his body intimately, the ripple of his abs, the strength and power coiled in the muscles of his arms. Wiping his hands on a rag, he arched an eyebrow at Ryder. *"If you ask me, your partner has a lot to do with your success rate."*

Ryder blustered and grinned. *"What? Hey, if I remember right, I saved your ass on that last call. You were too busy buttering-up the victim's daughter to notice the demon wasn't dead. I told yah, you gotta check the son's-of-bitches by poking them in the eye. If it ain't dead, it'll damn well blink."*

"C'mon, poke it in the eye? Next, you'll be tellin' me they can't breathe if they stop moving." Stefan's chuckle stirred an ache within me I thought had died months ago. As he tossed the dirty rag at Ryder's head, I focused on his eyes. Startling in their clarity, the azure radiance of those winter-sky eyes never failed to entice me. I knew the power at his core, the bitter chill of his ice element. But despite the immense amount of chaos energy he was capable of wielding, he hadn't been cold.

Reluctantly, I withdrew from the images and lifted my hand from the car to sever the link to the past. The brilliant sunlit workshop dulled to somber dust-covered reality. The retreat of the warm memory left me shivering. The ghost of Stefan's voice lingered for a few beats, but that faded until only the sounds of my breathing and the murmur of the city outside remained.

A weighty sadness siphoned the strength from my limbs. It had been a mistake to delve into the past. The memories only served to remind me of what I'd lost—of the mistakes I'd made.

A splatter of blood dripped onto the dust sheet, followed by another. I felt wetness on my top lip and tasted the coppery twang of it in my mouth and grunted a curse. Pain lashed up my spine, and a cry burst from my lips. I staggered back and bumped into the workbench, rattling the tools. A second slice of agony rode up my spine. This one turned my legs to liquid and dropped me to my knees. Blazing heat burned through my limbs and radiated up my back, over my shoulders, before drilling through my very core. The agony built, crawling beneath my skin as though it could burn my flesh from my bones. A third wave broiled up. Fire rolled across my flesh. I had a moment to realize my element had somehow broken through the Institute's drug-induced cage before the surge of chaos energy snatched my consciousness away.

Chapter Five

The beep of a heart monitor punctured my dreams and hauled me from the depths of unconsciousness. My thoughts still slumbered, reluctant to make sense of the scene around me. I tried to lift my arm but couldn't. Someone was holding me down. *Damien, no...* I gasped and jerked up. I was at the Institute. The heart monitor's sound accelerated, attracting my blurry gaze. A bank of monitors blinked and flashed down at me. Graphs jumped, and numbers ticked. I tried again to lift my hand. When it refused to move, I peeled my head from the pillow and saw why. Leather restraints fastened me to the bed. From my right wrist, an intravenous drip wove its way up my arm to a clear bag suspended beside me.

Ryder slouched asleep in a chair, his leg stretched out, and his head back. I swept my gaze around the small room as my molasses thoughts gradually organized themselves. I was in the Institute's medical facility. A normal hospital wouldn't have had a one-way observation window.

"Hey, Ryder." My voice came out more a hoarse growl than actual words.

Ryder woke with a start, saw me glaring at him, and smiled a sleepy not-quite-there grin. He sat forward and pulled a hand down his unshaven face to drag away the vestiges of sleep. "You look pissed."

I tugged on the restraints and arched an eyebrow. "You have about three seconds to untie me before I lose my cool."

His smile grew, and his eyes brightened. He'd actually been worried, which in turn worried me. What exactly had happened? He glanced at the vast mirrored window then back at me. His smile faded away. I wasn't getting out of here.

Dropping my head back, I scowled at the mint-green ceiling. The light wavered, and the room tilted. I blinked to refocus. "What did they give me?"

"Somethin' to keep you calm." Ryder bowed his head, finding his hands fascinating rather than meeting my eyes. "What happened?"

"I have no idea. How did I get here?" I remembered the workshop and mining the metal of the unfinished Dodge for memories but nothing else.

"I found you at the workshop."

I hadn't imagined the tremor in Ryder's voice. Nor did I imagine the worry lines pinched around his eyes. For once, he met my gaze and didn't attempt to hide his concern. Whatever he had seen, it scared him.

"I'm fine." I tugged on the restraints. "Or I would be if they'd let me out." A quick scolding glance at the window cleared my thoughts. I had no idea if anyone watched us, but it was likely. They were always watching.

Ryder rose from the chair, knees cracking. Considering that he always looked like he'd just rolled out of bed, he'd upped his game. His wrinkled shirt, rolled up sleeves, and creased jeans were the smartest thing about him. His ruffled hair jutted out in tufts, and his usually bright eyes were ringed red and bloodshot. "They reckon your demon is trying to... break out. That ain't ever happened before. Not during their experiments with Stefan, anyway. They..." A quick glance at the windows. "The docs aren't sure how to deal with it."

I snorted a laugh. "If my demon is trying to break through, I'd know it. She doesn't *try* to do anything. She does it."

Ryder shrugged. I frowned and instinctively reached into the void inside where my demon had once coiled like a cat in front of a hearth, but she wasn't there. Nothing of her remained. PC34—the drug the Institute used to inhibit her—did a damn good job. I'd not felt her presence since I'd almost swallowed enough elemental power to level half of Boston and nearly killed myself in the process. She was gone.

"She's not in there, Ryder. I'd know it. I wish she was. Whatever happened, whatever you saw when you found me, it wasn't her."

He searched my expression. "It ain't me you gotta convince."

Great. Adam. This was all he needed to lock me behind bars for another six months.

I growled and tossed my head back. "Dammit. I've done everything they've asked of me. Everything. Played their games. Danced to their tune. All the assessments and tests. The constant monitoring. I don't deserve this." The longer they kept me strapped to this bed or locked behind bars, the less time I had to retrieve Stefan from the netherworld. I had to believe he was still alive, but with every passing day, the chances of him surviving became less and less. He was powerful. I knew that, but he was also half human. I'd been raised there. He hadn't. I bit into my lip and blinked back tears. "They've gotta let me out, Ryder."

He clamped his jaw shut and laid his hand over mine. The sadness in his eyes told the same tale as the thoughts running through my head. He understood. He'd seen me fight my way through the Enforcer training, ignoring the jeers from my so-called peers, and I'd excelled to prove a point. Even without my demon, I wasn't to be trifled with. But where had it gotten me? Strapped to a hospital bed with another probationary period looming over me. That's where.

I squeezed Ryder's hand before letting him go. He left the room without another word. This was hard on him too, caught as he was between the right thing to do and the Institute. I didn't blame him for any of it. He'd tried to help me. He'd taught me everything to make me a damn good Enforcer. We both wanted the same thing, but until the Institute gave my demon back, I was a blunt instrument in their toolbox.

Closing my eyes, I thought of Stefan again. He'd lived like this, at the Institute's beck and call, all his life. Their pet hybrid. He'd hinted at how they'd used him. I could only imagine the hell he'd been through, and now they were going to let him die, knowing full well I could cross the veil and find him. Figuring out how to get him back was another problem. He'd trapped a Prince of Hell in the netherworld with him, using blood to seal the deal and preventing either of them from crossing the veil. I'd searched the Institute's library books but hadn't found a way to break that blood-bond.

I reached for my demon again, mentally calling out to her, but only silence waited.

After the Institute captured me and as time had worn on, I'd stopped calling her. The void at my center, once so debilitating, had become a necessary evil. I'd pushed all of the pain aside and focused on winning, but it had been so long that I'd become accustomed to her absence. They say time heals. It doesn't. It masks. I wore a mask of confidence—a mask of determination—because it was all I had left. Inside, I was a wreck, and Adam knew it. How he knew it, I had no idea, but he did. I could excel at all the physical tests, but none of it convinced Adam I was safe. Because I wasn't safe. I hadn't been safe since the night at the waterfront when I'd drained Akil, the Prince of Greed, of his power. I'd summoned enough of my element from beyond the veil to ignite a near-nuclear reaction and then snuffed it out instead of unleashing it. The fact that I was still alive was a miracle, and I suspected it was something to do with PC34. That night, my demon had ridden high on a wave of energy so vast, so consuming, she might as well have been a goddess. I'd slapped her right back down, shoved her in a box, and stuffed her away in some dark mental hiding place. PC34 kept her there.

When she came back—and she would—she was going to be pissed.

Chapter Six

"There's been another murder." Ryder peered at me from the driver's side of the car.

I climbed into the passenger side. "Then what are you waiting for?"

He peeled the car away from the curb outside the Institute and eased into evening rush hour traffic. I watched the city drift by my window: people going about their lives, unaware of the existence of the netherworld just a thin veil away. Ignorance is bliss, right? But ignorance can kill. Another murder. Could I have prevented it? Was I a coward for not telling Adam the truth?

I'd been out of my room—cage—for all of three days without incident. A few minor demon sightings had occupied my time, some house calls, note taking, report writing. All basic stuff. Ryder had worked the bigger cases, the demon interventions; when a demon needed its wrists slapped. Behave, go home, or die. The Institute didn't mess around.

"The victim is another woman." Ryder reached behind his seat and groped about in the foot well, found what he was looking for, and dumped a file into my lap. "Cheryl Munro. Another trainee."

I flicked open the file as Ryder maneuvered the car through traffic. A smiling headshot of Cheryl beamed up at me. Standard ID pose. She appeared to be in her early twenties, about my age. Her eyes were bright with the eagerness often seen in fresh Enforcers. They volunteer. Mostly. Many Enforcers, perhaps all, had witnessed the worst demons could do. That's how they found out about the Institute.

Ryder steered the car with his knees as he unwrapped some gum. "Coleman's on scene. Same MO. Same murder weapon." He popped the gum into his mouth.

"A chain..." I said, a little too softly.

"Uh-huh." Ryder tossed the packet into my lap. "You don't have to read it."

"I should." It could help. Just because I suspected I knew the demon responsible didn't mean I knew how to catch him. Any new information would help.

"You gonna be okay with this?"

"Yup." I popped a piece of gum into my mouth and bit down hard.

***

When Ryder pulled up outside the Atlantic Hotel, I kept my mouth firmly shut and my emotions nailed down. The Atlantic Hotel had played a large part in the chaos six months ago. It had changed hands since then, but memories still haunted it. I couldn't help wondering if the location was significant.

"You good?" Ryder checked me again as he climbed from the car.

"Uh-huh." I slammed the car door and jogged up the steps beside him. The foyer gleamed from floor to ceiling the way all luxury hotels do. Marble tiles, leather chairs, and glass doors bounced light in all directions, dazzling visitors with overt opulence. There was no sign that anything untoward had taken place. No doubt the hotel management wanted to keep it that way. It wasn't until we reached the eighth floor that things got interesting. Flashing our ID badges gave us entrance from the elevator area into a corridor. Cops loitered, giving us cursory nods of acknowledgement. Well, Ryder anyway. I was still the new face on the block and largely ignored.

Detective Coleman didn't look pleased to see me when he stopped us outside number 52b. He raked his gaze over me, measuring me for any sign that I was about to run screaming from the premises. Apparently satisfied, he slid his gaze to Ryder. Coleman was probably still angry because I was a) not entirely human and b) not telling him the truth.

"I need to warn you. It's not pretty." Coleman's voice held an abrasive edge as though he'd been up all night.

"Forensics finished?" Ryder asked, as if not caring in the least for Coleman's warning.

"Yeah. We're just waiting for you to take a look." He looked down at me, clearly not trusting that I could handle any of this. I grinned brightly. "Perhaps Miss Henderson should sit this one out?"

Ryder shoved my shoulder in a macho display of affection. "She's good."

I tried to plaster something resembling professionalism on my face but failed at hiding my smile. Coleman pressed his lips together, biting back whatever he might have next, and opened the door.

A stench like pennies and sewers wafted over us. I coughed and covered my mouth and nose with the crook of my arm. Whether it was the size of the room or the heat, I wasn't sure, but the carnage appeared ten times worse than the previous murder. The victim, or what was left of her, sat slumped against the bed. Much of her skin had been peeled from her muscles in methodical strips. Those strips had dried and coiled where they'd been arranged in orderly rows beside her. She'd been butchered—sliced up like a piece of meat.

My stomach lurched. I resisted my gag reflex and briefly closed my eyes. A flurry of guilt and fear crowded my thoughts.

Ryder hesitated ahead of me, unsure where to step. He glanced back, covering his mouth and nose in the same way I had. "Watch your footing."

I looked down and stepped gingerly around the shriveled pieces of flesh. "Jesus..." My vision wobbled. Tears blurred the vivid shades of claret and burgundy into a crimson river. The woman in the file, the bright young woman, didn't resemble the slumped body. My brain struggled to put the two of them together and in doing so, reminded me I could have prevented this.

My throat clogged. I staggered and reached for the wall. I tried to breathe, but an intangible weight crushed my chest. I turned and shoved past Coleman. Only outside the room could I breathe again. I didn't need to read the chain to know what she'd been through. He'd cut into her, probably with his claws. I remembered how sharp they were. He'd meticulously removed her skin, piece by piece. I could only pray she'd died quickly.

Coleman and Ryder followed a few minutes later. Ryder wiped beads of perspiration from his face. He sucked in a few fresh breaths through gritted teeth and then looked me over.

Coleman held out a plastic bag, the sides stretched by the weight of the chain inside. I snatched it from him and dumped it on the floor at my feet. Perspiration tickled down the back of my neck. I dabbed at my forehead with a cool hand, not bothering to hide my tremors.

"It'll be a marine chain," Coleman said. "Likely from the nearby docks. We found traces of salt on the previous one, along with demon DNA. This looks identical. Might even be cut from the same length. We'll know more once forensics is finished with it."

I made the usual cut and covered my fingers in blood before wrapping them around the chain. No amount of mental preparation could have shielded me from the horror I witnessed when the metal memories flooded my thoughts. She'd died quickly, but not nearly quick enough. He'd made sure of that. He had a knack for keeping human bodies alive against the odds. Over and over, he'd brought me back from the precipice of death.

I released the chain and stumbled back against the wall. "I know who's doing this." I mentally shoved back a threatening torrent of fear. The unwanted images swirled in my head, but I refused to focus on them long enough to give them purchase. I should have told Ryder everything. It probably wouldn't have saved her...but it might have. She'd suffered because of me.

Ryder and Coleman crowded closer. The two of them blocked out prying eyes, but I found their presence suffocating. I doubled over and placed my hands on my thighs.

"I knew him as Damien." The words fell from my lips, the truth tumbling forth. "He's a higher elemental demon, and I'm terrified of him."

I was bundled into a car and driven downtown. Within twenty minutes. I sat in an interview at the local precinct with Adam Harper, Detective Coleman, and Detective Hill grilling me every which way about Damien. I'd dropped a veil of indifference over me, retreating behind cold, hard facts.

Yes, Damien had been my owner. One of several, but he'd been the last. I'd killed him—or so I'd thought. An air elemental, he could use his element to suffocate, summon storms, and generally wreak havoc. But as demons go, he wasn't anything special, not even immortal. It wasn't his element that made him dangerous; it was his lust for pain. Coleman had tried to get me to open up about how exactly Damien operated, but even Adam stopped him there. I couldn't tell them what Damien had done to me. Much of it, I deliberately didn't remember. My human mind had trampled on those memories long ago for the sake of my sanity. To bring it all back to the surface now was more than I could face.

I told them what I'd heard reading the first chain. *You are mine, Muse.* He was killing newly qualified Enforcers to get to me. Somehow, he knew the Institute employed me. All he had to do was kill each new recruit until he either found me or his actions brought me out of hiding.

"Why now?" Adam leaned on the table while Hill and Coleman stood behind him.

Hill stood mannequin still, her arms clasped across her chest. She nodded in all the right places, but her eyes were cold. She looked at me as though she thought my being half-demon meant I'd brought this on myself. As if I somehow had a choice.

I sunk in my chair, shoulders hunched, and teetered on the edge of tears. There's only so many scars you can open before the wound starts to bleed again. "Because I'm alone. Akil's gone. I don't have an owner. As far as Damien's concerned, I'm fair game."

"Do you think this has anything to do with Stefan?" Adam asked.

"What?" I frowned. "No. Why?"

Adam's lips turned down. He held my gaze as though waiting for me to reveal something and then leaned back in the chair. The cheap plastic creaked. "Damien's getting his information from somewhere. Stefan seems the most likely source. How else would this demon know you're an Enforcer?"

I blinked rapidly. "Stefan didn't know that. He went through the veil before you got your hooks into me."

Adam waited a beat. "Your employment was inevitable."

I glared at him. My hands clenched into fists so tight that my knuckles paled. Heat flushed across my skin. I slowly adjusted my position in the plastic chair and straightened my back before leaning both arms on the table. "Stefan wouldn't tell Damien a damn thing."

"You knew Stefan for a week. He's in hostile territory, searching for a way out. You didn't part on the best of terms. Perhaps he feels he has no other choice. In his position, I'd use all available means of escape."

"You'd sell me out for a subscription to selfish-bastards monthly." I stood so suddenly my chair bounced back and clattered to the floor. "Yeah, I only spent a week with him, but I can guarantee I know him better than you ever will. Your own son wished you were dead, and I gotta agree with him."

Coleman must have sensed the interview spiraling toward physical harm. He stepped forward with a hand out, attempting to placate us. "Stefan has motive and means—"

"Motive? What? You think Stefan deliberately sent Damien after me?" A snarl rippled across my lips. The room contracted in on me.

"That's not what I meant, Charlie, and you know it." Coleman rubbed his forehead and puffed out a sigh. "We all need to calm down. Given that Stefan's trapped outside our jurisdiction, he's not my concern right now. Stopping Damien is. Charlie..." He paused, my narrowed glare giving him reason to hesitate. "We've got enough info for now. Go home. Get some rest. I'll call you if we need anything else."

A quick nod was all I could offer in return. Shivers rippled through me so damn hard I was afraid my voice would fail me.

Adam thanked Coleman and Hill for their time while I seethed by the door with rage simmering beneath my skin. I wished looks could kill. Adam was right about one thing. When I got my demon back, he was toast.

Chapter Seven

Tree branches tear at my bare arms. My sore feet pummel against the loose earth. I stumble and fall hard against a bank of gnarled tree roots. Pain arcs up my side, but it soon becomes lost in the agony radiating through me. Teeth gritted, I will myself back to my feet, and even though my lungs burn, and the air drags through my teeth, I somehow find the energy to keep running. This time, maybe this time, he won't find me.

A swollen moon, bruised purple by the wash of clouds in the night sky, watches over my escape. I've waited weeks for the full moon to rise. I need its light. Sometimes, the night is so thick it clogs my throat. Tonight though, the air is clean. It tastes like freedom.

Eyes watch from the shadows as I burst through the undergrowth. I jump fallen branches and weave around trunks of the ancient trees. The things that wait in the dark won't risk attacking. Not yet. But if I fall too many times... if I stop to catch my breath...

I'd rather be torn apart by lesser demons than return to him.

He must know by now that I've escaped. He'll be looking.

I look up through the skeletal branches. Aside from the moon, the sky is an endless black. Dipping my chin, I summon all my reserves and run faster. My leg muscles burn, and my chest tightens. I duck and dart, hissing as claw-like twigs snatch at my flesh. My wings snag behind me. I'm yanked back, pulled at an angle. Unbalanced, I stagger and fall into the branches' brittle embrace. Barbed creepers coil around my ankles. I kick out, but the vines twist higher and hook into my legs. A rumbling growl bubbles up from inside. Liquid fire flares across my skin. It washes over me. The creepers burn to dust in a blink.

A grumbling snarl ripples somewhere behind me. My heart leaps into my throat. I claw apart the smothering bushes and scramble free. Fire drips from my flesh and sizzles on the damp leaves. I'm on my feet. My leg muscles bunch, ready to spring forward. Something heavy and cold hooks around my wrist and yanks my arm back so violently I'm spun around and dragged off my feet. Face down in the mulch, the chain around my wrist tightens, almost wrenching my arm from the socket. I cry out and then try to gulp back a scream.

I'm trembling so hard I bite my tongue and taste blood. Tears sizzle on my cheeks. I barely made it to the shoreline. I ran so hard. I thought I had a chance this time. I thought I was free.

He's behind me. I can sense the whispering touch of his element crawling over my flesh. I don't want to see. My claws sink into the earth. I close my left fist around a handful of dirt. If I can blind him, maybe I can unwrap the chain... Because if I don't... If I can't get free. The things he'll do...

I tense, but his foot comes down on my lower back. He leans his weight into me, grinding my pelvis into the ground. Stones and roots dig into my ribs. His cool hand grips the rise of my left wing, and he laughs. The sound of that laughter clamps hold of my heart and freezes my thoughts. I try to turn my head to see him, but I only see his silhouette. The moon casts him in shadow. A shaft of light dances off a blade. He drops the chain and holds the scimitar high over his shoulder.

My thoughts scatter.

"I... warned... you." He spits the words down at me. His spittle vaporizes as it drips onto my back.

Begging won't stop him; my mewing only excites him. My best chance is to remain quiet and still. I pant. My lungs burn, but I try to keep the fear locked away, to hide it from him. He knows. Fire pools outward around me. Tiny *flames dance as they consume the fallen leaves. If I call the fire, his punishment will be worse. His grip tightens on my left wing. His claws press against the membrane. One by one, they puncture my skin. I flinch and swallow back my cries. He closes his fingers around a bone.*

"No, please..."

When the blow comes, a shock of agony jolts through every muscle in my body. My jaw locks, until the scream escapes, echoes in my ears, slices through my skull, and pierces the night. I buck beneath him. My body blazes, but it's no use. Hot blood spills over my back and sprays across my face, into my eyes, my mouth. Damien tosses something misshapen into the undergrowth. I can see parts of the thing protruding through the leaves. It doesn't make sense. What has he done?

He walks slowly around me and stops so close all I can see are his legs and the tip of the sword. Viscous black blood drips from its edge. My blood. He crouches down and coils the length of chain around his hand. "You. Are. Mine. Muse."

I can't see him clearly. Something is wrong. I can't feel the pain anymore. My entire left side throbs, but it doesn't hurt. Blood dribbles over my shoulder. I turn my head and try to focus, but my vision blurs. A filter of acceptance falls in front of my eyes. I struggle to focus, but I can see that my left wing is gone. Just a stump remains. Blood bubbles up and dribbles across my back.

I know what it is he threw away.

He laughs again. I close my eyes.

***

Tears are useless things; tiny droplets of salt infused water, insignificant and pitiful. I hadn't cried for Stefan, even when they'd told me he couldn't return. I hadn't cried when they'd stolen my demon from me a second time, when I woke with a yawning chasm of emptiness where she should have been. But I cried that night when the memories returned. I staggered retching into the shower.

Scalding hot water pummeled my pink and vulnerable flesh. Steam bellowed around me, and I cried so damn hard my body ached. I buried my head in my hands and fell back against the slick tiles. Sobs juddered through me. I slid to the floor, pulled my legs up against my chest, and squeezed myself into a tight self-embrace. I cried until my voice failed, and the water ran cold.

Adam, Ryder, Coleman and Hill, they had no idea what I'd done to escape my owner the first time around or what had been done to me. I'd barely touched on the details in the interview room and had no intention of laying my scars bare for them to pick at. Adam didn't need any more excuses to examine me under a microscope.

Still, I preferred them to Damien. The thought of him sent me into a fit of dry heaving. Not only had I—a lowly half-blood as far as any demon was concerned—done the unthinkable and killed my owner, but I'd trapped a Prince of Hell on the other side of the veil. It just so happened that Prince had been keeping the other demons away. Now he had gone, it was open season on me, and Damien hadn't hesitated. If he caught me, death would be preferable to his alternative.

Chapter Eight

Awaiting Adam's assessment of my situation, I wandered the Institute's many levels. The complex was a rabbit warren of old buildings and warehouses, all consumed over time by the sprawling embrace of the Institute. I'd been living on site for months and hadn't yet scratched the surface of its maze-like layout. On the inside, it bustled like a university campus with people coming and going from different departments and areas of expertise. Weapons, Science, Public Relations, Training. On the outside, it looked like an abandoned industrial park. Unusual graffiti riddled the outside walls, the perfect camouflage in a city environment. That graffiti looked right at home in the forgotten neighborhood of industrial units, but it also had intricate symbols etched into it which nullified elemental energy. No full-demon could pass through the exterior of the Institute. The magic didn't completely subdue elemental magic—they need to be able to use the demons they capture—it worked as a perimeter fence. I could only get through the barrier because of my half human body. The Institute knew what they were doing when it came to demons. Nobody could argue that.

My rambling brought me to the library. The room was called a library, but it was more like a store room. Rows of high shelving units housed countless books, mostly foreign and all antiques. Almost nobody used the library, not when all the information could be found on the Institute's cloud network. It had been forgotten and discarded, a victim of progress. I often visited it when awaiting some assessment of my behavior.

I poured myself some vending machine coffee. The machine hissed, gurgled, and spat. I noticed a handful of other people in the library. One young woman sat in one of the comfy chairs, legs curled under her, nose in a book. She flitted between a substantial hardback and a dog-eared paperback, and then scribbled some notes on a pad. Nica Harper was Adam's daughter, Stefan's younger half-sister. She and I had our differences, not least of which was the fact she blamed me for her brother's untimely departure.

She sensed me watching her and peeked over the book. I lifted my dishwater coffee. She made a face and shook her head, her blond ponytail swishing behind her, and then buried her nose back in the book. I settled into a chair next to hers and took a sip of my coffee. I grimaced. It needed more sugar. And real coffee.

Nica smiled and finally tore her attention away from the books. "Tastes like something died in the machine." It really did. "You've been doing well. Top of the class. You must be pleased." As she spoke, her face came alive, blue eyes brightening. She was one of those people who couldn't seem to sit still, as though she had surplus energy. If you spent enough time with Nica, her enthusiasm rubbed off on you. I missed that. I missed her. I didn't really have friends. Akil didn't count. Friends don't threaten to kill you with the intention of carrying it out. There was Sam… Akil killed him.

"The other Enforcers say I do so well because I'm half demon." I shrugged.

She nodded and closed the large hardback with the title *The Art & Implications of Summoning Demons* with a *thwump* that echoed around the library. "It's difficult. Stefan he... he had to fight every step of the way to prove himself. After a while, he just stopped caring what they thought. He never had to prove anything to me."

I dropped my gaze, and my coffee suddenly seemed very interesting. I hadn't expected to come into the subject of Stefan so quickly. "I'm sorry."

"It's okay." Her hand swept away the apology. "It was his choice. He did what he had to do."

"I know but, I..." I had told him to leave. Looking into Nica's face, I couldn't bring myself to admit it. "I was so angry. He should have told me everything." *Instead of piling lie upon lie, like bricks in a wall.*

Her eyes fluttered closed. She sucked in a breath and sighed. When she opened her eyes again, they sparkled with unshed tears. "He did what he could, and kept us both alive. Had Akil stayed, we'd be dead. And yeah, my brother lied to you, but sometimes you gotta do the wrong thing to do the right thing."

Ouch. I may even have flinched. She was right. I hadn't understood at the time, but now, with a bit of perspective, I knew why he'd lied. He didn't have a choice. But my realization had come too late. I'd told him I never wanted to see him again. Ever. I'd got my wish.

"I just miss him, you know." She picked a lose thread from her skirt. "When I was little, I didn't care that he was half demon—I didn't even know what it meant. He was just my brother. We looked after each other... We grew up here, did you know that?" I shook my head. "I had everything I wanted. College, proms, friends. Our father, Adam, he gave me everything I asked for, but when I talked about Stefan, he'd sorta... I dunno..." Nica's delicate fingers quivered as she tucked a loose lock of hair behind her ear. "It was as if Stefan didn't exist." She blinked, and a fragile smile lit her face. "But I'd always tell Stef about school... about friends and the crazy stuff we did. He never once resented me. He could have." Her words trailed off, and her gaze drifted for a few moments. "I taught him how to read. The Institute—Dad—they weren't interested in his mind. All they cared about was the ice demon inside him. But he was smart. He wanted to learn. This place," she glanced around us at the forgotten books and silent aisles, "he liked it here. I come here a lot. It helps…"

Nica fell silent, the echoes of her voice still rippling through the library. It was the most she'd said to me in months. I searched for a meaningful reply, something that would relay how I understood, how there was nothing we could have done. "It's pretty messed up, huh?" I failed.

When she looked up, her eyes glistened. "You don't know what it's like. You don't have anyone..." She paused, her focus softening. "He used to make it snow for me. This place has loads of hidden exits if you know where to look. We'd sneak out sometimes." She blinked and tilted her head back, her lashes wet with tears. "We'd go to the public gardens—to the George Washington statue, and it would start snowing." She swiped at a tear with the back of her hand. "I loved it. Snow is so... magical. He froze the frog pond once. You know the one? Where the little frog statues sit lookin' all pensive." She laughed softly. "We were going to try to walk on the ice, but someone saw us." Another tear escaped. "Freezing a pond in the height of summer wasn't normal. Daddy nearly..." Her words trailed off, her smile fracturing.

She didn't need to finish for me to guess what Adam might have done— nothing good. Stefan would have taken the blame. It was in his nature to protect; I'd witnessed his devotion firsthand. Nica was right; Stefan had done the wrong thing for the right reasons. Hindsight's a bitch.

She rolled her lips together as if to hide how her lips turned down. "But it's okay." She sniffed and nodded firmly. "We got away from Akil. It could have been a lot worse."

"I'm going after Stefan." I tried to hold her gaze, but she flicked hers away. "As soon as I get my demon back, I'm bringing him home."

Her eyes widened a little, the brightness there beginning to fade. "You know he's dead, Muse."

I shook my head. "No."

"He's never been across the veil. He's half human. You know what it's like better than I do, but I've heard enough. I've read about it." She glanced at the array of books on the table. "I've done my research. There are demons there who will chew him up and spit him out. Monsters the size of cruise ships. It's been months. Maybe...maybe if you'd gone straight away. But it's been too long. He's dead."

"I couldn't go. They took my demon." I shook my head and reached for her hand, but she snatched it away. "Listen. Just listen. My owner's back. He's looking for me, and he knows things only Stefan could have told him. About the Institute—about Enforcers. Adam thinks Stefan is alive. I'm getting Stefan back. You have to believe that."

"The Enforcer murders..." She blinked. Her pale blue eyes widened, and the color drained from her face. "Your owner is behind it?" She pressed her hand against her neck. "I heard the Enforcers talking... Those poor women."

"Yes. There's no other way Damien could know about the Enforcers. He's all demon, and as far as I know, he's never crossed the veil before. He wouldn't know how to catch a bus, let alone track an Enforcer, kill her, and then go back into hiding. Once Damien discovered I was alive and unclaimed, he would have used anything to get to me. Akil. Stefan. They have the knowledge Damien needed. I know, Nica. I do. Stefan is alive."

"Akil could have told him... You nearly killed Akil, Muse. I saw you. You were... something else; terrifying. Akil would want you dead." She spoke as though her thoughts were elsewhere. I wondered if she was remembering her days with Akil. The Institute had sent her in as a mole. He hadn't appreciated it. "He could have told your owner about the Enforcers. Couldn't he?" She pinned a hopeful gaze on me.

I'd thought about that. "No. Akil doesn't know the inner workings of the Institute. He might want me dead, yeah, but he doesn't know anything about Enforcers. It has to be Stefan." Could Stefan have told Damien everything? "I don't know why he would tell Damien."

"I do. He tried to help you, and you told him to go to hell." She bit into her bottom lip and swallowed hard. "I can't believe you. He's gone. He's not coming back." She gathered the books and tucked them into a canvas bag. "Even if he's alive, which is highly unlikely, he can't cross the veil again. He's trapped there with Akil. That was the key to stopping Akil from coming back. Stefan's trapped there in a world filled with demons who want him dead. Jesus, Muse, open your eyes." She turned and glowered at me. "You need to let go."

I watched her stalk out of the library and slumped back in my chair. Stefan and Nica had been close. Nica had been

Stefan's lifeline to the outside world. When he'd taken Akil beyond the veil, he'd left behind the only family he'd ever had—a sister he loved. He'd known it was a one way trip. And I'd told him to go to hell.

Chapter Nine

The demon's scales shimmered beneath the streetlights. His scaled armor rattled, and he hissed a warning. He blinked inner eyelids over round green pupils and bolted down the suburban street. He had wings bunched against his back, but for whatever reason, he wasn't using them. Head down, I dashed down the sidewalk after him. He swerved around a mailbox and leapt over a picket fence.

Things had taken a turn for the worse rather quickly. *A routine call,* Ryder had said. *Drop by on your way back. Form filling exercise.* The demon had known what I was as soon as I'd climbed from the non-descript Institute Nissan. The curtain in the front window of the house had twitched. From there, things went south before I had a chance to knock.

Mister Average had exited that quaint clapboard house with enough swagger in his stride to make me hesitate and reach for my gun right before his entire man-suit peeled apart to reveal the demon inside. Despite being an Enforcer, I hadn't actually expected to come face to face with a seven-foot, winged-demon on a leafy suburban street. He lunged forward, lower jaw splitting apart to reveal four writhing tendrils, each tipped with barbs, then hissed a warning and bolted. Considering his armored bulk, he ran like the wind.

I took the picket fence in a leap and chased his shadow around the side of a house, into the back yard. He didn't head out the back gate as I'd expected, but plowed straight through the glass sliding doors and into the house.

Evidently, the demon knew the owners, and they'd invited him in sometime in the past; for coffee, maybe.

I jabbed at my cell. Without needing to make a call, I sent an alert to HQ letting them know the situation was about to get out of hand. They'd be all over this place in minutes. Broken glass crunched beneath my boots as I stepped through the shattered doors into a lounge. The house was dark except for a few blinking lights from various electronic gadgets. It would take a while for my eyes to adjust. I reached inside my jacket and unclipped the Baretta Pico from its holster. I cupped the little gun in a firm grip. Normal bullets wouldn't keep a demon down for long—that was what the jet-injector in my left pocket with its dose of PC34 was for. Bullets, however, were an effective deterrent should this demon decide I'd make a tasty early evening snack.

I checked the hall and listened. A clock ticked somewhere to my left, and the boiler hummed. A board creaked above me. I was light on my feet, but each stair groaned a protest as I made my way to the second floor.

At the top, I paused. I didn't have back-up, and my eyes weren't fully adjusted to the dark. I wasn't sure of the demon's lineage, but I could bet my month's wages on him having better night vision than me.

Muffled shuffling and a few awkward bumps behind a closed door revealed his location. He was waiting. I had two choices: wait for back-up, or take him down myself. Training told me to wait, but there was more at stake than following the guidelines. If I could take this demon down, on my own, Adam would have to admit I was ready to qualify as an Enforcer. He might still withhold my demon, but it would be another step toward freedom.

"This doesn't have to get nasty." I kept my voice level, trying to instill some calm authority. I didn't quite nail it, probably due to the fact I was about to go toe-to-toe with a demon twice my size. "I don't know why you ran, but if you've done nothing wrong, you don't need to worry. Why don't you come out, tell me your side, and nobody gets bumped back across the veil."

More shuffling accompanied a rattle of scales. "You'll kill me." He must have reapplied his man-suit because the voice sounded human and afraid.

"Not unless I have to." I flexed my slick grip on the gun.

"Your kind don't ask questions. You shoot to kill. I know." His words tumbled out so quickly that he barely took breaths between them. "It was that Missus Donaldson. Wasn't it? Always sticking her nose in. I just want to stay here—that's all. That's not going to happen now. No way. I'll have to leave. I can't go back. I can't. It's been too long. Too long."

I inched closer to the door. "Like I said. We don't kill unless we have to." I pressed my back against the wall and reached my left hand down to the handle, gripping the gun in my right. A car screeched to a halt outside, then another. Once the heavies arrived, the demon was toast. "Let me walk you out of here, and you'll have your chance to plead your case. Fight me, and the Institute will take you out, or worse."

"Is it t-true?"

I pushed down on the handle. "Is what true?"

"They capture us; run tests, like we're animals."

I hesitated, hand lingering on the handle, door almost released. I didn't know the answer for certain, but I knew what they'd done to me and some of what they'd done to Stefan, and I suspected we were the lucky ones. I could have lied and told him everything would be fine, that the Institute was reasonable, that they wouldn't hurt him, but I couldn't do it. Maybe I felt something like compassion for him. Demon to demon. "Yes."

"Then you can't have me."

I flung open the door and ducked inside, swinging the gun around while taking in the child's bedroom with its Disney character bedclothes and bright wallpaper. I pinned the demon in my sights. He reared up to his full height, shook off his man-suit, and stretched badly deformed wings out behind him. Those green eyes fixed on me right before he sprang forward.

I fired, and the little gun kicked in my hands. The heat from my element poured into my veins and thrust fire into my muscles. The influx of raw elemental power snapped down my spine and jerked away my control. I protectively recoiled in on myself, my demon assailant momentarily forgotten. He rammed me up against the wall. His barbed tongues thrashed at my face. My hand slipped on his scales, but I couldn't get purchase to shove him back. I dug my nails in and tried to keep him at arm's length, but the tongues still writhed too close to my face. I wedged the gun under his jaw and pulled the trigger. The bullet blasted through his skull, jerked his chin up, and threw his head back. He fell away from me into a heap on the floor.

Ripples of fire rolled down my legs and seeped across the floor. A pool of flame reached for the demon's body and lapped at his arm. His armored-fingers twitched, muscles retracting from the heat. Fire laced around each digit, exploring, tasting. It wasn't an attack, more a curious investigation, but it shouldn't have been happening at all. I had no control over it.

I jabbed the toe of my boot into his torso. He didn't move. Even after a gunshot to the head, you can never be too careful.

Car doors slammed outside. Boots hammered on the sidewalk.

I couldn't let the Enforcers see me like this. I dashed into the bathroom at the back of the house. The fire's embrace wrapped tightly around my body, pulling back from flammable surfaces like a creature with its own consciousness. I opened the window just as the bathroom door opened.

Ryder shied away from the heat, arm up to shield himself. Orange light danced over him.

I backed away. "Don't tell them."

His expression tightened, lips parting. He would have to tell the Institute. Of course he would. It was his job. His life. I was his responsibility. He didn't need to say it. I read the truth on his face.

I held out a hand. Liquid fire rippled across my skin and twisted around my fingers. "Don't come near me. I can't control it. It shouldn't be happening." He chanced a step closer. "Don't! Please. I don't want to hurt you."

"Muse..." There were others behind him, more witnesses.

I felt the window at my back and eased my hand through. "I mean it. Stay back." I ducked through the window and jumped. The impact with the backyard jolted through my legs. I used the pain to drive me forward and ran. Not unlike the demon I'd chased down, I ran from those I knew would hurt me. The men and woman back there, they'd see demon, not colleague.

I burst through the rear gate, flames spluttering, and dashed down a path toward a park. The Enforcers were behind me, shouting orders, coordinating their efforts to round me up. Pain sparked up my side as though someone had taken a sword to my flesh. I staggered and fell to a knee. The hand I planted against the path to stop myself had blackened to the color of soot. My nails lengthened and gleamed like black glass, becoming obsidian talons that curled into the dirt. I was changing, revealing the demon, but I still couldn't feel her. She was silent. Gone. This shouldn't have been happening.

"Don't move!"

I swung the gun around and fired. Ryder's left shoulder jerked back, rocking him off balance. The snarl on my lips wasn't my own. He brought his gun up and narrowed his gaze down the sight. A dark stain spread across his shirt, and his left arm hung limp at his side, but his aim didn't waver. "Muse, I can't let you go," he hissed through gritted teeth. "You're a danger to yourself and others."

Tearing my gaze away from him, I focused ahead, into the park, and the trees beyond. Launching to my feet, I ran, expecting to hear the crack of a bullet at any moment, the sudden flash and burn of a bullet piercing flesh, but it didn't happen. He let me go.

Chapter Ten

There were places in Boston—and in most capital cities—
that an Enforcer only went if they were looking for trouble,
like sending a cop into gang territory. I knew about the
demon sanctuaries: parts of the city that harbored arriving
demons, acclimatizing them to this world, but they were
beyond my pay grade. I'd never visited one before. That
was about to change.

I had a measly amount of cash in my pocket, a gun with
limited ammo, and an unreliable elemental issue. Where
else could I have gone? The Institute would lock me up
and knock me out. They'd run tests from which I might
never wake up. No thanks. At least the demons kept it
simple. Yes, they all wanted me dead. A half-blood was
about as low in the demon food-chain as you can get.
There was probably a bounty on my head for killing my
owner (despite the fact he was still alive) and for taking
down a Prince of Hell. But I could use my reputation as
armor. They would know my name, and would think twice
about tackling me, at least to begin with. A half-demon,
trainee Enforcer in demonville, without her demon, had
about as much chance of surviving as a kitten in a lion's
den.

The Voodoo Lounge is the sort of backstreet club that
tried very hard to be trendy but fell just short of the mark.
Bathed in neon lights, it wasn't shy about its presence.
Inside white plastic glowed beneath ultraviolet light, and
multicolored light rained across split level dance floors.

I slipped unnoticed into the crowd and ordered a drink
at the bar. The congregation on the dance floor rippled to

the dance music. Demons masquerading as humans moved differently than the real deal. They didn't waste energy. A human woman might tap her nails against the bar to the music, for example, but a female demon wouldn't bother unless it served a purpose. In the company of others, they sprang into motion, but a demons liquid gestures and smooth stride give them away. They're good though. You have to know what to look for. Demons have spent just as long pretending to be us as we've walked upright on this earth.

The crowd at the Voodoo Lounge was perhaps eighty percent demon and all dressed in human suits. The crowd moved in one heaving mass of bodies, like a flock of birds evading a predator. It was surreal and deeply disconcerting.

The Institute could shut places like the Lounge down only when the clientele were caught breaking the law. It was a losing battle. Another demon gathering point would open up down the street within weeks.

I was there because I needed someone outside of the Institute who could figure out why my element was on the fritz.

"Hello, sweet thing." The woman who leaned casually against the bar beside me was the sort of beautiful bought beneath a surgeon's knife and just as fake. If the flawless latte tone of her skin and plump kiss-me-quick lips didn't trigger a few mental alarms, her iridescent eyes would have. Her navy blue trouser suit was tucked around an hourglass figure and flared over shapely hips. Stiletto heels hitched her height up a few more unnecessary inches so that she towered over my petite frame. Her dark hair, pinned back from one side of her face, exhibited an electric blue streak.

My skin prickled. I didn't need a sixth sense to know she was demon. Too beautiful to be real, she didn't exist in the same world as the rest of us. If I'd had my demon, I could have extended an elemental touch—a demon handshake—and gauged what sort of demon she was. But all I had to go on was my gut reaction.

"Don't I know you?" Her words rolled syrup-like off her lips.

"Maybe," I smiled and took a sip of my drink. Fear would get me killed. Demons smell it, taste it on you, and it drives them wild. Chaos adores fear. "You might be able to help me. I'm looking for a doctor."

Her plucked eyebrows arched. "Does this look like a clinic?" She flicked long pianist fingers at the crowd before curling them back into her palm. I suspected her claws would be sharp.

Things were still at the light-hearted let's-check-each-other-out stage, but I knew they could turn sour at the wrong word or gesture. My human senses were beginning to sound all sorts of alarm bells. I knew demons. I'd spent the majority of my life among them. Something about her felt different and not in a good way.

I held her gaze, watching a smile writhe across her lips. To her, I was little more than a bug. She might even have been considering squishing me, but she probably also mulled over the chances of the Enforcers finding out.

"Are you a cop?" She leaned closer.

"Not exactly. I don't want any trouble. I just need some help."

"How about you tell me your name?" The tip of her tongue slid across her lips.

A lie could get me killed as quickly as fear. My intentions here were amiable, and intentions are key when negotiating with demons. "My name is Muse."

A single eyebrow jumped, and the corner of her lips hooked up. "Oh." She threw a glance over my shoulder before dragging her attention back to me. "I can help you."

I didn't dare turn around to see what or who she'd been looking at. This was between me and her. "What's your name?"

"Carol-Anne." She extended her delicate hand. I took it in mine and winced as she clamped her fingers closed. "Nice to meet you, Muse." She grinned, flashing perfectly white teeth behind blood-red lips.

I followed her through the crowd, acutely aware of eyes turning on me as we walked. So far, so good. I was still alive and hadn't yet had to prove I could cut it among the killers. Had this been the netherworld, I'd have been fighting for my life from the start. Thankfully, things are done a little differently on this side of the veil.

Carol-Anne invited me to sit in a mezzanine lounge suspended above the crowd. It was no coincidence that we looked down on the heaving throng of customers. Intention, remember. Demons have a purpose for everything. This balcony view was a declaration of status on her part. She either owned this club or was among the higher echelons of those who did.

Draping her body in the corner of a plush couch, she patted the cushion beside her and crossed her legs. "Sit."

We were alone and tucked out of sight. She could quite easily dispatch of me without anyone ever knowing. I'd disappear. No family for the Institute to send a note to thanking them for their sacrifice. Just poof. Gone.

"Sit," she said again, this time more forcefully.

I perched on the edge of the couch cushion, angled so I could leap up and dash down the stairs. Maybe I was being paranoid, but half demons who weren't paranoid were already dead.

As satisfied as a cat curled on its favorite cushion, she blinked slowly. "I know who you are, *Muse*. Nobody forgets a name like that. Named by your old owner, I hear. As though you inspired him. Is that right?"

Not many demons knew that. "It's true."

"What is it about you that could inspire, I wonder?"

I raised an eyebrow. "You'd be surprised."

Her laughter trickled through the air like water in a brook. "I'm sure I would be. Tell me, Muse, why are you here?"

"There's a demon doctor around here, goes by the name of Jeremiah, or Jerry. I need to speak with him."

"Why?"

The music and the noise from the crowd rose and fell below us like the sound of waves crashing on a beach, but they could have been a million miles away. Our little suspended corner of the club felt comfortable, close, and homey, the sort of place you'd curl up with a good book.

Whatever power she had, it worked on me, easing beneath my mental armor and evicting my concerns.

"That's between Jerry and me."

She grinned. "Jerry answers to me. If you want something from him, you come through me. He's also very precious. Demons are often *mistreated* at hospitals. They don't know whether to patch us up or call a priest. Plus, our kind has a tendency to... lash out when misunderstood. Jerry is a valuable asset, not just to me, but for the entire demon community. I will not have him put in harm's way, and given your history, I'm inclined to protect him...from you."

It was my turn to smile. "I'm not all bad."

Her grin faded, and her eyes cooled. "Half-blood turned Enforcer? You're about as bad as they get. You'll be lucky to leave here alive unless I escort you out."

Oh. I pinched my lips closed. "Look, I didn't come here to cause trouble. I need his help."

"What's in it for me?"

I only had the clothes on my back and about five dollars in my pocket to bargain with. There was something else... I closed my hand around the jet-injector in my pocket—PC34—and plucked it from my pocket. The size of a spool of thread, it didn't look like much, but it packed a devastating punch. A quick jab to exposed flesh, and the demon who found themselves on the receiving end would soon be face down in the dirt.

"Is that what I think it is?" Her eyes widened, and her tongue darted across her lips.

"Just the one." She reached out a hand. I pulled back. "Take me to Jerry, and you can have it."

Carol-Anne's eyes narrowed, and something liquid swirled in her irises. "You have a deal."

***

It had rained while I'd been inside the Voodoo Lounge. The club's garish neon lights reflected in the parking lot puddles. The rain had since stopped, replaced by a foggy drizzle swirling around the streetlights. I tucked my hands into my pockets and walked beside Carol-Anne. She stepped around potholes, her dainty stilettos staying dry. My boots didn't warrant such careful footwork.

I dropped behind her as we crossed the parking lot and passed between two panel vans. The van door to my right slid open. I snapped my head up, caught sight of the two heavies in the back, and tried to lurch away. A gnarled hand struck out and wrapped around my upper arm. A fractured cry of alarm puffed from my mouth as he dragged me off my feet and into the back of the van. Another hand smothered my nose and mouth. I tried to bite down, but a strip of duct tape pressed across my mouth. I reached for my gun and felt their hands riding roughshod over me. My fingers fumbled against the grip. The gun snatched away, leaving my fingers stinging.

I lashed, kicked, thrashed, and bucked. My heel crunched against something semi-soft and I heard one of the men curse.

"For hells-sake, she's half the size of you two." Carol-Anne loomed in the van's doorway. Her impressive *Cosmopolitan Magazine* silhouette rippled in the low light as it peeled away to reveal her true appearance. The gray-skinned demon stood maybe six feet, her body elongated, limbs gangly, ribs protruding. Her fingers were narrow talons, like crabs' legs. Water bubbled up through open pores and trickled over her flesh. Great, a water elemental. And there I was without my demon.

She slammed her hand into my chest and pinned me down between her two henchmen. Her rigid lips parted. Rows of piranha-like teeth bristled in her mouth. A fin fanned down her back, its barbed points dripping a viscous substance.

I tensed to kick, but she wrapped her spindly fingers around my thigh.

"It's in her pocket," she gurgled. Water dribbled from her lips and splattered onto my chest.

I tried to buck again, but my arms were pinned to the van floor. I couldn't move. All I could do was glare, and I made damn sure Carol-Anne read my intentions in my eyes.

She laughed, a tinkling wet sound like water bubbling from a tap. "What a disappointment you turned out to be."

Calling my demon did nothing. I hadn't really expected her to come, but it was worth a try, considering my element's behavior the night before.

One of her guys found the injector. She snatched it from him with a liquescent cry. "Tie her up. She's another's property. He'll want her back."

Panic flushed through my veins. Did she mean Damien? Adrenalin sparked off all number of instinctual fight or flight reactions. My element finally came, rolling out of the dark void inside me like a backdraft devouring the insides of a building. In one great heave of chaotic energy, fire burst over my skin and ignited the two men flanking me. Their screams fuelled my fury.

Carol-Anne recoiled. The air quivered with heat and vaporized her liquid sheen. Her gray skin tightened around her bones like shrink wrap. Steam bellowed between us. All of my demon came then. She thundered toward me, a heaving malevolent darkness bursting from obscurity to expand every cell in my human body with her hunger. The pressure of her rising up severed my grip on reality. She evicted my humanity with one backhanded mental blow. My conscious thoughts fell back. It shouldn't have hurt, but it did; she tore through me with no regard for my sanity. It was wrong. We were one and the same, but she came at me—through me—as though I was the enemy.

My one ruined wing burst from my back and stretched outward to butt up against the van roof. My demon embraced my body with flames, superimposing her smoldering flesh over mine, blurring the lines between my normal appearance and hers. She devoured the fragility of my body, driving steel rods of power through my body.

I swung my glare toward the wide-eyed Carol-Anne as the tape over my mouth melted away. I could kill her. The demon in me, she wanted it. Death. Destruction. Chaos. But it wouldn't stop there. She wanted them all dead. Everyone. Everything. I felt her summon warmth from the buildings around us and the earth below us. If I didn't rein her in, she'd call it all, and I wasn't entirely sure I could stop her from using it. I wasn't even sure I wanted to.

I sprang from the back of the van and slammed into Carol-Anne, knocking her back against the other van. She wailed as flames burned across her skin. Torrential rain began to pound us from above. It fizzled and hissed against my sweltering flesh.

I wrapped my hand around her throat and squeezed. My wing stretched high behind me, funneling the fire skyward. "Take. Me. To. Jerry." I snapped each word through clenched teeth while desperately clinging on to the one tiny thread of control I had left.

She nodded.

I released her and stumbled away. *Burn them. Burn it all.*

My whole life, I'd walked a line; it's called control. Sometimes, it was obscured by so much emotional debris, I could barely see it, but it was always there. If you understand that chaos, by its very definition, is uncontrollable, then you'll realize the line was everything to me. If I stepped off, just for a second, the lure of chaos would sink its claws in, and I'd be free. Chaos desires freedom. It abhors control. I couldn't afford to let it win.

I splayed both hands on the roof of the nearest car. Fire flowed through me, cascading down my arms and into the metal. The roof buckled, sagged, and melted. Once the interior caught, fire roared from the windows and licked higher. I let it all go, let it wash through me, out of me. It was that or swallow the energy back into myself, and given the state of my demon, I wasn't sure she'd let me live through that.

Only when I'd spent the chaos and the car was fully ablaze, could I regain some measure of composure. I very delicately packed my demon away, back inside her mental box. Regaining control felt like clinging to the edge of a cliff. A crazy urge to let go came over me, that same crazy voice that sometimes wondered what it would be like to drive a car off a cliff or jump from a tall building. You know the trip only ends one way, but it might just be worth it. The voice, her voice, my voice, it wanted me to let go.

By the time my demon retreated from my skin and the flames around me died, I'd stepped away from the blaze and was ready to collapse from exertion. Carol-Anne watched me closely. Back in her woman-suit, she brushed a spec of soot from her shoulder and humphed something like reluctant admiration. She wouldn't press my buttons again unless I revealed a weakness. Considering my buttons were my weakness, the possibility of a long night ahead was a very real one.

"I'll have that injector back now please," I said, surprised at the clarity of my words.

Her two men stumbled from the back of the van, sodden clothes steaming. She returned the injector and my gun. Her gaze searched mine as the sound of sirens pierced the night. She hadn't sensed the power in me because it hadn't been there. She wouldn't feel it now either. It should have been a constant presence at my core. She and I both knew that. Something was very wrong with me. I hoped Jerry had some answers.

Chapter Eleven

Jerry was not the sort of man I'd been expecting. When I'd read about a doctor who treated demons, I'd assumed he'd be the academic type, and with a name like Jerry, surely he'd be a cheery, approachable kind of guy.

Jerry was built like a pro-wrestler. His wife-beater shirt stretched thin over obscenely butch muscles. Intricate black tattoos marked every visible inch of flesh. The markings swirled and dipped around his forearms, wove over his biceps, and rode across his shoulders. Even his face was marked. His eyes drilled through a ski-mask of symbols. Jerry did not look at all like a Jerry.

He glared at me in such a way I felt sure he expected me to wilt and die. I blinked back at him. I'd survived a childhood of torture, faced Hellhounds, and drained a Prince of Hell. Jerry didn't scare me. It helped that he was human, at least as far as I could tell. My senses weren't tingling.

"Jerry," Carol-Anne snapped, "let us in."

He grunted, turned his huge bulk in the doorway, and stalked into a poor replica of a waiting room. Plastic chairs formed a neat row down one side of the room. Dog-eared magazines looked as though they'd been scattered into the room at random. The lone light bulb barely penetrated the thick gloom, and I had to wonder whether I was looking at shadows or dirt on the floor. Or maybe blood? I couldn't smell blood, at least not beneath the stifling odor of antiseptic.

Jerry led us into an empty examination room and flicked on the lights, bathing us in a glare so bright it made the stainless steel surfaces of the table and washbasins look brittle. Carol-Anne maintained her flawless appearance, her skin mannequin smooth. I could only imagine what I looked like. Haggard and edgy probably.

"What's she?" Jerry's bass voice rumbled against my rib cage. He jerked a thumb at me and leaned back against the polished steel work surface, avoiding eye contact.

"A puzzle." Carol-Anne skewed her liquid eyes at me. "A half-blood with some control issues."

Jerry's eyebrows jumped, an expression which I took to be one of surprise, and then he gave me an up-and-down visual assessment, taking in my unassuming appearance. "A half-blood?"

The depth of his rumbling voice curled and teased its way beneath my façade of resilience and planted seeds of uncertainty about good ol' Jerry.

He folded his stout arms over his chest. "Well aren't you somethin'... How are you hiding your power?"

"I'm not." My voice sounded high and prickly compared to his. "Let's get something straight. I'm not an easy morsel you can chew up and spit out, as Carol-Anne here will testify, so don't get any funny ideas. I don't want trouble. I just want to know if you can help."

As I spoke, his smile grew until he practically beamed at me. "You're the half-blood they're looking for."

"Yes." There were others like me, but they were few and far between. Half-bloods are generally killed at birth or sold as playthings to lesser demons. Few survive into adulthood, and those who do are usually damaged beyond repair. Stefan had been the only other half-blood I'd ever met.

Jerry's chuckle rolled out of him and flowed through the room like a melody. If he wasn't demon, he sure as hell was something because his laughter disarmed my instincts with impossible ease. I found myself liking him. Hell, I was about ready to roll over and let him tickle my belly. Resisting the urge to melt into a pool at his feet, I flicked my hair back and planted a hand on my hip, setting my face into a scowl. "What are you?" I grumbled.

"A vet."

Laughter lodged in my throat. "A vet?" I coughed into my hand. "Really?"

"And other things. But mostly a vet." He seemed aware of how ludicrous it sounded because those penetrating eyes sparkled with silent laughter. "So, half-blood, what do you want from me?"

"Call me Muse."

His smile died a slow languishing death on his lips, and the laughter snuffed out of his eyes. "Muse. Holy-hell. You're the half-blood who ruined the Prince of Greed." He shot a look to Carol-Anne. "You brought her here?"

"She didn't leave me much of a choice. Plus she has something for you." She gave me an encouraging nod.

I wondered about how he'd described what I'd done to Akil. *Ruined* seemed like an odd word. I'd drained him and kicked his ass back to hell, but ruined? Did he imply Akil was still around but was somehow desolate? I hadn't considered what had become of him. I told myself I didn't care. But Jerry's definition picked at a mental scab, threatening to peel it off and reveal my fear that Akil was plotting his revenge. Jerry and Carole-Anne were watching me, waiting for me to reveal my trump card. I filed thoughts of Akil away for later and held out the injector. Jerry's eyes widened.

"PC-Thirty-Four," I said. "I've had this crap in my veins for over six months, and it's playing havoc with my demon. I'm sick of waiting for the Institute to free me, and events have... forced my hand. So I'm here, talking to you, to see if we can...work something out."

Jerry dragged his hand across his chin then scratched at his cheek. "You're a hot potato right now, Muse. I could hand you over to half a dozen named demons, and I'd be generously rewarded. Reckon you're on the run from the Institute too?"

I'd put money on those demons he mentioned being my owner and possibly Akil, not to mention demons that just wanted me dead for breathing, oh—and my charming immortal brother. Have I mentioned him? Form an orderly queue to kill the half-blood.

"You could try." I flicked a glance at Carol-Anne, who pursed her lips. "But I don't think you want it known you're the type to talk. Demons get spooked pretty easy, and all of them have secrets I bet you get to hear, right?"

"And if they find out I've had an Enforcer in here, what do you think they're gonna do?" He made a derisive sound in the back of his throat then crossed the room and took the injector from my hand. His eyes bored through the mask of tattoos and locked onto me. For a few seconds, a cool, creeping, slither of power swept over me, and then he looked down at the injector in his hand, and the elemental touch was gone. "I tried to help a half-blood once... He died. I've never seen a man so screwed up in the head. The scars on his body... He was more animal than man. Poor bastard." He placed the injector on the counter beside me and looked down into my eyes. Did he know what I'd been through? He couldn't know the details, but if he knew half-bloods, he knew how the demons liked to *ruin* them. "You got balls coming into this part of town—coming to me. You're gonna get yourself killed, half-blood. Until then, sure, I'll help you. I like a challenge."

Carol-Anne nodded her agreement. "Can I trust you two not to kill each other?"

Jerry grunted an 'uh-huh,' but I deliberately held Carol-Anne's gaze. "Back in the parking lot, you said I was another's property."

She nodded. "When you're done here, come and find me. We'll talk." She'd lost her allure now that I'd seen her true form, but she had gained some of my respect. She hadn't retaliated with all her available element in the parking lot, and for that I'd given her a few points for control. Had she come at me with as much force as I was ready to wield, we could have leveled the club and surrounding buildings. She'd sensed the chaos in me and refrained. Carol-Anne and her demon were smarter than they looked.

After Carol-Anne left, Jerry asked, "How long did you say you've had that drug in you?"

I took a leveling breath, trying to focus on the now. Sinking back against the counter, I rubbed at my forehead.

A dull ache throbbed at my temples. "Six months." My hand shook. I tried to hide it, but Jerry saw. He would have heard the weary sigh in my voice anyway.

"That's a long time without your demon."

I nodded and rolled my shoulders. "Do you know much about half-bloods?"

"No." The single world came out like a growl but with no ill-will behind it. "Rarer than hens' teeth." He appeared to be quietly assessing me. "You got control issues and you think PC-Thirty-Four is behind it? I can help you, but not here. Somewhere public."

"Why somewhere public?"

"Because you're not gonna to like it."

Chapter Twelve

Starbucks was the last place on earth I'd imagined I'd be sitting next to Jerry. It was an hour before closing. A few other customers had laid claim to the comfortable chairs. Jerry and I found a quiet corner. He even bought me a latte, anticipating my need for a caffeine kick.

"Okay, listen up." He leaned forward like a football player hunkering down. His bulk and swirling tattoos could be considered intimidating, but his luscious voice countered the bulldozer effect of his appearance. He'd confused the barista, who hadn't known whether to fear Jerry or swoon.

I took a welcome sip of coffee and inhaled the aroma. "I'm listening."

"I get no sense of power coming off you... at all. But I know it's in there. So we have a pissed off demon is my guess. She—it's a she, right?" I nodded, licking my lips and let him continue. "Forget the PC-Thirty-Four—there's something else going on, or you wouldn't be asking me for help."

I mulled over how much to tell him. I had the potential to wield an extreme amount power, and not just in a demon way, more of a god-like way, if I drew from beyond the veil. Some demons knew this about half-bloods, most did not. I'd only recently become aware of it myself. "How much do you know about me?"

He leaned back in the chair, filling it. "I know you sent Akil—Mammon the Prince of Greed—back to Hell." Something like admiration shone through his tattooed mask.

Technically, Hell with a capital 'H' didn't exist. One man's Hell is another's Heaven. Hell was a catch-all term for the netherworld beyond the veil. "Do you know how I did it?"

"No."

"I pulled every ounce of his element from him. I drained him dry." I had guzzled a Prince of Hell's entire wealth of power; summoned every last drop right out of his body, leaving him unconscious and spent. The tremendous load of power had nearly killed me. "But I couldn't release it without leveling half of Boston, so I drowned it. Dumped myself in the harbor." I shrugged. "Somehow I'm still here to talk about it."

"That's when the Institute recruited you?"

Recruited me. Right. More like they fished me out the water and incarcerated me. "Something like that. I've not been able to reach my demon since that night. But earlier, I had a little scuffle with Carol-Anne, and my demon came then... but she wasn't right. I had no control whatsoever. " I tapped my temple. "No communication. There's something else too... Nose bleeds, headaches. Like there's a pressure building in my skull."

Jerry sat motionless with just his eyes moving as he read my face. The tattoos masked his features, making him tricky to read. "You realize, half-bloods are impossible. A human body shouldn't be able to contain an elemental demon. It's physically and mentally impossible. Something about how you and your demon are tied together goes beyond scientific explanation. You shouldn't exist. It's a wonder you're not a jabbering lunatic."

I sometimes contemplated whether it would easier if I was. "I try not to think about it. Doesn't change anything. I'm here—despite the odds."

"I can help you reason with her, but I can't bring her back. You've got to get PC-Thirty-Four out your system. There's no way around that. Can you get your hands on the antidote?"

I grinned. I'd thought about stealing the antidote, but it was kept locked away in the heart of the scientific department. "You can't just walk in and take it. Finger print scans, retina scans, voice recognition. Hell, they'd ask for your DNA if they could get away with it." Adam could get it with ease.

"Your demon is screwed, Muse. We can reach out to her, try and calm her down. It won't solve your problems, but it might prevent you from lashing out and killing someone."

Like the thugs in the van. I tried not to think about how easily I could have killed them. They'd been lucky a water elemental had been on hand to douse the flames. "How do we reach her?"

"Hypnosis."

I blinked. "What...? Now?"

"Yeah. I didn't think you'd want me try it somewhere without witnesses."

Good call. No, I most definitely would not want to be hypnotized alone in a room with this guy. Sure, he had a voice that could melt arctic ice, but that didn't mean I was going to let him poke around inside my head while I clucked like a chicken.

I eyed him suspiciously. "Is it safe?"

He gave his answer some thought. "Usually."

"Do you routinely hypnotize demons?"

His wolfish grin tucked in his cheeks. "Among other things. I'm just gonna... relax you, see if we can tempt her out."

Well, it beat being tied to a bed and drugged up to the eyeballs. I told Jerry to hit me with his best shot. He sat beside me and angled his chair toward me. It all felt rather peculiar. "You're just going to relax me?"

"Yeah, no funny business." His deep voice rumbled.

"No offense, but you work with demons on a daily basis. I'm not sure I want to trust you."

"You think I'd be alive if I screwed over my patients?"

"Is that what the tattoos are for? Protection?"

"Yes."

I frowned. "Alright, let's do this. But shouldn't we have a safe word or something?"

He laughed and told me to lean back and close my eyes. I didn't expect hypnosis to work, but I was willing to give it a try. What was the worst that could happen? I listened to the seductive bass tone of his voice as he told me to imagine the safest place I could. That in itself was no mean feat. The concept of safe was not one I was familiar with, so I tried to picture somewhere I felt happy, a beach with my bare toes scrunched in the sand, the sea breeze on my face. I let the sound of the sighing waves chase away my fears and lift a ton of burden from my shoulders. I tilted my face to the warmth of the sun and closed my eyes.

Jerry's voice ebbed and flowed, lapping at my consciousness. I couldn't hear the individual words, but I felt the effects of them. The sun warmed me through, lifting my mood. I tasted the salt air on my lips and sighed. Was this what freedom felt like?

A shadow fell over me. I opened my eyes. The sky above had darkened. A bank of storm clouds rolled in off the sea. I might have shivered, but the warmth from the sun hadn't faded. I looked at my hands and watched curiously as sprites of fire danced across my palms. I knew what loomed on the horizon. Lifting my gaze, I saw a huge pair of eyes burning through the clouds, their irises swirling with molten fire. An enormous blackened hand reached out.

I jerked myself awake and darted my gaze around Starbucks. I was alone. Jolting up in my seat, I scowled. Jerry had left me. Everyone had gone. Hadn't they noticed the sleeping girl? Surely the barista...

A demon stood at the counter, rapier claws tapping on the glass cabinet as she eyed the paninis. I identified her from the single ragged wing relaxed behind her. When extended, it would tower over her at twice her height, but without its opposite, it was useless. I was on my feet and inching forward without realizing at first that I'd moved. Her scorched skin fizzed with dancing embers, as though lava flowed beneath the crusted surface of her flesh. She had a definite feminine physique, curved and lean like a panther, built for agility and speed.

As I came around the edge of the counter, she turned her amber eyes toward me. A smile peeled her lips over curved ivory fangs. Two horns swept back against her skull. They might've resembled jet-black hair if it wasn't for their sharp tips kicking out a little behind her ears. Her face vaguely resembled mine, the way a sister's might.

She gave her wing a twitch, dislodging a dusting of ash that sprinkled the floor at her bare feet. She slowly faced me. Her eyes looked me over with curiosity, like the slightly bored gaze of a cat observing its owner go about her daily routine. She didn't appear angry or frustrated. We were one and the same. I knew what she felt because I felt the same. We were kin. Connected on a cellular—possibly a metaphysical—level.

I took a step closer and lifted my hand, reaching for her. I couldn't help admiring her. Despite missing a wing, she really was a creature of deadly beauty. Perhaps all the more beautiful for the scars.

She snapped her head to the side and fixed a furious glare over my shoulder. "He's here." She hissed and recoiled, back arching and hackles rising. A growl rumbled beneath her words and sparked a blaze of horror in me. I glanced back. The swift motion unbalanced me and sent the coffee shop into a spin.

I flung open my eyes and gulped air. Jerry's vice-like grip clutched my arm. My fingers dug into the arm of the chair so hard I'd snapped a nail. A devastating ache pounded against the insides of my skull. Jerry told me to breathe slowly, to calm down, but I couldn't. A man stood in the doorway. His ankle-length black coat sparkled with rain. He didn't look dangerous, but he did look out of his time and place. As his dull eyes scanned the crowd, he swept back his shoulder length, tar-black hair back from his hawkish face. I'd seen that face before: the solid cut of his jawline, his hollow cheeks and dead eyes. I'd felt the elation strum through him as he'd choked the life out of his victims.

I sprang from the chair. Jerry bellowed my name. Nothing could have slowed me down, not even Hellhounds. I'd have welcomed a game of tag with the hounds again if it meant escaping him. I scooted around tables and shoved chairs and people aside in my blind rush to get away. Throwing myself through the opposite exit, I stumbled onto the sidewalk, and launched into a sprint. I darted across the road. A horn blast didn't slow me down. Head down, arms pumping, I ran until my lungs scorched and my leg muscles burned.

***

The Stone's Throw was unusually busy. Although most establishments wouldn't class seven customers as busy. The television blathered from high above the bar while a pair of young men played pool. The clatter of the balls rattling in the table pockets set my teeth on edge. A couple deeply engrossed in one another ate fries at one table. The remaining customers propped up the bar. I worked my gaze over each of them, assessing for threats before reaching my intended target.

Ryder hunched over the bar. His left shoulder sagged beneath his jacket. A pang of guilt undermined my resolve as I approached from behind, taking a wide arc around the empty tables to avoid catching his eye. I eased my trembling out-of-breath body onto the stool beside his. He slid his gaze from an empty shot glass in front of him up to me. His chin bristled with stubble. His tight red eyes didn't lighten at the sight of me. They hardened, and I got a sense of what a demon must feel when they look into Ryder's eyes right before he pulls the trigger. The little pang of guilt I'd felt earlier tightened a knot of regret.

He waited a few seconds, snorted a curse, and straightened. I immediately clutched the gun inside my jacket. His frown cut deeper. "You ain't gonna shoot me again, lil' firecracker."

I might. He couldn't know the turmoil churning my thoughts. Given how I must have looked—hair bedraggled from my sprint through the rain, my eyes constantly darting back at the door—he should have figured something was up.

My hand lingered on the gun. "I don't trust you."

Ryder shook his head with a bark of laughter. He lifted his shot glass and hailed the bartender. "I take my job seriously, Muse. An' right now you're a tickin' bomb."

I tilted my head to get a look at his wounded left arm inside his jacket. "You're not on the job."

He quirked an eyebrow, let the bartender refill his drink, and drawled, "No, I'm not *on the damn job*, thanks to you." He set the drink down on the bar and glared at it, jaw working as though chewing on his next words. "You know," he said, facing me, "I did everything I could to help you, and this is how you repay me?" He gestured at his arm in the sling. "Dammit, I thought we were friends."

I released the gun and slouched against the bar. I bowed my head. My hair fell forward, curtaining my face. I couldn't see his expression and didn't want him to see mine. "I'm afraid, Ryder. So damn afraid. I'm alone, and I'm so messed up. I need my demon back. I need her. Can you get me the antidote?"

"No." The shot glass rattled on the bar.

I tucked my hair back and carefully lifted my gaze. I expected to see disgust, but he hadn't judged my words. He looked back at me, waiting, expectant, but not criticizing. "I can't do this anymore."

His lips had turned down. "I don't know much about you, but I never figured you one for givin' up."

He was right. He didn't know me. I barely recognized myself. I held Ryder's gaze, determined not to look away. "My owner is out there. I saw him. He will find me and the things he'll do to me... you have no idea...the things he's done..." I flinched but didn't pull away. "I need my demon back. Adam had no right to take her from me. I can't survive like this. I've got a target on my back, and the Institute can't protect me." I paused to control my rapid breathing. Ryder held my gaze as though he knew I needed his strength. If he looked away, if he pitied me, if he judged me, I'd fold. "This isn't a game. Those other women had it lucky. He killed them within hours and butchered them when they were dead. Believe me, Damien can make death last a lifetime. I don't want to have to go through that again, Ryder." My voice cracked. "I can't." My sight blurred. "I won't."

He absorbed my words. His fingers teased around the rim of the shot glass. Finally, with a ragged sigh, he straightened and raked a hand through his hair. "Shit, Muse. I wanna help you, but Adam is the only one who can get you that antidote."

"Can you get me inside the Institute without spiking an alarm?"

A muscle jumped in his jaw. He knew what I was asking. If he did this for me, his devotion to his career would be in question. I'd never met anyone who lived and breathed the Institute quite like Ryder. He had nothing else.

When he finally met my gaze, resignation softened his eyes.

"Please," I said.

He leaned closer. "If I do this for you, I want a guarantee you won't rain fire down on the Institute, or on Adam."

I tore my gaze away and grimaced at the thought of holding back. The one thing I knew my demon and I agreed on was our mutual hatred of Adam. I'd dreamed night after night of the things I would do to that bastard when I got my demon back. He'd reared Stefan like an animal, sent Nica in to spy on a Prince of Hell, and he'd nailed me to the floor by stripping my demon from my soul.

"You hate him. I get it. But you know the Institute is important. Hell, Muse, you've see the number of demons crossing over, same as I have. We need the Institute. Tooled up, you could destroy Adam, the Institute, and everyone in it." He knew me better than I'd thought. "Did you know they use you as an example of what a Class A demon can do? They rank you right up there with the Princes. What you did to Akil that night on the pier, the power you and Stefan threw around... Don't use that against us, Muse. You're better than that, better than the goddamn demon inside'a you. I need your word, right here, that you won't turn against the Institute. Ever."

"The things Adam's done. He locked me up like an animal, treated Stefan like a lab rat —"

"I know what he did to Stefan. Better than you do." Ryder lowered his voice. The corner of his mouth turned down in a snarl that didn't quite make it to his lips. "If you want your demon back, you gotta give up on revenge. You gotta work with us, Muse, not against us."

"Okay," I grumbled.

"Look at me."

I pinned my stare on him and growled. "Okay."

"Give me your word, as a friend."

I rolled my eyes. "Alright! The Institute is safe."

A restrained smile twitched across his lips. "And Adam?"

"Yes, dammit, I won't touch him. Cross my heart and bake a demon in a pie, but you gotta get me inside the Institute. Tonight."

He grinned. "Then let's do this."

Chapter Thirteen

Ryder snuck me in by walking me through the front doors with black canvas bag over my head and my hands cuffed behind my back. *Just a transfer from New York,* he'd said, and the guards bought it. Why wouldn't they? Ryder was an Enforcer, his record squeaky clean, his reputation preceded him.

I could have walked in myself, but considering how I'd left things with the Institute, I'd likely find myself tranquilized and shoved in a cage before I could say "Boo." They didn't suffer out-of-control demons lightly. I wouldn't have put it past Adam to have me euthanized for my own good.

Ryder uncuffed me as he walked me through the administration level. He tugged off the bag, and we fell into step beside one another. I reached inside my jacket and removed my gun from its holster. I flicked off the safety and loaded a round into the chamber. A few employees glanced my way, but we'd reach Adam's office before anyone thought to raise the alarm. Hopefully, they'd assume Ryder had everything under control.

We stopped outside Adam's office. I heard the bastard inside. A one sided conversation indicated he was on a call. I sucked in a breath, trying to chase away my nerves, then jabbed the gun in Ryder's side. "I'm sorry."

He jerked, body tightening, and glowered at me. "Muse..."

I gripped his shoulder and leaned the muzzle into him. "Open the door." I didn't have time to tell him this was the only way to keep his rep intact. From the disgusted look on his face, I could tell he wouldn't buy it anyway.

He shoved open the door. Adam, phone to his ear, glanced over as I marched Ryder inside and kicked the door closed behind me. "Hang up."

Adam hung up the call and slowly placed the handset on his desk. His hand dipped beneath the roll edge of the desk. I knew, from one of my early fresh-out-of-the-cage attempts to lunge across the desk at him, that he had a gun in the top drawer.

"Keep your hands on the desk." I didn't sound as angry and fucked up as I felt. I was getting my demon back. Everything would be back to normal once she coiled inside me. I'd be whole again. Free? Maybe not free. I still had a psychopathic owner after me. The Institute would probably go back to wanting me penned in, poked, and prodded to their hearts' content. But it would be okay because I'd be me again. How I should be. And anyone who tried to hurt me could go to hell.

Adam splayed his hands on the desktop and held my stare. He rolled his lips together, moistening them, but otherwise sat perfectly still.

Ryder had lifted his hands a little, making it clear the position he was in. He breathed slowly. If he wasn't already wounded, he might have attempted to tackle me. He still might. I didn't want to hurt him again, but I could.

"This has gone on long enough." I made no attempt to hide the tremor in my voice. Ryder could probably feel me shaking through the gun still digging into his ribs. "I'm not your property, Adam. I am not chattel to be traded, or a beast to be studied. I've permitted your tests. I let your doctors poke and prod me. I've done everything you've asked and more. It's time you gave me my demon back."

"No." He barely looked ruffled at all. The slight pinch around his eyes and firm press of his lips indicated he was angry, but he certainly wasn't afraid. He had never feared me. That was a mistake.

"You don't seem to understand how desperate I am. I'm more dangerous to you now like this. My element is breaking through. It's unpredictable and chaotic. I can't control it. I've nearly killed two men already. Give me the antidote."

Adam drew in a breath. "If I give you the antidote there's nothing to stop you from laying waste to everything I've worked for. I will not have you destroy my life's work. The Institute is bigger than you, Muse. It's bigger than me. I can't jeopardize that. Certainly not for you."

A growl bubbled up the back of my throat. "I have no interest in hurting you or this place. I need her back. She's a part of me, Adam. You just don't get it. Do you? I'm worth more to you whole. If you want a demon on your side, you've got one. I promise you that, but if you don't give her back to me, I'm as good as dead. Damien is here. I've seen him. You know what he can do. If I'm without my demon, he'll tear me to pieces, and he won't stop at me. He's got a taste for it now. He'll kill again and again. Is that what you want?"

Adam bowed his head. "How can I trust you, Muse, when you're holding a gun to your handler?"

I couldn't decide whether to smile or snarl. "You were never going to give her back. Were you?"

He stood slowly and glared right back at me. "I'm in the business of stopping demons, not harboring them."

I swung the gun around and aimed it at his head. I could pull the trigger and do the world a favor. I wanted to.

"Muse..." Ryder warned. He stood a few strides off to my left, poised to lunge.

"Pick up your phone, and make it happen, Adam. I'm not leaving here without my demon."

"Kill me, and you never get her back." So calm. So confident in his conviction.

My finger twitched, just a little. Ryder inched closer. I flicked a warning glance in his direction then glared at Adam. "Do it."

He reached down and picked up the phone. His fingers trembled as he dialed the internal number. He lifted the handset to his ear and barked the order I needed to hear. "I need you to bring an injector of PC-Forty-Two to my office. Yes, I understand. Do it now." He ended the call and tossed the phone onto the desk. The immense weight of disappointment on his face considerably brightened my mood.

"You're dangerous." He said it like an insult.

"I know." I grinned. "But you don't need to worry because I'm on your side. I meant what I said. I'll kill Damien. I've done it before. I'll do it again. Then I'm going to get Stefan back."

The mention of his son's name clouded his face. "Dangerous, impulsive, and stubborn. You're nothing like Stefan. Despite his affliction, my son was a good man. You, I don't know what you are."

I resisted the urge to say, "Your worst nightmare," despite it being particularly apt. He probably read as much from my smile. "I never asked. If you despise demons so much, how did you manage to get close enough to one to get her pregnant? Stefan's mother, Yukki Onna? The Snow Witch?" A twitch of restrained emotion went through him. My gaze flicked down to where his right hand closed into a fist. I'd hit a nerve, and by the looks of it, a deep, painful, raw nerve. I planned on hitting it harder. "I hear she's very beautiful. Did you fall for her? Your dirty little secret perhaps? Did she break your old heart? Is that why you hate demons so much?"

"You—" He bit the words back, swallowing his anger with them. "Don't presume to know my past, Muse."

My lip curled. I still trembled but not with fear. "You're a fake. You hate demons so much, and yet you managed to screw one to get yourself a hybrid son." It was a low blow, but if I couldn't hurt Adam any other way, I could certainly verbalize what I thought of him.

Adam came around the desk, bearing down on me within a few strides. I still had the gun on him and stood firm, holding it out at arm's length until the muzzle wavered close to his forehead. His wide eyes and flared nostrils said it all. At least we had hatred in common. He believed I'd shoot him. I'd never killed anyone before. Only my owner, and I'd screwed that up. Did I have it in me to pull the trigger?

A knock on the door pulled me out of my darkening thoughts. Ryder checked me. I nodded, and he opened the door. Nica yelped as he grabbed her by the arm and tugged her into the office, quickly closing the door behind her.

She stumbled between Ryder and Adam. "Oh my god... Muse... What're you doing?"

"Give me the antidote."

Nica looked at her father, but Adam only had eyes for me. She stepped forward and held out the injector. Keeping the gun trained on Adam, I snatched the injector from her palm and jabbed it against my neck. Relief spilled through me. The drug simmered through my veins.

A slight itch crawled beneath my skin. I tilted my head and rolled my shoulders as the fizzling sensation spread down my arm and across my chest. I'd had this happen once before and knew it hurt like hell. Before, my demon had been banished for a few days. This time, months had passed.

I became very aware of three people waiting for me to buckle. The itch beneath my skin smoldered. Unpleasant heat bubbled through my body. I lowered the gun and flicked on the safety before attempting to tuck it back into its holster. I missed.

Adam took a step closer.

I snapped my head up and backed against his bookshelf. "Don't touch me. Just let it happen. If you touch me or try and restrain me in any way, I can't guarantee I won't hurt you." A white-hot blaze of pain snapped up my spine, throwing my head back and locking my jaw together. I dropped to my knees. The gun skittered from my hand across the floor. Ryder snatched it.

Slumping forward onto my hands, I felt the chasm inside of me swelling outward, opening to embrace the impending release of power. She was there; a coiled predator lurking in the far reaches of my mind, stalking the fringe of my thoughts.

"Hold her." I heard Adam bark the order and sensed Ryder beside me, but he didn't touch me.

"No," Ryder said. "She's right. Let her do this."

"Goddammit, hold her down."

"Back off, Adam. I got this," Ryder growled. I felt his presence and smelled the gun oil on his clothes, the alcohol on his breath. When he spoke, it was a soft whisper in my ear. "Don't make me regret backin' you up, Lil' Firecracker. Control her."

I got the distinct impression that if I didn't, he wouldn't hesitate to put a bullet in my head. It didn't matter either way. She was coming, and if I couldn't control her, we were all dead.

Heat both smothered and swelled over me, filling me up until my demon broke the surface. She stepped from the unknown, from nothingness, into my heart. I gasped. A sudden thrill of power danced through my veins. Sparks jerked my mortal body. My puppet master element pulled the strings attached to my nerve endings. She laughed. I laughed. The room throbbed with energy. The building sizzled. The city outside buzzed with the promise of power. I had it all at my fingertips, could summon it into my heart and release it into the wild. The lust for chaos stole my breath away and wrenched reason from my mind. She wanted power. She wanted to burn it all; to slice open the veil and summon the fires of hell to dance for her. So did I.

She laughed again and pulled me onto my feet. I saw the three of them standing across the room. Ryder had the gun trained on me. Nica leaned into her father, tucked protectively against him. *Burn them,* my demon purred. *Burn them all.*

I smiled and allowed my demon to manifest. They would see her image shimmer over my mortal form, not entirely there, but real enough. They could never see all of her—too human to witness the truth. My one wing stretched high and flapped once, sending a scorching blast of air swirling about the office, lifting papers. Chaos thrashed at my core. It would take little more than surrender on my part for my demon to call enough heat and flame to burn the Institute to the ground. Just one moment of acceptance. It flirted with my thoughts, called to me, lured me closer to the precipice of madness with promises of freedom. They couldn't stop me. It would be easy. It would be divine.

I snarled and stood tall. Dying embers spiraled loosely around me like moths fluttering around a campfire. Ryder eyed me down the length of the gun, his finger hooked over the trigger. He looked into my eyes. He'd see the demon there, the fire. He might even see the madness bubbling in my mind. And he could pull the trigger.

I sucked in air through my teeth, hissed deeply, and eased the thirst for chaos back where it belonged, deep behind my human barriers. She didn't fight me. I had feared she would, but she seemed content to curl up at my core and rest, until all I could feel was a tiny filament of fire. I was complete again.

I blinked, licked my lips, and ran my hands through my hair; gathering my self-control around me. "Okay then. Put the gun down, Ryder. We need to find Damien before he kills again."

Chapter Fourteen

The woman—what was left of her—had been propped up against the massive trunk of an ancient oak tree, arms and legs posed at awkward angles, like a discarded doll. Foxes, stray cats, and all the other city critters had feasted on her remains while the city slept. It wasn't until dawn broke that she'd been discovered in the park by a jogger. The sickly cloying odors of death hung in the stagnant air. Mist hovered around the trees and wisped across a nearby shallow pond.

The tug of tiredness dulled my senses, numbing me. I'd been up the majority of the night briefing a handful of Institute officials on Damien, keeping my emotions in check behind a detached professionalism that I hadn't known I was capable of. While we'd been talking, Damien had been killing.

I'd told the officials everything I knew and given them the caveat that demons behave differently on this side of the veil than they do on their home turf. They're restrained here, governed by laws they don't understand. Unless a demon has enough clout to bend reality, they usually try to blend in—until their efforts to disguise themselves fail.

Damien wasn't there to blend in, but he wasn't out to create chaos either. He was treading carefully, making sure he couldn't be caught, feeling his way. His premeditation was something I hadn't anticipated. The Damien I'd known hadn't needed to tread carefully.

"There's something different about you." Coleman had finished talking with Detective Hill and joined me at the fringes of the crime scene. A strip of tape cordoned off the area around the body. The forensics team was inside, meticulously recording each drop of blood or speck of disturbed leaf mulch.

I leaned out around Coleman and watched Hill return to the incident van in the nearby parking area, where many of the Boston PD coordinated the investigation. I got the distinct impression Hill was avoiding me.

Coleman tucked his hands deep into his coat pockets. His shoulders slouched. His expression was grim. The damp air had settled in his hair and on his face. "Definitely something different..."

I smiled. His human senses were picking up on my newly returned demon. "I thought you were meant to be a detective?" I didn't want to get into a conversation about my demon, where she had been, and what it meant to have her back, especially with a detective who had no reason to sympathize with demons. "Where's the chain?" I'd already walked the scene.

"No chain. Early indications are he used the chain to restrain her but took it with him."

"That's different."

"He may have been disturbed. The other victims were attacked in private residences. This one, he'd been watching. He followed her back from a late night drink with some friends at a bar not far from here." Coleman must have read an unspoken inquiry on my face. "She has receipts in her purse. We've already confirmed with the bar owner that she was there."

What d'yah know? Coleman can detect after all. I nodded and wondered what Ryder would make of the scene. Wounded, he was technically on desk-duty. Having his arm in a sling wouldn't have stopped him from coming, but Adam had ordered him to stay behind to discuss my situation. What that meant exactly, I wasn't sure, but for now, the Institute seemed content to let me roam free.

"Any witnesses?" I asked. The park sat at the heart of Boston and as parks go, wasn't huge. Someone must have seen something.

"Hill is checkin' out a few leads, but nothing yet." He removed his hands from his pockets and tugged on a pair of woolen gloves. "Charlie, has anyone considered that this guy might have a source inside the Institute?"

"Yeah. Adam was onto it straight away. They've locked down all the IDs of the Enforcers, but the people who work there... I just can't see it being them. Most have dealt with demons in the past and not in a good way. They're the most professional people I've ever known, and they take their work seriously, I mean cult-like seriously." A few Enforcers batted around the motto "committed to the core," and they weren't wrong. "It could be someone there, but I doubt it. There's another, more likely source, beyond the veil. A half-blood. We think he might have given Damien the information."

"Half-blood?" Coleman frowned and held up a finger. "Wait, don't tell me..." He glanced up, searching his thoughts. "A hybrid, right? Part demon?"

He'd been doing his homework. "What the demons call a hybrid, yeah. Like me. Half demon." I waited for him to cringe or shrink back.

He nodded, as if reaffirming something in his mind. "We should talk. About demons, I mean. I could really use your expertise."

I didn't answer immediately. His request had thrown me off-guard. I'd assumed my half-blood nature had spooked him, but I'd been wrong. "I'm not sure the Institute would appreciate it. I'd likely get my wrists slapped for revealing classified information."

He smiled, and the smile seemed to lift a hundred pound weight off his shoulders. His eyes brightened, and his face softened. I caught a glimpse of the man behind the badge. "You don't strike me as the type to care."

"I er... I'm..." He must have seen the surprise on my face because he held up a hand, an indication there was no need to defend myself. I hadn't realized he'd been paying attention, at least not close enough to pick up on my distaste for Adam. It didn't take a detective to figure out how much I hated that man.

"You got everything you need?" he asked, attention back on the task at hand. The smile had gone, leaving me wondering if I'd seen it at all.

I took one last look at the victim, giving her a respectful nod before turning my back on her. I had my notes and relevant photos. I'd go over them all again back at the Institute. Coleman fell into step beside me. I got the impression he wanted to ask something, so I let the silence linger between us.

It wasn't until we were beside my car that he asked, "You've been to the netherworld?"

My smile barely touched my lips. "I was raised there."

"What's it like?"

Someone from the incident van called him over, but he waved back at them without looking. He watched me closely.

How to explain the netherworld to someone who's never seen it and if they were lucky, never would? "It's like here," I said, "but ruined—in more ways than one." A flicker of puzzlement narrowed his eyes. He wanted to know more, but I wasn't sure he could handle it. Some things are better left unknown. "Do you really want me to tell you?"

His gaze wandered somewhere over my shoulder into the trees beyond. "I've seen what demons are capable of. In the last few years, it's got a whole lot worse. If I knew where they came from, maybe it would help me understand it all."

"If it's understanding you want, you won't get it from demons. They're chaos, pure and simple. You could try to figure out the whys, but it won't do you any good."

"They must want something? Why are they coming here? Why so many? What's happening in the netherworld that makes our home so damn appealing?"

"They've always been here," I said carefully, wondering where he was going with this.

"Yeah, but something's up. A few hundred maybe, in the past… Enough to spark fairy tales and rumors, but now? Something is changing. The equilibrium is in flux, and don't tell me it isn't. I'm the one fending off the press when another rumor surfaces." He stepped closer. I lifted my chin and met his keen eyes. "Where is it all going? What's their end-game?"

I didn't have an answer for him. I knew no more than the average rookie Enforcer. As a half-blood, I'd spent my days trapped away from the ebb and flow of demon existence. Even Akil had dodged around the details whenever I'd asked for more. He'd promised to tell me. I didn't know then that his promises were worthless.

"I... I don't know." I lowered my voice to a whisper. "But I think you're right. The status quo is changing."

Coleman glanced behind him at his colleagues mingling back and forth. Hill wasn't in sight. "Look, I don't suppose you want to grab a drink sometime?" When he faced me this time, his gaze wandered nervously. "I'd like to know more. You know, get a handle on the creatures whose mess I'm clearing up. You guys—Enforcers—you get to track 'em down and send them back. I just... I want to know more. You come in, brush it all under the rug, and me and my people are left out in the dark. I don't trust the Institute, and I don't think you do either."

Mental note: Watch what I say around Coleman. He's smarter than he looks.

"More demons are breaking through," he said. His severe expression cut deeper. "The Institute isn't doing enough. Sooner or later, it's all goin' to come out, and it'll my people in the firing line. I want to be ready when it happens. The Institute doesn't care."

Oh, they cared. I didn't have clearance to visit the medical and weapons divisions, but I heard the whispers. They were experimenting on demons in a big way, searching for weaknesses, learning all they could, but it wouldn't be enough.

"They're working on it," I said, by way of avoiding the truth.

"Just a coffee," He brushed his thumb across his chin. "Maybe I give you some theories, and you tell me if I'm in the ballpark or way off field?" He waited, saw my frown, and said, "Think about it."

Spilling classified information would probably get me knee deep in trouble with the Institute. Which wasn't necessarily a bad thing. If I could piss off Adam, I'd be happy. Plus, he was right. He deserved to know more.

He walked back toward his colleagues.

"Hey," I called. He glanced back. "Give me a call when you get off. We'll talk."

He dipped his head in a tight nod and then jogged back to his colleagues. I unlocked the car, muttering to myself, when a dash of movement across the parking area caught my eye. The mist swirled between the skeletal trees but I couldn't see or hear anything out of place.

I glanced back at the crowd of officials within shouting distance. Coleman was deep in conversation with a uniformed officer. It wouldn't hurt to take a quick look at the edge of the clearing. I plucked my gun from its holster. A tingling of energy fizzed at my fingertips, my element stirring as my senses focused. I'd missed that little tug of power from my demon back-up.

My boots crunched on the loose gravel as I crossed the clearing. The blanket of mist smothered the city noises. My steady heartbeat drummed in my ears, and my level breathing sounded too loud in the quiet. A trickle of apprehension shivered down my spine.

The quiet became so thick I could almost taste it. It was the kind of quiet that crawls across your skin, the quiet when the crickets stop chirping, and the air hangs motionless. The mist dampened my face and spritzed my hair. I placed my left hand against the nearest tree-trunk and sharpened my senses. I smelled the damp earth and looked down to see overturned leaf mulch. I wasn't alone.

A twig snapped somewhere ahead. I took a few light steps forward, then paused and glanced back. The mist had closed in behind me, obscuring the parking area. The cops weren't far, but I couldn't see or hear them. I'd just take a few more steps, not too far.

I blinked ahead.

Damien stood a few strides into the trees. Detective Hill knelt in front of him. He'd hooked a blood-encrusted chain around her throat and pulled her back, tight against him, like a hangman holding the noose. Her wide eyes pleaded with me. She clawed at the chain, trying to pry it free. Her mouth opened and closed, but no sound escaped.

Damien's ashen face might as well have been a mask. His eyes were cold, like those of a shark. His element wove around me, the ghostly touch of air, not quite there, like a whisper in the dark. It eased around my ankles and slid up my legs. I felt the touch of power embrace my waist and tighten my chest.

I had my gun in my trembling hands but no memory of grabbing it. I clasped both hands around it, but the tremors migrated through me. I could do this... He was just another demon masquerading as a man. My aim wavered. I licked my lips and shifted my stance. *Just aim between his eyes and pull the trigger.*

"Muse..." he growled. His voice was different spoken from a human mouth. It rumbled and rolled, growled and hissed. He said my name like a curse. It barely sounded human at all. "I will kill her." He worked hard to form each word and spat them out as though human speech disgusted him.

I tried to swallow, but my throat constricted. Hill's eyelids drooped. Her mouth worked. Her eyes rolled back.

"Damien..." I gasped. "Please..."

Now he smiled. At least the corner of his lips twitched, but those dead eyes didn't brighten. He liked to hear me beg. "Drop the weapon."

My demon twisted. Her fear swirled in my head, mixing with mine. I couldn't move. My body wouldn't obey the screams in my head. Shoot, run, drop the weapon, do something, say anything, but I couldn't. My breaths came in short sharp gasps. Sickly chills spilled across my prickling skin. He was my owner. I belonged to him. I'd tried to kill him. I was terrified of him.

His eyes narrowed slightly. He tucked his chin in and drilled his gaze into my soul. "Obey. Me."

I opened my mouth to beg, but my breath rushed out of me as though I'd been punched in the stomach. I staggered and reached for the nearest tree. My chest heaved. I tried to suck in air that wasn't there. I fell to my knees, gun forgotten. It fell from my hand. I clawed at my own throat, trying to work non-existent oxygen into my lungs. My chest burned, lungs bursting. Damien denied me the air I needed to breathe.

Fire burst from my flesh and tried to cocoon me in a protective barrier, but it spluttered and gasped, dying out with a *pfft* noise. I fell onto my hands. Pressure built inside my head. My sight blurred. The dark of unconsciousness loomed in my peripheral vision, pulsating with the beat of my racing heart.

The abrasive metal chain hooked over my head and wrapped around my throat. Damien yanked my head back so hard he pulled me up onto my knees. I saw the trees swirl and caught sight of Amanda Hill face down on the ground. As my eyes fluttered closed, I wondered if she would live.

***

I pried my eyes open. Burned, black trees crowded around. Above their spindly branches, the sky swirled purple and red in black, like mixing ink.

I dragged the sickly sweet air through my teeth, trying to breathe in the soup of elements in the swollen air. Blackened skin layered over my human flesh. Obsidian claws tipped my coal black fingers. My clothes were gone, stripped by the harsh onslaught of elements in the netherworld. I was demon, and I was home.

I flung my wing out and tried to sit up. Damien yanked on the chain around my neck and drove a knee into my spine, leaning all of his weight onto me. My trembling arms gave out, and I collapsed under the weight of him. The chain links clinked tighter... tighter...

"You are mine, Muse." His voice, harsh and heavy, bored into my skull and emptied out the horrors I'd worked to keep hidden. My memories spilled out of their unlocked box. Everything he'd done, the pain he'd wrought, the agony of an existence among demons, it all came rushing out in a surge of unfiltered emotion.

I desperately summoned my element from the alien world around me, tearing it up from the earth. I mentally reached for the veil, knowing another world of power lay just beyond: the human world. I could summon it all and blast Damien into fragments of smoldering flesh, but the chain tightened, and my thoughts muddied. I tried to reach out in hope, clawing at the pieces of my mind, to ram them back into place, but the darkness came, and my element retreated. The chain pulled tighter. Damien's growls rumbled. Tremors reverberated through his knee embedded in my back. He bowed forward and pressed his cool face against mine. "It has been too long," he said, and the blissful embrace of darkness overcame me once more.

Chapter Fifteen

Wood-smoke and the smell of damp earth tickled my nose. I sneezed and jolted fully awake. Fear tried to spur me into action, but as I attempted to sit up, pins and needles shivered down my arms. My wrists were bound behind me. I rolled onto my back, crushing my one tattered wing awkwardly beneath me. Stone walls on all four sides penned me in. A closed timber door seemed to be the only way in and out. Above, I saw the moss-covered underside of a thatched roof. I was in some sort of hut.

Netherworld air encircled me. It filled my lungs and embraced my demon body. The air I dragged through my teeth strummed with frequencies beyond human interpretation. Power. Chaos. *Home.* A fire smoldered in a grate at the opposite end of the hut. I sensed its familiar warmth reaching out to me even though the fire had died down.

I sat up and became acutely aware of my demon appearance. My skin had burned to black. Ash dusted from my flesh, like the wood ash crumbling in the grate. Embers twitched beneath my skin. My veins pulsed like rivulets of lava. If I'd been in any doubt about my new location, my all-over demon transformation provided all the proof I needed. Bubbling panic threatened to spill from my lips. Crude, maniacal laughter rang like bells in my head. If I let it, the madness would consume me. I'd curl into a ball and succumb. I'd beaten this before. I could do it again. Stronger. Faster. More powerful. I had the tools I needed. I could do this. I had to do this.

If Damien doesn't get me, Val will.

No, no, I couldn't think like that. Thoughts of my brother wouldn't help. Damien was unlikely to tell anyone he had me. Not yet. Val would not yet realize I was back on home soil. Would Akil know? Surely not. A Prince of Hell must have other things to worry about. But what if he knew? He'd want revenge. He'd want a lot of things. He'd have to pick a number and get in line.

Dammit. I could do this. If I could just slip out of the restraints around my wrists... I called to the fire in the grate. The tiny flames licked higher, tasting the air, answering my summons. Focusing my will on the brackets holding my wrists, I pooled the heat there and tugged, but they didn't break.

Muttering a curse, I twisted my joined wrists around my side to get a good look at them. The shackles had been cut and shaped from a hardwood. They should have combusted when I'd focused on them. On closer inspection, I could see why that hadn't happened. A string of curiously swirling symbols entwined the cuffs, symbols similar to those adorning the walls outside the Institute. They prevented elemental magic from crossing them. Great, if you wanted to hide a building from demons or tie one up in your hut.

Plan B. I clambered onto unsteady feet and staggered toward the door. Turning sideways so I could reach the wooden latch with my hands, I flicked it open and bumped my shoulder against it, shoving it open. The netherworld vista spread in front of me like an elaborate canvas of dark surrealism. The perpetual half-light muddied my adjusting eyes. Hues of purple and black swirled and mingled like bruises on a beaten landscape. A vast forest carpeted a bank of hills to the right of the hut. On the opposite side of the valley, the forest had been scorched, leaving the trees naked, black and brittle, their branches like skeletal fingers reaching toward the sky. In the distance where the valley cut scored through, a bulbous moon hugged the shimmering surface of an ink-black ocean.

I'd forgotten how devastatingly beautiful the netherworld was.

A hollow baying rolled up the valley. My skin prickled, and my heart hammered faster. I'd heard those hounds before. I shrank back into the warmth of the hut and clicked the latch down. Shutting the door and ignoring the fact I had a realm of demons out to get me didn't make it any less real. I would need an ally and fast if I had any hope of surviving. I padded bare foot back into the relative safety of the hut and tried to search my memory for something I could use.

The last time I'd been in the netherworld Akil, better known as Mammon the Prince of Greed, had taken me under his wing. He'd taught me how to summon my element, and with that knowledge, I'd killed Damien. Turns out that part had been a lie. No surprise, given Akil's penchant for bending the truth. For all I knew, they'd planned it that way.

Disgust turned my stomach. Could Akil have deliberately misled me about Damien's demise? Surely even Akil couldn't fake revulsion as keen as his for Damien. He had despised my owner. When I'd wanted to hurt Akil, I'd compared him to Damien and watched the infallible Prince lose his cool. That kind of hatred can't be manufactured. But things had changed. I'd crossed Akil. Could he be helping Damien? I shook the thought away and with it the fear of what a partnership between the two of them could accomplish. I thought I'd known Akil once. I'd been wrong, wrong about a lot of things it seemed.

Damien would be back soon. He wouldn't risk leaving me for long. I could run. It was tempting, although I was just as likely to be picked off by any number of the horrors lurking outside the hut as I was to be killed by Damien inside it. Until I got the cuffs off, I couldn't protect myself, and even then the chances were slim. One problem at a time. First, the cuffs. I'd need a weapon to pry them off.

The hut had a stool in one corner, two bowls by the fireplace, two hand carved spoons, and a misshapen jug on the floor beside a bed of straw. The only thing I could use was the fire itself, but even if I could plunge my hands into the flame, it probably wouldn't burn the cuffs, because of those damn symbols. Worth a shot though.

I tried to angle myself so I could dip my hands into the flame. It took a bit of maneuvering, especially with my single wing pulled against my back. I needn't have bothered. The fire just licked at me like an eager puppy, its affection useless. I growled my frustration. Damien would be back soon, and his idea of a reunion was not going to be pleasant. I shivered. Ashes dislodged from my wing and dusted the earth. Okay, if I couldn't get the cuffs off myself, then my only other option was to get Damien to release them. To do that, I'd need to lie.

I crouched down in front of the fire. I'd lied to a Prince of Hell once. It hadn't been easy, and I didn't exactly succeed, but it could be done. I had my ways of using those around me, just as I'd been used. Sex and lies. I didn't like to do it. It reminded me of what I was: a demon's property, something to be used and discarded. I'd been raised to believe I was chattel. Why should it hurt? Or perhaps I was kidding myself. My time away from the netherworld had taught me much. Self-worth was one of those lessons.

Lying to Akil would be easier than manipulating my owner. Damien terrified me on a primal, gut wrenching, bowel loosening level. I'd be lucky if I could look him in the eyes without collapsing in a quivering wreck at his feet. You can't argue with terror. It robs you of all control, snatching coherent thought right out of your body, so you become an animal fuelled by instinct alone, and if those instincts tell you to drop and roll, you do it. I'd have loved to have bravery at my disposal, but it wasn't going to happen. I wasn't heroic, just a half-blood pet, bought and sold among demons until one tired of me enough to put me out of my misery. Sure, I'd had my eyes opened to the truth in the past six months, but that didn't change the fact I'd happily scream obscenities at Akil, or shoot a Hellhound between the eyes, instead of standing up to Damien.

But I had beaten him once before.

When I thought I'd killed him, I'd had Akil standing right behind me. I'd failed. Damien was still alive, and I technically belonged to him. I clicked my sharp teeth together as a nervous purr vibrated through me. The more I went over my options, the faster my heart fluttered. Things were different now. I wasn't the same half-blood Damien had sliced a wing from. I wasn't the same woman either. Fifteen years. Ten with Akil and five on my own. I'd escaped. I'd moved on. I'd lived, but Damien had the power to tear it all down around me.

Whispering voices plucked me from my rapid descent into fear. A particular voice, to be exact. Whispers fluttered about my head. Were they real? I cocked my head to the side and listened.

"Muse, Charlie Henderson, friend: I invite you to share this place and time with me..." The voice quietened and almost disappeared completely, but I'd heard enough to recognize Ryder's drawl. Only he could summon a demon and still make it sound as though he was reading from the back page of a newspaper.

I closed my eyes, reaching out with my senses.

"I summon Muse, Charlotte Henderson, friend... Damien's chattel."

That last inclusion sunk a hook into my gut and wrenched me from the netherworld, dragging me back through a blur and depositing my sense of self opposite Ryder. He glared back at me behind a dancing candle flame. The image sputtered. Colors snapped. I lifted my hand and realized, with an oddly detached thought, that I could see through my skin. I wasn't really with Ryder. Physically, I sat huddled in front of the fire in Damien's hut, hands tied behind my back, but the summoning had worked enough to tug my consciousness into Ryder's time and place.

I smelled gun oil and blood, and breathed the scent of Ryder into me. I could almost taste him. All demon, I drank him in with all my senses. The man looking back at me had old eyes, an old soul. I heard his drumming heartbeat and measured breathing, but his exterior appeared gravely calm. It's not every day you summon a friend and look her demon-self in the eyes.

It takes spilled blood and intent to summon a demon. The little flame held the key to anchoring me in the human realm, but the hold was fragile and could be snuffed out at any time.

Ryder leaned closer to the flame. "We're doin' everythin' we can to get you, even some shit I never thought Adam would agree to. Hold on, Muse."

My gaze darted around, expecting to see others. I couldn't see beyond the confines of the candlelight. Darkness loomed, waiting to suck me back in. "Hurry," I breathed. The candle puffed out. The summoning failed. The link broke, and I was slammed back into the netherworld with all the finesse of a sledgehammer.

I doubled over by the fire in the hut and tried to control my short, sharp breaths. My vision swam, and my head throbbed. Half-human, I wasn't made for metaphysical mind-jumps into different realms.

The touch of *his* gaze crawled like spiders legs across my flesh.

Terror drained reason from my mind. Fire fizzled beneath my skin. Superheated dust shivered from my flesh. I pulled my torn wing against my back and folded it around my side as though it might protect me. I hunkered down and heard pitiful whimpers tumbling from my lips. The dreadful mewing wouldn't stop. Sweat vaporized. Shame trembled through me. I had wronged him in the most terrible way possible, and I deserved to be punished. Sickened by my own disgusting behavior, I dug my claws into the palms of my hands, deliberately cutting myself. I deserved the pain. My head swirled with rage, fear, and shock. The surge of emotions poisoned all rational thought, turning my strengths against me, rendering me weak and pathetic.

At the sound of his rumbling laughter, salty tears boiled on my cheeks. I could only hope that he'd kill me now. A quick death would be a blessing. The invasive touch of his element slid over me. Fingers of air glided over my shoulders and down my back. I clamped my eyes shut and strained to control the trembling. He made a sound, like a dismissive snort. His element slid carefully, purposely, down my thigh, probing, reacquainting, and then wound around my one remaining wing, slipping beneath it to my chest. He stamped a foot, and a whimper slithered from my lips. Finally, after seconds-minutes-hours, he uncoiled his elemental tendrils from around me, so that I could at least breathe again.

"It has been too long." His voice grated against my brittle state of mind as he injected the words into my thoughts. He had a gruff accent that I'd not noticed before. My time away from him, from everything, had afforded me the chance to forget. Now that luxury was over. This was a time for remembering who and what he was. I pressed myself against the ground, hoping the earth might open up and gulp me down.

When I finally found the courage to lift my eyes, I saw him standing tall, filling the space between floor and ceiling. His muscles quivered like the flanks of a horse. Every inch of him dripped demon masculinity, but he was more animal than man. Noticing my attention to his bunched, leathery wings, he flexed them a little, lifting a gust of wind that blasted through the hut and spluttered the fire in the grate. I was built for speed, but he was every inch a beast of strength. Bulging veins snaked down his taut arms. His shark-gray skin didn't glisten as it should and after blinking to refocus, I could see why. His flesh was mottled, its once smooth surface dulled by scarring—the unmistakable curdling of healed burns.

My lips parted. I'd done that to him, and the scars weren't minor. In the firelight, I noticed how they curled up one leg and around his waist. Although he hadn't fully opened his wings, I saw the shadows dancing on their uneven surface. I tried to swallow, but my throat clamped closed.

He won't let me live.

When I flicked my nervous glances over his face, his glowering expression slammed the realization home; I wasn't getting out of this alive. Whatever Ryder had planned, he'd better do it fast.

Damien rushed me. He scooped a huge hand around my neck and thrust me back against the stone wall, pinning me there with a possessive roar. Jaw clamped closed, I turned my head away, not wanting to see the fury knotting his features.

"Thank you for your parting gift." He licked the air with a forked tongue and then dragged its moist leathery touch up my cheek, lapping at the remnants of my tears.

"I didn't..." I choked and wheezed, unable to draw enough breath to form words.

His nostrils flared. He breathed in my scent, lips quivering in snarl. "Humans die so easily. You, I can make last. I know you." He slid his free hand around my waist and leaned his crushing weight against me. "I know how to break you." His storm-grey eyes filled my vision. "And I know how to make it last an eternity."

"I..." Hands clamped behind my back and wedged against the wall, I couldn't pry his fingers from around my throat. If he wouldn't let me speak, how could I even begin to reason with him?

My element rolled over my flesh and coiled around him. He'd feel the touch of it the way I'd felt his, as though a warm hand caressed his skin. My eyelids flickered closed, chest heaving, lungs ready to burst, but I eased the touch of my element further. Tendrils of power coiled around his legs, writhing up his thighs and over quivering muscles. I couldn't call fire, but I could extend the essence of my power out to him.

He pressed his lips hard against my cheek and growled through his teeth. I coiled the energy around him, into him, seeking the source of his element. I couldn't draw his power from him, not like I had Akil. Damien's air element opposed mine, but I could distract him. I drove my ethereal touch deeper and discovered a seething well of darkness.

The grip around my throat eased enough for me to snatch a breath. He brushed a cool leathery cheek against mine in a curiously feline gesture. "I feel you inside me, my Muse."

I fluttered my eyes open while sinking my element further inside him, circling the dark well of his soul, tentatively stalking around its edges. Damien was damaged in a way I had no hope of reaching. A substantial primal madness pulsated inside him. I'd known he was sick, but I hadn't realized how deep the corruption went.

He released my throat and slid his hand over my shoulder to find my wing-stump.

Now I could breathe. I could speak. "I had no choice," I wheezed. His cold hand slid over the healed bone where he'd sheared my wing from my body. I winced, the memory of the assault slicing through me. I spat out my lies. "Akil—Mammon—he forced me to hurt you."

Damien's hand withdrew from my stump and rested on my shoulder. He leaned back. Gray eyes searched mine. Hell-knows what he saw there, perhaps exactly what he wanted to see. He pulled back and lowered me to my feet. I slumped against the wall and drew my wing back around me. I held his searching gaze, sensing I'd stumbled upon something I could use. "What could I have done? He wanted me for himself. I'm nothing. I could no more go against his wishes than I could yours. He's a Prince of Hell... I had no choice." He read the desperate tone of my voice as despair, which of course it was, but for entirely different reasons than the one I'd just manufactured.

"Mammon is Prince no more." Damien spat on the ground.

I gritted my teeth, and my jaw muscles jumped. I refused to let his revealing words rattle me. *Buy it Damien. Just hear what you want to, that your beloved pet, your work of art, your muse, didn't turn on you.*

"I was always yours," I said. My legs gave out. I dropped to my knees. "Your muse."

His jaw set. His lips turned down. His eyes pinched into narrow slits sharp enough to pierce through me and sink into my soul to discover the truth. "My muse..."

"Always." *Please, please let him believe me. I don't want to die here...*

He knelt before me and clasped my face in his cold hands, locking me in his unwavering stare. I saw hope in the briefest flicker of light in his eyes and the gentle parting of his lips. He wanted to believe me.

I flung the touch of my power inside of him and locked it around the throbbing darkness. Lashes of tainted energy spiraled around mine and tangled with my touch, pulling me further into him. I gasped and twitched. His dark dragged me down. What the hell was he doing?

"Are you lying to me?" His grip on my face tightened. He could crush me. He was capable both mentally and physically of grinding my skull to dust.

"No." I squeezed the simple denial through my clenched teeth as he pulled me deeper in to the terrifying unknown.

"You are mine. You were always mine. You will always be mine." Dry lips smothered mine. His forked tongue pried my mouth open. I clamped my eyes closed, still trying to tug my ethereal touch out of him, but he wouldn't release me. Every time I plucked a piece of power free, an eel-like tendril reached out and snapped it right back down. Screams burst inside my head.

His hands rode over my shoulders and down my back. My skin prickled. His roaming left hand rode up my wing. His toxic touch ignited memories that burned against my flesh. I realized with dreadful certainty that I wasn't escaping him. Nobody was coming to save me. I would have to endure the worst he could do all over again.

Ryder, someone, anyone... Don't let his happen.

Chapter Sixteen

Damien was right.

He knew how to break me.

The creature I had once been, the tiny insignificant half-blood, she'd never really left me. I'd told myself she'd died with my owner, but those lies returned to haunt me. I had despised her, the old Muse—the slave, the piece of meat—and shoved her down into the smallest corner of my mind, wrapped her in fifteen years' worth of denial and left her there to rot. That would have been fine, except I hadn't anticipated Damien's return. Perhaps, had I known he still existed somewhere, I could have prepared myself. I had no defense. I'd spent over a decade painting over the emotional cracks, every time they showed through my carefully constructed veneer of reality. I'd focused on remaking myself into something new and clean, bright and fresh. A human woman. I had a job, friends, an apartment, a cat. I watched *Lost* and swore at the ending. I wasted time drinking lattes in Starbucks. I sang in the shower, painted my toenails bright red, and dyed my hair, only to regret it in the morning. I had good days, when the sun warmed my skin and I couldn't hold back the laughter. I had bad days, when I struggled to make enough money to pay the rent on my workshop. It all came together and created something so acutely real that I'd forgotten the years of slavery at the many hands of many demons.

Damien hadn't.

He unmade me. The woman I'd become—the happy, independent woman—she'd been a dream. I knew that now. Akil hadn't saved the wretched little girl at all. He'd left her to wallow in her own filth and dream up fanciful images of a world that didn't exist. What good was freedom if all it achieved was the agony of having it ripped away? If I'd never known what it meant to be free, Damien couldn't have hurt me the way he did.

I felt the break of dawn snap through the morning air even though I couldn't see it from inside the hut. I lay on my side and watched logs crumble to ash in the grate. I was alone except for the scurrying of sharp-eyed-needle-point-legged critters skittering across the floor.

The ghost of Damien's touch bloomed in the bruises beneath my skin. My hands, still clasped behind my back, were numb. I wished the rest of me felt the same. My wrists throbbed where the skin had rubbed raw. An abrasive burning ache radiated through all of me, alternating between teeth-gritting agony and wretched, feverish trembling.

I couldn't escape his ozone smell. The sickly sweet scents of vomit, perspiration, semen, and blood surrounded me. My gut churned. Had it just been my body he'd invaded, I might have been able to scrape myself off the floor and find it in me to rage at him—given time—but he'd pulled me inside his rotten, rancid core. His poisonous touch had sunk beneath my skin, unraveling as it went. He picked apart my hopes and dreams, and drowned them beneath his lust, greed and hunger. When he couldn't take any more—when I'd fallen silent and retreated into a numb husk of myself—he'd thrust his element into me. He invaded all of me, poured himself into my open wounds and smothered my strength, my will, my soul. Not done with soiling my insides, he broke down my rapidly diminishing barriers by pounding into me. I did nothing as he ruined me inside and out. Satisfied and spent, he discarded what was left of his half-blood slave in a stinking puddle of muck.

Fifteen years to make Muse the woman. A few hours with Damien to unmake me.

When the woman in white walked into the hut, I didn't care who or what she was. I wasn't entirely sure she was real. I didn't trust my senses and was afraid, if I moved, my body and mind might shatter.

She knelt before me. Her skin sparkled in the dawn light spilling through the open doorway. She wore a delicate, translucent gown, through which I watched the light play across her female physique. I felt her cool touch feather across my cheek. Her brilliant-blue eyes flicked over my used body.

A small dagger, its surface a brittle blue, glinted in her hand. A flicker of a thought briefly offered me some relief. *Perhaps she will kill me now.* But she reached behind me, and after a few stokes of the blade, tossed my shackles away.

"My sweet thing..." Her voice chimed with a delicate melody.

I reached out a trembling hand and touched her face. Ice spidered across her cheek. A bitter chill sprinkled down my fingers. I hissed and pulled back.

"Come, Little One." She slipped her arms beneath me and lifted me as though I weighed nothing. "He will return soon enough, and it would be best if he did not find us here." I buried my head against her cool shoulder. Closing my eyes while curled up in her arms, I could pretend I was safe.

***

Her heartbeat held the same lullaby quality as her voice. I listened to its gentle rhythm as she carried me away from the little hut on the hill and away from Damien's reach. Time passes differently beyond the veil, measured by the weight and taste of the air. Dawn and dusk aren't reliable and can be manipulated by the most powerful of demons, hence the body becomes attuned to what it can measure. As the air lifted and thinned, I suspected we'd been walking for roughly an hour.

She asked me if I could walk when I lifted my head to take a look at our surroundings. I nodded and let her lower me onto unreliable legs, then walked beside her. We'd arrived at the fringes of a lake. The azure waters matched the woman's eyes. She was a demon, but she'd chosen to appear human to me. Either she didn't think I could handle her true appearance, or she was hiding her true form for other reasons. Even human, she was a breathtaking figure of serene beauty. Snow white hair cascaded in gentle curls down her back. Her pale skin glowed and shimmered beneath the morning light, as though she'd been sprinkled with sugar. Her oval face and delicate cat-like almond eyes exuded a warmth her cool touch couldn't detract from. She didn't watch as I waded into the water and washed the filth from my skin. She didn't see my tears.

It would take more than water to cleanse his touch from me.

We walked for long enough that my body stumbled. My muscles seized up. My legs trembled. I wondered if I might just as well lie down and rest when we finally reached a pebble beach. A quilt of snow had settled over the edge of a forest. Light refracted through icicle-tipped tree branches. The temperature plummeted as we ventured toward the snow. My breath misted in front of me, and my skin glowed warm in response. I pushed ahead; the air rippled around me. The ice attempted to suck the warmth from my flesh. My element flared.

The white woman smiled over her shoulder at me. "It will not hurt you."

That was easy for her to say. I hung back as she walked over the snow. Her light footfalls barely left a single imprint.

I retained a little of my element and kept it close against me. My heat-wrapped feet promptly melted holes in the snow, making my progress a little awkward. Before long, we reached a grove frozen in ice. The ambient light slithered across brittle surfaces and fractured into tiny rainbows which danced like sprites around us.

"Would you mind?" She gestured at a stack of kindling in the center of the grove.

I obliged with a flick of my hand and ignited enough of the wood to start a fire. I assumed it was for my benefit.

"Wait here," she said. "I'll return."

I melted the snow a few feet back from the campfire and sat with my legs drawn up, chin resting on my knees. My body throbbed with unpleasant heat. All things considered, I was lucky to still be breathing, but I didn't feel lucky. I felt filthy, like a soiled rag. At one time, I had lived with this night after night for as long as I could remember. Damien's control had been the whole of my wretched existence. But this time, Damien's violation mattered on a visceral level. I knew my worth. I was strong. Powerful. Capable of great things. More than that, I was a woman. A living, breathing, human being. An entity all of my own. Why–how had I let him do this to me?

I curled my claws into my palms and pierced my skin again, wincing at the fresh pain. But something in that new pain relieved the horrid depth of anguish and disgust in the pit of my stomach. It was a clean pain.

The white woman returned, carrying a tin pot of something. She hung it over the fire. Within minutes, I smelled a sweet but sharp odor rising from the warming water, like eucalyptus and tea tree oil, cleansing but with a kick. Only my eyes moved as I watched her stir the concoction. Her lips seemed to be pulled into the most delicate of smiles at all times, as though she were listening to music that nobody else could hear.

She poured some of the mixture into a tin cup and handed it to me. "Drink."

I sniffed at the steam rising from its surface and wrinkled my nose.

"It will take the pain away."

"I'm not in pain," I shot back.

"Drink." She smiled.

What was the point in denying the truth? I lifted the cup to my lips and sipped. The tea tasted bitter, but as the warmth rolled down my throat, softness spread through my muscles.

Satisfied, she sat on a snowy tree stump. Her gown resembled a gossamer veil. It barely existed at all. I could clearly admire the curves of her dainty body beneath. When in the netherworld, demons rarely craft themselves clothes, real or illusionary. Why would they? Clothing restrains. It restricts. Demons need to feel the elements around them, feel the air against their flesh, the earth beneath their feet. It's different in the human world. When I revealed my demon there, she layered herself over me, clothes and all. On the other side, anything human doesn't survive for long. My clothes had fizzled away the second I stepped through the veil, as would anything I had with me. Full demons could manifest clothes when and however they pleased. I didn't have that luxury. My human half wanted to cover up my vulnerability, but my demon was in control. She slapped my insecurities down.

"I must apologize. I wish I had found you sooner," the white woman said.

The tea scalded my lips, but I welcomed the heat. "How did you find me?"

"He wouldn't have taken you far. I know where our world layers your Boston."

He could have. He could have wrapped me in his arms and taken to the air. We could have been half way across the netherworld in hours. She seemed to read my mistrust because her blue eyes softened sympathetically.

"He would not wait to claim you again, Muse."

Claim me. I shuddered and gulped down more tea. "I couldn't stop him." I closed my eyes and felt his abrasive touch roam over me. It had taken years to lock the memories away, to stand tall and walk proud, as though I hadn't been beaten into submission both mentally and physically. Now the memories were back, mingling with new ones, and I teetered on the edge of madness. "The restraints—I tried to summon—" I licked my lips and flicked my gaze to hers. She looked back at me with quiet dignity. I silently ordered myself not to fall apart. Not yet. "I had to make him believe I was his again. I had no choice. It was all I had... I couldn't..." I bowed my head and bit into my trembling lip. Words wouldn't suffice.

"I know. You do not need to explain. You are alive. Wounds will heal. Drink. You are safe here. For now."

He would find me again, and I had no idea how I might react. I could tear into him. With the restraints gone, I could summon the fires of hell, draw the heat from this world and the human realm. I could funnel it all into his soul and burn him from the inside out. But it wasn't that simple. If I lost control—which was highly likely—there was a chance the sheer weight of power would destroy me.

"He did something..." I pressed the palm of my right hand to my chest. "Inside."

She blinked slowly, her smile falling away. "*Tamashii rokku...*" she whispered, and then for my benefit said, "He's claimed you—inside?" She tapped her chest. "He has locked your soul?"

I didn't know what that was, but the look of barely restrained horror on her face was already conjuring up likely scenarios in my mind, none of them good. Perhaps I should have felt something, fear maybe. I didn't. I just felt empty. "I tried to reach out to him with my element, to distract him, but he pulled me in. There was something inside him, something dark, it dragged me under, and then he was inside me." A surge of nausea rolled over me. I gagged and pressed the back of a hand to my lips, blinking back tears.

I watched her throat move as she swallowed. She came forward, knelt before me, and took my free hand in hers. My blackened skin pulsed with fiery veins against her delicate, icy touch. The cool touch of her element slid across the back of my hand and up my arm. I recognized that elemental touch but couldn't pin it down. "You and he, you are joined. As one."

"I don't understand."

"He cannot do this to you unless you are willing."

I snatched my hand back. "I wasn't willing."

"Willing or not, you let him in, Muse. He's tied your soul to his. If anything should happen to either of you, the soul will join its mate. You are as one."

My chest tightened. Bile burned my throat. "There's a way out?"

She looked away. "I... do not know."

I cleared my throat and threw my gaze skyward. Curdled clouds drifted across the lilac sky. "There's a way." There's always a way out of these things. Isn't there? I might have been raised among demons, but I'd been deliberately sheltered. I knew more about the human world than I did the netherworld. Soul-locked. I never knew such a thing existed.

"I didn't let him in," I growled.

I'd shut down once he'd made it clear what he wanted. My mind retreated while I let him use my body, but even cowering inside my own subconscious, I hadn't been safe. His power had plunged deep inside to depths I didn't know existed. He hadn't done that before. Before, it had all been physical abuse, but fifteen years ago, he hadn't known what I was capable of. He'd thought of me as a plaything, below him on the demon social ladder. Six months ago, I'd rendered a Prince of Hell impotent. I could pull the power of two worlds into my being. Things had changed. No wonder he'd claimed me. It made him powerful in return.

I gulped back the swell of rage and agony, but it still leaked into my voice. "There are rules, right?" I snarled. "There must be some sort of order here. Otherwise you'd all be tearing each other to pieces."

"Yes, the Princes dictate order, but they are unlikely to help a half-blood."

We fell quiet. Slowly, methodically, I finished my tea and managed to keep it down. The warmth of the mixture soothed my aching limbs and sore bruises. The mental damage would take a lot more than herbal tea to heal. I couldn't afford to dwell on it now. If I fell apart here or lost control, something bigger and nastier would likely take the opportunity to bite a few chunks out of me.

With the lid firmly on my broiling emotions, I looked up at the white woman. "So what do you want?" She might appear to be the model hostess, but no demon did anything out of the kindness of her heart. It's not their way. If they can screw you over, they will, and appearances are always deceiving. The white woman had saved me. She looked like a dazzling angel, which often meant there was a devil hiding beneath.

"My name is Yukki Onna. You will reach my son." She straightened as if waiting for my challenge.

I recognized her name and realized why I'd felt a familiarity in her icy touch. Nica had once told me about

Stefan's mother, an ice elemental, more commonly known as the Snow Witch. I wasn't sure what I'd expected, but nothing quite as otherworldly beautiful as she appeared to be.

I looked up. Thunderous clouds smothered the lilac sky. "I'll happily find Stefan, but I don't know where he is." Snowflakes spiraled around us.

"I know where he is." She turned her head and cast her gaze out across the lake. Snowflakes nestled in her hair and kissed her cheeks.

"But you said..."

"Do you have family, Muse?" she asked. I almost laughed. It depended on what her definition of family was. She didn't give me a chance to attempt an answer. "There is no stronger tie that binds, but ties can readily knot. And easily strangle."

Apparently, her definition of family complimented mine.

She sighed and refocused on me. "My son is beyond my reach." She looked down at me, tears freezing the moment they skipped from her eyes. "This is my price."

Chapter Seventeen

The netherworld heaves with vicious creatures. The shadows harbor countless nasties that will quite happily take a chunk out of you while you look the other way. Night is even worse there. In the dark, the lesser demons come out to hunt. Anything smaller than them is prey. Survival of the fittest plays out every time the sun sets. Only the strong, the quick, and the resourceful make it through even a single night.

Yukki Onna wouldn't answer any further questions about Stefan. It didn't matter. He was alive. After so long, I had confirmation he'd survived, not just speculation and theories. After the events of the last few hours, a heady dose of hope was exactly what I needed.

While Yukki Onna refused to talk about her son, she did explain how the Institute had summoned her and asked her to find me. She'd agreed, on the understanding I reach Stefan. I wondered if Adam had anything to do with the deal. He and Yukki Onna had a history, and considering how he'd reacted to my crass accusation in his office, his feelings—good or bad—were clearly still raw. I was tempted to ask Yukki Onna, but I had no idea how she'd react to mention of Adam. Knowing him as I did, I suspected their union may not have been a happy one. His hatred of demons seemed at odds with the image of the two of them together.

"Yukki Onna..." I stood beside her on the beach. The waters of the lake lapped at the polished pebbles a few feet ahead of us. A warm breeze teased through her ivory hair and tugged at her gown. "You don't need to appear human for me."

"But you are half human."

I smiled. She meant to protect me. "It's okay. My demon protects me here. I can see all of you without... passing out."

She gave a little shiver, and my vision quivered. Her image blurred out of focus. I blinked and refocused. Her gown dissolved, revealing a crystalline female figure. Light swirled beneath her skin like a genie in a bottle. Four-pronged gossamer wings unfurled behind her. They briefly beat the air too quickly for me to see each stroke. A dusting of snow fell from their trailing edges. Her white hair became a brittle mantle, glistening with spikes of ice.

She shook herself all over. Snow spilled to the ground. I smiled. She was as beautiful as a winter's morning, but like all things truly beautiful, she had a deadly glint in her eye. I got the impression Yukki Onna was not a demon to be crossed. Ice burns as readily as fire.

"Night will be on us soon." Her voice took on a brittle, tinkling edge.

I noticed a dagger and rapier sheathed at her hip. In comparison, I felt decidedly unarmed. My one shredded wing wasn't going to be of any use either. I had power— lots of it—but wielding it was tricky at the best of times. These were not the best of times.

Yukki Onna withdrew the rapier. "Take it."

I weighed the sword in my hand, testing its balance. As a blacksmith, I'd made rapiers, but hers was impossibly light, like a steel feather in the palm of my hand. Clasping it tightly, I felt the cool touch of ice seep into the heat of my hand. "It has power."

"Yes. She is named Kira-Kira. She will look after you. She belongs to Stefan. Or would have, had he been returned to me...as promised."

Trying to read her expression felt a little like trying to see faces in clouds. I thought I saw regret pass across her features before she masked it behind a half smile. I flexed my grip on the sword, acquainting myself with the balance. "Won't my element play havoc with the power?"

"If it does, use the pointy end."

I glanced up and saw her crooked smile. Blue lips ticked into her cheeks. Her eyes were alight with the promise of conflict. I knew then where Stefan did inherited his thrill of the fight and quick wit. All we had to do was survive long enough to find him while avoiding my soul-locked owner, and staying below the radar of Mammon and my ruthless brother, Valenti. I couldn't help thinking our chances of survival compared to that of a snowball's chance in hell.

**

As soon as the sun bowed out for the night, the forest embracing the grove came alive. Insects chirped and chittered. Shadows sighed, and the breeze hissed through the trees. I felt the crawling sensation of eyes on me but couldn't locate their source beyond the dancing glow of our campfire.

Yukki Onna perched on the stump. The liquid light beneath her skin lent her an iridescent glow. She had clamped her wings closed behind her, their skyward tilt as rigid as the rest of her body. We hadn't discussed the possibility of attack; there really was nothing to discuss. It was inevitable.

I clutched Kira-Kira across my knees. It had been a long time since I'd had to fight the lesser demons for my right to walk their lands. They would sense any weakness and smell the humanity on me. I had the blood of Asmodeus in my veins. My father was a longstanding Prince of Hell, but while they might smell my lineage, the scent wouldn't dissuade them for long. I was damaged goods, and they wouldn't be able to stop themselves.

At least Asmodeus wasn't on the list of demons who wanted me dead. In his mind, I simply didn't exist. I was little more than a bug on a windshield to him, something he could wipe from existence with little more than a hand gesture. Thankfully, he didn't care for me dead or alive. Unfortunately, my brother didn't feel the same. Family, eh, can't live with them, especially when they plot to kill you.

A muffled scurry in the snow behind Yukki Onna jolted her to her feet. Her wings splayed. Her element stirred, charging the air around her. I stood slowly and drilled my glare into the thick cover of darkness. The wild netherworld elements tingled across my skin.

The rattle of armored plates spun me around. The substantial bulk of... something swept through the undergrowth. The bushes rustled and then settled. Yukki Onna caught my eye and smiled.

I splayed my left hand toward the campfire behind me. The flames roared higher. In the darkness beyond the firelight, countless pinpricks of glowing eyes glaring back at us. Something large, black, and snake-like burst from the bushes. With a yelp, I skipped back just as black fangs the size of my forearms plunged through the air. I thrust the sword out, but the point skipped off the lesser demon's snout. It twitched its trailing whiskers and chittered, sounding oddly like laughter. It pulled back and lifted its elongated head, snorting hot air. I'd been wrong. It wasn't snake-like. I'd seen smaller versions of the demon on Chinese take-out boxes; more Oriental-dragon than snake.

Gathering my element, I cast the rippling power down my arm and flung a whip-like tentacle of flame at its face. The demon roared and recoiled from the blistering heat. The tail swept out of the dark to my left and hooked my legs out from under me. I fell backward and hit the ground hard with a grunt. Steam coiled around me. I was out of practice and feeling it. The bristle-faced demon planted talon-like feet either side of me and bowed its head. I brought the sword around in one heaving arc and slashed the sharp edge of the blade across its jaw. Black liquid spurted from the wound. The demon swung its head around and slithered back into the undergrowth. I didn't think for a second it had given up.

As I rolled onto my side. A smile crawled across my lips.

Yukki Onna was surrounded by a pack of Sasori demons. Half scorpion, their torsos loosely resembled a humanoid form, but below the waist they were all arachnid. They skittered and scuttled about Yukki Onna.

Black lacquered pincers snapped at her wings. She danced back, delight bright in her blue eyes. She let loose a flurry of dagger-like shards of ice that rapidly peppered the beasts.

The cacophony of cries as the lesser demons scrambled away would alert any nearby beasties to our melee. I blasted a few of the Sasori as they attempted to flee. Their scorpion bodies twitched, cries pitching high. Where they fled flaming through the dark, I caught sight of half a dozen eager hunks of quivering demon-muscle complete with murderous gazes loitering in the shadows.

Something swooped down from above. I ducked in time and winced as a curved claw tore through Yukki Onna's delicate wings. She flinched away and thrust a blade of ice into the sky. Seconds later, the winged demon landed with a thwump beside our roaring campfire. The shard of ice protruded from its arrowhead skull.

A breath of air against my neck alerted me, and I spun, launching a wave of fire at the thing hunkered over me. The dragon demon was back. It huffed at me, green eyes narrowing. I realized exactly what it was: a Larkwrari hatchling, thankfully only a fraction of the size of an adult specimen, which could reach Boeing proportions. It bared black half-moon fangs and spat viscous mucus over me. The fire simmering across my skin blanched white. My element unexpectedly surged through me. I laughed at the thrill of the inferno firing off the pleasure receptors in my brain. So it wanted to play with fire. That, I could do.

Gathering an element is like breathing in when you've been starved of air. It's invigorating, rejuvenating. The power swells and flows and fills every part of you. It's alive, the very essence of chaos. When it comes, it does so in a way that tips you over the edge of ecstasy and a wild, unrestrained sense of freedom. Calling it was just half the thrill ride. Using it spoke to the chaos swirling at the very center of me, chaos and the raw hunger for more. I spun it around me, whipping up a firestorm, my demon body blazing white at the eye. The whiskered demon stamped backward, thinking twice, but I had it in my sights. I blasted a ravenous wave of energy over it. I tasted its death in the flames as though I'd plunged my hands into its chest and crushed the living essence to dust with my bare hands. My child of fire devoured everything, leaving only ash swirling in the wind.

There's danger in the lure of chaos. The power had the strength to topple my control and overflow my precisely constructed mortal barriers. Every time I called it to me, let it flow like molten lava through my veins and ride roughshod over my better judgment, the potential to lose myself in it danced around the fringes of my mind. *Burn them all.*

Something snatched at my ankle. I twisted and plunged Kira-Kira through my assailant's soft underbelly, and then flung its hound-like form aside. Another flew at my head. I caught the reflection of fire in its black eyes before I incinerated it with a flick of my wrist. Ash blasted my face. A throaty intoxicated chuckle laced with madness bubbled from my lips. Shortly after, I stopped seeing individuals as they tried to take me down. They became insignificant shadows dancing through the flames. Each and every one, I reduced to ash with little more thought than a throw-away gesture.

Eventually, the lesser demons stopped their onslaught and cowered back. Flames writhed over my body as I watched them slink off into the dark with a new fear burning in their dull eyes.

I stood, feet planted with Kira-Kira in my right hand hissing its displeasure at being drowned in heat. I wanted more. Rage strummed through tensed muscles, fanning the flames at the heart of me. I sensed Damien inside me: a darkness sitting cold and lifeless amidst the lure of chaos. Closing my eyes, I sought his touch. I could burn the bastard out of me and cauterize my soul. I couldn't physically claw it out, but I could sink metaphysical tendrils into the parasitic touch and pull it free.

"Muse..." Yukki Onna's cool voice drifted through the maelstrom.

I twitched but ignored her. Fire blanched across my flesh.

Just a little deeper. I wove my element through me, seeking the seed he'd planted, intent on destroying it like I had those pathetic lesser demons. I could turn his touch to ash, blast him from my being. *Deeper...* I didn't notice when I fell to my hands and knees. I cast my power further into the dark, riding its weaving, reaching, tendrils. My cocoon of fire withdrew into my skin. My demon peeled apart and exposed fragile human flesh. I barely registered the precarious reveal. All I could see was the poison latched onto my core like a parasite. I reached out to it, clenched it in ethereal hands– A blinding flash of agony ripped through me. A scream punched from my stomach, through my throat and out.

Yukki Onna had taken my face in her hands and launched a surge of her own elemental touch through me. Her ice shocked me out of my mental surgery with an explosion of pain. Power snapped down my spine. Jagged blasts of energy bolted across my flesh. My demon burst from my skin. Fire roared, and I slammed a blast of heat into Yukki Onna's chest, flinging her away. She caught herself midair with a sweep of her wounded wings and dropped to the ground. I blinked.

I'd tried to kill her.

She pressed a hand against her chest and shuddered. A fresh dusting of snow drifted from her wings. I'd burned her. The smell of scorched flesh hung in the air. I wasn't sorry. I didn't care. I felt nothing. I glared at her and saw only another demon armed for battle. A rival. A challenger. It was only Kira-Kira throbbing in my hand that distracted me enough to recall what I was doing crouched on all fours. A gasp of delayed surprise puffed out of me. What was I thinking? I wasn't, that was the problem. The demon had done the thinking.

Rivulets of water gathered speed either side of me, on their way down to the beach. Around me, the blanket of snow had all but vanished. I'd melted her picture-perfect ice grove.

Yukki Onna's smile was gone. She straightened up and weighed whether I might attack again.

"I'm sorry..." I was, but a smile slid across my demon lips. I hadn't meant to hurt her, but I'd wanted to. I still wanted to. *Burn her...* It wasn't her. She'd done nothing wrong. It was me. I couldn't rein in my desire for chaos. It skipped around my control, flirting with freedom, and I teetered on the edge of letting it go. *Oh to let go of it all... The pain, the anguish, the shame and disgust... Just let it all go. Embrace chaos.*

"You should leave. Now." Yukki Onna narrowed her dazzling eyes. She tightened her grip on the dagger.

She was right. I couldn't stay. Not like this.

"Go."

Chapter Eighteen

Beneath the moonlight, the naked forest shivered. The trees had been stripped bare. The carpet of needles and dried leaves crunched under foot as I passed beneath clawing branches. The brittle bark on each misshapen tree trunk had been flayed clean on one side. Some ancient trees had toppled, and the fallen giants all faced the same way, like a graveyard of timber. Others had snapped in two. Something catastrophic had blasted through here. I couldn't sense any residual use of elemental magic. Whatever it was, it had taken place days, if not weeks, before. Battlegrounds like this were not uncommon. Lesser demons weren't the only ones that squabbled over the scraps of their prey. When the big boys got involved, the landscape often bore the scars.

After leaving Yukki Onna, I followed the edge of the lake, stopping only once to take a drink and wash off the dried blood from my scratches. My mind stilled, my desires sated. For now.

I felt eyes on me, even if I couldn't see the lesser demons hunched in the dark. If you aren't the hunter, you're the hunted. Hopefully the gleam of Kira-Kira in my hand would dissuade the majority of demons from attacking, but my missing wing would mark me as damaged, that, and my distinctly human odor. I'd pulled off some powerful stuff back at the ice-grove, but I had no desire to lose control again. Not so soon. There's temptation in chaos. If I made a habit of answering its call, I might never return from its alluring embrace. Madness beckoned.

Of course, I could have fled the netherworld and returned to Boston, crossed the veil and given myself time to lick my wounds, also known as hiding. But then what? Damien would find me and continue his crusade. Now that he had a taste for it, he wouldn't stop with me. No, I couldn't leave the netherworld. Wherever I was, he'd be with me. I had to get his tainted touch out of me somehow, and then I'd kill him, and this time the twisted bastard would stay dead.

Once I found Stefan, I could figure a way out of this mess. He knew more about demons than I ever would. Stronger, smarter, the half-blood who beat the system: he'd know what to do.

I was close. *Follow the lake to where the trees give way to steep tundra. That is where you'll find him,* Yukki Onna had told me. I trudged on. My pace quickened, and my rapid breaths misted in the cool night air. Stefan and I hadn't parted on the best of terms. He had lied through his teeth, but he'd also saved me from Akil's murderous intentions.

Stefan taught me how to draw power from beyond the veil, but he'd given me a gift more precious than potential. We'd shared a shower and a bed and each other. Sex, for me, was a muddle of emotion, needs and desires. As a child-demon, I'd understood sex as another way to hurt me. The act of sex was no different from the beatings, the mutilation, or the humiliation. It was life, just like every other wretched means of inflicting pain. After Akil had saved me, our relationship changed as I'd aged and he hadn't. Once I became a woman, he'd coaxed pleasure out of me where before there had been only pain, but even then, with Akil, it had been about control, his and mine. With Stefan, it hadn't been that way at all, although I hadn't realized at the time. I'd thought a great deal about the hours I spent with Stefan and what they meant to me. When we'd lain together, I'd been without my demon but Stefan hadn't. He'd held back. I knew it in his quivering muscles and fierce winter eyes. But he'd been gentle, so goddamn gentle that I'd growled and demanded more. His touch had been reverent, delicate, sensuous, and outright infuriating. Until it wasn't. We'd lost each other in those hours and found ourselves again. I'd wrapped myself so tightly in his arms that I didn't want him to let go. Ever. He'd woken something in me I hadn't known existed. He taught me I wasn't a worthless half-blood. Neither was I a frightened woman. He taught me by way of his touch, his snowflake kisses and the warmth of him, that I could be loved. And it was only the beginning. I knew if we came together again when I was whole—demon and woman— the exquisite combination of elements would be divine but dangerous. We'd flirted with something forbidden in those hours. Fire and ice. Wrong, but so right. In the months since, a day hadn't passed without my thoughts finding Stefan and wondering if he was alive, if he was okay, if I should have been so hard on him, if I'd been wrong to blame him. If I loved him.

I'd forgiven him for his lies, but had he forgiven me?

I paused near the edge of the dead forest and rested my hand against the desiccated bark of tree. A curtain of greens, blues and purples twisted and thrashed silently across the canvas of black sky. It was magnificent, but it wasn't natural, not even for a world as twisted as this one. I'd seen pictures of a similar phenomenon; the aurora borealis. This was no aurora. It was raw elemental energy: the veil. It pulsated above the ragged landscape, danced like watercolors in the rain, and throbbed like an open wound.

I left the cover of the forest and climbed upward over a rubble-strewn incline toward a vast cliff face. The frozen ground beneath my feet hissed gently against the heat seeping from my flesh. A cool breeze teased around me. Ahead, I made out a barrier of bushes. But as I drew closer, I realized the barrier wasn't natural at all. It was ice. It towered over my five-foot-nothing and bristled with obscenely sharp spines. I reached out to touch one. It pierced my fingertip before wilting away from my heat.

The ice barrier stretched around the foot of the cliff face. I couldn't see over it, and there didn't appear to be a way in. Some of those javelins of ice were as long as I was tall and had been packed so tightly they were virtually impossible to penetrate. I walked along the perimeter, trying to find a spot where I could wriggle through. The shards gleamed and rippled under the moonlight. They creaked and groaned as though complaining.

With a resigned humph, I lifted my hand and focused a surge of heat at one spot on the barrier. Ice-shards wilted and warped. Water trickled over my feet. A small hole opened, just large enough for me to duck through. I straightened on other side of the barrier and gaped. Ice had crystalized over the ground and up the cliff-face. The plateau beneath my feet resembled etched glass. Vast geometric patterns, like those found in magnified images of snowflakes, shimmered just below the surface. The sound of cracking ice snapped through the air like gunfire.

Ice had devoured the rock face. Jagged spikes jutted outward, deterring anything that might attempt to climb down. The defenses, the rock face, the plateau: it was a killing ground. Kira-Kira shivered in my hand and strummed with power. Above, the elemental light show dipped and swayed. Earthen greens mingled with liquid blues. I swallowed. My wing shuddered.

"Stefan...?" In the near silence my small voice carried, but only the cracking of ice responded.

I stepped onto the plateau. A yawning cave drew my eye. Icicles hung from the mouth like fangs. Water dripped from their tips only to refreeze as it hit the ground, forming a lower jaw of teeth. Sword clenched in my hand, I stepped into the darkness inside. "Stefan?" I whispered. A gentle breeze teased across my warm cheek, and my skin prickled. The weight of his power pushed against my back. I turned, and caught a glimpse of moonlight cascading through multifaceted ice wings before a shard of ice tore through my wing membrane.

I pulled my wing against me and crouched low, poised to retaliate. I hissed a warning. The ice demon took a few more strides before stopping to glower at me. I barely recognized him. His distinctively masculine physique bristled with splintered ice. Where his mother shimmered like frosted glass, he glinted sharply in the moonlight. His eyes blazed electric blue. Restrained power swirled in his irises. Pale blue lips, dusted with crushed ice, pulled back in a sneer. His wings arched high behind him. Each frozen feather held a lethal razor's edge, and as they grated together, they sang like the chiming of distant bells. His beauty terrified me.

"It's me," I whispered.

He flicked a hand and flung a wave of ice splinters at me. I ducked low and hissed as they passed too close. He gathered an ice javelin, called it forth out of nothing, and locked those surreal eyes on me.

"Stefan," I growled. "Stop."

If he heard me, it didn't register on his face. A little curl of his lips hinted at a grin, but it was a twisted mockery of the smile I'd dreamed of. He lifted the javelin over his shoulder and launched it at me.

I reared up and blasted heat toward him in time to meet the javelin midway. It splintered into countless pieces that vaporized as they rained over me.

The snarl on his lips rumbled the ice. The ground shifted. I staggered. A shard of ice erupted from the earth beside me, too close for comfort. I jumped back, arms flailing. "Stefan, goddammit... It's Muse." With a hasty flap of my wing, I regained my balance and drew more of the heat from outside the ice fortress. A torrent of warmth funneled through my body. With a quick pushing gesture, I summoned a tumbling wave of fire and shoved it toward him.

He dropped to a knee. A shield of ice bloomed in his hand. He braced against the wave. Fire splashed over him. His shield sagged, its edges curling. Water pooled. I was beginning to realize what Yukki Onna had meant when she'd told me to *reach* Stefan. There wasn't going to be a friendly chat.

He glowered at me over the warped rim of his shield, and with a roar of rage, he swept up a carpet of bristling spikes and flung them at me.

I spilled ravaging heat over my body, cocooning myself in blue flame, and swept my wing around me, crouching as water splashed across my flesh. My fire spluttered, hissed and spat. Sweeping open my wing, I growled back at him with every bit of demon bass-tone I had.

He sprang off his back foot. I locked my stance low to the ground, teeth gritted, wing out-stretched, and braced myself. He slammed into me, driving me back. My feet skidded across melting ice. His arctic embrace sucked the heat from my flesh. Water fizzled between us, steam sputtering, ice cracking, and fire spitting. Our elements butted up against one another, entangled in a deadly battle of opposing forces. I tried to coil my element around him, but the strength of his retort slapped me down. His brittle glare pierced me. Those eyes held no recognition whatsoever. He was gone. He shoved me off the plateau. I tumbled over myself until I landed sprawled on my front, face down in the frozen dirt.

He stood, wings spread, stance rigid, the sky behind him alive in a dramatic display of color. He had more power to call. So did I. I hoped that he wouldn't go that far. I'd already tasted chaos a few hours before and didn't want to chance it again so soon. But if he pushed, I'd push back.

I got to my feet and brushed loose gravel from my superheated skin. "You stubborn son of a bitch," I muttered. Deliberately pooling fire in my gaze, I lifted Kira-Kira. "Recognize this?" My voice echoed across the plateau. "Do you remember your mother?"

He huffed and turned his back on me. Fragments of ice crumbled from his wings and tinkled melodically against the frozen ground.

"Stefan. I'm not going away." I stomped up onto the plateau. "Don't walk away from me. You have no idea what I've been through. Don't test me."

Something in my words clearly struck a nerve. He stopped and glowered over his shoulder. Wicked light danced in his eyes, followed by a throaty laughter that I almost recognized. But it was wrong. He was wrong, twisted somehow. This demon wasn't the Stefan I'd known. The man I could have loved had gone. The bitter bite of winter in those eyes smothered any trace of humanity.

I flung the sword aside and collected fire into my palms. "I know you're in there."

"Bring the fire, half-blood." He laughed. "You'll die like the others."

The threat sent a shiver of trepidation through me. I lifted my hands and summoned it all. There's heat in everything that holds life: the earth beneath us, the rock face behind him. It was nothing like the reserves in the city—Stefan's ice had chased away much of it—but enough remained for me to sculpt to my will. I let the fire spin inside of me, around me. I twisted it around me and whipped up a storm of bubbling liquid heat.

Stefan moved closer. His fingers twitched. His wings shivered behind him. His power blazed bright in his eyes and rippled across his blue flesh. Tendrils of energy seeped from inside him and thrashed at the air, licking, tasting, reaching. He looked every part the demon: devastatingly powerful, potentially the most powerful demon on this side of the veil. Besides me.

The twirling maelstrom lifted me off my feet. The crazed, cackling laughter bouncing around us was mine. "Ready to dance?" My voice growled and boomed at the same time. My demon rode high. She breathed it all into her, into me. She consumed every last drop of heat from the land, compressed it into a ball of power at our center and fed the madness.

Stefan dropped his stance. The ground around him rippled. The ice plateau cracked, reshaped, and undulated at his will. Ice funneled up from the earth. Branches of it climbed higher and wove together, creating, shaping, building. Jagged shards snapped and locked into place. Two monstrous humanoid ice beasts with wisps of blue smoke for eyes clawed their way out of the towers of ice.

This was new.

I clasped my hands in front of me and formed a sphere of white-hot heat and launched it through the firestorm. It plunged into the torso of one of the beasts. The hideous avatar shuddered, planted itself onto all fours, and charged. Dropping to my knees, I thrust out both hands and funneled a blast of heat at its face. The absolute force of power melted the creature in an instant, but the momentum it carried continued in a gush of ice-water that drenched over me. I spat out a cry. My fire spluttered and died.

The second beast sensed its moment and thundered forward on four legs of dirty ice. I pointed my hand high and tore a hole in the veil with a slice of my claws. I could smell the human world, hear its glorious thrum of life, taste the sweetness of air.

"Stop!" Stefan hissed.

The creature planted two stocky legs on either side of me. Its stumpy snout snorted blasts of cool air against my reaching hand. In the next moment, its bulk collapsed, dumping rocks and snow on top of me. Briefly, I was entombed. Panic twitched through me, but before it could hold the snow melted and simmered off my skin. Stefan came forward through the rising steam. My gaze pinned on his. I withdrew my hand from the small tear in the veil, allowing the wound to heal and vanish.

Stefan picked up Kira-Kira and stopped close enough to me that the air tightened with the touch of frost and burned my throat. He pointed the tip of the sword at my throat. "Leave."

I flinched. "No."

"Leave before—" He snapped his head up, eyes narrowing to focus on something behind me.

He didn't get to finish his warning. A hurricane force gust tossed him back and pinned him against the rock. His glorious wings shattered. Fragments of ice rained against the plateau. The wind picked up, and the debris we'd churned in our melee blasted Stefan. He let out a frustrated cry, hands clutched into fists as he tried to lift himself. Then the wind dropped, and Stefan plummeted to the ground.

Damien stalked through the gap in the ice barrier. His vast, bat-like wings whipped up a storm. Scrambling backward, I stumbled onto my feet, breathless and riddled with paralyzing fear. He flapped his wings and rose with surprising grace to the edge of the plateau where he slid his dead eyes to me and waited.

I glanced back at Stefan. He lay motionless, covered in a thin blanket of ice. I wanted to call out to him, to let him know I needed him, now more than ever. If he was in there, if the man I knew still existed, I needed him to help me. The words never came.

"Come." Damien held out a hand.

I lifted my chin and faced him. I'd used all the heat available to me. If I wanted to fight him, I would need to call from beyond the veil. If I fought him and won, what would happen to the part of him he'd locked inside of me? Could I survive him rotting at my core? I wanted to kill him. I knew I could. My fingers twitched as I imagined summoning the molten rock beneath the earth's crust. I'd drown him in it. I grated my sharp teeth. For what he'd done to me and to those other women, I'd take my time when I killed him. He'd scream, and I'd like it. I'd burn every inch of his skin off his flesh and make sure he lived through it.

No. Not yet. I needed him to live for now if I was going to be free of him. I took a step forward and then another. With each step, it became easier. I lifted a black, fire-veined hand and let him close his cool grip around mine. Inside, I locked the most fragile parts of me away and slipped a mask of control and indifference onto my face. He pulled me against him and closed his arms around me. *Shut it down. Shut the pain down. Bury it all inside*. His wings beat the air. My nostrils flared as his ozone scent—like burned electrical cables—filled my head. I rested my head against his mottled skin and squeezed my eyes closed. My body would heal. The memories would fade. They had before. I could survive this, but he would not.

As the wind tore at my face and Damien carried me higher, I opened my eyes just enough to see Stefan's motionless body below. He wasn't dead. He couldn't be. We were both powerful creatures, but our half-human bodies were our weaknesses. And in some cases, our strengths. When Damien had flung Stefan against the rocks, he could have killed him. I couldn't think that. I'd come so close to finding him, and yet Stefan hadn't been the man I remembered. I was too late.

I closed my eyes and listened to the beat of Damien's wings. Perhaps Nica was right. Stefan was gone.

Chapter Nineteen

The cities of the netherworld resembled those of the human realm the way that higher demons resemble people, but the reflections are distorted, twisted and broken. Cobbled streets could turn to asphalt when you rounded a corner. Thatched cottages leaned against glass covered high-rises. I'd tried to explain it to Ryder once, and the best I could come up with was it felt like being lost in a theme park at night. Something about the absence of life, the eerie familiarity, and inherent touch of darkness felt deeply malevolent, as though the air and the buildings were all alive. Why Damien had brought me there, I could only guess, and I suspected it had something to do with parading his new toy in front of his peers.

We entered what appeared to be a banquet hall. The vaulted ceiling gave the place a cathedral-like ambience. Torches flickered high up on the walls, and soot hung heavy in the air. A sea of demons rippled. The smell of burned rubber assaulted my nose and coated my throat. The smell of demons. I pulled my wing tight against my back and fell into step behind Damien's bulk as he carved a path through the crowd. A few hisses reached my ears. My skin prickled. Several demons spat at the floor by my feet. I kept my eyes firmly on Damien's back, between his wings, where his muscles bunched and flexed. Demons of all shapes and sizes mingled. Claws glinted, talons clicked. The exploratory touch of elements slid over me, fire, earth, ice, air, and something different, an oily element. They all licked at my skin. The power-thick air choked the back of my throat. I fought the urge to gag and gulped the air down instead of breathing it. It was a tinderbox of energy. The potential for madness quivered through the crowd. An unsettling urge to call my power and lash out at them tingled at the tips of my fingers. It would undoubtedly result in my death, but it might just be worth it. I knew these thoughts for what they were: the chaos talking. The unsettling thing was, I liked those whispers. I wanted it. I'd spent no more than two days as a full demon, and already the urges had found purchase in my thoughts. Stefan had spent six months trying to resist.

I stumbled into Damien as he stopped ahead of me. Where his skin brushed mine, slithers of air probed. My stomach flipped, threatening to drop me to my knees and spill my guts in front of a demon horde.

"Go," he grunted. "Wait for me." He stalked off toward a gathering of demons, leaving me exposed in a hostile crowd.

Any number of the demons surreptitiously watching me would've liked nothing less than to plunge a dagger into my back or tear out my throat. Probably both. I reeked of mortality. A half-blood. An abomination. With just one wing, coupled with my puny human size, the odds were against me. I backed up and bumped into a water demon who huffed and bubbled a growl at me. Head down, I turned and cut through the crowd, heading toward the outer wall. If I could avoid eye contact, there was a chance they'd ignore me. I was so low on their radar that they shouldn't even acknowledge me.

I slipped out a side door and breathed the comparatively clean night air. I'd stumbled out of the hall into what appeared to be an abandoned town square. A dry fountain at its center sprouted a few purple saplings. I crossed the open ground and sat on the fountain's edge. I skipped my gaze over the shadows layering the streets and houses huddled around the square, looking for potential threats. I was alone. A few blazing torches hung in brackets along the walls. The only noise came from the mass of demons congregated inside the hall, a low rumbling of gruff voices and strumming energy.

I took a few moments to gather my wits. My thoughts invariably fell to Stefan. Yukki Onna could have warned me. I hadn't expected him to be the same Stefan I'd met in Boston, but I hadn't quite expected him to be so far gone either. I'd looked into those eyes and seen only ice. He had to be in there somewhere, but it was going to take more than a polite hello to reach him. I'd hoped he'd at least recognize me, but all he'd seen was a half-blood fire demon trespassing on his territory.

He'd lost control. Out of the two of us, I would never have expected it would be Stefan who would succumb to the lure of chaos. He was always so perfectly in control. He'd worn his control like armor. Not anymore. Ice was his armor now.

"Muse..." I knew that voice. The last time I'd heard it, he'd threatened to kill me and had very nearly succeeded. I slid my gaze to Akil, blinked, and faced ahead again. In those few seconds, time screeched to an abrupt halt. When I closed my eyes for a second time, I saw a blazing imprint of him in my mind as his warmth radiated across my skin. He leaned against the fountain, all subtle charm and masculine potency. Soft hazel eyes belied the monster inside the sculpted avatar of a man. He'd fashioned himself a slate-gray suit, probably for my benefit. Ten years is a long time to live with someone, longer than most marriages last. He saved me once, tutored me, released me. Or so I'd thought. I had loved him as a savior and then as something more carnal. Knowing he stood beside me now, I had to rein in a terrible desire to fling myself into his arms and bawl like the lost little girl Damien had roused in me. It helped to remember Akil was a murderer.

Eyes still closed, I bowed my head. Something was wrong with the imprint in my mind. My memory of Akil didn't match the man on my left. In Boston, he'd carried an infallible confidence, as though he existed outside the rhyme and reason of mortal man. Anything he wanted— women, wealth, influence—it all danced to his Pied-Piper tune. The extent to which he could manipulate others was one of the reasons I'd left him, thereby sealing my fate. Nobody walks away from the Prince of Greed. But that suave bastard had been lost somewhere among the ravages of the netherworld. The man beside me, alluring as he was, had lost his luster. I examined his mental imprint while time continued to stretch thin. His dark hair was longer than I remembered. He'd slicked it back, lending his features a severe intensity that declared 'cannot-be-tamed' without him having to say a word. His white silk shirt had dulled to an over-washed gray. A few buttons were missing. A thread had unraveled at the collar. Even his jacket hung askew. Handsome features hadn't done him any favors in the netherworld. He was a man on the edge: a beast barely contained inside an alluring male vessel.

I opened my eyes and speared him with my gaze. A tentative smile flirted with his lips, but the fire in his eyes touched my soul.

Akil was the very essence of fire, and my demon adored him. He wore raw elemental power like a mortal man wears cologne, and my demon was hopelessly addicted to him. It was my human half that detested how manipulative, destructive, and downright evil he could be. My humanity kept me real, and it was my humanity that sparked an inferno of rage inside me when I finally decided how to deal with him. He'd killed a friend in cold blood, stabbed him through the chest without a shred of remorse. He'd tried to kill me. I knew what I felt for Akil.

I sprang at him. My fist connected with his jaw. I wasn't thinking. I was in no fit state to reenact our battle on the waterfront. He grunted and pulled back in time to avoid a second punch that would have broken his nose. Inhuman growls and snarls rumbled up from my depths. I drew my right arm back again, but he snatched my wrist. No matter. I swung an open palmed slap with my left hand and raked my claws down his face. He snarled and caught my other wrist. Blood welled in the gashes. It warmed me to see how I'd hurt him. I wanted more.

I twisting and pulled, but his hands clamped tighter around my wrists. He tugged me forward and tried to envelop me in an embrace. My bruised demon-skin prickled at his touch. I stamped on his scuffed black shoes and jerked a knee toward his groin. He twisted in time to avoid the blow.

"Stop," he growled.

I wasn't listening. I didn't care. It wasn't about Akil. Some part of me had shattered. I wanted to drive my fists into his chest—into anything—over and over again until whatever I hit crumbled to dust. Or I did. My veins pulsed with heat, and my head throbbed. My jaw locked. I ground my teeth together so hard my face ached. I snarled and snapped, bucked and kicked. I managed to get a hand free and wildly lashed out, connecting with his shoulder hard enough to stagger him.

He caught my free hand and yanked me back against him. His muscular arms encircled me. I tried to writhe free, but every movement gave him leverage to squeeze me tighter into his chest.

"Stop, Muse." He hissed against my cheek.

My heart thumped in my ears. "I'll kill you." I spat the words, but I wasn't entirely sure they were meant for Akil. I could have pulled the fire right out of his soul, but I hadn't. This was for me. My eyelids fluttered closed. I twitched and jerked, but my strength had fizzled away. He closed his arms tighter around me, holding me so close I could hear and feel the beat of his heart.

"I need you." His lips brushed my shoulder, his words cool whispers against my hypersensitive skin.

He smelled of cinnamon and cloves, a spicy warming scent that reminded me of the only home I'd known. I slumped in his arms and bowed my head against him. His crushing grip loosened, his arms relaxed, but he still held me close. I wanted to hate him, I knew I should. Maybe, somewhere inside my ruined mind, I genuinely did. But right then, after what had been done to me, Akil's embrace felt like freedom.

He radiated a background thrum of power. My fire responded in kind. He'd called to my demon. That was why I'd found a way out of the hall. She—I—had sensed him. It irked me that he could still have any effect on me, but considering the storm of rage, shame, and fear in my head, I had other issues to worry about.

His hand on my lower back splayed. He slid his touch around my waist and eased me away from him. I didn't want to let go and certainly didn't want him to see the fear in my eyes. If he thought me weak, I wasn't sure what he'd do. Six months before, I'd tried to kill him. He'd tried to kill me. Did that make us even?

He hooked a finger under my chin and tilted my head back, leaving me no choice but to meet his gaze. His eyes smoldered. He breathed hard through his teeth, but it wasn't anger I saw on his face. Concern, perhaps, hid in his furrowed brow and narrowed eyes. Was that even possible? The cuts across his cheek stitched back together before my eyes.

He dared to touch my face. A trickle of heat danced through my cheek. I snapped my head back and glared up at him. "Don't touch me. You don't get to touch me." I shoved against his chest and extricated myself from his grip.

He maintained a perfectly unreadable expression, but the eyes betrayed him. They harbored an empty sadness so intense it stalled my anger. Akil didn't do sad eyes. He was steel, an unyielding pillar of strength. For a fire demon, he was damned cold. Sad eyes weren't in his skill-set.

"What has he done to you?" he asked quietly. He reached out a hand, perhaps expecting me to take it.

I staggered back. He couldn't touch me. Not yet. My thoughts whirled inside my head. I wanted him to touch me. I wanted those arms to close around me and for him to whisper once more how he needed me, but I hated him. Didn't I? A blubber escaped my lips. I covered it with a snarl and paced a few strides back and forth. I couldn't bear the thought of hands on my skin. I closed my eyes and flinched at the devastating memories marching through my mind. I couldn't pack them away. Old horrors mingled with new ones. I paced.

Akil watched me closely. His gaze wandered over my naked demon body, lingering where the bruises throbbed and cuts healed.

He'd gained a few creases around his eyes, additional worry lines that aged him. Laughable, considering he appeared to be in his thirties but was, in fact, timeless. Had he appeared to me in his true form, as Mammon, I'd likely have lashed out with all the power I had. Nothing about his appearance was an accident. He'd sculpted that body, all steel and honey, to lure in unsuspecting victims.

"What are you doing here?" My words lodged in my throat. I had to growl them out one by one.

"Damien seeks my presence." Akil ran his fingers across his jaw and winced. "He means to challenge me. It is why all these wretched demons gather." His voice gained an abrasive edge and with it an undertone of an accent that both intrigued and alarmed me. The changes were subtle. Had I not spent ten years with him, I might not have noticed them, but Akil was different.

"Why now?"

"Apparently..." He took a breath and winced too. "I stole you from him." He fingered his ribs through his shirt. I'd landed a few well-placed punches.

"I told Damien you made me try and kill him. That it was your fault." I eyed him closely for his reaction.

He fought a smile, lips twitching. "Whether you or I attempted to kill him, it's little more than semantics. We failed."

"How could you not know he still lived?"

He bristled. "I was with you in Boston. Whether he lived or not did not concern me. He was-is insignificant."

Rage twitched through me. I shoved it back. "It concerned me."

"Damien is a degenerate beast. I'll end his existence soon enough."

A jab of pain stuttered my heart. "Don't kill him." I spoke so lightly I wondered if the breeze might sweep the words away before Akil could latch onto them.

He frowned. "Why ever not? I've no idea how he came back from death last time, but it won't happen again."

I gritted my teeth to stop them from chattering and pinched my lips together, hoping to hide their quivering.

He'd noticed I'd stopped pacing and probably saw something in my expression that tipped him off. "What did he do?" His voice dipped lower, flirting with threats.

I remembered Yukki Onna's words about how I must have somehow let Damien inside for him to be able to soul-lock me. My skin itched with shame. "He did something, inside." I scratched my claws down my arms, barely noticing the cuts I left behind. "He's inside me."

Akil tipped his head. His eyes narrowed to sharp slits. He took a step toward me. "An infusion? Muse—" He enclosed me in a sudden embrace so uncharacteristically affectionate, that it didn't occur to me to pull away. I melted against him, flinching as the hardness of his body tugged at unwanted memories of Damien. Akil could take me away from everything, from the netherworld. He could hide me from the worst of it all here, where I understood very little, and nothing understood me. But he understood. He'd saved me before. He could do it again.

Akil pulled away first, a knowing smile sitting easily on his lips. "I can help you."

"How?" I breathed, lightheaded. "I can feel him now. It's awful. It's like something's eating me from inside. Akil, I didn't ask for this. I didn't let him do this to me. You have to believe me. I just..." Memories of Damien's violation blurred in my eyes. "I was trying to stop him. I reached into him. It was all I could think of to do, but he caught me and pulled me under." Anger, fear, disgust; the words used to describe the maelstrom of emotion spinning inside of me came easily, but they meant nothing.

Akil took my hands and nestled them against his chest. "I know you. There's no way in this world or the other that you'd have let him inside, which means his control is tenuous. An infusion, or a soul-lock, it's... a permanent connection, a spiritual agreement between two demons. To force it upon you weakens the bond considerably. But—" He leaned in, lips so close I could nip at them. I bit my lip and drew blood. He pulled back, just out of reach, and searched my face. His cinnamon and cloves scent filled my head. A warming sensation came over me as though I could curl up beside him, warm and comfortable. But not safe. Never safe.

"But," he sighed, "I need you to help me."

"Yes," I breathed; thoughts broken and body numb. *Just take me away. Make it all end. I want to go home.*

"I must return to Boston, but I'm prevented from doing so by Stefan." I instantly pulled back. He tightened his grip on my hands. "When he brought me across the veil, he bled us both, tying us together. I can't go back, and neither can he unless we go together. Once through, the blood-bond is broken."

I licked my lips and shrank back. "I've seen him. He's lost."

"I know." A glimmer of recognition briefly touched his eyes. "He's dangerous and exponentially powerful. But you and me, Muse, together we can subdue him. Once we get him through the veil, I can release you from your bond with Damien."

I frowned. "Why not release me now?" The sooner I had the touch of Damien out of me, the sooner I could concentrate on healing the ragged mess he'd left behind.

He arched an eyebrow. "I need leverage, Muse. Otherwise, there's nothing to stop you reneging on our deal." Blunt, but true. Any trust we'd once shared was long gone, burned to ash along with my misplaced love for him.

"Damien will follow us back to Boston. He's already killed people there. He has a taste for it now."

Akil planted a finger on my lips. Sizzling heat pooled beneath his fingertip. A nervous purr rumbled from the back of my throat. His eyes widened a fraction. "Once the infusion is undone, we will kill him. He's nothing compared to you. He knows it. It's why he bound you to him. He believes he's trapped you."

I wondered why Akil had never done the same. He'd had me wrapped around his finger for years. He could have infused me, and I'd never have known what it meant. What did it say about him, that he hadn't? *No. Don't go there. Don't start thinking he's not as bad as he could be. Don't go there again.*

"Wait. You want me to break you out of the netherworld?" Something was very wrong with this picture. "All of this is happening because of you. Once I get you out, there's nothing to stop you from turning on me again. You're stuck here now because you tried to kill me. I told Stefan to trap you. You wouldn't have stopped. You killed Sam. Do you remember? I know what you think of me, all of me. You look at me now, and you see demon, but what about when we're out, and I'm human again? That hasn't changed. Have you? Or are you still a selfish, murdering bastard?"

He took a few moments to let my words sink in. Probably trying to come up with some bullshit about how he'd changed. When he met my gaze again, he said clearly, "I don't have it in me to be sorry for my actions. An apology would be meaningless, but I regret the outcome. I regret how I hurt you. That was never my intention. I only ever wanted the best for you."

The best for my demon, he meant. He regretted being trapped on this side of the veil, but he was right, he didn't have it in him to be sorry for his actions. He was not human. His words were about as close to an apology as I was ever going to get. They sounded like the truth, but Akil had a way of bending the truth just short of a lie.

I shook my head and chewed on my lip. "I can't trust you again." Akil had issues with my human half: deep, terrifying, murderous issues.

"Then don't trust me. I'm not asking for trust. We both want the same thing: to get Stefan back to Boston and Damien's claws out of you."

I wasn't going to be able to get Stefan back on my own. The blood sacrifice had sealed them both on this side of the veil. Whatever happened, Akil was a part of the solution. "Okay." I watched his eyes brighten. "But if you cross me again Akil, so help me, I'll find a way to kill you this time."

His eyes lit up at the prospect, as though he'd accepted a challenge I didn't even know I'd issued. "I'd expect nothing less." Only demons can get a cheap thrill from a death threat.

"This doesn't mean I forgive you. You can distract my demon all you want with all that power and promise you exude, but my human half doesn't forgive and forget as easily."

He held out a hand. "I'm not looking for forgiveness."

I studied his outstretched hand. Agreeing to work with Akil was like dancing with the devil. One wrong step, and I'd be half-blood mincemeat. I'd only been on the earth a few decades. He was an eternal being crafted from the soul of fire, pure elemental chaos. He could dress himself in a man-suit, walk like one, talk like one, but the thing inside him was all needs and wants. I'd forgotten that before. It wouldn't happen again.

A searing gust of wind blasted us. I flinched and flung my wing up, shielding my face. Akil staggered back. Something lashed out at him. He raised his arm to bat it aside. A rattling length of chain coiled around his wrist. Damien's element snagged a hook into my chest. I heard growls and the snapping of teeth and realized it came from me. My chest swelled, bone and flesh wrenched sideways as the metaphysical hook dug deeper.

The howling gale tore at my wing membrane. I peered through ragged tears at Akil. He leaned back, dragging the fist-sized links of chain with him, and began to change. His human mask peeled apart. The suit, shirt, and flesh unraveled. Mammon, the Prince of Greed, emerged. He curled vast coal-black wings around him. Embers danced through the veins of his wing membranes like crimson fireworks lighting up a night sky.

Damien had said Mammon was a Prince no more, but the demon revealing himself before my eyes might as well have been. His huge bulk towered over me. Power throbbed through every muscular inch of him. Sparks danced in rivulets beneath his skin. He hunkered down, broad shoulders heaved forward against the wind, and then he flung his wings open and launched himself skyward. The chain snapped. Twisted links pummeled the ground around me. Mammon was gone, but it wasn't over.

The wind dropped as suddenly as it had arrived. I swung my gaze across the square at the approaching hordes of demons and found Damien. He reserved a snarl entirely for me, and despite the roaring cries from the demon-crowd, a thunderous rage rumbled up from my depths. He knew I'd lied. Either that, or he was just pissed I'd been talking with Akil. Either way, I was going to pay.

I sought a way out, but the once-quiet square had flooded with demons. Their malevolent stares slid over me, each one of them eagerly anticipating the battle to come. Lightning fractured the sky. A second later, thunder shook the ground. Where the hell was Mammon?

The demons formed a ring around Damien and me. Their caterwauling grated across my skin and dug claws into my skull. Gleeful baying stoked the fire in my belly, rousing my power. I cast a mental net outward and pulled every molecule of heat toward me. The demons jostled at the edges of my vision, sensing the energy. I marked a few fire demons in the crowd and plotted them on a mental map in case I needed to tap them for power.

Damien stalked forward. His scars rippled beneath the torchlight. "Obey me, half-blood whore."

The flaming torches behind the throngs of demons flared higher, stoked by my summons. Chaos energies swelled. I could have flung insults back at him, but words were redundant. He would see the fire in my eyes and the twisted sneer on my lips. The rippling crowd bayed, hooted, and jeered. I could taste their lust for chaos as it spiraled in the air. My fingers tingled with the need to wrap them around Damien's neck. The demon part of me embraced what would surely result in reckless devastation. I wanted it. Madness crooned in my ear.

Damien's laughter rumbled like the thunder above. He threw his arms out and summoned his element in one huge intake of breath. The gale lashed my back, toppling me forward and snuffing out my flame. In horror, I looked at my arms. Delicate veins of fire sputtered. He was stealing the air my fire needed to breathe.

A jet of heat, flame, and molten energy rolled over Damien. I snapped my head up. Mammon funneled a blast of heat through his arms. His wings blazed brightly as he beat the air. I had a moment to think—yay! —when my lungs tried to leap out of my throat. No air! I gasped and slumped forward. Mammon's flames spluttered. He tried to maintain his height above us, but he was failing.

Damien stood tall and proud, wings flung back, chest thrust out. A leering smile slashed across his face. His sharp teeth glinted. Coils of dust-filled air twisted around him. "Your fire is nothing without the air it breathes."

Mammon stumbled to the ground and staggered back against the fountain. Chips of mortar crumbled beneath his claws. Could he lose against Damien? No, but he couldn't kill him either. Not while Damien's soul-lock poisoned me. Akil's black fathomless eyes locked on mine for a heartbeat too long, and then he summoned an ethereal broadsword into his hand. I'd seen the sword twice before: a weapon crafted of elemental energy. It could only be wielded by the Princes. From the way the crowd of demons cowered like scolded dogs, I wondered if Akil had just revealed something they hadn't expected.

Blue flame licked up the intangible blade. Mammon thrust the weapon toward Damien, but my owner spun a length of chain in the air, looping it around the blade and yanking it up so that he and Mammon collided in a clash of quivering muscle and thrashing wings. Mammon had the strength, the blade, the prestige, but Damien had help.

Just as I found I could breathe again, the demons—what felt like all of them—barreled into me. My back cracked against the fountain. Something vital inside my chest snapped. Intense pain rushed up my right side. My vision pulsed black for a moment. I yelped like a wounded animal, kicked out, and flung a thrashing demon back. He flailed his arms, about to fall, when his two leathery murder-in-their-eyes demon buddies righted him. They rushed me as one. A wave of rage broke over me. I roared. The sound of my own fury terrified me. It was alive, crawling into my bones and peering through my eyes. The fragments of my humanity were swept aside. I became wholly demon.

A fist cracked across my face. I ducked a second blow and snapped my teeth at the demon. He rammed a fist under my chin. My head jerked back. He fell on me; teeth and claws, biting, tearing. His jaws clamped around my neck. Another demon gripped the rise of my wing. Another clawed at my arm. Others fell on me. I kicked, thrashed, and snarled. More came. I caught glimpses of teeth, of red cat-like eyes, and felt trails of spittle and splatters of blood hiss against my flesh. They tore into me.

A superheated tsunami of energy clamored up from the depths of my soul. An elemental geyser rumbled through my core. Power bubbled and broiled, lashed and spat, as it wove its way through every cell in my body and tore through my pitiful attempt at control. The volcanic blast of energy crashed over my mortal restraints and detonated a shockwave so intense it vaporized the demons on top of me, and it didn't stop there. I bucked, and the energy spilled forth, devouring all it encountered. It chewed up the earth, the fountain, the demon bodies and their elements, and churned the remains into a pyroclastic storm front.

When I finally came back to myself, body aching, bruised, and bloody, I sat at the epicenter of a bomb blast. Some of the nearby buildings had been reduced to rubble. Smoke drifted lazily from the debris. An inch thick layer of dust coated everything like dirty snow. The fountain was gone, as were the demons. All of them. Mammon? Damien?

An erotic lick of energy rode up the length of my spine. I gasped. Pleasure ebbed and flowed, arching me over, rolling me toward the edge of ecstasy and back again. I trembled, but not from fear. I liked it. The power. The loss of control. The result. I'd killed them. Blasted them to smithereens. Liquid laughter spilled from me. I looked up to see the veil torn. Crimson lights shivered and rippled around a wound in the very fabric of reality. I'd pulled the energy from the human world, but I had no memory of drawing from the veil.

I severed the link and rubbed ash from my eyes. The veil twitched and snapped closed, the lick of power dying with it. I'd lost control in a big way. I smiled and then cursed. "No, goddammit... I'm not my demon."

I coughed, throat hoarse and lips cracked. The dust tasted metallic. Or was that blood in my mouth? I tried to sit up and swallowed a ragged cry as pain lanced up my right side.

When I saw Mammon wading through the ash to reach me, I almost didn't believe it. He'd gained a tear in his wing, and a gray dusting of ash clung to his side where I assumed he'd been wounded, but otherwise he looked unharmed... and aroused. His onyx-black lips pulled back over fanged teeth in a leering grin. His midnight eyes had widened, and I could quite clearly see how his formidable body trembled. Holy hell, I'd made the Prince of Greed tremble.

He knelt beside me. Ash swirled around us like smoke. "Are you hurt?" His guttural voice resounded inside my skull, harsh and unforgiving.

I blinked, my eyes gritty. "I did this." A question? A statement? I wasn't sure.

He lifted his head and looked at the devastation. When he met my gaze again, I saw a glint of admiration there, and something more: unfiltered, raw need.

I felt sick and coughed, then winced as my chest burned. "I think I'm broken."

"Come." He wrapped his huge hand around my upper arm and drew me against his chest. He shivered. A low purr resonated through him and tugged on the trailing strings of my lust. He folded his wings around us both. The air pressure pulled tight and snapped. He was taking me away from the epicenter of madness; peeling apart reality so we could step through to another place. I didn't last more than a few minutes and collapsed unconscious in his embrace. My dreams filled with the sights and sounds of bubbling heat and searing flesh and then nothing but the dark and the quiet.

Chapter Twenty

"Damien's still alive." Akil's voice was human once more. "He fled prior to your pyrotechnic display, likely sensing your intent through the infusion." He snarled something in another language and then spat. "Coward."

I was listening to Akil, filtering the frustration from his words, but his voice drifted. I lay on my back, sprawled motionless beside a campfire, but my head floated elsewhere, drifting as though I could close my eyes and slip off into a dream. I watched the stars blink silently to one another and then realized they weren't stars at all, I was looking at the glow from tiny demon eyes. Sprites flitted above the clearing. I remembered where I was. This wasn't Boston. It was hell.

"I thought I'd killed you." My dreamy, dislocated voice bobbed untethered about my thoughts.

He made a dismissive sound in the back of his throat. "Quite the opposite."

"Damien's smarter than I remember." Was this my conversation, or was I listening to someone else?

"He has something worth fighting for."

I turned my head and admired Akil seated beside the campfire. He had one leg drawn up. Brittle leaves clung to his creased suit-trousers. In the dance of firelight, his silhouette held me spellbound. He sat too still to be human, of course, but that didn't stop me from losing my thoughts in him. His dark eyes absorbed the firelight so that nothing reflected in his irises. Shadows played across his face, lending his expression a grim severity. A dangerous smile teased the corners of his lips. My muddled thoughts plucked random scenes from my past and tossed them in front of my conscious thoughts.

I clung to the incongruous memory of the time Akil had introduced me to metalworking. We knew I had an affinity for metal, but when I'd tagged along on a visit to a local blacksmith Akil had hired to craft some gates for his house on the outskirts of Boston, I'd taken more than a passing interest in the harmony between metal and the sweltering temperatures of the forge. A fifteen minute visit turned into three hours while the blacksmith showed me his trade. Akil's presence blended into the background, but he didn't once take his eyes off me. In three hours, I learned more than most students could in weeks. The blacksmith was impressed. He asked Akil, who was masquerading as my uncle at the time, if I'd like to become an apprentice.

What was my subconscious trying to tell me? Why were my thoughts corralling warm and fuzzy memories?

I tore my gaze away from Akil and sighed, then flinched and hissed at a jab of pain. I reached for the tender area down my right side. Something thick and clammy clung to me. I looked down at myself. Wadded leaves plastered against my skin. I peeled them back. A viscous substance tried to pull the padding back into place.

"I'd leave those on a little longer," Akil advised.

"What is it?" The slimy leaves slipped from my hand and sprang back into place, molding themselves snugly against my flesh.

"Leaves from the riegen plant. They're poisonous, but they also secrete a powerful healing agent."

"Poisonous?" My vision blurred, and my head seemed packed with cotton.

"Just a little." His lips ticked. "You'll be fine."

I should have cared that he'd drugged me. For all I knew, he was deliberately weakening me for his own malicious purposes, but I couldn't have cared less. Disjointed memories swam through my mind, scenes of fire and flame accompanied by unending demon screams. Some of those screams were mine. Closing my eyes, I tried to find the important image, the one where I reached for the veil prior to incinerating a crowd of demons, but my aching head and inability to concentrate conspired against me. At least the madness—and ecstasy—I'd experienced while trying to protect myself had gone for now.

A rickety hiss rose up from the undergrowth. I jolted upright and nearly fell onto my face. Akil didn't turn. He barely even flinched. His element pooled around him. Then he growled a bubbling growl that sounded wrong rumbling from his mortal lips. The sound of it triggered the memory of an aroused Mammon striding toward me. I shivered.

Whatever loitered at the edges of the firelight must have decided against attacking because a new quiet settled over the forest. Akil relaxed the flow of his element, letting it fizzle back into the earth.

Yukki Onna and I had fought off an attack, and while it hadn't been difficult, it certainly hadn't been a walk in the park either. Akil had deterred whatever lurked in the undergrowth with a single growl. Lowering myself back onto the bed of leaves, I propped up my head and stared at him. Something fundamental in him had shifted. I couldn't place exactly what looked or felt different. Perhaps the touch of his element had altered, but he wasn't the same demon I'd lived with in Boston. "What happened to you?"

His gaze checked mine, and then settled again on the firelight. "Demon's aren't born Princes. We earn the title." He paused. The fire spat and hissed. "When Stefan trapped me here, I was weak."

I had to fight my own guilty conscience not to look away. His weakened state had been my fault. I'd drained him of his power, gobbled it all up. The high I'd experienced while draining him had been euphoric. Perverse pleasure assailed my body, spiked my heart rate, and shortened my breaths. I wanted to experience that again. I closed my eyes and drove the sensations away. *Still half-human... Still have control... But for how long...*

"Within seconds, they were on us. Stefan... fought with exceptional control. He got away. I, on the other hand, did not." Shadows gathered across his handsome face and twisted his expression into something dark and menacing.

"They take great pleasure in ripping a Prince off his throne."

An apology fought its way up my throat, but I gulped it back down. I had nothing to apologize for. Akil got what was coming to him. Perhaps that was the change I sensed in him: a humbling. Akil met my gaze. In the amber firelight, I couldn't quite read his expression, but I sensed a flicker of power reaching out to me. He stood and ambled over to sit behind me. Drawing my wing against me, I rolled onto my back and looked up at him. My focus blurred, head light, and thoughts adrift.

"Too much time in the human realm weakened the power I had here." His gaze roamed over me. I felt the heat in those eyes fall against my demon skin and might have purred. Damned demon attraction.

He stroked the trailing edge of my wing with his fingertips. "I've been working on getting my title back."

How exactly you worked on becoming a Prince of Hell I had no idea, and I didn't want to know. I rested my head on his thigh. He ran his fingers lightly over my shoulder. Where his touch eased across my skin, a comfortable heat pooled. The memory of Damien tried to muscle its way into my thoughts, but it soon floated away, like everything else drifting in my head.

"I would have killed Damien had he not been infused with you," he said. "I could end his meager existence quite easily."

I wished he had. A rude, stabbing sensation in my chest reminded me of my unfortunate predicament. "If Damien dies and I'm still tied to him, what happens?"

"His essence would find a home inside you," Akil replied without hesitation.

I'd already tried to lever the touch of him out of my insides with painful results. What would it feel like to have all of that hideous misshapen darkness at my core?

I focused on Akil's light-fingered touch. In my drug-induced state, I imagined everything was going to be okay. If I closed my eyes, I could will the horror away and pretend we were back in Boston until an ache pounded my side, and a throb of something darker beat inside me. "How is it done? I mean, how will you get him out of me?"

"There are two means by which one can reverse a soul-lock. The first is extremely painful and would likely result in your death."

I lifted my gaze and saw from the slight frown on his face that he was about as keen on that option as I was. "The other?"

He cast his focus back to the fire. "The second is…less painful."

The second option didn't sound like a bag of laughs either. Whatever it was, it would have to be done. I couldn't live with Damien's seed inside me. Option One would be preferable to that. "How is it the Princes are the only ones who can reverse a soul-lock?"

"Only those with unwavering control ultimately claim the title of Prince. Control is what will be required to unravel the threads of Damien from inside you. It is… delicate."

"So, you're a Prince again?" I asked with a little too much enthusiasm. Mentioning Damien's name was enough to make me nauseous.

"Yes, but I'm weaker now than I have been in… a very long time. They will continue to challenge me."

"Like sharks?" I asked. He frowned a little, forcing me to explain. "You keep swimming or you die."

"Not all sharks…" Akil danced his fingertips down my arm, smiling a knowing smile. "What you did, Muse…" He settled his hand on my chest, over my heart, and for a few moments, I let him sink his ethereal touch through my skin. "It was glorious." Admiration gleamed in his eyes.

That was where he and I disagreed. I plucked his hand away. "No. What I did was out of control."

"It was necessary."

Maybe. "What if that happens in Boston? What if I'm cornered, and I react like that again? I could kill hundreds of people and not even know I'd done it…until afterward."

From the confusion in his eyes, I realized he wasn't capable of understanding why such a thing would concern me. All he saw was a demon brimming over with power.

Demons don't concern themselves with collateral damage. In fact, they thrive off it. Chaos. I was under no illusions. Akil wanted my demon. He wanted the reservoir of power dammed up inside me. We both knew it. It wasn't a secret, not any more. He looked at me, his eyes devouring my demon. He'd always wanted her, probably from the first time he'd seen me all those years ago, cowering on my knees in front of Damien, a bruised and battered thing. *Like a butterfly crumpled in the hand of a child,* he'd once told me.

I turned my head away and lost my thoughts in the firelight. Akil trailed his hand over my shoulder, down my arm, leaving sensuous threads of power behind. The lure of sleep cushioned my fears and chased away the conflicting needs and truths, but not before I clung onto the one fact Akil couldn't refute. "You killed Sam... I hate you, Akil. I need you to free me of Damien..." I didn't finish with, "that's all," but he heard it.

"I know." There was a knowing downward tilt at the end of his words, and I wondered again if it was sadness. I couldn't kid myself about Akil. I wasn't that woman. Not anymore.

"I'm so tired..." I whispered.

"Rest. Heal. You will need to be well if we're to subdue Stefan. He will not come easily."

Stefan... Had he lost control the way I had? Was that why the elements crowded the sky above his cave? If he had, I wondered what would be left of him should we manage to get him back where he belonged. What if nothing of the man remained? If I got him back, could I control him? What if I was clinging onto a hopeless, dangerous dream, just as Nica had said? *It was time to let go.*

"Sleep," Akil whispered, fingers swirling across my skin. "You are safe."

Chapter Twenty One

Two demon 'days' passed before I could move without gasping in pain, but it was probably no more than a few hours back in Boston. Time works differently in the netherworld, night and day are not fixed points. While resting and healing, I began to realize how little I'd known about Akil. He taught me how to be human. It seemed ludicrous at that moment, especially considering how I considered myself human first and foremost, but when I arrived in Boston, I barely knew how to cross a road without getting mowed down by traffic.

Those early days were a blur of disjointed memories. Not only was I coming to terms with murdering my owner—a crime for which the demons could have executed me—but I was learning to be human in a strange new world. I had looked up to Akil. Hell, I'd virtually idolized him. He taught me how to channel surf on a TV, how to hail a cab, how to eat with cutlery. I was the proverbial child raised by wolves, only my wolves were demons. Wolves would have been kinder.

Akil had power. He had influence in a world that rewarded such things. It was a strange realm where people cared for one another, where someone might take the time to ask how your day was and listen to the answer, where communities came together. We took it for granted, but the human spirit is unique and fascinating. I began to learn just what it meant to be half-human. I thrived. I embraced humanity and its quirky idiosyncrasies. I grew into a human female, a woman. But while I reveled in the joy of newfound freedom, Akil began to lament what I'd become.

He lusted after my demon, and I'd shut her away alongside the memories of the life I'd left behind.

Now, as I stole moments to watch Akil, to really listen to him, I realized with reluctance how wrong I'd been. He was only ever a demon. He could only be demon. I had expected him to play by human rules, but that was never going to happen. You don't blame a predator for killing its prey. It's the natural order of things. Considering the destruction and utter devastation he was capable of, Akil had showed consistent restraint until he'd snapped and tried to get back the demon he'd lost.

He wasn't to blame. I was. I'd been too human to see the truth.

***

Akil could have transported us into Stefan's territory, but we agreed Stefan might not react well to a sudden attack. So we approached through the dead forest. Ahead, in the distance, through the naked branches, the writhing aurora of power rippled in the late evening sky.

"How do you feel?" Akil glanced back at me. The air was still, and although he'd kept his voice low, his words echoed through the skeletal trees.

"I'm okay." My ribs still ached, and an occasional twinge of pain jabbed rudely at my chest where Damien's metaphysical soul-lock sat heavily on my heart, but otherwise I felt rested and raring to snag Stefan and get the hell out of Dodge. I also had countless questions burning on the tip of my tongue. In the two days I'd spent healing, I'd been trying to wrap my head around where I was and who I was with.

I studied how Akil stalked through the trees ahead. He moved with purpose, weaving around flayed trees and ducking below low-hanging branches. He had a liquid grace, as though he could adapt his body to any environment, even dressed in a tired suit. It felt at odds with how I remembered him: a professional businessman, surrounded by modern trappings, the epitome of charm and success. Here, he had a gritty edge and a hint of wildness.

It took me a day of quiet watching to realize why. He was home. This was where he belonged. Despite spending my early years in the netherworld, it would never be my home. He'd spent a hundred years in the human realm, give or take few decades, but the rest of his eternal existence had played out in the netherworld. Could I really say I knew him at all? What's a hundred years to an immortal being? A blink? What had he done in those years? What kind of creature was he, really? I'd never asked, never needed to. That was about to change.

"Is there a King?" Of all the questions I could have asked, such as "do you still intend to separate my demon from my flesh?" I could guarantee he didn't expect that one. *Start easy.* Once I had him talking, I planned to pounce on the other more pertinent questions.

"Mm…" He shoved a branch away.

"What does that mean? Mm?"

"You're awfully talkative."

I glared at his back. "You think one question is talkative? You ain't seen nothing yet. Damien didn't like to hear me talk. Then I was with you in Boston, and I wanted to forget about the netherworld. So I didn't ask question—"

"Wisely so." He covered ground in one step that took me two.

He brushed a branch aside, stepped around it, and released it. I got a face full of twigs as it smacked me in the head and chest. I spat out a curse and wrestled free. "The Institute doesn't know anything about the hierarchy, just myths and rumors. There are seven Princes… So, is there a King?"

He snapped the next bough off at the junction with the trunk. "Do you think any one of those Princes, me included, would answer to a King?"

"How would I know? You've never told me anything about the Princes." I waited, hoping he might elaborate. He didn't. "You haven't answered my question."

He stopped, straightened, and glanced over his shoulder, shooting me an expression of curious amusement. "Observant, aren't you."

I pulled up short. "Is there a King?" I hadn't really cared for the answer, but now he was being evasive, and I wanted to know why. Did he just not like me asking questions, or was it the subject I'd chosen?

"Sometimes."

I frowned. "Sometimes?" What was this, a lesson in vagueness?

He angled his body to face me, giving me all his attention. The feather-light touch of a smile flicked across his lips. "Why do you want to know?"

"I've been kept in the dark all my life. I intend to change that, and I'm starting now, so why don't you just give me a straight answer?" Was he playing with me? His expression seemed to say so, but as always with Akil, there was the threat of something darker lurking behind his relaxed posture.

"There was a King." He watched me closely, assessing, waiting.

"What happened to him?" I eyed Akil warily, the same way he observed me.

"The Queen killed him."

My mouth fell open. "There was a Queen?"

He laughed. The delicious sound of it wove through the trees before the silence gobbled it up. "There *was* a Queen."

"Wait, don't tell me… The Princes killed her?"

He inclined his head and arched an eyebrow. "Now you are thinking like a demon." A purr rumbled beneath his words. Was it the memory of the Queen's death sparking delight in his eyes?

I swallowed, aware I was poking a sleeping tiger. I wanted answers… "So, how come there's *sometimes* a King?"

"The netherworld is changing." He turned away, allowing me to heave out the breath I didn't realize I'd been holding.

"Meaning?" I sensed the candid moment slipping through my fingers. I fell into step behind him again, dodging wayward branches springing in his wake.

"I will tell you everything once we've returned to Boston." His clipped tone shut me down. End of discussion.

At least I got some answers out of him. It was a start. So there had been a King, and a Queen. Both now dead, leaving behind Seven Princes. As the Princes don't inherit their titles, I assumed it was the same with the King and Queen. They must have earned their 'crowns'. It was a sobering thought. The Princes had disturbing reputations. Just how bad did you have to be to sit at the top? The netherworld was a cauldron of chaos. I only knew about a fraction of what must exist on that side of the veil, but I intended to change that. I meant what I'd said to Akil. I needed answers.

Spindly branches tugged at my wing. "Something big went down here..." I yanked my wing free.

"Yes it did." No hesitation.

"Was this you?"

A few more steps and he said, "Partially."

I assessed the dead forest with renewed interest. "You've tried to get Stefan out before, haven't you?"

Akil stopped and faced me. His hair wisped about his dark eyes as he drew them across the devastation. "It's best you go in first. Wear him down, distract him, do whatever you must to exhaust him, but don't rile him up so much that he draws from the veil..." The rest didn't need to be said. It also went without saying that I was to keep a lid on my own little party trick for fear I might kill us all. Happy thoughts.

"The last time I was here, he created an ice beast..."

"I'll deal with those." He blinked slowly. "Keep him focused on you at all times. He's unlikely to kill you. Me..." An eyebrow twitched. "He'll try to kill me." No ifs, buts, or maybes.

Akil moved to turn away, but I caught his wrist. "What if Damien shows up?"

He smiled down at me and caught himself reaching out to touch my face. "He has no need to. He knows exactly where you are." He lowered his hand, placing it over my heart. "He'll wait until we are separated." He tensed to pull away when I tightened my grip again. This time, his smile faltered. "What is it?"

It was insane, it went against all of my better judgment and my gut feelings, but I didn't want Akil to get hurt. How do you stop yourself from loving someone even when you know they're incapable of loving you back? No matter how many times I reminded myself of the monster inside him, it made no difference. What is it they say, love is blind? In my case, it wasn't just blind. It was oblivious, foolhardy, and outright suicidal. Maybe this need wasn't as neat as love. Perhaps I was so thoroughly ruined that Akil looked like a reasonable alternative to the horrors cohabiting in my life. Love was an excuse. Love was tidy. Neat. I didn't love Akil. What I felt for him was messy and confused, slippery and self-serving. My guardian, my killer. It wasn't love.

"Just be careful." I released him. "If Stefan snaps the way I did at the fountain, I'm not sure either of us will survive."

Akil clasped my face in his warm hands. He was suddenly so close that I breathed him in and gasped. His element bloomed around his hands, through my cheeks and cascaded down my neck, over my shoulders. I instinctively cast my element around us. The warm liquid touch of his power caressed my demon skin. I could drink him in, let our elements blend together as one. I knew it would be maddeningly pleasurable. But as those old desires and needs vied for control, the specter of Damien's abuse lingered. I bit into my lip, tasted blood, and held back. Fear doused the fire in my veins. The spark of need snuffed out as quickly as it had come.

Akil's nostrils flared. He eased back, dark eyes narrowing. "Stefan won't hurt you. He loves you."

He released me and turned away in time to miss the grimace on my face. For a few seconds between breaths, I'd wanted to meet Akil's lips with mine, to melt against him and taste the exotic spiciness of him on my tongue. Had it been a test? Was he trying to reel me back in, or had he withdrawn to protect me? The lust I'd felt had been real, even if it had only lasted a few fleeting moments before fear had pushed it out. He would have sensed my need when I'd thrown my element around him. *Stefan loves you...*

I felt wretched; as though, in wanting Akil, I'd betrayed a part of me and somehow soiled Stefan's memory. Trudging behind Akil, I shivered and pulled my wing around me. It had to be my demon that caused these despicable feelings toward Akil. She never had been able to resist him. In fact, everything he'd done, the betrayal, the threats, all it did was remind her how thoroughly demon he was and how much she liked it. He could have lured us in, but he hadn't. What did that mean?

The sooner we escaped the netherworld, the sooner I could be free of my demon's desires. And of Damien and Akil.

Chapter Twenty Two

The bristling ice-teeth at the mouth of the cave were as welcoming as the last time. I could have sent out a little elemental heat and melted the prickly barricade, but decided to try to keep the power to a minimum for now. I stepped awkwardly through the spikes and gingerly lifted my wing out of the way.

Inside the cave, the walls shivered beneath the caress of evening light. The cold crept beneath my skin and gnawed at my bones. I clenched my teeth to stop them from chattering. I couldn't see Stefan or any sign of habitation. Within a few strides, the light died and the darkness fell in from all sides. Maybe he wasn't here. But then where else would he go?

"I don't want to fight you." My words tumbled over one another in a drawn-out echo, then abruptly fell silent.

I straightened and flinched as my wing brushed against a bitter snag of ice. I lowered my right hand and summoned an orb of fire into my palm. Warm orange light spilled outward, licking over slick surfaces.

He sat in an alcove, head bowed, bright blue eyes drilling into me. His demon skin didn't glitter as it had before, but he still rippled an incandescent blue. His face, virtually free of ice apart from a dusting around his jaw, was set in anger. His wings had gone, but that only meant he wasn't fully charged and ready to attack with all of the elemental power at his disposal. I'd seen the wings shatter when Damien had tossed him against the rock face, but Stefan's wings weren't tangible like mine. I assumed they could be remolded.

Despite the snarl frozen on his lips, I took the lack of wings and toning down of his ice armor as a good sign. I tried to smile, but couldn't get it to stick to my lips. "Do you remember me?"

He sprang out of that hollow and had me by the throat so quickly my vision spun. He pinned me back against the cave wall. Ice hissed and sizzled against my back. The urge to pool heat into my limbs nearly broke me, but I gulped it back and snuffed out the orb in my hand.

He leaned in so close I could see the rough shards of ice in the blue of his eyes. "I remember you." He didn't sound too happy about it.

I flinched as needles of ice tried to creep their way from his hand into my throat. Already sore from the jaws of the demon who had grabbed me around the neck, I really didn't need more injuries to add to my collection. "Will you hear me out?"

He stepped back and shoved me toward the cave entrance. "Leave."

I stumbled and flung my wing out, regaining my balance. "Do you remember the Hellhounds you saved me from?"

A snarl rippled across his lips.

"What about the time you killed a demon who tried to jump my face at Akil's party? Do you remember that?" An uneasy chill spread through me. Behind him, his crystalline wings began to form; layers of ice stacking over one another, each building on the next until they butted up against the cave ceiling; razor-edged angel's wings.

"Get out," he sneered. "I will not warn you again."

My breath formed clouds of mist as the temperature plummeted. My throat constricted. The air burned cold as I breathed it in. "Do you remember the Institute?" I rasped. He flinched, his memory likely snagging on a fragment of his past. "Our time together there. Just you and me... Stefan... do you remember us?" I did the most ridiculously dangerous thing I could do and shook my demon from my skin. I wouldn't have long. Human flesh isn't designed to be exposed to the elements of the netherworld, but all I needed were a few precious seconds for him to see me as he knew me. Not as a fire demon, but as Muse.

My demon skin slipped free and turned to dust at my feet. Vulnerable, pink human flesh prickled in the cold. I tried to appear impressive in all my vulnerable humanity, but the shivering dashed any chance of that. "It's me," I stuttered, surprised at the fluidic tone of my voice. "Just Muse."

His cool gaze clinically assessed my naked body.

He could have killed me. I had nothing, no armor, no power. It would take precious seconds to call it all back to me, and in that time, he could fling a shard of ice at my heart, or my head, and I'd be dead.

His gaze drifted, memories likely bobbing to the surface of his thoughts, and then, when he focused again, he said softly, "Muse."

"Yes." I could have laughed, if my core body temperature hadn't dropped to dangerous levels. "You know me. I'm here to help you. To take you home." I couldn't hold out any longer and welcomed the demon back into my flesh. Her warmth drew an audible sigh from my lips.

He frowned and glanced behind me through the mouth of the cave. "What are you doing here?"

"I'm here for you." I chanced a step closer and froze as he pinned me rigid with his chilling glare. "Come with me. I can end this. I can get you home."

"No you can't." He shook his head. "There's only one way."

I hadn't expected to break through his armor of ice. The plan was to get him out in the open where Akil and I could overwhelm him, but he'd surprised me by recognizing me, and now I had to tell him the truth. Or lie.

"I found another way." I tried to keep my expression hopeful. "Please. Come back to Boston with me. To Nica."

Resignation softened the hardness around his eyes. He relaxed, cool marble-like muscles quivering with the sweet release of tension. His wings sagged, and his shoulders slouched. I stepped forward, thinking he might fall, but he reached for the cave wall and planted a hand there to steady himself. He whispered something so quietly that I moved closer again. His winter aura shivered over me. He brought his head up. Tears glistened in his eyes. I ached to touch him, to hold him, wrap my arms around him and tell him everything would be alright. But it wasn't over. I had to get him out, and he had to face Akil.

Stefan's lips quirked into a crooked smile. It warmed those arctic eyes. Relief flooded through me. He was alive in there. Stefan, the man, the mortal man, he still lived inside that icy armor. For six months I'd waited for this moment, fearing all the time that I'd be too late.

"You came for me..." he said.

I reached out a hand but withdrew a little as the heat flared against the bitterly cold air surrounding him. Fire and ice. Two opposing elements. Two ill-defined half-bloods. Energy simmered the air around him, rising off his smooth muscles in a haze. When we'd lain together, PC34 had locked my demon away. I'd been virtually human. Even then, his revering touch had awoken something bigger than the both of us, an elemental promise of danger mingling with delight. Now, with our demons riding high, the lure of chaos strung tight between us. It was forbidden. Fire and Ice. It was wrong, but damn it felt so right.

"Will you come with me?" I asked, between breaths.

He grinned and straightened, taking a breath and inhaling the energy broiling around us. "You took your sweet time, Muse."

The human part of me did a little mental leap for joy as I recognized the dry humor I'd missed so much. "Let's go."

Everything was going well. Stefan was beside me. We were going home. That was until we emerged beyond the cave mouth and found Akil waiting on the plateau.

I drew breath to explain, but it was already too late. Stefan's element surged outward, spilling over me and flooding the surface of the plateau. The cold sucked the warmth out of my flesh, wrenching a gasp from my lips. Akil's human form burst apart in an explosion of heat. Mammon stretched his wings, took to the air, and roared.

Stefan's physical form bristled with ice. His wings jolted outward, bolstering his size. Each filament splayed apart, their tips glinting sharply beneath the writhing light. His bellow shook the ground at our feet. He summoned a carpet of ice from the plateau and heaved it toward Akil. Swords of ice swept upward, waves frozen as they crested, driving Mammon back.

I took one look at Stefan behind his frost armor and knew he wouldn't listen, no matter what excuses I had. There was murder in his eyes.

Mammon's vast wings beat the air. Wildfire raced across their membranes and embraced his colossal form. I knew, without doubt, Stefan would try to kill him, and if Stefan drew from the veil, he would likely succeed. I itched to intervene, but the massacre at the fountain stalled the battle urge. What if I lost control again? I'd kill Stefan and wouldn't even know I'd done it, until it was too late.

They raged at one another in a breathtaking display of fire and ice. Stefan stood behind rapidly melting barriers, launching a barrage of shards at Mammon. He moved with blistering accuracy. Many of the ice daggers simply drowned in Mammon's retaliating blasts of heat, but Mammon couldn't target them all. Those that got through peppered holes in Mammon's wings. He lost height.

I watched helplessly from the sidelines. Pulse racing. Mammon's draw of power tugged at the element coiled inside me. Stefan's ice encrusted home didn't lend itself well to reservoirs of heat. Mammon couldn't draw from the veil. Only half-bloods have that talent. If he didn't find a source of heat, he wouldn't last long.

Stefan, on the other hand, could draw from the wintery mountain slopes. He had already shored up his defenses with enough ice to put up a fight that would deter most demons. This was his battleground, and he had the advantage.

I had hoped Stefan would hold back, knowing he had to return with Akil if he was ever going to escape the netherworld, but he clearly wasn't thinking ahead. Or maybe, in his mind, that solution wasn't one he could live with. I had to do something. They needed each other alive.

A bolt of ice slammed into Mammon's shoulder. He grunted and dropped to the ground in a crouch. He pulled his tattered wings in close. Flames broiled over the surface of his flesh. His outline blurred inside a cocoon of fire. Stefan backed up, but he wasn't giving in. He opened his arms, palms up and the ice slumbering around us reared up. The ground trembled. The air tightened, thinned, and the cold took a bite out of us. My veil of heat contracted.

The wind picked up. Cold air rushed down from the slopes, carrying with it a blast of snow. The white-out rolled over me. I leaned into the blast. Mammon's fading orange glow flared ahead, but his fire was dying. His element spat and hissed its displeasure, as did mine. He had more in him, but he continued to hold back. He couldn't risk hurting Stefan.

I squeezed my eyes closed and bowed my head into the wind. Snow pummeled me from all sides. The wind dashed ice and snow against my skin. The storm roared like a living thing. It howled and groaned, rumbled its fury. I'd known Stefan was a force to be reckoned with, but I'd never witnessed it.

I released the hold on my element, letting it spill over me. Immediately, my skin blazed and rippled with heat, creating a haze through which the snow couldn't penetrate. I burned like a beacon of light among the impenetrable gray. Mammon's ethereal reach lashed out of the storm and threaded through me. I steadied myself, pulling back so I didn't fall to my knees. My summoned heat dragged through my muscles, out of my body, into Mammon.

I turned my head away as a fresh blast of heat gobbled up the storm from the inside. The wind dissipated, leaving only a few lazy flakes twirling through the air. Lifting my gaze, I saw Mammon standing over Stefan. He had summoned the elemental sword and pressed the tip against Stefan's chest. Stefan lay sprawled on his back, ice armor melting, limp wings pinned beneath him. Their gazes locked, and Mammon lifted the sword.

"Akil!" I sprang off my back foot, heart leaping into my throat.

Mammon slid his black eyes to me. Stefan flung his head back and fixed his arctic eyes on the waves of energy rippling in the sky. The veil tore open like a bolt of lightning searing across the sky, and raw elemental energy gushed through the wound between realms.

I stumbled as my element surged, rearing up, ravenous and wild.

Stefan thrust out his hand. A lance of ice followed the movement and plunged through Mammon's chest. Mammon jerked back, muscles shivering. Impaled, he looked down, his demon expression difficult to fathom, but the flicker of fear in those dark eyes was undeniable. A funnel of energy spiraled from above, rode over Stefan's body, and danced down the lance. Ice cracked, jumped, and twisted as it wrapped around Mammon. With a snarl, Mammon swung the sword down and shattered the lance. Free of Stefan's weapon, Mammon stamped back. The wound in his chest glistened with ice, and as I skidded to a halt beside them, delicate spider webs of ice laced across Mammon's chest.

Mammon wavered and dropped to a knee, the impact cracking the ice beneath him. He should have been aglow with fire, but instead the embers dancing in his veins gradually fizzled to nothing. The elemental sword fell from his grip and vanished before it hit the ground. The veil still gaped above us. Stefan lay back, breathless and trembling. Propped up on his elbows, he watched Mammon. His smile twisted into a sneer. A thin threadlike string of power lashed between them. Energy danced down the line, feeding the ice spreading across Mammon's dark flesh.

"Stefan, stop." I begged, caught between them.

Mammon fell forward onto shivering arms. His wings slumped. Ice groped where his wing-tips rested against the ground. More ice climbed up his legs. It snagged and pulled at him. Nothing of his fire remained. I couldn't feel the pull of his element, just the cold.

"Stefan." I stood in Stefan's line of sight. The thread of power wove through the air beside me. "Stop". He wasn't listening. He didn't even see me. Those eyes gleamed like diamonds, cold, hard...empty. I moved closer, standing over him. The ice would kill Mammon. Without Akil, I couldn't be free of Damien. Without Akil, Stefan would never be able to return to Boston. "Don't hurt him, Stefan." He looked right through me.

I couldn't return to Boston without Stefan. I'd promised Nica I'd get him home. I owed it to her. I owed Stefan. But this demon wasn't Stefan. Stefan was better than this, better than me, better than the Institute. I swallowed a brittle knot of grief in my throat and poured all of my fear into one single word. "Please."

A shadow passed over his face. His bright eyes pinched closed. When he opened them again, the dazzling glow melted away. But it wasn't relief I saw on Stefan's face. I couldn't be sure what it was. Disgust? Horror? He looked at me, saw me, but something I'd said or done had wounded him. More than that, it had crushed him.

The string of power collapsed. I spun and bolted for Mammon. In the two strides it took me to reach him, I'd summoned what power I had and poured it over him. My element latched onto Mammon's cold body, and spilled heat back into his veins. I gave everything I had, let it wash through me and into him. I'd call from the veil if I needed to. Mammon needed to live.

The ice that clutched hold of Mammon by the legs, arms, and wings peeled back and melted away. Sparkling shards retreated into the earth, and as the fire I fed him took hold, steam coiled in the air. Mammon lifted his head. Thick lips pulled back over jagged teeth in a wolfish grin. He shoved me aside as easily as scolding a puppy and grabbed Stefan by the neck.

"Wait! What are you going?" I demanded.

Stefan barely fought him. As Mammon's huge claws locked around Stefan's throat, the veil snapped closed above.

Stefan fell limp, head lolling to one side. Mammon straightened and growled, "He will live." He snorted a satisfied sound, pumped his wings, and glared at me.

Within a few blinks, he'd shaken off his demon guise, replacing it with the mortal man. Akil's shirt was torn and bloody, his hair a tousled mess. His eyes burned. "We need to leave," he said, breathless and rigid. "The energies stirred here have caught the attention of the Princes. We must avoid their intervention at all costs."

I nodded. My voice had completely abandoned me. Turning my back on Akil, I mentally opened a cut in the veil and reached toward Boston.

Chapter Twenty Three

The hole in the veil spat us out somewhere along the leafy cobble streets of Beacon Hill. Brownstones towered over the three of us and blocked out much of the pale blue sky above. Long shadows stretched from parked cars. Briefly disorientated, I stood motionless and let the ambience of the city wrap around me. The air slipped easily across my lips. I could hear the constant noises of city life and feel the beat of the city through the ground. A swell of unexpected joy jolted me back into my human skin.

I took one look at Akil's bloodied shirt, my own filthy naked body, and Stefan's blood-encrusted nakedness, and realized we needed to get off the street before someone called the cops. Akil leaned Stefan against a house wall. I was about to join him when I noticed a woman walking with her toddler up the steep hill toward us. They hadn't noticed us; yet.

"Wait here." Akil took a step and vanished in a sizzle of static.

I spat out a curse. The bastard. I knew it. I knew I couldn't trust him. I crouched beside Stefan. "I'll kill him if he doesn't come back." Stefan's entire body trembled. His eyes were clamped closed, and his lips pulled thin over gritted teeth. A sprinkling of perspiration beaded on his face and chest.

Akil appeared beside me with a metallic snap of air. I almost jumped out of my skin. He dropped a pair of jeans, leather ankle boots, and a sweater in my lap and tossed a blanket over Stefan.

"Where d'you—" I tugged on the garments with frantic hands.

"Department store. Petty theft."

"We need to get moving. If we can wake him..." I stopped planning. Akil looked back at me, weary eyes worried. When I glanced at Stefan, I saw why. Webs of ice wove around him. His body twitched as though an electrical current pulsed through his muscles. Eyes squeezed closed, he clamped his teeth together and growled, the sound fraught with agony. "Stefan..." I reached out to touch him, but Akil pulled me back.

Veins of ice snaked up the building behind Stefan like slow-motion lightning. It twitched and lashed over the brownstone façade. The ground beneath my bare feet frosted over. "What's happening?"

"He's cut off from the elements. His demon wants freedom." Akil tried to draw me against him, but I tugged free. He shot me scolding look that seemed to say, *don't be an idiot.* "When I brought you here, Muse, it took months for you to rein in your demon."

I remembered those early months as a swirl of conflicting emotions. I shivered. "But he's always controlled it before." I tried to prevent the outpouring of panic from flooding my thoughts, but it felt a little like plugging a dam with a cork. Stefan had always been the pillar of control. I was a walking disaster compared to him. He'd had the sort of control over his demon I could only dream of.

Akil shook his head. "It's been too long."

I heard the woman talking with her young son as they neared. At any moment, they'd notice us.

"It's been six months," I said. Six months was a long time to live entirely as a demon. I'd let my demon trample all over me after a few days, but Stefan was stronger than me.

Akil tilted his head and gave me an odd sort of expression, as though he couldn't quite believe me. Had I said something wrong? His eyes narrowed, and then widened again. "Here, yes. But time passes differently beyond the veil."

Realization jabbed me in the gut like a physical blow. Of course. It had been six months for me, living in the human realm, but Stefan's time would have passed more slowly. I should have known that.

"It's been years, Muse," Akil said, his voice soft with a sympathy I didn't know he was capable of.

Years. Stefan thought I'd left him there for years. *You took your sweet time, Muse.*

A snowflake drifted aimlessly in front of me and settled on Stefan's blanket.

"Is he okay?" The woman and her son stopped a few strides down the street from us, close enough to see Stefan in the midst of a seizure. I glared at her; she flinched, the horror I felt likely clear on my face.

"Look, Mommy, snow." Her little boy giggled and reached out a chubby hand to catch a flake.

His mother, dressed for summer in an above-the-knee flower-print skirt and short-sleeved top, looked as though she was about to shush her son when she noticed the snow flurries spiraling in the air. She forgot us for a moment and threw a confused glance up and down the street.

Akil gripped my shoulder. "The best place for him is the Institute."

I shoved him off me. "No. He can't go back there like this. If they suspect he's losing it, they'll lock him up. Or worse."

Stefan bucked, cried out, and the sheet of ice shattered. His human appearance shimmered and rippled. The full transformation was difficult for my human eyes to see. If his demon manifested here and he called his power, there was no telling what he might do.

"He needs help." The mom fumbled in her shoulder bag.

"Wait." I held out a trembling hand. "Please. Don't call anyone." She had the cellphone in her hand, thumb poised to dial. "Please, just... just don't. Let me think…"

"Hey, it's snowing," a man said, from somewhere behind me. I looked up at more people ambling from their front doors. Some frowned at the snow flurry. Others gawped. It was snowing in summer. Why couldn't Stefan be a water-elemental? Rain in summer wouldn't have been so bad. Rain, I could bluff. Snow blew any excuses I had out the water.

"Muse," Akil growled. "If not the Institute, then where?"

The mom jabbed at her phone and lifted it to her ear. "He's one of those demons, isn't he?" She gathered her son against her side and backed away.

Dammit. A ripple of unease spread through the swelling crowd. Ice sparked over Stefan and snapped across the sidewalk, reaching for the people. One of the men lifted a cellphone. Some snapped pictures, others made calls. I searched their concerned faces. They would call the police, who would call the Institute.

"Please..." I raised my voice. "It's okay... He's just... He's...." The crowd didn't care. All they saw was a demon about to lose control on their street. There were children here, families, they were doing the right thing.

I had about four minutes before the Institute Enforcers would appear. I couldn't let them take Stefan away. They'd destroy him.

I searched Akil's mildly concerned expression. He could have abandoned me. We were back in Boston. He had the freedom he wanted, but he stood waiting for me to make the right call. I'd expected him to vanish the second we breathed the Boston air. Yes, we'd made a deal, but a part of me had always assumed he'd drop me the second he became a free demon again.

"Help me get him to safety," I said carefully, as though my asking this of him would spook him into tipping his proverbial hat and bidding me farewell.

He nodded. Akil could bend reality around him, rendering him and everything he touched virtually invisible. He'd once walked me out the police station in full view of the cops, and nobody had seen a thing. That same talent enabled him to hop from one place to another in seconds.

"Where?"

"To a vet." I took Akil's hand. "I know what to do."

Chapter Twenty Four

Jerry's veterinary clinic was closed. Not surprising considering the late hour. The sun had all but vanished, and the streetlights were blinking on. Akil put a bit of muscle into the door and broke in.

The Voodoo Lounge was a short walk from Jerry's clinic, but I didn't want to walk into a demon sanctuary with an unconscious Stefan. We left him sprawled across the waiting room chairs. As soon as he came into contact with the chairs, ice bloomed across the floor and up the walls, like mold in a time-lapse photo. At this rate, it wouldn't take long before the entire room resembled a freezer.

I followed Akil out and let my gaze linger on Stefan before closing the door behind me. Akil had suggested he stay with him. I'd snorted and didn't dignify his words with a reply. I didn't trust Akil as far as I could throw him. The Prince of Hell would likely hand Stefan over to the Institute, or worse. No, Akil was staying right beside me. I'd have handcuffed him to me, if I had a pair. On second thought, maybe not handcuffs. He'd like it.

I shook the unwanted image of an aroused Mammon from my head, wondering if I'd ever be free of that disturbing memory, and told Akil all I knew about Jerry. He listened quietly, nodding in all the right places. We didn't have time to talk about the infusion, and even if we did, I wasn't sure what I'd say. Once Stefan was safe, Akil had agreed to free me of Damien's soul-lock, but what would happen after that? Damien was still out there. He'd come for me. Free of the soul-lock, I could—I would—kill him.

The relentless beat of dance music drummed against the walls of the club as we approached the neon lit entrance. The doorman raked his gaze over Akil, his attention drawn to the blood stains. He looked me up and down, expression thoroughly bored. A trickle of an elemental touch slid over my skin when he dove a little deeper than physical appearance. Done with me, he did the same to Akil and jolted upright. Had his face just drained of all color? With a wordless nod, he allowed us entry.

The early evening crowd was thin. I glanced back at Akil and saw him reading the anonymous faces. All looked human, but only a handful of them were. The rest moved with the fluid grace of netherworldly things. Under the sliding lights, my human eyes had trouble focusing on the demons for more than a few seconds. The touch of power summoned goose bumps across my arms, as it always did. I shrugged it off. Considering I'd survived a netherworld riot, annihilating countless demons in the process, this should've been a walk in the park. Akil appeared mildly amused, no more, no less.

About to look away, I noticed his step missed a beat. He winced and pressed his hand against his side, catching my eye. *It's nothing,* those eyes said.

At the bar—the music too loud for softly spoken words—I glared at the dark stain on his shirt and met his calm expression with a concerned one of my own. He smiled, and gave me the smallest of nods, before leaning against the bar. I wasn't convinced. His shoulders slumped. Stefan had skewered Akil with a lance of ice. In his true form, as Mammon, Akil might've been a tough bastard and immortal, but the lance must have wounded him, and considering the events of the past few days, he had to be feeling the strain. I was.

I ached in every conceivable muscle, even in muscles I didn't know I had. My demon was rammed back into the flesh and bone of my squishy and fragile human body, and I felt all the physical damage. Demon flesh absorbs much of a half-blood's battle-scars, but not all, and not those that aren't physical.

I ordered a vodka and coke and gritted my teeth as I waited for the bartender. Neat vodka might be asking for trouble, but damn I needed something. I kept my face turned away from Akil. The physical tiredness would pass, as would the other aches and pains, but the tugging sensation behind my ribs, where my heart raced? That wasn't going away. Damien. The darkness of his touch seeped putrid poison through my veins. Just the thought of something of his, some part of him, metaphysical or not, sitting inside of me made my flesh prickle and my stomach lurch. I couldn't think too long about it without wanting to run and hide in the darkest corner of the quietest of places, where I could bury my head in my hands and cry. What Damien had done to me was a violation of the most penetrating kind. I shouldn't have been surprised. The act of violation was his specialty, but nausea still burned the back of my throat every time I sensed him inside me.

Akil watched the expressions drift across my face. I gave him a bright, utterly unrealistic smile. He didn't buy it and narrowed those dark eyes, attempting to scowl me into an explanation. He knew me too well, even after the months we'd spent apart. Six months for me, years for him. Years for the both of them. Stefan was suffering now, because I'd waited too long. I should have forced Adam's hand months ago.

"I didn't realize—about the time. I should have."

Akil leaned in close. "The passage of time is unique for each of us. This curious fact is felt a little more keenly in the netherworld."

His shoulder brushed mine. Heat lapped gently down my arm. I met his eyes and wondered if he truly had changed since threatening to peel my flesh from my bones to free my demon. Could demons change? Could a Prince of Hell change? Everything I knew about them, it all pointed to a simple 'No'. Demons don't change. They are eternal beings, constructs born from the elements of chaos. Chaos doesn't change.

I wanted to believe Akil had changed. He seemed different, softer, somehow. But I'd been down that road before, and I wasn't falling for his soft hazel eyes and suave exterior again. Back in my mortal flesh with my thoughts grounded in reality, I had the strength to stick to my guns. My demon still wanted to jump his bones. That wasn't going to change either, but the squishy human me had control now.

Akil searched my face for any clue of my thoughts. Whatever he saw there, it didn't erase his frown. "Once Stefan is safe," he said, perhaps sensing my doubts, "I will free you of Damien. That was our agreement."

I lifted vodka and coke to my lips. "I'll believe you when it happens." I watched him closely and took a sip. He dropped his gaze, ageless eyes harboring a touch of sadness. Then he flicked his head up and focused behind me.

"We have company," he said flatly.

Carol-Anne parted the crowd and glided toward us. The hem of her blue silk dress rippled over her dainty shoes like water over pebbles. The fabric hugged her languid figure, accentuating lean legs and luscious curves, before rising up to cup her breasts in a strapless corset. She'd pinned her dark hair up, leaving just the one electric blue lock twirling free. The caress of her power trickled over me, and I dampened down my jealousy. It helped to remember the fish-like demon hiding inside that human suit, but even so, her manufactured beauty turned heads.

I was about to grumble something to Akil along the lines of how we both looked like we'd been washed up on a beach when I saw the twitch of a smile on his lips. "Let the games begin."

He pushed away from the bar, moved around me, and extended his hand to Carol-Anne. Her radiant smile shone only for Akil, and her pace quickened. She took his hand, bowing low before him. "Mammon."

He touched her lightly on the head and let her rise. He lifted her hand to his lips and skipped a kiss across her knuckles, his eyes fixed on hers. "Carol-Anne," he purred.

His voice had slipped into its lowest tone, the one he used to deliver secrets and promises. I might have turned my back on the both of them to finish my drink had I not been fascinated by their exchange.

"You should have notified me of your arrival." She touched her hair with the hand he'd kissed and twirled the blue lock around her finger. Her cheeks warmed. I could practically smell the hormones wafting off her. "It's not often we have a Prince among us."

"Yes, well, as you can see," he gestured at his bloodied shirt, "we've been otherwise occupied. I apologize for the unscheduled arrival." His words came out clipped and precise, his exotic accent gone, reminding me how easily he could put on an act for the benefit of those around him.

"No need." She batted his comment away with a flick of her hand. "And so I see you have Muse back by your side." Carol-Anne's gaze barely lingered long enough to acknowledge me.

I wanted to say something about Akil being at *my* side but swallowed my pride in the spirit of getting the job done. "We need to see Jerry," I grumbled.

I slid my gaze back to Carol-Anne. She pinned her stare on me with unadulterated disgust. I frowned back at her. Sure, we'd clashed swords a little. I might have torched her two men, but in demon terms, our tiff had amounted to little more than foreplay.

She checked Akil, taking note of his bloodied shirt. "Are you wounded?"

"Yes," I said.

"No," Akil winced, then covered my slip by offering Carol-Anne a confident smile. "It's nothing."

"Then why do you need Jeremiah?" She mirrored Akil's smile. "I'm sure I could help with your wounds, Mammon." She inched closer to Akil and draped an arm over his shoulder, her dress ruffling around her. She walked her long thin fingers down his chest. "A little water can do wonders for the heat of wounds."

Akil made no attempt to pull away. He eased his hand around her waist and pulled her close. I chose that moment to return to my drink. "Get a room."

I heard Carol-Anne purr in response to my suggestion. My stomach hardened. My teeth squeaked as I ground them together.

"Your pet does not appear to appreciate our teasing, Mammon."

Anger rolled up my spine and jolted me upright. "I'm not his pet." I glared at Carol-Anne's body still glued to Akil's. "We don't have time for this." Stefan was in agony, and Akil was copping a feel. "Where's Jerry?"

Her blue eyes danced as laughter bubbled up her throat. She and Akil parted. He did a damn good job of appearing delighted by her. He wouldn't meet my glare, and instead, fixed his gaze over my shoulder. The smile was real though. Real and curious and sly.

I coiled heat across my skin. "We've been here before Carol-Anne, but the last time I wasn't in control. Things have changed. I don't want to start anything, but I'm very capable of burning this bar down around you."

She absorbed my threat for a few moments, glanced at Akil, and then laughed a soft trickling chuckle. "You stand beside a Prince of Hell and threaten me when I have done nothing to incite such a display of anger. You insult both Mammon and me, little half-blood."

"Akil is with me on this." At least I hoped he was. "So tell us where Jerry is, or you'll answer to the both of us." Akil stood off to her side, face impassive, watching me lose my cool. He hadn't said or done anything to help. A thought hooked into me, an accusation I'd once thrown at him before: he liked to watch me squirm on a hook.

Her laughter cut off. "I do not answer to you," she snarled. "And your so-called Prince cannot lift a finger to protect you. You are bound to another. Mammon has no claim over you. You're a half-blood pet playing games with higher demons you do not understand."

Finally, Akil moved closer to me. "Carol-Anne, I would think carefully before you assume to know who you're dealing with. While it is true I have been... indisposed of late, I have reclaimed my title." He leaned casually against the bar. "Ask yourself, why I would ally myself with a half-blood while in such a precarious position?"

She didn't think before answering. "Because you're a fool, Mammon. You've spent so long in your human vessel that you've become blinded by their inconsequential ways. She makes you appear weak." As soon as the words left her mouth, I caught the brief widening of her eyes, saw her lips part, and heard her draw in a tiny gasp.

Akil's element bristled. I couldn't see it, but I felt his heat prickle against my skin, and so did Carol-Anne. She rippled her top lip in a snarl. Her beautiful face contorted in a purely inhuman manner. Akil hadn't moved. He still smiled, still leaned against the bar, but the elements stirred around us. A few people in the crowd had stopped mingling and turned toward us, sensing the draw of energy.

"I have to admit," Akil said, "I had my doubts over the years, but I've seen what Muse is capable of, and her talent is magnificent. Perhaps you are unaware of the massacre in the netherworld. News will reach you soon enough." He paused, possibly remembering how I'd gone nuclear. His nostrils flared. His eyes widened. His element throbbed in the air. Oh, he remembered alright. "Muse incinerated a crowd of several hundred demons. She could make short work of you. So shall we dispense with the theatrics? Tell me where Jerry is now, while we all still have a measure of control."

"I don't believe you," Carol-Anne hissed. "She is unstable...nothing but a human girl playing with fire. She's a disgusting freak, a demon contained in human flesh, it's repulsive."

Akil was on her. He locked his hand around her throat and threw her down on the bar. She had enough breath to yelp before he clamped his hand closed and choked off her air.

"You speak of disrespect." He leaned over her, intimately aggressive. "You disrespect me and her. Muse is not to be so easily dismissed. She is quite capable of turning your insides to ash before you can draw breath to apologize. You will give her due respect, and you will tell us now where Jerry is, or I'll let her burn your beautiful human vessel off your demon-skin and watch Muse broil your insides. Do you understand?"

I wasn't sure whether to hoot and cheer or nonchalantly admire my nails. We'd drawn quite a crowd. Those who had been surreptitiously observing us now openly watched the confrontation play out. Nobody was likely to interfere, not while Akil had his power coiled around him.

Carole-Anne's eyes darted across Akil's face, lingering on his eyes, where sparks of energy burned. Her appearance wilted around the edges. Her flesh sagged as she fought to stay in control of herself. One hand gripped Akil's forearm, and the other clawed at his hand around her throat. She could easily call her power, and manifest her true appearance, but it would be a sign of weakness in front of a Prince. Besides, summoning her power wasn't going to help her. She was beaten, and she knew it. Everyone in the club knew it. You don't throw down with a Prince of Hell unless you have the power to back it up.

Something cool and smooth eased around my ankle. I glanced down, but of course I couldn't see the element entwining around my leg. At first, I assumed it was just the touch of Carol-Anne's element. It felt like cool water on hot flesh, but Carol-Anne's touch had been sharper. This was something else. My gaze seemed to be drawn behind me into the crowd. The hairs on the back of my neck prickled as I scanned the anonymous faces. The demons felt it too. The crowd stirred, and the music cut so suddenly the silence throbbed in my ears.

I stepped closer to Akil. I opened my mouth to ask what was happening. He shoved off Carol-Anne with a muttered curse and corralled me against the bar. "Don't talk. Don't move." I had the sense he wanted to say more, but he turned his back on me and blocked my field of vision. I peeked around his arm and caught sight of a tall figure moving through the crowd. The demons stumbled against one another to move out of the way. Some ducked out the main doorway, making their escape.

When I finally laid eyes on the woman the crowd appeared to revere, a bolt of energy danced up my legs, funneled into my spine, and damn near wrenched a cry from my lips as it pierced my skull. My legs wobbled. I clung onto the bar and tried to ride out the pain without drawing attention to my sudden weakness.

Akil's hand found my hip, but he didn't turn. He settled his hand against my waist, holding it there to steady me. His warmth seeped through my clothes and into my skin. It helped clear my head enough that I could focus on the woman who stopped a few strides from Akil.

I'd never seen anything like her before. She wore a combination of leather and steel plates. She had a short sword strapped to one leather-clad thigh, and a dagger hooked through the thick leather belt riding her hips. Her auburn hair had been pulled back into a tight braid, yanking her features back so that her eyes, cheekbones, and chin all seemed perfectly aligned and symmetrical. Perversely perfect.

I closed my eyes. An ache throbbed through my skull and down my neck. When I opened my eyes again, the figure hadn't been a woman at all. How had I mistaken him for a woman? He still had the braided red hair, the same oddly feminine face, but he was heavier. His broad muscular arms looked like the sort to wield a sword with deadly accuracy. Armor clung to him like a second skin. He tossed a glance left and right. The crowd shrank away. He fixed his liquescent green eyes on Akil.

My head buzzed. My vision blurred. My own element tried to rush my skin. I held it back, shoving my demon back into her box before she could make herself known. Like Carol-Anne moments before, I didn't want to appear to lose control so easily.

Carol-Anne had slipped off the bar and regained some of her composure, although her hair was mussed and her dress was askew. She dropped to a knee just ahead of Akil and bowed at the feet of the armored man. She didn't speak. Nobody had said a word.

The armored man tilted his head, the gesture akin to a satisfied wolf admiring its prey, marking future hunts. He pointed a gauntleted finger at me as I peeked from behind Akil. "That… is quite the plaything, Mammon." His voice carried to every soul in the club, his tone one not used to being argued with. Clearly, he was the sort who gave orders.

That! I knew better than to growl, and besides the pain in my head dashed my anger.

I did, however, manage to hold his emerald gaze for all of three seconds before the pounding headache forced me to avert my eyes.

"Levi..." Akil's purr resonated to a depth my mortal hearing could barely detect, setting my teeth on edge. I'd not heard him purr before, not quite like that. I'd've called it a nervous purr, but nervous and Akil were two words that should never be present in the same sentence. "May I have the pleasure of introducing you to Muse?"

Akil stepped aside and left me exposed, slumped over the bar, head drooping, struggling to stand and barely able to focus. I don't know what Levi saw when his green eyes drank me in: a twenty-something woman dressed in ill-fitting clothes with wild eyes and a harassed expression. But he didn't waste time assessing my physical appearance. He went straight for my demon. I almost caught sight of the wave of power rising behind him. My mortal sight captured the quiver in the air, right before he plunged his element into me.

I should have screamed, but the overbearing thrust of energy wrenched my voice away. This was no curious exploration. Levi threw enough ethereal power into my human skin to render me useless.

Akil dropped his gaze. I saw him to my right, head hung low, turned away from me, and then Levi's power rode over me so completely that I no longer saw anything but the whirling torrent of water which had swallowed me whole. Swept up in the whirlpool, I recognized the drowning sensation, having nearly drowned twice before. It didn't matter that I was dry as a bone or that my own element spun in chaos around me, unable to find direction in my terrified thoughts. I couldn't remember my own name, let alone draw from the veil and direct my power at Levi. He could have torn me apart on the elemental level, and I had no defense against him.

When he finally let me go, I fell to my hands and knees, coughing up non-existent water from my lungs. My skin and clothes were clammy with perspiration, but the rush of water I'd experienced hadn't been real, at least not on a physical level.

"A curious thing." Levi flung out a hand, twisted it palm up, and then beckoned me with his fingers.

My arms and legs worked as though they possessed minds of their own. I rose off the floor like a wooden puppet, dancing on the end of Levi's strings. His half-smile quirked one sided. His lips parted, and he peered at me through wet lashes. He controlled my human body, and those emerald eyes made wicked promises.

I snapped my head up and summoned my demon. She came willingly, spilling into every cell, planting her strength and power into my limbs. Looking through demon eyes, I saw what Levi really was. Behind the armored-man, towered the ghost of a vast sea-serpent. His scales glistened beneath the writhing lights. His elongated snout bristled with whiskers jutting from his chin. One long barbed fin rode down his back, probably all the way to the end of his tail somewhere far back in the crowd. He had wings bunched against its sides. Levi's demon form eyed me curiously.

"Levi..." Akil spoke up, but stalled under Levi's glare.

I stood my ground, pulling back against his summons, leaning away from him, as he held a coil of power around me.

Whatever Akil was going to say, he'd better hurry. Left any longer, and I was opening the veil and throwing every damn molecule of fire I could find at Levi.

Akil moistened his lips and took a step closer to Levi, holding out a hand. "Wait."

Levi's smile was too broad for his face. Too many teeth gleamed behind his thin lips. The demon image behind him chuffed a laugh. "Mammon. Did you think you could keep this little morsel for yourself?" As Levi spoke, his voice fractured in two, human and demon, an echo over an echo that bounced around my fragile skull.

"Just..." Akil struggled to find the correct words. A rigid expression of concern cut into his face. Akil didn't know what to say.

Holy hell, I was on my own.

I fixed my heated glare on Levi. "Akil introduced me, but I don't know you." My words felt gritty and abrasive against my tongue. I was suddenly thirsty. My throat was parched, lips dry. Water, I needed water.

Levi visibly shivered, and immediately the suffocating weight of power in the room began to ebb away. "You will." He took a few strides forward. His human guise shimmered and contorted. On his last step, I found myself looking at a warrior woman once more. Man and woman, both and neither. It messed with my already fragile mind.

I lifted my blackened hands, claws glinting. "I don't know why you want me, but I can guess. Can we perhaps, do this another time? I mean... you're immortal, yes?" The female Levi didn't answer me, just smiled an empty smile, like a queen smiling at her subjects. "Time means nothing to you, but I'm asking you for time. Surely you can forgo a little time before we do this again... whatever this is." I had no idea what I was doing. I didn't know the correct way to address other Princes, which, by now I'd assumed Levi was, by the fact he/she made Akil quake in his shoes.

The she-Levi flicked her green eyes to Akil, who flinched under the weight of her glare. He hadn't dropped to a knee like Carol-Anne, but he wasn't far from it.

"Very well." Levi's voice alone cleansed my mind and satisfied my thirst. How was that possible? "Mammon, I am obliged not to interfere in your undertakings, but a creature as powerful as Muse should not rest with you, Prince of Greed."

Akil glowered back at her, hands clenched at his sides. "And you believe you have the right to her?"

She snorted, as though offended. "No. You misunderstand me. I am not here for my own desires. I'm here for Asmodeus, her father by blood. Not even you can dispute his claim over her. Muse shall return to her father as it should be."

Akil smiled. "He was content to throw her away as a child, but now she's come into power, he wants her back." He grunted a demonic curse. "Does he know she's *infused with another*?"

Levi's face paled. Her image shimmered before she regained it again. "Easily undone." She dismissed.

"Just so." Akil's reply sounded equally blasé.

Levi and Akil exchanged wary glances, and I felt like a pawn in a game of chess. "Well Levi," I snapped, words and their implications buzzing through my head. I could filter it all later. Right now, I needed breathing space. "Another time, perhaps?"

Levi bowed her head. "Another time, half-blood."

Carol-Anne jerked her head up. "Wait, don't leave me with Mammon." I couldn't see her face, but I didn't need to. The tremor in her voice said enough. "We have a deal. You promised to protect me."

Levi gave Akil what amounted to an eye-rolling glance. She gestured absently at Akil for Carol-Anne's benefit. "Mammon will not harm you. He is weak. He would not dare interfere with one of my subjects. Give Muse what she wants, and let them leave. She is not to be harmed. Do you understand?"

Carol-Anne's head bobbed in agreement, and with that, we watched Levi turn, take a few steps into the crowd, and dissolve into fine droplets of mist that swirled and drifted beneath the multicolored lights.

The presence of Levi's power lingered long after she'd gone. For a few moments, nobody spoke. The seconds ticked on, and then the music burst across the dance floor. The crowd began to move, stirring back into life. Carol-Anne climbed to her feet and turned on the spot. She adjusted her hair and brushed down her dress.

Akil joined me at the bar. His shoulders slumped, and his eyes had dulled. He hitched himself onto a bar stool and ran a hand through his hair, ruffling the dark locks with his fingers before slouching forward. Eyes closed, he dragged his hand down his face and growled low in his throat.

I shook off my demon, packing her neatly away inside of me. Carol-Anne gave me a curt nod of acknowledgement, which I took to mean she'd be back, and then she disappeared in the crowd. Glancing askance at Akil, I wasn't sure where to start with my questions. The one I settled on surprised even me.

"Are you okay?"

He dragged his gaze up to meet mine and mustered an insignificant smile. "Of course."

"Is it the wound? Are you hurt?" He looked away, but he wasn't escaping so easily. I leaned back against the bar so I could look into his face. I reached out a hand, hesitated, and then rested it lightly on his arm. The warmth of his element soaked through his shirt, into my hand, and wound up my arm. "No lies. Tell me the truth."

His face softened. His gaze dropped to my hand on his arm and then flicked back to my face. "The Princes are difficult. Levi knows how weak I am. He won't hesitate to take my title from me, should it benefit him. Likewise, the others, should they discover I'm wounded..."

I eased my hand off his arm and undid a few buttons on his soiled shirt. Akil made no attempt to stop me. He watched my face.

I peeled his shirt back. The fabric clung to a ragged puncture wound on his right side of his chest. The puckered flesh wept blood. A mottling of bruises bloomed across his muscles."Akil..." I hissed. "Stefan did this?"

He tugged his shirt from my grip and buttoned it up. "It's healing. There's nothing to be done."

I scowled at him. "Why didn't you say?"

"When?" He smiled. "It's not important. It will heal in a few days. Stefan needs your attention more than I do."

"That's very noble of you, but I need you to get Damien out of me. You're no good to me unconscious." He looked offended that I'd suggest such a thing could happen. "Levi is bad news, isn't he... she... whatever it is?" I grimaced and shook the eerie commanding touch of him from my body. "He controlled me..."

Akil closed his eyes and drew in a deep breath. "He has physical control of human flesh. Leviathan is one of the

First. He wields authority the way most demons wield weapons. I cannot protect you from Levi. Or from your father, Asmodeus, for that matter."

I fell quiet and watched Akil watching me. He looked as exhausted as I felt. "He controls human flesh... So if I'm demon around him, he can't control me?"

"Levi has many ways of controlling those around him. I suggest you do not defy him."

"You mean, do as he says?"

He inclined his head. "If you want to survive with your mind intact."

"I'm done bowing to others." A growl tried to claw up my throat.

A tiny smile skimmed his lips. "Defiance will get you killed."

"What's the alternative? A lifetime groveling at their feet? Asmodeus, Levi, you?"

"I would never— "

"Control me? What were you doing for ten years, Akil? Huh?"

The weariness on his face tempered to steel. "I think you'll find your time with me was a fucking fairytale compared to the alternative." Splinters of fire blazed in his eyes.

My heart quickened. There was a time I'd have feared that look in his eyes. It wasn't fear amping up my heart rate. Goddamn demon desires. "Until you tried to kill me. What kind of fairytale ends with the Prince trying to flay the Princess?"

"Is that what you are? A Princess?" Laughter danced with the light in his eyes.

"Go to hell."

He pursed his lips then worked them together as though fighting his own words. "I wasn't aware the fairytale was over." He snorted a laugh.

I crossed my arms and shot him a look. "You're in denial."

"Denial? I'm the Prince of Greed. I don't recognize denial."

"I noticed."

He laughed deep genuine laughter. The sound of it eased between my defenses, slid like honey across my skin, and fuelled the spark of my desire.

I looked away. Where the hell was Carol-Anne? Rolling my shoulders, I ignored Akil's chuckles. I was more disgusted with myself than with him. After what he'd done, how could I let him turn me on so easily? I could blame my demon all I wanted, but the hunger for Akil wasn't all hers. I thought of Stefan and welcomed the ice back into my soul. "Why is Levi both man and woman?" My voice sounded cold, hard.

Akil noticed my abrupt change of tone. He flicked his gaze to me, caught the warning on my face, and wisely looked away. "Why wouldn't he be?"

I rolled my eyes. "You owe me answers. So spill."

He brushed a thumb across his lips and leaned on the bar. The laughter had fizzled away, as had the touch of fire in his eyes. "I do owe you answers. You will need them if you are to survive Levi. He is the Prince of Envy. He appears in the form he thinks will offer the most coercion. Our vessels are tools. Think of it like camouflage. He exhibits a multitude of ways of achieving his desires."

"Is that what you are, Akil? Camouflage for Mammon?" I pounced on the question, eager for information I could use. I'd been too long in the dark. Knowledge was my beacon now. I watched his reaction closely. The fractional narrowing of his eyes gave him away, but that was all. He masked it quickly with a smile that said I couldn't possibly understand.

"Try me." I said, as though he'd spoken aloud.

"You sense weakness, don't you Muse?"

"What?"

"I'm wounded and weak, and you're exploiting that fact."

Is that was I was doing? "You think because I'm asking questions, I'm trying to screw you over?" Was this new weaker-Akil paranoid?

"You've never asked before."

Before... Before when I had my head buried in the sand. Before, when I was trying to live a normal life, and he'd decided I wasn't worthy of one. Before Damien reminded me of the pitiful creature I had once been. "I'm asking now. So answer me."

He moistened his lips. "Our vessels are webs, designed to attract and entrap, so that we may consume."

Consume? I filed that one away to process later. "Am I talking to Mammon or some sort of construct? Are you even real, Akil?"

He chuckled and smiled. "Am I talking to Muse the woman or the demon?"

"The woman. But I'm different. I'm a half-blood, demon and human at the same time. You're just demon."

"Just demon..." he echoed. "Mm..." He licked his lips and focused on his fingers tracing an invisible symbol on the counter. His fingertips scorched the wood.

I inclined my head, moving in closer. This was dangerous territory. I'd never asked Akil to explain himself. He'd always skimmed over the details of how the netherworld worked, and I'd blinded myself to the truth of my darker half. Things had changed. I was a tiny fish in a pool full of sharks. Levi had made that clear. I needed Akil to be straight with me.

"Do you really want to know?" He lifted his eyes. The fire was back. An amber hue ringed his darkening irises. Mammon was inside those eyes. He cast the liquid touch of his element around me, warming me through without moving a muscle. He licked his lips, slowly.

I swallowed and locked my teeth together. "Distraction tactics, Akil? Did I cut too close to the quick? Answer my question, is Akil real, or is he just Mammon's puppet?"

He was on his feet and pressed against me so quickly I couldn't prevent my sharp gasp. The taste of him, spices and warmth, danced across my lips and warmed my tongue. Liquid heat flooded my veins. I fought it, but the press of him nearly unraveled my control. Akil tilted my chin up. I flinched away. If he made me look into his, I wasn't sure I'd escape. He caught my jaw and forced me to meet his dark amber-ringed eyes. He smiled a hungry smile and breathed in deeply. A shiver rippled through him. I arched against him, not wanting to give in, but struggling to hold on. He bowed his head and whispered against my lips, "You are more than capable of playing their games. Once Stefan is safe and I've removed Damien's infusion, we have much to discuss." He slowly shifted his hips, grinding against me. I inhaled sharply. He breathed me in. Mammon's preternatural gaze burned through his human eyes.

"Let. Me. Go." I didn't want this. Damn, I wanted this. He'd hurt me on so many levels, screwed me up in so many ways, and all I wanted to do was pull him down and devour him whole. On the bar if we could. What the hell was wrong with me?

Damien's seed chose that moment to pulse its dark poison through my chest. I tensed. Memories fluttered in front of my eyes. Cold slick hands on my scorched body. I splayed my hands across Akil's chest and soaked up his warmth. Would Akil's fire erase Damien's touch? Could his warmth burn away the memory of Damien's abuse?

"Did you think the answers would come easily?" He released me and stepped back a few strides. I slumped against the bar, head spinning, legs weak.

His gaze raked over me. "You were my responsibility, and I failed you." He straightened his shirt cuffs. His tone had changed, his words colder somehow. His body too. He'd shut the emotions from his face. "I have much to make up for. Don't I?" Akil, the man was back, and he wasn't happy.

I wasn't going to argue, not least because I was afraid my voice would fail me. "Yes."

Chapter Twenty Five

Akil and I walked in silence either side of Jerry's generous bulk. Akil wasn't a small guy at well over six feet tall, nor was he thin. He had enough physical muscle to make most women forget themselves. Jerry towered over him, all broad arm muscles and sturdy legs. He made Akil look like a lightweight.

Jerry had grumbled a greeting back at Carol-Anne's club, and only once outside had I suggested he join us back at his clinic rather than wasting time explaining what awaited us there.

No more than an hour had passed inside the club, but the weather had turned. A bank of mist rolled in off the waterfront. In that hour, I'd faced a Prince of Hell who could summon my human body against my will—with a hand gesture no-less—and I'd learned that Akil was wounded, weak, and not the man I'd thought he was. Or was he? All things considered, the night could only get better. Right?

I knew the situation was about to take a turn for the worse when I heard the blip-blip of a police siren and watched the marked car race down the narrow street and take the turn into the same street as Jerry's clinic. I swung a glance over my shoulder as a silver Nissan raced on by. I caught sight of the plates. An Institute car.

Panic tugged at my demon. My element simmered around me. Instincts kicked in, and my heart pounded. I didn't stop to explain what the car meant and bolted into a run.

At the corner, before I could burst around the wall and run right into an Enforcer free-for-all, Akil grabbed me around the waist and hauled me back, pinning me against the wall.

"Hey!" I shoved against him, only to be slammed back again.

"Stop," he hissed, leaning into me. "You can't go running in there. Think about it. They know you've been in the netherworld. They aren't going to welcome you home, Muse."

I glared at Akil, watching the dusting of embers swirl in the irises of his dark eyes. "Stefan's back there. If they take him..."

Two more cars buzzed by. Akil eased off me, but he kept a hand pushing on my shoulder. "I'll distract them. You find a way inside, and get Stefan away from here."

Could I trust Akil to do this? There was that word again: trust. I growled at him. What if he didn't come back?

Jerry gave a grumble of agreement. "There's a back door. We can slip inside while the Enforcers are preoccupied with Mammon."

Jerry and Akil gave each other a nod of agreement, but I didn't like it. Akil was already wounded. He might think the Institute people were impotent when it came to higher demons, but they lived and breathed their profession. One Enforcer wouldn't be enough to bring down a Prince of Hell, but several might. There were ways to trap him. Subdue him. They'd like nothing more than to get their hands on a Prince.

"Akil..."

"Just get him to safety..." Akil released me, and without a second glance, he strode around the corner.

"Dammit." I poked my head around the corner after him.

Police and Institute cars blocked the street. Blue lights strobed off the neighboring properties. Mist hung heavy in the air, smearing the lights and cushioning the sound of sirens. Jerry's clinic had a thick crusting of ice covering its facade. That must have been what alerted them. I counted four Institute cars but couldn't pick the Enforcers out of the crowd milling about the front of the clinic. If Ryder was there, he'd recognize Akil.

Akil sauntered closer. Nobody paid him any attention. A uniformed officer busied himself trying to keep a small line of bystanders back. I couldn't hear what he was saying, but the public were listening to him, nodding enthusiastically. If he was telling them about demons, they were about to get some firsthand experience.

Akil stood at the back, three people away the front. He must have felt my gaze drilling into him because he turned a little, so I could see his smile, and then he let the man-suit fizzle away. Fire devoured his figure. Hue of orange and red firelight blazed higher. His human outline swelled. Much of the transformation was lost to my human sight, as it would be to those around him, but they'd see fire and flame. They'd feel the terrible crushing weight of power, sense it pulling the warmth from their bodies while at the same time blasting them with heat. Human senses would prickle their skin, hike their adrenaline as instincts kicked in.

It didn't take long for the screaming to start. People ran, terrified of the monster in their midst. I had a moment to hope Akil wouldn't hurt anyone, and then I wondered what on earth I'd unleashed

Jerry pulled me back just as the gunshots reverberated down the street.

"C'mon." He led me through a pedestrian gate. With each gunshot that boomed through the air, I winced. Normal bullets wouldn't kill Akil. They'd hurt his human vessel, but would likely bounce off his true form, if the heat didn't melt them first. Knowing that he was impervious to bullets didn't prevent me from worrying though.

Jerry strode ahead, weaving around trash cans, garage bags, and an old couch. I followed, listening to the bellowed orders. I heard fire roaring like an animal with its own hungers. Akil—Mammon—could thread fire through a needle. His control put mine to shame. I might have drained him of power, but I had no idea how to use it once it was in my possession. Mammon was a creature born of fire. A construct of pure energy. If fire could live and breathe, if it had a conscious, with needs and desires, it would be Mammon. I told myself that worrying about him was pointless. He could look after himself.

Jerry plucked a key from his back pocket and slipped it into the lock of the back door to his veterinary clinic. Frost dusted the entire door. Jerry gave me a 'ready' look. His warm breath misted in the bitterly cold air.

I rubbed my arms, nodded, and followed him inside. The darkness hit me first, and then the terrible teeth-chattering cold wrapped itself around me and sucked all the heat from my exposed hands and face.

"About now would be a good time to tell me what the hell is going on." Jerry fumbled about in the dark ahead of me.

"The man we left in here, he's a friend. Stefan's a hybrid, like me, but he's been in the netherworld for... a while." My teeth rattled as I explained. I held out my right hand and coiled my element around it to ignite a flame over my palm. The warm orange glow spread a few steps ahead, far enough for us to see where we were going. Shifting firelight slid across ice-coated walls.

Jerry slipped and cursed. He grabbed at the doorframe leading into the waiting room and waited for me to catch up. I squeezed by him, hand held out in front of me and stepped quietly into the tunnel of ice that had once been a waiting room. The walls, ceiling, and floor gleamed. My firelight slid off the slick surfaces and bounced around the small room until it came to rest on Stefan slumped against the far wall. Had I not known any better, I'd have thought him dead. Legs drawn up, arms locked around them, hugging his knees to his chest, head bowed, he didn't look real, more like a statue in a winter-garden. Cold, hard stone, frozen forever.

"What's wrong with him?" Jerry whispered behind me.

"He can't control his demon." I kept my voice low. Moving closer, feet aching against the ice-covered floor, I crouched down in front of Stefan.

"What do you expect me to do about this, Muse?"

"It's not what you can do... it's what you have." I lifted my enflamed hand close to Stefan's face. Diamonds of ice sparkled in his hair. He looked brittle, like a fragile thing that might burst into countless pieces. Outside, the gunfire had tapered off in the distance. Either that or the thick ice had soundproofed the room.

Jerry shuffled behind me, and I sensed he'd left the room but couldn't tear my gaze from Stefan. "Are you in there...?" I whispered.

I switched my flame to my left hand and reached my right out to lay my fingers gently on Stefan's head, sliding my hand down his ice-smooth hair. A snap of power lanced between us, jolting my hand back and cracking the ice encasing him. His entire body jerked, a spasm riding through him, driving his head back and legs out. I gasped, reeling back, and landed on my backside with a jarring thump. The fire in my left hand snaked up my arm, recoiling from the cold and seeking my embrace.

Stefan opened his eyes and locked his glacial glare on me. His lips twisted into a sneer.

"Wait... Stefan... It's me... Listen—just listen..." I was yammering, but he didn't look as though he was in any mood for listening. Still human, barely, his power gathered around him. I couldn't see it, but I felt its frosty bite nip at my flesh. "Stefan..."

"What have you done?" His demon voice grated through me, words spoken directly into my mind where my own demon snarled in response.

"I brought you home." I stuttered. The air in the room had thinned, making it difficult to breathe. Frost dusted my clothes. The fire wrapped whip-like around my arm began to spit and hiss its displeasure.

"You brought *him* home." Stefan got to his feet. Ice cracked and crumbled off his naked body.

I scrambled to stand, not wanting to be backed against a wall. "Listen, okay, Akil had to come back through—"

Stefan thrust out a hand, and I found myself pinned against the wall by a trident of ice. Two of its three prongs fitted neatly around the neck. I fought the urge to summon my fire, fearful of where any retaliation might lead the both of us. Between us, we had enough power to level a city. Stefan leaned into the trident, driving its prongs further into the wall. Ice clung to my neck. His boreal eyes pierced my defenses and scored my soul with rage. He could kill me. I hadn't thought it possible. I'd thought he was still Stefan, the man who had saved me in more ways than one, but that man was gone.

Jerry jabbed the PC34 injector against Stefan's arm. The sub-sonic jet easily pierced his skin. Stefan hissed, yanked the trident free, and rounded on Jerry. But as he took a step, his balance wavered. He reached for the wall, missed, and fell against it.

I knew all too well what it felt like to have your demon torn from your insides. He would experience a soul rendering agony that no physical wound could inflict. His demon would fight. It would sink its talons into his mind in an effort to cling on to freedom, but the drug would win, and those talons would slice through Stefan's mind, ripping gashes in his consciousness that would leave him weak, disorientated, and so very vulnerable. I'd never forget it, and neither would he.

Stefan slid down the wall. Water dripped from above and poured down the walls. The source of the arctic temperature had gone. In the heat of a summer night, ice wouldn't last more than a few minutes.

Stefan's eyes, once so brilliant, dulled to a washed blue, almost gray. He looked at me, his crushed expression driving a lance of guilt through my chest. I'd done this to him. It didn't matter that Jerry had been the one to administer the drug. It had been my idea. I'd done to him the same as the Institute had in the past, the same thing he despised them for. I'd taken from him the only strength he had. I'd betrayed him. Me, possibly the one person he trusted, the person who was meant to save him. I'd condemned him, and it was all apparent in his crumpled expression.

The unmistakable *thwoop thwoop* of helicopter blades beat the air outside.

"We need to leave," Jerry said. "Muse. Now. We gotta go. Either leave him here for them, or we take him with us, but make the call now."

"We take him," I croaked, then reached down to slip an arm around Stefan's waist and hook his arm over my shoulders. He didn't protest, nor did he resist. Eyes open but unseeing, he let Jerry and me prop him up and carry him out the back door.

Chapter Twenty Six

The back rooms at The Voodoo Lounge resembled individual lounges. I didn't know what went on behind the closed doors, and didn't want to. I heard a few growls as we passed by and battled my imagination to ignore them. Carol-Anne shepherded, Jerry, me, and the virtually unconscious Stefan, into one of those rooms and closed the door on us, saying she'd let us know once she'd discovered what had happened to Akil.

By now, the arrival of the Institute Enforcers a few streets away had scattered most of the club's demon clientele. They were smart enough to know when to scurry back into hiding, returning to their pseudo-normal lives.

Stefan lay motionless on a couch, blanket draped over him, unfocused gaze fixed on a point beyond the wall. I watched the rise and fall of his chest from my position in the corner. Jerry leaned against the wall beside the one door, arms crossed. His tattooed face was a grim mask. I couldn't help feeling I'd done something terrible. Stefan was dangerous. Without control, he could get himself and others killed. I'd only wanted to protect him, to give him room to breathe. He'd spent years in his demon form, day and night, fighting off a world that wanted him dead. I knew what it was like to let chaos control you, to feel the demons watching you every second, every minute, of every hour, but I didn't know the horror of trying to survive there, not as he had. I'd always been protected by owners. Life had been hard—a freakin' understatement— but it had been my life, and I knew nothing else. Stefan didn't have that luxury. He'd gone through the veil as a mortal man who happened to have a demon half. He hadn't known what it would take to survive there. He didn't know the rules, the games. And his demon would have thrived.

I lowered my gaze to the tiled floor. From the information I'd gleaned while working my way through the ranks of the Enforcers, I knew Stefan had been raised by the Institute. He'd probably learned how to shape and throw ice daggers before he could walk. He hadn't had a childhood. He'd been molded, tuned, honed into a demon-killing instrument, but he'd always been human, his mortal self firmly in the driver's seat. Beyond the veil, in the netherworld, his demon would have broken through his restraint within a few steps. You can't stop it. They know they're home. Stefan would have needed his demon to protect his fragile human flesh. He would have fought the hordes of lesser demons with everything he had. The battles would have raged only until the demons pulled back to regroup. In that moment, Stefan would have realized that his demon had control and liked it.

Imagine the ability to let go of everything. To step back from the expectations of life, let it all slip through your fingers as though none of it mattered. Your doubts, your fears, your weaknesses, all of them falling like grains of sand into the wind. It feels like freedom, but it's an illusion. The lure of chaos is a powerful one, perhaps more so to a half-blood, as our human halves are geared for control and restraint. Chaos whispers to us in the darkest of hours, in the depths of night. It promises the blissful indifference of freedom, and all we need do is let the demon win.

Stefan would have fought it. He would have tried to rein it in, but after days or weeks, his strength failed him. His demon bewitched him, coiled his human half around its glistening claws and crushed the vestiges of control in the palm of its hand. In order to survive, his demon had controlled every aspect of him. With every demon he must have slaughtered, his lust for chaos would have grown. Until it became all he knew.

I'd had no choice. If Stefan couldn't control himself, nobody could.

And I understood now why the Institute had injected me with PC34 all those months ago. Adam had been right. I was dangerous. When they'd dragged me out of the marina waters, they were handling the human equivalent of a nuclear bomb. They'd had no choice.

I didn't thank them for it, and Stefan wouldn't thank me. I'd torn out the half of him that had kept him alive in the netherworld. He'd lost the power, the protection, and the blissful ignorance that chaos provides, and I'd been the one to steal it from him.

I bowed my head, hiding my face from Jerry. And to add insult to injury, Stefan had gone through all of that for me, and what had I done? I'd thrown his sacrifice in his face by bringing Akil back through the veil.

Akil burst through the door in a flurry of motion, barely breaking his stride. Bloodied shirt untucked, face twisted in a grimace of pain, eyes ablaze, he scooped up Stefan. "Get up, Muse. We're leaving."

I scrambled to my feet and helped him lift Stefan. "I know where Stefan will be safe."

Akil nodded, teeth gritted. He threw Jerry an acknowledging glance and slipped my hand into his. Did he tremble? I met his eyes and saw the embers swirling in their darkness. He squeezed my hand gently. The room fell out of focus. The anchoring touch of his power whirled around me, twisted up my legs, and coiled around my waist. I closed my eyes, not wanting to see the dark tendrils of ethereal energy enveloping me. Darkness dragged me down. Akil's power smothered and embraced me. I locked a location and an image in my mind, one I knew Akil would remember.

Lake house.

***

Akil's power unraveled around me outside the white-clapboard lake house. I tasted the mountain air on my tongue, brisk and fresh. The scent of pine cleared my lumbering thoughts and roused memories from the last time I'd been here. Hellhounds, gunshots, calling another world's worth of power from beyond the veil, the memory of Akil running a sword through Sam's chest—it hadn't happened here, but I'd discovered the memories slumbering in a sword and my perception of Akil changed forever. This place had made a lasting impression. Even the wind through the trees whispered a reluctant greeting.

Akil stumbled beside me. He fell to his knees in the mud. Stefan's weight threw me off balance. I staggered and heaved Stefan's dead weight against me. Jeez, he was heavier than he looked. I grunted a curse, leaned into Stefan, puffed my hair out of my face, and offered Akil my hand.

He took it without meeting my eyes and dragged himself back to his feet. Sharing Stefan between us, we managed to get him inside the house and up to a bedroom. Akil left me with Stefan without a word. What was I meant to do with him? Stefan just lay there. Every couple of breaths, he'd blink, but otherwise he lay still and silent. I couldn't bear it. I couldn't stay with him, not after it had all been my fault. Nica would know what to do. I would need to get in touch with her. She'd be able to help.

Descending the newly replaced staircase—a rampaging Hellhound had wiped out the last one—I walked through the open-plan lounge area into the kitchen with its wall of panoramic windows, also newly replaced for similar reasons. The view beyond the glass and down to the water's edge had taken my breath away last time I'd been there, and this time was no different. I was city girl at heart, and just the amount of inky black night sky with its countless shining stars rendered me speechless. The milky light from the crescent moon rippled across the vast expanse of lake, rimmed by towering pine trees as far as the eye could see.

"Muse."

I jumped and spun. Akil sat slumped in a chair beside the dining table. In the low light, his eyes smoldered. He clutched at his chest where a seeping wetness soaked through his shirt.

I moved to his side and eased his hand away, so I could unbutton and open the shirt. His eyes searched my face.

His breathing sounded labored. He couldn't summon his element here. All of the interior walls in the house had been covered in the restrictive symbols, blocking our abilities. I peeled the blood-soaked shirt away from his chest, revealing two puncture holes in his left side. The wound on his right where Stefan had stabbed him still gaped, but it didn't appear to be bleeding. Akil must have read the fear in my eyes.

"It will heal..." His deep voice bubbled, words slurred behind a liquescent drawl.

I moved around him and pinched my lips together. Blood plastered his shirt to his back. "Lean forward." He obliged slowly and waited, holding his breath as I slid his shirt off his shoulders and down his back. An exit wound had torn a ragged hole in his lower back. "Jesus..." There was so much blood that the air tasted like copper. "Akil, you still have a bullet in you."

"I know." He dropped back in the seat with a growl that should probably have been a cry of pain. "It's most... uncomfortable."

"If it's an Institute bullet, it could reduce your ability to heal yourself." I'd once watched Stefan empty a clip into Akil, and he'd got up from that, as right as rain within a few hours. Something had changed. Either Akil was too weak to repair himself, or the Institute had been using bullets designed specifically to nullify elemental power. I'd heard rumors about special bullets but had never seen them. Ryder would know.

Akil closed his eyes. His right hand shook as he rested it on the dining table beside him. He fought to breathe. I saw it in the stuttered rise and fall of his chest. "Akil..." A sudden, horrible thought trampled on all the others. "Can you die?"

His lips twitched, and he opened his eyes. The embers were gone, and those eyes, those soft hazel eyes, belonged to just a man. They widened with surprise and sadness.

He breathed hard. "Not the death you're thinking of."

I didn't believe him. I'd come to expect lies from Akil. Perhaps it was the quiet resignation in his voice, but the barely concealed fear in his eyes sealed it. "We have to get the bullet out."

Panic tried to muscle its way into my thoughts, but I refused to give it leverage. Instinct kicked in. I shoved my emotions to the back of my crowded thoughts and focused. "Okay, right, tell me if you think you're gonna pass out." I tugged open the cutlery drawer and upended it on the countertop. Knives, spoons, and forks clattered across the counter and fell beside my feet. I grabbed a few knives and tested their edges. Did I know what I was doing? No. But I wasn't letting him die on me. It didn't matter if our definitions of death differed. Akil didn't die. That was a fact of life. The elements don't die. They fizzle out, they change shape, they dissipate, but the energy is always there. I knew what he was saying. He might not die, but he'd change. He'd be gone from me. Without Akil, Damien's repulsive seed would root inside me.

"I'm weak, Muse." He sighed. "This vessel is tired."

"Shut up." I glared at him. "At least put your hand on the wound, apply some pressure, stem the blood flow. Do something."

He obeyed and then after a few beats said quietly, "They say you're my weakness."

"Since when have you cared what anyone says?" I searched for something sharp, long, and thin, but all I could find was a barbecue fork. My surgeon's tools consisted of a knife and a barbecue fork. It was hopeless.

"But they're wrong. You're my strength."

I looked at Akil and frowned. He smiled. Goddamn him. "You aren't dying on me. Okay? Do you understand? You don't get to screw up my life and then die. Not until I'm finished with your sorry ass. Get up." I tossed the implements aside, crossed the kitchen, and caught his free hand. "Get. Up."

He peered up at me, tiredness tugging his eyes closed.

I slapped him hard. The loud crack snatched a snarl from his lips and stung my hand. "Get out of that chair. We're going for a walk."

"Muse…" His voice trailed off. I cracked a fist across his jaw and received a snarling growl in response. His eyes widened, embers flaring.

I tugged on his arm. "If I can't cut the bullet out, I can burn it out. So get off that damn chair, and pull yourself together. You're supposed to be an ageless creature of chaos, and all I'm getting right now is sulking city boy."

Laughter brightened his eyes, but the pain seized the sound before it could reach his lips. He rose, wooden and awkward, and fell against me. *Keep it together,* I warned myself. Seeing Akil like this, vulnerable and barely able to stand, gnawed away at my subconscious thoughts, eating into the most fragile parts of my mind. Yes he was a killer. But damn him, I owed him so much. Akil wasn't meant to be weak. He was a force of nature. A constant. He would always be there like the sun, the stars. He couldn't leave me. It wasn't possible.

I half dragged, half shoved him out the front door. When he fell, I scooped him up and cursed him. Blood coated my hands, making my grip on him slippery. I struggled to hold him. Several times, we almost tumbled together.

We managed a few staggering steps off the track and into the tree cover before he fell and refused to get back up. He rolled onto his back, eyelids drooping. I planted my feet and snapped the reins of control inside my head, freeing my demon. She knew what was happening, knew my fear, what it meant probably better than I did. I flung my hands down and summoned the heat from the earth at my feet. Energy flowed up. My demon wrapped me in her scorched embrace and sealed my vulnerable humanity away behind her fiery armor.

He can't die. I didn't know if she was saying it or I was, but we agreed. I needed him to free me of Damien. He wasn't dying on me. Not today.

I tore open the veil with a jagged, need-driven thought and reached beyond. The writhing flow of heat came willingly. Fire and light whisked around me in a whirlwind of chaos. I could have taken more, could have lost myself in the madness of desire for power, but the human heart of me pulled back from the abyss.

Akil watched with dull eyes. The reflection of flames danced in those dark orbs, but his own fire had vanished. Panic wrapped its icy grip around me. *I'm too late.* I dropped to my knees and planted scorched hands on Akil's chest. Flames washed across his body in an undulating ripple of heat. The tear in the veil poured power through me and into him. It lashed against my demon flesh and strummed into Akil.

It seemed as though hours passed, but could only have been minutes. Akil snapped open his eyes. His chest expanded. His body arched, and right before my eyes— beneath my hands—his human body dissolved into the mass of obsidian muscle that was Mammon. The Prince of Greed latched both hands onto mine and fixed ageless eyes on me. I faltered. The power funneling through me stuttered.

Mammon's black lips rippled in a snarl. I tried to pull back, but his huge claw-tipped hands sealed around my forearms. *Don't...* I warned him, not needing to speak the words for him to hear them. He laughed. His sharp teeth glistened. He yanked me closer. My world shrank into his eyes. The dark in there knew me. It hungered and drew me down. I managed to jerk away, but his grip tightened.

With a curl of my lip, I sealed the veil shut and abruptly severed the rush of power he fed from. The withdrawal of power hit him like a slap in the face. His features twisted into a bitter mask of disgust. I'd deprived him of power, an almost endless supply of fire and heat. The Prince of Greed wasn't pleased.

Neither was I. He wasn't going to let me go, but I'd done enough cowering at the feet of demons who thought themselves better than me. I leaned into him. My gaze burned into his. I kicked my leg over his waist to straddle him, and with my hands still planted on his chest, I began to draw my power out of him. We must have looked quite the sight. Compared to him, I was a tiny insignificant thing: a pitiful half-blood. But I wasn't afraid of him. Not anymore.

The swell of power filled me up, bolstered my defenses, and shored up my strength. Mammon had been here before. He knew I was capable of draining every last drop. I could draw all of his princely power right out of his body and take it into my tiny insignificant demon self. I'd done it before, and I could do it again. I wanted to do it again. I grinned.

His black eyes widened. His nostrils flared.

He flung me aside with a sweep of his arm. I felt the rush of wind and instinctively landed in a crouch, one hand steadying me against the ground while the other clung onto the thread of power that sucked my element back out of him.

"Muse..." His grumbling inhuman voice summoned my wicked laughter.

"You don't own me, Mammon." I rose up and snapped the tendril of power between us, severing my link to him. "Nobody owns me." I leered at him, knowing full well I had won this fight.

He stamped back a few steps and shook his behemoth body, giving his vast wings a few token sweeps before clamping them closed and pulling his true form back into his human vessel. I watched with demon eyes as the whip-like tendrils wove together to form a reborn Akil. He'd lost the lines around his eyes and had gained a gilded glow in those infinitely dark irises. His bloodied and torn clothes had undergone a similarly dramatic transformation. His crisp white shirt hung open. All traces of blood on his chest had gone. The wounds and bruises, which had marred his bronze skin, had vanished, as though they'd never existed. He was once more the epitome of seduction, all clean-cut lines, proud shoulders, raw masculinity, and curious knowing smiles.

He strode toward me. An aura of energy radiated around him. The ground sizzled beneath each step. Hunger burned in his eyes and tugged a crooked smile across his lips. A fluttering in my chest shortened my breaths. I knew what he wanted. Need burned fiercely in his eyes. Akil and I shared the same element, the same thirst for raw power.

Born of fire, he and I were too alike to deny the desire raging through us.

He was on me, around me, in me. When I gasped in surprise, I breathed his power into my lungs where it bloomed through my chest. His lips smothered mine. His hand clamped the back of my head and pulled me into a frantic kiss. All demon—human doubts and fears locked away—I fell into that kiss with no hope of escaping. My demon wanted him on a primal level. I molded my body against the steel hardness of his. I dragged him closer, tighter, as though I could crawl inside his skin. Our elements entwined and laced together until I could no longer fathom where my element began and his ended.

I rode my hands up his lean arms and dug my fingers into his muscular shoulders. The fabric of his shirt denied me access to his skin. I needed to feel the warmth of his delectable flesh beneath my touch, to soak him into my pores. I growled my frustrations. He made a deep sound in his throat, somewhere between a growl and a groan. I shivered. I slipped my fingers into his hair and pulled his mouth to mine. He tasted of things forbidden, of sweetness and spices that danced on my tongue. I nipped at his lips. His ragged breathing matched mine. His unyielding body writhed with me. I could gorge myself on Akil. Let him fill me up until I could take no more.

He backed me against a tree and growled something in a language I didn't recognize. They were old words, words with power and weight. I quivered with raging desire. The seeking touch of his element threaded through me, as if seeking my darkest desires. I felt the electric thread of power probing, fingering, exploring. I faltered, blinked. Pain splintered in my chest. He clasped my face in his hands and held me firm. The pain melted away. The embers in his eyes swirled like a firestorm. Pinpricks of red danced against an endless black. I tore his shirt open and roamed my hands over his shoulders and down the sculpted curve of his back. His exquisite power teased up my arms, flowed through me, and pooled wet between my legs. Words tumbled from my lips, demands that needed to be met. I pulled him hard against me. My racing breaths snagged. I felt his ready hardness. He growled, said something foreign and maddening, and I mashed my mouth to his. I tasted, teased, drove my tongue in, and devoured him.

When the pain twitched in my chest again, I gasped and fell back from Akil's heat-saturated touch. I pressed my hand against my chest, where the driving pain pierced me. Incoherent thoughts vied with the madness of lust. I slumped forward against Akil. His arm slipped around my waist and a hand gripped my shoulder. He spoke a string of words into my ear, barely pausing to breathe, and with each beat the pain hammered harder.

"Stop..." I gasped.

"It has to be this way." His hurried breaths touched my cheek, cooling flushed skin.

No. What was he doing to me? I couldn't think clearly. My head filled with fears, needs and desires. I ached for his touch. I wanted to feel all of him around me, inside me, but an icy slither of fear had worked its way into my thoughts. He whispered indecipherable words into my ear. His hand splayed across my hip and dove lower. His warm fingers found the heat pooled between my legs. The pain and fear subsided. Hunger once again smothered my doubts.

Something he said, one of the weighted words, hooked into me. A twitch of energy danced down my spine, jolting my head back. I'd heard the word before. Damien had spoken it to me the night he'd made sure I knew who my owner was. The night he'd torn into my mind and flesh and soul-locked me. I could see him now, hear those words on his lips, feel his slick touch kneading my simmering flesh. As he'd driven himself into me over and over, pounding my flesh and my soul, he'd growled out those same words. I didn't know what they were, but I knew what they meant. It didn't matter that Akil whispered them into my ear and made the words sound like promises. It was still an invasion.

I planted both hands on Akil's chest and shoved him back. He staggered a few steps away from me, passion ablaze in his eyes. "Muse, let me do this..."

"No." The snarl that followed was a warning. Our gazes met, both of us aflame, ridden by desires we could barely control. He had a frenzied look in his eyes. He panted hard, then clamped his mouth closed and breathed hard through his nose. His hands clenched into fists at his sides, and for a moment, I thought he was going to ignore my rebuttal and carry on regardless of my denial.

I trembled from head to toe. My wing quivered, and my body tingled. My mind swam with the memories of Damien's touch. Nothing dampens desire faster than disgust.

"It has to be this way," he said between breaths, "to undo his hold. You must let me in." He moved a step closer but froze as he saw me recoil. His lips turned down. He closed his eyes and sucked in a deep quivering breath. It was an attempt to regain control. When he opened his eyes, the embers had gone. I wanted to believe him, but how could I? I'd let him in once before—invited him—and he'd screwed me every which way.

I leaned back against the tree. The bark hissed beneath the touch of my superheated flesh. Even as demon, I couldn't fight the memories of Damien. He had invaded my body, sunk his poisoned tendrils into my heart, and planted his seed. The violation burned like acid in my gut. I couldn't let Akil do the same, and I couldn't explain it to a demon—a Prince of Hell. He wouldn't understand.

Akil tensed. He wanted to move closer. I saw the battle raging between his body and mind. The Prince of Greed wasn't used to being denied.

I summoned an animalistic growl from the pool of rage gathering at my core. "Do not touch me. If you take one goddamn step closer, I'll empty your body of heat so fuckin' fast you won't be able to light a match for weeks."

To make matters worse, he actually looked confused and wounded by my brush-off. "I can help you." He scowled, as though this was my fault, and I was merely being stubborn.

I shook my head, words locked behind gritted teeth. He could help me, of that I was certain, but he could also tear out what remained of my tattered soul. I didn't trust him enough to let him in. I'd never trust him like that again. I might have brought him across the veil, but I did that to free Stefan. I might have saved him from the demon equivalent of death and recharged his batteries by doing so, but that didn't mean I would let him get close to me. I needed him to do this for me, but not yet. I hadn't realized it, but I wasn't ready to let Akil, or anyone, inside.

"I haven't forgotten what you are, Akil." Slowly, carefully, my demon withdrew from my flesh, slinking off into my subconscious now that her desires weren't likely to be sated. Once the blackened armor of her skin fizzled away, I stood against the tree, human once more, clad in ill-fitting clothes, beyond exhausted.

Akil glared at me. He'd stopped trembling, but a medley of anger and confusion played across his face. "Are you content to let Damien control you for the rest of your life?"

My lips turned down in a grimace. Akil didn't get it, but what was I expecting? He was as demon as they get, a creature of needs and desires. He wouldn't understand why I couldn't let him touch me. "I'm not ready."

"You can get over it when you're free of him," he snarled.

I would have laughed if I'd had the energy. He was right of course, if this was all about the practical, but the fears inside my head weren't reasonable. I couldn't simply pack the pain away for another day.

He glanced back at the house, as though something had drawn his attention. Whatever it was, it didn't last. When his gaze found me again, those damned hazel eyes were laden with sadness. "I do not understand."

Those four words cut to the very heart of my pain. I squeezed my eyes closed and fought back the tears of frustration and anger because I didn't want him to see how much this—his understanding—mattered to me. Why couldn't he listen to my words, or see what was happening to me? Why did he not realize what it meant to be broken so badly that nothing might fix me again? Dammit, I wanted him to fix me, and the worst part of it was, he could—but I couldn't.

Akil moved away. I watched him walk back toward the path. Tears skipped down my cheeks. He turned, looked me over for a few seconds, and then smiled. "I pity any man, demon or otherwise, foolish enough to believe he owns you."

He left me then, alone with my fear and disgust. I listened to the breeze sighing through the trees, and my thoughts gradually calmed. I hadn't stopped fighting since Damien had dragged me back across the veil. I'd been battling my fears from that day to this one. If I stopped now, I was afraid I might collapse in a heap of emotional wreckage. If I wanted Damien out of my life for good, then I had to let Akil in. It was fact. My choices were Akil or another Prince of Hell, but that wasn't going to happen. As the Princes went, Akil appeared to be one of the more amicable ones. To move forward, I needed to let go of the fear. How? How was I meant to ignore what Akil was, what he'd done, what he could still do? He'd used me before. There was nothing to stop him from doing it again. He wasn't a man. He didn't regret. He wasn't sorry. He'd screw me and throw me away just as Damien had.

I tried to wipe the tears away, but more took their place.

I wasn't escaping Damien. If Akil was my only option, it wasn't an option at all. There was no hope of freedom for me. No cure for what Damien had done.

I couldn't think like that. If I lost all hope, I was afraid of what I might do. When I was a tiny young thing in a world that wanted me dead, I had hope. I hadn't even known what hope was, but I'd had it in spades. I'd dreamed of a day I'd be free. It's what kept me alive. Akil had once provided an illusion of freedom. I had to believe true freedom was out there: the freedom to make my own choices, the freedom to walk my own path without others trying to steer me toward their desires. I had hope, and when it all boiled down to nothing, hope was all I had.

I dried my face with my sleeve and trudged back to the lake house. I needed to focus on what I *could* do, and that was helping Stefan. Nica would be able to watch him. She'd want to know he was alive, and she would know what to do. Besides, Nica was the closest thing to a friend I had. Her brother was back. Everything was going to be okay.

Maybe.

Chapter Twenty Seven

The lake house was quiet on my return, as quiet as an old house could be. The floorboards groaned, and the stairs creaked. With no sign of Akil, I took the opportunity to finally shower and wash off the burned rubber smell of the netherworld. My human exterior had fared pretty well on the other side of the veil, thanks mostly to the protection afforded by my demon. I barely had a scratch to show for my ordeal. She couldn't protect my mind though. In that department, we were sorely in need of help.

Dressing in some jeans and a snug-fitting, sleeveless top left from my last visit to the lake house, I towel dried my hair and headed back downstairs. The sight that greeted me in the lounge stopped me in my tracks. Stefan sat in the couch closest to the stairs with his back to me and an arm draped over the cushions. He didn't turn, so couldn't see the shock on my face, but Akil noticed. He leaned against the wall beside the front door, arms crossed. His gaze flicked from Stefan, to me and then drifted toward the kitchen from where the majority of the light pooled into the lounge. He appeared to be bored. I knew better. He leaned close to the door, knowing he might need a quick escape route. And he stayed standing, to save precious seconds should Stefan lose his cool.

Electric tension sizzled in the air. The last time they'd stood in this room together, Stefan had emptied a clip of .50 caliber bullets into Akil's chest. For them, it had been years ago. I was sure they'd collected a few more mental souvenirs from their time in the netherworld. Akil's lackadaisical expression didn't mask the simmer of power radiating around him. The symbols on the wall prevented him from calling his element, but it broiled just below the surface. Stefan, of course, couldn't do anything remotely demonic, not with PC34 in his veins. I was almost afraid to move around the couch and look him in the eyes—afraid of the expression I might find on his face.

Stepping lightly, I moved around the couch and kept my gaze on Stefan. He'd dressed in black jeans and dark blue V-neck sweater over a pale blue shirt. His platinum blonde hair hung loose in damp tendrils, wet from the shower. Like me, he would have wanted to wash off the netherworld. Perhaps it helped him feel half way to human again.

When his eyes met mine, I froze. His lips twitched, hinting at a smile. I could breathe. He didn't look furious. He just looked like Stefan: the same relaxed posture, same crooked smile, the same Stefan I'd seen while reading the metal in his workshop and scrounging for memories that weren't mine. A day hadn't gone by when I hadn't thought of him. I had so much to say, so much to apologize for, but now he was here, and I couldn't remember any of it.

"Demon got your tongue, Muse?" His voice held a serrated edge, as though he'd not slept in weeks. It would take a few days to kick the guttural demon brogue.

Something cool and sinister prickled the back of my neck, but in a blink, it was gone. He looked right at me— into me—and those crystalline eyes pinned my runaway thoughts to the back of my skull. I couldn't find my words. I didn't know where to start.

"You're okay." Not such a slick comeback, but at least I managed actual words.

His fingers tapped a few beats on the cushions. He looked away. "I will be." Those words sounded simple, but his eyes hardened, and his fingers curled into a fist.

I stole a glance at Akil. He hitched an eyebrow, indicating he'd caught the tone of Stefan's words, but otherwise he was staying out of this.

"Stefan..." I licked my lips and moved to sit on the edge of the coffee table in front of him. The presence of Akil behind me warmed my back like an open fireplace. I tried to ignore it, and focused on Stefan. He half-smiled, but his brittle eyes belied that easy smile. "I'm sorry," I said softly. "I had to..."

"I know." He leaned forward as though he might reach for my hand. I balked and shifted back. His touch had once ignited a pins-and-needles dance of power beneath my skin. I didn't want it..., not then. Too much chaos already flirted with madness in my mind.

Stefan's face tightened, touched by a frown, before he smiled too brightly and leaned back.

I looked down at my hands in my lap. "I didn't want to hurt you."

"It's done." His cool gaze focused over my shoulder at Akil. Before I could glean much from Stefan's expression, he locked it down behind a frozen mask of indifference. What had transpired in the dead forest? I knew there was no love lost between them. They'd both played each other in an attempt to save the ones they loved, and that was before they'd been trapped on the wrong side of the veil together.

"Muse has been soul-locked," Akil said flatly, evidently deciding to cheer us all up with hard facts. I glowered over my shoulder at him. He barely noticed me, and only had eyes for Stefan. "So perhaps we can put our differences aside until her owner is dealt with."

A muscle jumped in Stefan's jaw. He returned his gaze to me. "I thought you killed your owner?" He sat too still, wound up so damn tight he could snap any second. I almost wanted him to explode and launch at me with the accusations I deserved. It might diffuse some of the tension suffocating me.

I sighed and got to my feet. "I thought so too. I burned him—before. I thought it was enough, he's not all that powerful, but we didn't hang around long enough to '*poke him in the eye*.'"

Stefan's smile vanished. He tilted his head and eyed me curiously, no doubt wondering from where I'd gleaned that fragment of his past. He bounced his attention from me to Akil. "How did you let her owner soul-lock her?"

So he knew what a soul-lock was. No surprise, Stefan was twice the Enforcer I'd ever be. He made catching and killing demons look like a walk in the park. "It's complicated." I halted Akil before the two of them could lock verbal horns. "It happened. That's all that matters, and he'll be coming for me."

I told Stefan what I could and filled in the most recent events, deliberately skipping over those I found most painful. He could fill in the blanks himself. He stayed quiet as I went through my meeting with Yukki Onna and how she'd helped me. If she meant anything to him, he hid it all behind cold eyes. As I explained how I'd annihilated a crowd of demons, he bowed his head and ran his hands through his hair. By the end of my tale, where Akil had decoyed the Institute to save Stefan's ass, Stefan was on his feet and pacing the room.

"I have to get back to the Institute."

"No," Akil and I replied together.

Stefan stopped and frowned at us. "This is out of control. Forget the part, Muse, where you brought a Prince of Hell back to our world for dubious reasons." I tensed, but he didn't let me draw breath to defend my actions. "Someone is communicating with Damien, giving him the names and locations of Enforcers. That information is only available to a handful of people."

"It wasn't you?" I asked.

He cut me a scowl so hard I flinched. "When you found me, did I look as though I was on friendly terms with a demon, any demon?"

My memory plucked a random image of him, all bristling ice behind his fortified cave entrance. "Well, no...but—"

"Did you think I'd been trading stories around the campfire?" Okay, sarcasm. He was getting angry.

"Well, no, I didn't think you'd give up information willingly. I thought maybe they'd..." I trailed off as his glare intensified to looks-could-kill territory.

"If Damien can't find you Muse," Stefan gestured at the symbols adorning the walls, "he's going to go searching for those he knows are close to you. Who's next in line?"

I didn't hesitate. "Ryder." Ryder knew me better than anyone. It was his job. If Damien wanted information on me, outside of the Institute, he'd find Ryder. Ryder was a tough bastard, but the chances of him going toe-to-toe with a psychotic Damien and surviving were slim.

Stefan closed his eyes and took a few steadying breaths. "Then Damien will hit the Institute."

"Why?" I asked. No demon would be foolish enough to strike at the heart of the Institute. Even if they could get through the protective symbols, it would be suicide.

Stefan opened his eyes. "Because Ryder won't talk. He'd die before he told a demon anything. Damien's only option is to go back to whoever's feeding him the information. Someone on the inside."

"But who?" Stefan's words came back to me. Only a handful of people had access to the information. Oh my god. Adam. Did Adam hate me that much? "Stefan... Do you think Adam would do this?"

He sunk a hand trembling into his hair. "I don't know. He's capable. He'll do anything if it benefits the Institute. You can rely on him for that, if nothing else."

But why? Why would Adam go to the trouble of employing and training me only to release Damien? Adam was ruthless to the core, but would he employ a full-demon to get what he wanted? Surely not if it endangered his precious Institute. Maybe his intentions had started out good, and then Damien had slipped his leash. Demons had a knack for twisting circumstances to suit themselves.

Akil had been remarkably quiet through all of this. I looked at him now. He appeared to absorb the quiet, as though savoring my anticipation. I was looking to him for answers, and by the gleam in his eye, he liked that feeling.

He moistened his lips and straightened his cuffs. "It would seem you have a dilemma."

Stefan made a sound like a restrained growl, and the waning tension snapped back into the room, charging the air with static energy. Had I not been there, I was certain they would have tried to kill each other. At least they had that in common. "What would you suggest?"

"Muse, you can't trust him." Stefan bit off his own sentence, as I threw his look-that-could-kill right back at him.

"Split up," Akil suggested. "Stefan, stay away from the Institute. Given their extreme prejudice against poorly controlled demons, I'd hazard a guess they'd lock you away the moment you stepped across their threshold. Your talents —and mine—would be better spent helping this Ryder. Muse, return to the Institute. Warn them. You're fresh from the netherworld, so they're more likely to believe a warning coming from you. Be careful though. They're just as likely to lock you up."

I nodded. "He's right." And caught Stefan's glare of disgust.

"Taking orders from him now? He's a liar and a murderer, but if you want to go ahead and believe his lies again then sure, why not? It's not like I gave up years of my life to keep that son-of-a-bitch away from you."

His sharp words cut my thoughts off in one ruthless pass. "Stefan..." He held up a hand and tossed me a scathing glance. Clearly, we had a lot to talk about, but not now. Not yet. There would be time to heal wounds once this was over. Ryder was about to receive a firsthand introduction to Damien, if he hadn't already.

Chapter Twenty Eight

Akil deposited me a short walk from the Institute's innocuous warehouse complex. I'd lost all track of time. Above Boston's skyline, light pollution leeched into a starless night sky. A touch of rouge against the dark sky to the east suggested we had perhaps an hour before sunrise.

I zipped up my jacket and turned back to regard both Stefan and Akil. I wasn't entirely sure they could be trusted in one another's company. Akil had convinced me that, should Damien already be with Ryder, Stefan would need his help. He was right again. I'd rendered Stefan elementally impotent, although he was still entirely capable of bringing down a demon without his element. He'd have a better chance with Akil beside him. Plus, Akil couldn't enter the Institute. I almost wanted to see it. It'd be like throwing a wolf into the chicken coop. Besides, they wouldn't listen to a Prince of Hell, even if he could somehow breach their graffiti-symbol defenses.

Still, looking at the two of them standing on the sidewalk, bathed in the glow from a streetlight, I couldn't help feeling I was doing the wrong thing. Stefan's gaze was slippery. He ground his teeth and shifted restlessly, hardly bothering to conceal his loathing for Akil. Akil, on the other hand, carried an easy stride, as though none of this could penetrate his infallible exterior. Back in top form, he had no reason to worry. Nothing fazed a Prince of Hell, or so I'd thought, but I'd seen a different side of him, and the heat in his eyes told me he knew as much.

"Can I trust you to not to kill each other?" I kept my voice low in the hushed quiet.

Stefan snorted a laugh and muttered something about Akil not being able to kill him the last dozen or so times he'd tried, and Akil arched an eyebrow, as though I'd wasted my breath asking such a ridiculous question. It was enough to convince me they'd temporarily hold back their mutual distaste.

"Be careful." Akil lifted a hand. The lingering touch of his element coiled around my ankle and wove higher. He could have closed the distance between us in a few strides if he wanted to. I saw it in the rigidity of his stance, but he held back. For a few seconds, I wondered why, and then realized his self-restraint was for Stefan's benefit. Akil's actions said more in that moment of hesitation than any words could have mustered. *He cared.*

I nodded briskly. "I'll be fine. If they get twitchy, I'll bring the fire."

I cast my gaze past Akil at Stefan. If he waited much longer, he'd start pacing. By the flick of his fingers against his thigh and the sweep of his hand through his hair, he was clearly itching for a fight. "Take care of Ryder. He's been good to me."

Stefan finally pinned his arctic glare on me. Even robbed of his element, the look he gave me had me tightening my coat. He dipped his chin in a sharp nod of acknowledgement, but the chill he'd wrapped around himself intensified my doubts.

Akil noticed my concern, even if Stefan didn't. "Go. Once we've ascertained Ryder's safety, I'll return."

With little else to say and the seconds ticking on, I took a few steps back, drawing out my goodbye while I committed the image of the both of them to my memory. Utterly useless at anything resembling a goodbye, I turned and marched away without saying any of the dozen or so farewells in my head. It wouldn't be for long, I told myself. Everything was going to be fine. When I glanced back, they'd both gone.

Flicking my collars up and tucking my hands deep into my pockets, I upped my pace to a jog and rounded the street corner toward the sprawling, concrete warehouse.

***

"Hey, Muse. Thought you were AWOL?" The guard behind the outer doors watched me sign in and plant my thumb on the ID pad by the door.

"Yeah, short vacation in the netherworld. There's no place like home."

His gaze rode me like a devil on my shoulder until I was through the reinforced steel. I could be damned sure he'd alert Adam to my presence. My return would spike a security alert; hopefully nothing too heavy. It might wake a few Enforcers and put them on stand-by, but Adam wouldn't risk spooking me. He'd want to hear me out. The head of operations was always ready to hear information he could use.

The Institute halls and offices were quiet but not empty. I attracted a few curious glances from the nightshift staff. Many would know me by name. Having a demon in their midst, even half of one, didn't sit too well with the majority.

The sound of my boots thumping the carpet seemed a little too loud in my anxious mind, as did the hum of the computers and occasional tap-tap of fingers on a keyboard. A ringing phone just about made me jump out of my skin before I calmed the hell down. Nothing untoward was going to happen. I had every right to be here. I was helping them.

Yeah, and the last time you'd told them that, they'd pumped you full of PC34 and threw you in a prison cell. Okay, so I had reason to be on edge, but there was no point wallowing in anxiety. I was a multi-realm she-devil capable of incinerating a crowd of demons at the snap of my fingers. I didn't need to fear the Institute...

A shaft of light cut across the hall from below Adam's office door. I rapped my knuckles against the panel, expecting Adam's bullet-quick 'come' to fire back at me. When the invite didn't come, I glanced up and down the hallway. Alone, I helped myself inside the comfortable office. Adam wasn't there. The desk-light illuminated a spread of papers. A half empty glass of water sat beside the keyboard. A computer tower hummed out of sight.

Wherever Adam had gone, he'd been away from his desk long enough for the computer to doze off and condensed water to gather around the base of the glass.

A blue file rested on top of the others on his desk. Its tag read: Subject Beta. I reached out and flipped open the cover. In the few seconds it took to scan the covering page, I picked out several key words: Subject Beta. Muse. Volatile. Akil Vitalis. Class A demons. Threat Level Red. *Sam Harwood.*

I scooted around the desk and turned over the covering pages. Sam had been my friend. Akil had killed him. Why was his name in a file on Adam's desk? What the hell was Subject Beta? I skimmed over Adam's handwritten notes and peeked under sticky-notes. There were dates and events from years ago, long before Stefan had walked into my life and blown my workshop to smithereens. Stefan's name didn't appear to feature at all. Half a dozen pages consisted of progress reports signed by David Ryder. More documents bullet-pointed my past with Akil. They knew the date Akil had brought me through the veil. I noticed the name of the school I'd briefly attended before a demon had tried to kill me in class. Numerous sightings... Pictures of me as a skinny teen tucked into Akil's embrace at the Aquarium; his eyes fiercely protective while I gawked at the penguins. Subject Beta...was me. In Adam's handwriting, there was mention of an Operation Typhon, whatever that was. There: Sam Harwood... Deceased. There was another name beside it; Jason Bywater. Who was he? What was Operation Typhon?

A shadow passed by the office door. I tensed, ready to spring back and plaster an innocent expression on my face. The door stayed closed. I puffed out a sigh. Adam could be back any minute. Even if he wasn't, I needed to find him and warn him about Damien. I didn't have time to waste. I grabbed a few pages from the file and fed them into Adam's copier. I plucked each newly printed copy free and tapped my foot as more churned out. Something Adam had said... "Your employment was inevitable." I thought he'd meant from the moment Stefan had revealed the existence of the Institute to me, but what if it went back further than that? Just how long had they watched me? And why? Did Akil know? Was he in on it? I remembered his scathing comments months ago about the insolence of the Institute. Had he been referring to something else besides Nica being sent to spy on him? Had the Institute put Akil up to saving me from Damien all those years ago? I'd thought he'd found me because he wanted me... Had the ten years we spent together been a ruse? Was he part of the Institute's grander plan? Akil wanted my demon, and I'd assumed that had been his motive all along. Could there be other motives behind his actions? Was he just following orders? It would explain how a wretched half-blood girl belonging to a vile demon had appeared on a Prince of Hell's radar in the first place.

I plucked the last sheet free, folded it, and tucked them all into my jacket pocket.

Surely Akil wouldn't be under the thumb of the Institute. I'd seen nothing that suggested the Institute had their hooks in any demon as powerful as a Prince of Hell. I couldn't imagine Akil bowing to anyone, especially the Institute. He despised them more than I did. There was no way he'd work for them. It wasn't possible. It wasn't in his nature. I knew him. Akil did everything for Akil. Yet, I didn't trust him. He was secrets and lies. Could the Institute have bargained with him? They'd convinced Yukki Onna to find me. They weren't beyond bartering with demons for the greater good.

Suspicions chased doubts around my head. I growled at myself and mentally shoved it all to one side to examine later. Adam wouldn't answer my questions, but the new more vocal Akil might. When this was over, we'd have a nice long chat about the Institute, Operation Typhon and Subject Beta, and what the hell he knew about all three.

I couldn't wait any longer for Adam to return and decided to check the library. There was a chance I'd find Nica there, squirreling away her private time in research. Besides Adam, there wasn't anyone else I trusted with the information. Plus I wanted to tell her Stefan was alive and well—perhaps not as well as he could have been, but we had him back. It was a start.

She might already be aware. The Institute had been called to an unseasonable ice incident at Jerry's, and Mammon had crashed their party. Adam would have been informed of Mammon's sudden appearance and would have surmised Stefan was back on this side of the veil too. That didn't mean he'd told Nica though. He was just as likely to keep it all a secret in the hope he could whisk Stefan away for the benefit of the Institute.

I found my pace quickening as I navigated my way across the Institute's rabbit-warren to the library. The early hour meant I was able to pass undisturbed by the staff, but the security cameras blinked their green indicator lights at me as I passed. Always watching. The only place they didn't routinely observe was the storeroom-cum-library.

The library door gave a woeful groan as I shoved it open and stepped inside. I expected to be met with the evocative odor of old books, so when the metallic coppery smell of blood assaulted my senses, I froze. Instinct took over, senses kicking into fight or flight mode. The huge space with its cathedral proportioned ceilings and rows upon rows of books made seeking out the source of the blood difficult. The strip lights buzzed their stark inhuman glow down from above but still somehow managed to miss the valleys of shadows between the shelves.

I could see straight down four rows in front of me, but further afield either side of those shelves was a dead zone. A creeping sense of unease thread its way up the back of my neck. Someone watched me.

"Who's in here?" I called.

Beneath the monotonous buzzing of lights, the hiss of whispers reached me. I didn't even consider leaving to get help. Why would I? I could smell blood. Somebody was hurt. As an Enforcer, albeit a new one, I should have been well equipped to deal with this. I told myself this as I moved with deliberate care along the ends of the aisles.

The whispering abruptly ceased. I paused, tilted my head and listened. When the whispers returned, the sound had changed, turned into snatches of shallow breath. Someone was choking, fighting for their life. Fear fuelled a reckless burst of speed. Dread plummeted through my gut.

I caught hold of the end of the metal bookshelves and skidded around the end of the aisle, only to be brought up short when Damien's glare met mine.

All demon, he towered over Nica, forearm muscles taut from the strain of holding the chain looped around her neck, wings cast back to balance him. Her feet kicked uselessly at the air as she dangled doll-like in front of him. She'd hooked her fingers into the chain, trying to pry the links free. At half his size and strength, there was little hope she'd escape. She didn't see me, but Damien knew I was there. A rasping laughter hissed through his sharp teeth. A sharp stab of pain punched me in the chest. His poison writhed like maggots inside me. I gagged and staggered.

Nica's struggles weakened. He would kill her and wouldn't stop at her. He'd rip a swathe of destruction through the heart of the Institute. Whatever happened, I couldn't let him leave the library.

I crouched low and dropped the mental barrier holding back my demon. She roared through me in a blistering tsunami of heat. Blue flame devoured my human flesh. Veins of molten heat pulsated through my scorched black flesh. Blind, unadulterated fury fed the inferno roaring inside of me, rendering Damien's touch inside of me insignificant. Head down, wing up, I sprang at him.

He dropped Nica and rounded on me. He coiled the chain in his right fist. Twice my size and five times my weight, he could have tackled me, but I was agile, and when pissed off, I had a sting in my tail. He swung his fist down toward me. I ducked and twisted at the last second and caught the end of the chain. He tugged me back, heaving me off my feet, but I had my target. I threaded the flames through the chain, blazing the links white-hot. Fire lashed around Damien's fist and danced up his arm.

He bellowed and flung me to the floor. My breath exploded as I landed awkwardly on my side against Nica. He staggered back, arm thrashing in a bid to free himself of the chain. Globules of molten metal rained around us.

Damien stumbled back against the wall, his leathery wings pinned at awkward angles behind him. He snarled at the superheated chain and tried to wrench it free. White-hot metal clung to his claws.

I watched him writhe in pain, watched his hideously demonic face twist in agony, and I delighted in the thrill of seeing him suffer. I leered at him, unable to tear my gaze away. A sensuous touch of perverse glee touched my mind. The scene sharpened. The smell of burned flesh, the taste of it on my tongue, the blaze of disgust in his eyes—I committed it to memory, sharpened the sensations to a point, and pinned them to the back of my skull like a goddamn trophy. *Burn, Damien. Dance beneath my fire.* I could have watched him burn for eternity, but the chain loosened and slipped free. He swung his murderous glare back to me and roared.

I drew in a breath and gathered the Institute's residual heat. It came willingly, funneled up my legs, and devoured me. I shone with the will and desire of fire.

A living inferno reflected in Damien's eyes. "You are weak." He spat the words between us. "I know you…" He reached out his good hand and pointed a claw-tipped finger at my chest. "I. Am. Inside. You."

"You don't know me. If you did, you'd run." My demon spoke through me, for me. "You see me, I know you do. But you fail to recognize me. That wretched half-blood girl you abused for years, she's still here. She lives in me. She's a part of me, and I'm stronger because of her. I killed you once. I know what I am, and you're about to find out." I flung my arm out and cast a jet of liquid fire.

He dropped his stance low and summoned up a gust of air that diverted the jet of heat away from him. It splashed against the wall behind him and exploded outward. The wind whipped around us, scooped up my fire, and whisked into a firestorm. Books tumbled from shelves and were swiftly devoured by fire. Flames licked across the floor.

An alarm shrilled somewhere in my mind, behind all the rage and revenge. It was only when rain hissed and vaporized around me that I came back to myself. The sprinklers. I glanced up but could only see fire and ash spiraling above me. I had to stop this. The fire alone could destroy the Institute. I closed my eyes, just for a second, and re-called the fire into me. As I did, Damien dismissed the torrent of wind. The firestorm vanished as quickly as it had come.

High pitched alarms thumped inside my head while the sprinklers rained water over me.

Nica wheezed. *She's alive!* I kept my gaze trained on Damien. He cradled his right hand against his chest and returned my heated glare with his own, lip raised in a silent snarl.

"Muse..." Nica coughed. She wheezed a few words that I didn't understand. Then she lifted her head. I stole a glance and saw her tear streaked face and the welts around her throat. She mouthed, "I'm sorry."

Damien took a step toward us. She flinched and tried to pull herself away, using the bookcase behind us as leverage. I stepped in front him and spread my wing, hiding Nica behind me. "You don't touch her," I growled.

"She's weak of body." He hissed at me through sharp teeth. His dull gray eyes held no emotion. He was empty. "A pathetic creature. She thought to control me. I controlled her. She will die easily."

Nica controlled him? *Nica* controlled him!

Damien saw me falter. Maybe I gave it away in my stance, or something in my eyes betrayed my surprise. He laughed that horrible gut-churning laughter, and I lunged at him. He snatched my right wrist and tugged me clean off my feet. I pooled fire into my arm, flailing wildly in the air. I needed the veil... and reached out with my mind. His fist smacked into my jaw like a sledgehammer. I hit the floor hard and instantly blacked out. I wasn't out for long. Seconds—a few breaths. A mind-numbing throb thrummed across my face. Something was likely broken. I didn't have time to wonder what. He stamped on my back and clutched at my right wing, jerking it back hard enough to grind the bones. I screamed.

He crouched over me, leaning all of his weight into my spine, and hissed over my shoulder. "Defy me again, whore, and I take this wing." As if to prove his point, he curled his fingers around the bridge of my wing and tore it back. Bone splintered, and a pain exploded inside my skull with enough force to bury me in unconsciousness again. When I came around, Damien straddled Nica. His good hand locked around her throat. She'd fallen limp, her mouth open, eyes wide.

"Don't..." I tried to summon my element, but a combination of water from the sprinklers and pain muddling my thoughts robbed me of the clear intent I needed to call the heat. I shoved up off the floor onto quivering forearms. "Please, Damien..." What could I say to stop him? He'd already killed half a dozen Enforcers. He wasn't going to hesitate to kill Nica.

He slid cold eyes to me, and he loosened his grip on Nica. She sucked in a heaving breath.

"You have me." My teeth chattered. "You d-don't need to k-kill her."

He smiled, "So fragile... these humans." He dropped her body and bowed over her. He studied how she struggled to fill her lungs and observed the tears streaming from her eyes. He felt nothing for her. "Flawed." He breathed her scent, wings flexing behind him with a quiver of excitement. "She believes you killed her kin." He dragged his claws down her face. "I recognize revenge."

The weight of emotional baggage crushed me. "Damien..." I begged, trying to distract him from his lust for the kill. "Let her go. Do what you want with me. It's why you're here. You want revenge for what I did. I burned you. I tried to kill you. Let her go."

He made a purring sound, and I tasted bile at the familiarity of that noise. Sliding his good hand into Nica's hair, he locked it there and twisted. She wailed. He yanked her head to one side and bowed toward her neck.

"Don't!" I tried to get off my front and onto my feet, but my limbs refused to obey. I fell forward, hearing the gunshot from behind me. A hole punched through one of Damien's wings, close to the shoulder joint. He tore his head up, teeth, mouth and chin glistening with Nica's blood.

Adam stood at the end of the aisle, gun planted in both hands. He fired again. Damien roared, leaning back and calling his power. The ground beneath us rumbled, rattling the bookshelves, and then the wind thundered through the library like a bomb blast.

I saw Damien rise up but had to duck my head against the hurricane force winds buffering me. If Adam knew what was good for him, he'd run. I heard a few hollow gunshots bounce around me—the wind played with the sound—but I couldn't see anything beyond my own torn wing membrane.

Nica. Hunkered low, I crawled across the floor, hugging my broken wing against me to try to stop the wind from tearing it open. It hurt enough that every strong gust sent a wave of pain though me. Jaw clamped, head down, I crawled on until my hands sank in the warm pool of blood. She'd been bleeding before, but not like this. Half her shoulder was gone... a chunk of her neck too. She saw me. Her pretty face twisted in agony. Her wide blue eyes locked unblinking on mine.

I stretched my broken wing over her, shielding us both beneath the torn membrane as best as I could.

She sobbed and mumbled incoherently. Fresh tears streamed down her face. She mumbled my name, mixed with apologies.

"It's okay." I pressed my cheek against hers. "It's going to be okay."

She snatched each breath, as though they fled from her. "I... was wrong," she hissed, "I let him in, he said... he knew Stefan. That he'd tell me... about my brother." She clutched my arm, her grip cold against my flushed demon skin. "I thought... you were dangerous. I... thought... he would control you. I didn't..." Her words trailed off. "I didn't know he was... evil."

I gulped back a sob and draped my arm over her. I wanted to pull her against me and hold her close, but I was afraid I'd hurt her. "Stefan's alive... You have to fight this, Nica. Hold on. Listen to me... You brother is back. I brought him home."

Her grip on my arm tightened. She heard me. She knew. It would be okay, Stefan was back. Her brother was home. She would see him again. We'd survive this. We'd survived Akil together. We would win. But her hand fell away from my arm, and her breaths stopped snatching. I waited for another breath, for a whispered word, but nothing came. I pulled back a little and looked into her unfocused eyes.

"Nica?"

The gale force winds were fading. I felt the spider-crawl of Damien's gaze and knew he was watching, waiting for me. I barely registered the gunshots and screams from beyond the library. It all seemed so cursory, so needless. I locked my painful jaw closed and summoned the fire. It was nothing like the amount of power I was capable of, but it was enough to throw him back.

I lifted my head and growled out a warning. Stefan looked down at me, his face frozen behind a guarded mask of disbelief. Adam stood slumped by a hole in the wall that had once been a doorway, gun loose in his hand. There was no sign of Damien, but from the sounds of gunfire I knew this wasn't over. I still felt his pulsating darkness inside me.

"Stefan... I..." I wanted to tell him I'd tried to stop Damien, but he wasn't looking at me. His gaze, so cold, fell on Nica's motionless body. A fracture appeared in his expression, a crack through which I saw a lightning flicker of rage. He turned and strode toward the door.

"Stefan..." Adam straightened. Stefan shoved his father aside. He threw me a concerned glance and went after his son. I could see enough of the hall to watch as Adam managed to catch Stefan by the shoulder. Stefan swung around, gathered Adam up by the shirt, and pinned his father back against the wall with a snarl. I held my breath. The two of them didn't move. Stefan's snarling face was inches from his father's. My hatred of Adam paled in comparison to the revulsion on Stefan's eyes. Would he kill his own father?

Stefan shoved off of Adam and strode out of sight down the hall.

"Stefan?" Adam stumbled after him. "Don't do this... I can't protect you."

I didn't know what Adam's words meant and didn't care. I might have curled up next to Nica and let the

Enforcers deal with Damien, but the throb of his poison wouldn't allow it. I gave Nica one last look. Where had it all gone so wrong? She was so sweet, bright, and alive. She had the kind of unwavering courage I aspired to. Why had I not seen the hatred in her eyes when she looked at me? Why had nobody noticed her cry for help? How had it come to this? I dragged my hand down her face and closed her eyes.

My muscles burned as I heaved my weary body onto unsteady legs.

Damien's touch throbbed in my chest. Maybe they'd cornered him by now. I hoped so. Then it occurred to me: if they killed him, I'd never get his claws out of me. His putrid touch would rot inside me until the day I died.

I growled, and with a shake, shoved my demon back behind mental barriers. She didn't go easily and spat her desire for revenge inside my mind, but walking through the Institute all demoned-up was a quick way to get myself executed. Back in my human body, the pain of my broken wing had reduced to an ache in my shoulder, but the throb in my jaw continued to blaze across the side of my face.

My soaked and bloody clothes clung to me. Tremors locked my muscles tight. I clamped my teeth together, wincing at the pain in my face. My sense of self felt distant and detached. I was shutting down, going into shock. I couldn't afford to step back, not for one second, not while Damien roamed the Institute. I had to end this. I left the library and followed the sounds of rapid gunfire. I would end this—whatever the cost.

Chapter Twenty Nine

Damien hadn't been shy about throwing his weight around. He was little more than a moth compared to Mammon, but he had strength, and he'd used that muscle to rip a path of destruction through the heart of the building. I followed the devastation, sidestepping around islands of fallen ceiling, crumbling walls, and wading through drifts of papers and documents. He'd simply torn through anything in his way, including people. There was nothing I could do for the fallen, but I could stop him. He thought he was the biggest, baddest thing in this building. He was wrong.

I broke into a run, swerving to avoid a dangling strip light, and veered around people running away from the chaos raging ahead. If you've ever crouched in a storm shelter while waiting for the tornado to pass, you've heard the howling that accompanies the beast. It's a harrowing wail, as though the storm is a thing alive, and it's hungry. That noise drowned out the alarms as I drew closer to the conference hall where Damien was unleashing a tornado. The wind rushed from behind me and sucked through the corridor toward the double doors.

I stumbled through the doors. My hair whipped about my face, stinging my cheeks. I leaned back against the weight of the wind, seeking to funnel me toward the swirling vortex of debris at the center. Somebody shoved by me and escaped. Others clung to tables, fighting to hold on. Enforcers fired bullets into the maelstrom with no hope of hitting anything. Some were spray-painting symbols on the walls. It wouldn't be enough. A room of that size would need more protective wards than they could muster.

The ceiling let out a groan and collapsed. The funnel of wind gobbled up the falling tiles and metal framework, exposing the steel beams and underside of the roof. The tornado pulsed and swelled, then burst apart like a bomb. A mangled mass of debris slammed into me.

My skull buzzed. My ears rang. What the hell? I'd been standing near the doorway and found myself on the floor against the wall, with no memory of moving. I lifted my hand to prop myself up. My arm twitched. My hand didn't respond. A twisted fragment of steel protruded from my right shoulder. I had a few surreal seconds to wonder how that got there, before the accompanying pain fired off the appropriate nerve endings, and a garbled scream burst free. I curled my left hand around the shard, trembling so hard I couldn't get a grip. I wrapped my fingers around the serrated edges, tugged, and nearly threw up. The shard was stuck fast. I barely had enough strength left to stay conscious, let alone pull it out.

Damien did a slow turn in the center of the destruction, admiring his achievement. His cold dead eyes caught sight of me. My breaths stuttered. My heart pounded. I couldn't clear my head, couldn't pin down my thoughts into actions. My body wouldn't work. I floated somewhere outside my skin. If I passed out, he'd win. I had to stop him. There was no other option. It must end.

He spread his wings wide. Their span almost reached across the entire width of the room. He smiled and walked toward me. His swollen muscles quivered. I knew that look, the leering snarl, the raw expression of need. Clearly aroused, physically and mentally, he was high on the devastation he'd wrought. Had it been any other demon, I might have thought they meant to finish me, but Damien wouldn't kill me. Death was too final.

I tried to get my legs under me but only managed a few kicking scuffs against the floor before he wrapped his claw-tipped fingers around the steel shard and lifted me in front of him. Muscles and flesh tore in my shoulder. A mangled cry shot from the back of my throat. I didn't kick, didn't fight. I couldn't. The pain was too much. It took all my strength not to give in to the looming threat of unconsciousness.

He ground out the words through his misshapen demon mouth. "I. Like. To. Hear. You. Scream."

I had hold of the steel shard and tried to lift my own weight to ease the pain. He grinned and gave the shard a twist. A scream lodged in my throat. My vision bloomed red, my skull threatening to burst. I yelled inside for my demon to come, but she didn't answer. She'd never refused before. She was there. I could feel her writhing around in the darkness at the bottom of my consciousness, but she hid.

Everyone in the room was either dead or dying, and nobody had ventured through the doors. I was alone, skewered by Damien with no means of escape. I tried to think of something to say, some spark of genius that would make Damien drop me, giving me time to coax my demon back into my skin, but pain blinded all reason.

Damien gave the shard another twist. I jolted, back arched, jaw clamped shut, but the cry still squeezed through my teeth. *How much pain can the human body endure?*

He grinned. His leathery slate-gray face filled my vision. "They will all die," he purred. "Every. Last. One." His black tongue lapped at his lips. Glee widened his dull eyes. "You will watch."

His torso did a little hiccup and, the smile died on his lips. The glee in his eyes turned to puzzlement. I blinked rapidly.

He dropped me. I landed in a heap on my side, and another cry of pain escaped me. I twisted into a ball, drawing my knees up. I thrust my thoughts aside and dove inside my soul. My demon cowered. I raged at her, hooked metaphysical hands around her, and dragged her sorry ass out of hiding. She fought, but I had her by the scruff of the neck and threw her into my flesh. Fire washed over me. The pain in my shoulder faded away. I snatched the shard free and tossed it aside. The wound twitched and hissed as it cauterized. Only when I had all my relevant pieces in the right place, mentally and physically, did I look up.

Stefan had his demon back and wore it like a coat of ice-spiked armor. Frosted-wings fanned out on either side of him. He carried a spear of ice twice his height, and considering that Damien appeared to be bleeding from a neat puncture wound in his back, I took a stab at guessing Stefan had been the reason Damien had dropped me.

Damien snarled. "You." He pointed a finger at Stefan and lunged.

I gasped, expecting Damien to crush Stefan. He looked so fragile against Damien's heaving bulk of muscles, but I'd forgotten how fast Stefan was. He darted right, and twisted the spear into Damien's side, circling around as Damien reared up and roared.

Stefan backed up toward me. The temperature plummeted. The weight of his power had my demon shirking back. She'd had enough, but giving up wasn't an option.

Damien's lips twisted in disgust. "Worthless half-bloods."

When Stefan laughed, there was nothing jovial in its tone. His laughter chilled. It was cold. Empty. Even though I carried a coat of fire, I shivered at the sound. Stefan lifted his left hand and opened the veil a few feet above us. He gathered a swirling mass of azure power to him. It wove around his body, surging through him. He shone from within. A brilliant blue light writhed beneath his glacial flesh. He became a creature of ice. And madness.

I knew that lust. I'd let the power flood through me only a few hours before, when I'd drowned Akil in it. Pure surrender. A wonderful release. Nothing matters, just the element as it dances to your tune. Damien stumbled back. His wings bowed behind him as he watched Stefan call the energy from the netherworld into his soul.

Damien had good reason to be concerned. He eyed Stefan warily. "Kill me? Muse will be my eternal prisoner."

Stefan inclined his head. Chaos writhed in his arctic eyes. "I'm not going to kill you." Stefan's demon brogue sent shivers skittering through me. His words doubled, echoed, and reiterated. They hurt to hear. He flung the spear at Damien, who easily knocked it aside, but in doing so, Damien had missed the dozen or so daggers of ice that manifested in the air around him. They plunged into Damien from all sides. My owner twitched and bucked. He twisted in search of the deadly daggers. His wings fluttered, membranes torn apart. Crimson blood dribbled across his dull skin.

While we'd been engrossed in our battle, the Enforcers had piled into the room. They opened fire but didn't stop to consider who they were shooting at. They saw three demons. Never mind that two were technically on their side. A bullet punched into Stefan. He buckled, staggered, and went down. An arctic shockwave punched the air from my lungs and flash-froze my flesh. In a blink, the world turned icy-blue before releasing us all. The Enforcers fell back, shaking ice from their clothes.

Stefan wasn't moving. His wings had curled around him, cocooning him in ice. The veil stitched itself closed above us. Stefan had called enough power to bring about a mid-summers ice-age, but with no outlet, no focus, that power would devour him from the inside out. It would kill him.

I heard the Enforcers barking orders. A bullet slapped against the floor beside me. A numb acceptance smothered me in a comforting embrace. I got to my feet, snatched up the jagged piece of steel, and ran full force at Damien. In the confusion, the muddle of gunshots, shouts, and with the tumultuous power spiraling around the room, Damien didn't see me rushing him until the last second. By then it was too late. His eyes widened. He hadn't believed I'd do it. He thought himself invincible. I barreled into him and punched the shard into his neck. The bellow that boiled up from my insides poured out of me in a thundering roar. We toppled together.

There's a time for careful deliberation, for considering the consequences, but this wasn't it. I had him pinned beneath my tiny frame. In seconds, he'd knock me off him. I didn't hesitate. He must have seen the naked rage in my eyes, but even then he didn't fear me. I don't think he had it in him to be afraid. Hand clenched around the shard embedded in his neck, I leaned in, smiled, and cut his throat open. His lips parted in a silent howl.

I plunged the shard into his chest where his black heart beat. I drove that sucker home until every inch of the metal burrowed inside the wound. Blood bubbled over his chest, my hands, down my legs. His huge bulk twitched beneath me, but with his throat cut, he couldn't speak a word, which was why the laughter, when it wormed its way into my head, almost stole my killing-ecstasy. The bastard was smiling. I'd cut his throat and stabbed him, and he was smiling at me? The bubbling laughter rumbled through the fog of murderous rage. It hooked claws into my doubts and tried to undermine my resolve. But I wasn't giving in. Placing both hands on his chest, spreading my fingers wide, I thrust a wave of heat into him. This wasn't a conscious assault on my part. I was beyond that. I wanted him to feel pain like he'd dealt me, to wish his own life would end just to be free of the agony. I drove my element into him, filling him up with fire. Even as the embers devoured him from the inside out, as they crawled across his flesh, turning it to ash, I didn't stop. And still his laughter clawed at my skull.

I knew the exact moment he died. I felt the stab of his death like a gunshot to the chest. I jerked back as though struck. A crushing embrace closed around my heart. I could barely breathe. I slumped over and fell off Damien's smoldering body. I clawed at the floor, trying to reach clear air. He was dead. How could he be doing this to me? Something cold caught my ankle. I tugged, but the touch coiled up my leg.

I almost wished I hadn't glanced behind. A heaving cloud of darkness pulsated above the flames devouring Damien's body, and from that malevolent cloud, threads of power thrashed and writhed. As soon as I saw them, they rose up in one rippling tangled mass. I was looking at his soul. It plunged into my chest. I heard screams—my own—and fell back. The river of darkness flowed out of Damien and poured over me. Viscous poison streamed into my mouth, my eyes, my ears. It wrapped around me and seeped through my flesh, sinking into my bones. I drowned in his dark.

An Enforcer could have put a bullet in my head, and I would have welcomed it. Sometimes, I wish they had. Damien's infusion invaded all of me. The violence of its attack went beyond anything he could have done while alive. Imagine the blood in your veins replaced by acid. Imagine the comfort of your own thoughts torn from the safety of your consciousness and ripped to shreds before your eyes. His soul, or whatever it was, sliced me open, sunk its claws in, and tore out my center, quickly curling into a ball of rancid power, and made itself a new home.

***

Ryder's voice. He was telling someone to get back, threatening them, and from the desperation tightening his words, I knew his threats were real. I'd not heard fear in his voice before, but I heard it then. I blinked. He was beside me, my name on his lips. He couldn't touch me, but I didn't have the presence of mind to realize I was still demon. I looked up at him and wondered why he wore a thick winter coat and why it was snowing. The snowflakes didn't last long as they twirled and danced in the air around Ryder. As soon as they came close to me, the flakes fizzled to nothing. I would have liked to watch them swirl hypnotically in the air. They were calm and kept the screams in my head away. Of course, as soon as I thought that, the pain returned with a vengeance. Broken wing, bruised or broken jaw, puncture wound in my shoulder, and the thing throbbing dark and hungry in my chest.

I locked onto Ryder's face and stared at the smudge of blood across his cheek. Lines of reality sharpened into focus.

"...have to get up... Please, Muse...They're gonna kill him."

I blinked. Ryder's words drifted through the fog of shock. He continued to say something about needing me, but the snow distracted me. It was everywhere. I turned my head and frowned at the blanket of white softening the edges of the debris. Then I saw the hole in the roof and how the snow poured inside like a waterfall of white noise.

"Get up, Muse, goddammit!" Ryder snapped.

I closed my eyes and very carefully sealed the horrible darkness inside away behind tentative mental barriers, poking at it with minimal contact, as though my subconscious might catch evil from it.

With a shiver, I opened my eyes and dismissed my demon. The pain in my shoulder blazed and tugged a reluctant whimper from me. Ryder's eyes widened. I must have looked as bad as I felt because Ryder paled, and swore under his breath. He held out a hand.

I welcomed his help back to my feet and then again when I staggered like a drunk. My eyes rolled, my stomach lurched, and I fell back to my knees, retching. Could I vomit the dark out of me? My body wanted to. I dry heaved for what felt like forever. I was sick to my bones and hurt all over. Why would it not end?

"You need a doctor..." Ryder crouched beside me. Did he know what had happened? His eyes had hardened, but his expression hadn't. He attempted a smile and I very nearly pooled into a jabbering wreck on the floor.

"Muse?"

I couldn't breathe. I gasped again and again. Panic. Run. Hide. Dark pulsed inside my chest.

Ryder gripped my good shoulder and captured my gaze in his. "Muse... Breathe slowly. It's alright." He leaned in. "Pack the fucked-up shit away. Don't let it control you. I need you. Stefan needs you."

"I know," I mumbled. I was kneeling in two feet of snow inside the building. Bowing my head, I clamped my eyes closed. Pack it all away. Dig a hole and bury it. Deny it. My breathing slowed. The fear receded. "Where is he?" My voice sounded like it belonged to someone else, distant and throaty.

"Stefan's gone, but not far. There's a blizzard outside. The Enforcers are trackin' the eye of the storm. They're goin' after him. They'll kill him, Muse."

They could try.

I nodded. The movement felt as though I was dragging a bag of nails through my aching head.

Ryder helped me stand. I wobbled and hissed as my shoulder flared up, but at least I was on my feet. My body appeared to obey me again. I saw what remained of Damien on the ground behind Ryder. The ashes barely resembled anything humanoid. The snow hadn't settled on the grim pile. It stood out like the white tape outline of a body at a murder scene. My stomach lurched, and the hideous clinging parasite inside of me throbbed with a sickly heat.

Ryder deliberately stepped in my line of sight and ducked his head. "You can do this, okay?"

No. I shook my head. No, it wasn't okay. Ripples stuttered through my limbs. I wanted to blurt out that Damien wasn't dead, that he was inside me. I wanted to pick up the jagged piece of metal nestled in the pile of ashes and use it to carve him out of my chest.

Ryder gripped my good shoulder. "Muse, I get it. Okay. I get it. But you can't break down on me now. We have to find Stefan before the Enforcers do. Before he suffocates the city in snow. We gotta do that, an' I can't do it without you. Can you hold it together? Just for a few hours?"

Tears skipped down my cheeks. "Yeah," I croaked. I could, but it was going to be a close thing.

Chapter Thirty

Ryder hadn't been wrong when he'd said, "suffocate the city in snow." I caught snippets of news feeds on my way out of the building. Waiting for me outside was a world turned white. Temperatures had plummeted to -29 degrees. The sub-zero temperature would have been a record breaker for winter, but it was summer, and the people of Boston were demanding answers. Snow drifts had piled up against houses. The water in Boston harbor had hardened to ice a foot thick, crushing the hulls of the boats and ships moored there. The blizzard raged.

The Institute was in chaos. Alarms shrilled. The corridors brimmed with people either trying to get out or armed personnel trying to reach those in need. Ryder and I were buffeted along toward the exit. He explained over his shoulder in snippets that, when Akil and Stefan turned up on his doorstep, he nearly had a —insert a few Ryder-themed expletives—heart attack. Then the call came in from the Institute for Ryder to get his ass back to HQ. Muse was back, and the fire alarms had tripped, never a good combination. Akil had given them the non-corporeal lift back to the Institute and promptly vanished, much to Ryder's relief; *"If I ever have to get that close to the Prince of Greed again, it'll be too fuckin' soon. And I ain't ever doin' that Star-Trek teleportation crap again, yah hear? I feel dirty."* Once inside, Stefan had wasted no time retrieving the PC34 antidote. He'd threatened to kill Adam if they didn't give it to him. Needless to say, Adam now had a broken arm, and Stefan got his demon back. Like Damien, Stefan had cut a path of destruction from the medical department to the conference room where he'd found Damien skewering me, but unlike Damien, he hadn't killed anyone to get there, just put the fear of ice into those who tried to stop him. I took that as a good sign. To call this much power, he had to be drawing from the veil, which meant he continued to syphon off more power than he could handle. How long could he maintain control of his demon? Had he already lost control? If Stefan had let go of the reins, what could I do to stop him? He wasn't like Akil. I couldn't drain Stefan of power. We were two sides of the same coin, destined never to meet and yet so close.

Nobody prevented Ryder and me from leaving. The Institute teetered on collapse, but I had no interest in helping them. If anything, they'd brought this on themselves. They were lucky Stefan hadn't decided to turn the Institute into the arctic. He could have. He probably should have. *He might still...*

We stepped out into a land of white. My brain could hardly wrap itself around the fact that three feet of snow had settled over Boston like crisp white icing on a wedding cake. My boots crunched through the white stuff, and the cold sucked the heat out of my flesh. I instinctively wrapped my element around me, keeping me warm. So cold inside... where the darkness waited.

We walked to where the backstreet joined one of the main arterial roads. People shivered beside their cars, many sat huddled inside, engines running, fending off the arctic temperatures. The early morning rush hour had been captured in ice. Nobody was going anywhere.

"...a Boeing overshot Logan International," Ryder was saying. "There were three hundred and twenty seven people on board." Ryder paused, and when I met his stare, he didn't need to finish. "He's outta control, Muse."

Someone had to stop him, but I wasn't sure that someone was me. "I'm not going to hurt him. I can't."

"They'll kill him." Ryder looked pained. Anxiety twisted a knot inside me.

I turned my back on Ryder and trudged through the snow. My centrally heated footfalls melted the snow beneath my boots. Ryder fell into step behind me. I heard his teeth chattering and the rustle of his coat, but otherwise, the street was quiet. "Nica's dead," I said, keeping my head down.

Ryder waited a few beats. "I know. Adam briefed us. I… can't believe it. Stefan saw her. Shit. What a fuckin' nightmare. Muse… I need to say this…" Ryder sucked in a breath. I tensed and stamped through the snow. He puffed out a sigh. "I'm sorry I couldn't get you outta the netherworld sooner… Adam didn't want to summon Yukki Onna. I told him I'd quit."

The change of subject stalled me. I stopped and looked back. "You said you'd quit?"

His mouth turned down. He dropped his gaze. "I knew what that sick son-of-a-bitch would do to you… After what you said at Stone's Throw… I had to do something."

An unexpected sob wedged in my throat. I tore my gaze away and gulped down the rising emotion. My lip quivered. I pinched my mouth closed and squeezed my eyes shut. If I cried now, I wouldn't stop. Ryder had saved me. I met his eyes and fought to keep the raw emotion from my face. "Thanks." My voice cracked. "Yukki Onna did enough. She got me away from him. I was… I was gone. If you'd done nothing… I'd be dead. So thank you, David Ryder, you soppy bastard."

He grinned. "I wasn't gonna let Adam give up on you the way he did Stefan."

I turned away, grateful for diversion of our conversation before things got too blurry-eyed. I slogged through the snow. "Stefan just needs our help." It occurred to me that David Ryder, the hard-as-nails Enforcer was here, with me, not with the Institute. The Institute was his life, but he'd made his choice. I glanced over my shoulder at him, catching his eye.

"Where are we going?" He hugged his coat tighter around him. Snow settled in his hair and melted on his face.

I looked at the wash of gray above us. Falling snow obscured any traces of the sky. Further ahead, not far from the financial district, the sky lightened. "I know where he is."

"What happened, Muse? This ain't Stefan. I've known him for years. He doesn't do this... He's the most level-headed guy I know. He's always been dangerous... But he's never let loose. Never."

"The netherworld happened." We passed suited-up commuters trying to dig their cars out of the snow. Nobody could have prepared for a white out in summer. "Stefan was raised here, on this side of the veil. He's spent his entire life controlling his demon, but it doesn't work like that beyond the veil. A human body can't survive unprotected in the netherworld for long. The demon takes over. It protects us, wraps us up in demon bubble wrap. There's no choice. It just takes the reins. Stefan would probably have fought it to begin with, but after time... the demon always wins."

"Fuck."

"After long enough, you start thinking like a demon. The human half sits on your shoulder, whispering about self-restraint, emotions, and wrong versus right, but the demon doesn't give a damn about any of that. It wants. It hungers for chaos. Stefan wouldn't have realized what was happening. He would have needed the demon to begin with. You don't get through a night there unless you fight your way up the food chain. The weak get eaten. He survived, and to survive you gotta be the biggest, baddest thing in the forest. I saw him Ryder. He... He'd become demon. No half measures. He's always had it in him to be top of the food chain."

Ryder mumbled something colorful. "Can you help him?"

I wasn't even sure I could help myself. I was putting on a brave face, but one wrong move, and the madness clawing at my skull would break out. I tried not to think about it, about what sat rotting inside me and focused instead on the task at hand. Could I help Stefan? I hadn't done a great job of helping him so far.

"What's that?"

Ryder's question snapped my head up. We'd walked for ten minutes and were nearing Atlantic Avenue. The glass fronted skyscrapers towered above us, some swathed in clouds of swirling snow, but over the Public Garden, the sky had cleared to a gray-blue, and at its center, danced the veil in all of its liquescent glory. If Ryder could see it, then so could the rest of Boston, and the big-fat secret the Institute had tried so hard to cover up was out of the bag. *Hey, people of Boston, you know those rumors about demons? About a world neighboring yours that's filled with the monsters from your childhood nightmares? Well, looky here. What's that great big smoking gun in the sky?* Adam would be having heart palpitations.

"Is that the Northern Lights? This far south?"

Technically, the Northern Lights or the Aurora Borealis is the veil.

"That's the veil," I replied, repeating the words cool and calm in my head. I could see it clearly too: ribbons of color undulating to a silent song. Usually the veil is invisible to the human eye, and I'd need to call my demon to see it, but not today, not while Stefan continued to draw power through it.

"Shit, really?"

Stefan had held the veil open longer than I thought possible. I'd only ever been able to draw from it for a few minutes before it collapsed on me. A few minutes were enough. In that time, I could consume enough of my element to incinerate a horde of demons or heal a Prince of Hell. What was Stefan planning to do with it all?

As we approached Atlantic Avenue, I broke into a jog and within a few minutes, Ryder and I entered the Public Gardens. We weren't alone. Police cars, marked and unmarked, were parked around the snowy grounds. Some had been there a while. Snow had banked up against their wheels. I recognized the non-descript Institute cars mixed in among the rather more obvious armored vehicles and their black clad squad members. A ring of tape cordoned off the George Washington statue, or rather where the statue should have been. All I could see was a vast globe of glacial blue ice. Its curved dome encompassed the entire monument. Directly above, where the swollen snow clouds crowded around a perfect circle of blue sky, the veil twitched and rippled like a wounded snake.

Ryder stopped beside me as I tried to get a feel for the scene of orderly chaos around us. The snowfall had slowed to the occasional wayward flake.

"Ryder." Coleman jogged toward us. He had on a thick padded jacket zipped up to his chin.

Ryder smiled tightly and nodded in the general direction of the circus. "You know who's doing this, right?"

Coleman glanced at the opaque globe. "Yeah, your old partner. We've been briefed." He slid his gaze to me and chanced a gentle smile. "Hey…" His greeting trailed off when he noticed the blood splatters on my clothes and the ragged hole in my jacket shoulder. "You don't look so good, Charlie…"

"I'm really not." I smiled brightly. *Seething dark.* I flinched. "Who briefed you?"

"Adam Harper. He's on his way from the Institute."

"If you let Adam in there, you might as well say hello to a nuclear winter."

Coleman shook his head. "It's out of my hands. This is demon protocol. You guys hold all the cards. We're just here to keep the public back. The Institute knows what they're doing. Right, Charlie?"

I winced at my own words coming back to haunt me and looked away. A crowd-control barrier had been set up a few hundred yards back from the globe. The press jostled at the front of the line, snapping away with their zoom lenses. Dammit. That was my day job splashed across the front pages.

"Can you get me closer?" I asked.

Coleman's lips ticked at the corner into something like a grimace. "I'm… not sure throwing fire on this situation is going to help."

My glare said, *don't fuck with me - not in the mood.* "Hey, you just said this is demon shit, so let me deal with it, okay."

Ryder made a noise in general agreement. "She's right. At least give Muse the chance to talk him down. If you or the Institute go at him, all hell's gonna break lose." He scratched at his eyebrow and glanced at the veil. "Maybe literally."

Coleman flicked his eyes to the veil writhing silently in the sky above. "Alright, but Charlie- Muse, whatever your real name is, please, don't make this worse."

I arched an eyebrow— meaning to convey how could this possible get any worse? —when I began to wonder if I was about do exactly that. Neither Ryder nor Coleman knew my precarious state of mind. That was my little secret. And with the veil throbbing with energy, all I needed to was reach for it and let go. Just let go. *Whispering dark...*

I shook myself free of the chaotic lure and approached the ring of cops sealing off the monument.

"You still on for that coffee?" Coleman called, his tone hesitant.

I glanced back, watched him raise his eyebrows expectantly, and gave him a smile. It was the least I could do. The last time I'd agreed to join him for coffee, Damien had jumped me in the woods and whisked me off to the netherworld. I wasn't making any promises, but the thought of it, the normality of relaxing with a coffee in friendly company —even if it was to talk demons— anchored me, gave me something real to cling on to. I was going to need it.

Chapter Thirty One

The temperature plummeted as I ducked under the police tape and approached the globe of ice. Even wrapped in my element, a shiver trickled down my spine. I fought the urge to look up into the veil, but I felt the power of it washing over me, raising the fine hairs on the back of my neck, calling to my demon. I had no intention of bringing her to this party. I didn't trust myself.

Up close, the curved wall of ice appeared even more breathtaking. I had no idea how Stefan had done it, but he'd sculpted a perfect sphere of thick ice around himself and the thirty-eight foot tall statue. The globe shone a deep blue. I couldn't see through it.

I laid my hands lightly on the ice, ignoring the throb of pain in my shoulder. The flash from a camera distracted me briefly. No doubt that picture was already being uploaded somewhere and my name dredged up from public records. Whatever happened here, the world was watching. I focused on the back of my hands and pushed a tide of heat into my flesh. The ice peeled away from my touch. I had no idea how Stefan would react. Softly-softly was the plan of action.

The ice fractured. A crack snapped and twitched up the curve of the globe. Another joined it. The ice hissed and groaned, then splintered and tumbled apart, leaving a jagged hole. The thing had walls two feet thick. Substantial enough to stop a bullet.

I stepped inside. My gaze briefly wandered over the proud bronze statue of George Washington on his marching horse and then fell to Stefan sitting on the ground. He had one knee drawn up. He leaned back against the granite pedestal, head bowed. The fall of his hair obscured his eyes. He would have looked entirely human but for the slight touch of frost glistening in his hair and clothes.

The hole in the ice globe gave an audible sigh. The ice around the breach shimmered with patterned fractals. Geometric pieces of ice slotted together until the hole vanished, and the globe was complete again. Stefan had control of his element the likes of which I could only dream of. But at what cost? He sat as still as ice. The sounds of my breathing seemed too loud in the near perfect silence. Did he even breathe?

His fingers twitched and tapped against his leg. "Did you kill my sister?" He kept his head bowed.

"What? No!" I gasped. "Why would you think that?" I tried to keep my voice level, to hold the emotion back, but I didn't have the strength to mask it all.

"I don't know what to think." He turned his head. His eyes swirled an iridescent blue. My breath caught in my throat. He looked netherworldly, his human only skin deep. His demon glared at me through his eyes. "I saw you with Akil...by the lake house. Before you lie, you should know I learned a few things while away. Your father, Asmodeus? He's the Prince of Lust. So go on and tell me how it wasn't what it looked like—how you couldn't help yourself."

I sucked in a tight breath. He'd seen me pump Akil full of power, watched me call from the veil and funnel it all into Akil, and then afterward, when Akil had tried to pry Damien's touch out of me. It would have looked intimate. For a while, it had been. Lust. I hadn't known my demon-father was the Prince of Lust. Akil had neglected to mention that pertinent fact in the ten years I'd spent with him. The jigsaw puzzle of my mind shifted, and a piece slotted neatly into place, but now was not the time to examine the picture it made. Not that it mattered. Stefan had already tarred me with my father's heritage.

I smiled. He wouldn't believe me. He'd made up his mind. "It really isn't what you think. Akil was hurt, and I needed him to—"

"You injected me with PC-Thirty-Four." Every word clipped. Electric tension prickled my skin. He trembled with the effort of control and glared at me.

"I had to. It was for your own good." I knew what I'd done was wrong, but what choice did I have? What was it Nica had said? "Sometimes we do the wrong things for the right reasons."

"You have no idea..." He choked the words back and tore his gaze away. "You had no right."

"This isn't about me."

He barked a cruel laughter. "This is all about you."

He jumped to his feet. I tensed and stole a few backward steps, but he didn't approach. He stood regarding me with a twisted mockery of a smile, head tilted to the side. "You didn't bring me home." He sneered. "You brought *him* home. Akil. I just tagged along for the ride, right? Because you couldn't have one without the other."

"No. Yes, I mean..." I glared back at him. Why was he twisting everything around? It hadn't been like that. "Yes, I needed Akil to get you out of there. I needed him to free me of Damien too. I was soul-locked, remember? I didn't bring either of you back lightly. I get it, Stefan. Dammit, I spent the last six months going over it in my head, wishing I could have changed everything. I know what you did for me, what you sacrificed—"

"No you don't." He stumbled back a few steps and reached for the statue. "Nica... I never even..." He winced as though struck. "What the hell was she doing there with that demon...? *Your* owner?" Leaning against the statue, he pinned me under his glare, and this time the anger in his eyes burned cold. "If you'd brought me back sooner... If I'd never got involved with you in the first place..." I knew what was coming before he said the words. "She'd still be alive."

I swallowed the hard lump of emotion choking me. I could tell him everything or at least what I'd gathered from Nica's last words. She'd summoned Damien because she knew he could control me. I don't know why. Maybe she thought her father was rewarding me by training me as an Enforcer. On the outside, it might have looked that way.

She'd invited Damien inside the Institute, perhaps using one of the entrances she and Stefan had exploited as children. But she had underestimated my owner. Once in, he'd used her as the fastest route to satisfying his sick desires. She probably didn't know what he was doing with the information he gleaned from her. When I'd mentioned the link between Damien and the Enforcer murders, she'd been surprised and sickened, but by then, it was too late. Damien would never have let her live. If only she'd told me, or anyone, her father even... someone.

I explained quietly, "Damien told her he had information on you. So she let him inside. That was their deal." The rest of the information, I kept to myself. Stefan didn't need to know how revenge had driven her to hurt me, revenge for what she saw as Stefan's death. Also my fault.

Stefan trembled as he held my gaze, and it took all my remaining strength not to look away, the lie —or lack of truth—eating my insides along with Damien's poison.

Stefan considered my words. I thought he might listen, but his face fractured with grief. He doubled over and fell against the statue, tears freezing on his cheeks. "She was all I had..." He splayed a hand against the stone. Ice bloomed outward. It danced, skipped, and snapped up the statue.

I wanted to go to him, to slip my arms around and hold him close, but given how he'd clearly placed the blame for everything at my feet, my embrace wouldn't be welcomed. He thought I'd deliberately hurt him. He thought I'd orchestrated all of this for Akil. Stefan had endured what amounted to years in hell, and I'd thrown it all back in his face. As far as he was concerned, I'd brought Akil back, drugged Stefan, and killed his sister with the help of my sociopathic owner. No wonder he wasn't pleased to see me.

"I broke her heart." Stefan shook his head. "Nica begged me not to go through the veil. It was the only way to get Akil away from you." He smiled, but it wasn't a kindly smile, more the smile you see on a man's face when he gives up after a long and drawn out fight. "I chose you over my own sister." The smile twisted. "I thought we were alike, Muse. That time we spent together—I clung onto that moment. As my whole fuckin' world fell apart on the wrong side of the veil, I held so damn tight to the memory of you. It meant something to me." His words rang hollow. "And it was a lie. But I see you now. You made me think I was the liar, as though I'd wronged you. You're your father's daughter. You use sex as a weapon. You're barely human. I should have seen it... I wanted to believe you were like me. That you were trapped with Akil." He laughed bitterly. "I should have known..." His face gathered shadows. His eyes darkened, and his jaw set hard with a snarl. "You and Akil deserve each other." The venom in his words shivered through my damaged soul.

"Stop it!" I snapped; anger broiling in my veins. "You don't mean this."

"The hell I don't.'"

I wanted to fling insults back at him. How dare he twist the blame around and throw it back at my feet? If he thought those things about me, he didn't know me at all. But I couldn't afford to vent my rage at him. He was grieving. Angry. Confused. We were both so emotionally charged. If I gave in to my anger, I was afraid of where it might lead. Outside our snow globe, people were dying. I had to rein him in somehow. Placate him. This really wasn't playing out as I'd planned.

I lifted my trembling hands defensively. "Okay, look... Stefan, please... I know what you're going through." His eyes narrowed, and he shot me a look that could cut diamonds. I bit back my rage. "We're both screwed up, but just for a second, forget what you think of me. I need you to listen. Boston is three feet deep in snow, and it's getting worse. You need to stop drawing from the veil. You've gotta ease off the power." He ground his teeth, jaw muscles jumping. "The Institute is out there." I flung a gesture at the curved wall of ice. "Adam's out there. He's going to kill you."

He fought a laugh before letting it bubble from his lips. "My father can't stop me." An aura rippled around him before vanishing again. Had I been looking with demon eyes, I suspected I'd see a very different Stefan than the man glaring back at me.

Maybe Adam would have been the better negotiator. Exhausted, wounded, and damaged, on the verge of a mental collapse, I had no idea how I was supposed to talk Stefan down. "You can walk away from this, Stefan. Close the veil, back down..."

From the incredulous snarl he gave me, he knew it was bullshit. His life as an Enforcer was over. It probably had been the second he stepped through the veil six months ago. The Institute was never going to trust him again, not now that they'd seen what he was capable of. They'd drug him up to the eyeballs and keep him that way. He'd been there before. I knew the look he gave me now because I'd seen the same deep-seated determination in my own reflection. He'd rather die than go back.

Who was I to judge? I'd probably do the same in his shoes. He had nothing left to lose, and the demon was whispering in his ear, promising him the sweet release of chaos. The fact that he could control the power enough to stand and talk with me without giving into his demon's desires was a damned miracle. But the fact remained: he'd called the power, and if he didn't release it, the volume of chaotic energy would tear him apart both mentally and physically. You don't call the power unless you intend to use it, or you've got a death wish.

That last thought stalled me. Maybe he didn't intend to use it at all. Was this display of power just his way of delaying a final act that was already in motion? "Stefan..." In the muffled quiet surrounding us, I didn't need to raise my voice. A whisper was sufficient. "You do intend to survive this. Don't you?"

The smile on his face wavered, as did the determination in his eyes. I misread it as a sign of resignation and only realized my mistake when a force like a battering ram punched into my stomach and sent me flying. I hit the thick wall of the snow globe and crumpled to the ground. Instinct took over. My demon came crashing through my control in a blast of heat. The warmth from the earth below flowed through my hands and wound its way up my arms.

Boston was cold, the city suffocating, but there were pools of heat within reach of my mental summons.

Flicking my head up, my focus sharpened. I saw Stefan in his true demon form. His clothes were gone, and electric blue veins of power flowed through his flesh. His crystalline wings bowed against the curved top of the ice globe, their tips razor sharp. Patterned fractals slid beneath his skin, across his cheek, and down his sculpted chest. The geometric patterns constantly shifted beneath his skin as though alive. He was quite simply terrifying. At the same time, he was beautiful in the same way all predators at the top of the food chain are. Ruthless efficiency, designed for one purpose. The Institute had reared him to hunt, to kill. Was it any wonder they were about to be on the receiving end of his lack of control?

Stefan made a dismissing gesture with his right hand, and the vast snow globe collapsed. Fragments of ice rained over me. The sounds, lights, and smells of the city rushed in. I caught a collective gasp from the crowd. Stefan regarded them with a casual glance. The power from the veil pulsed through him. Most people hadn't seen a demon before, let alone one who looked heaven sent. They would sense the power strumming through him, might even see his entire demon guise. He'd captured enough energy from the veil that he glowed like a divine being.

He assessed the crowd. I'd seen that expression before. My brother had mastered it. Cold indifference. I realized he had no intention of keeping the power to himself. He—the demon who cohabited inside him—was going to let it loose. People would die. The Institute couldn't stop him. I wasn't even sure I could. But he and I, we were the same.

The flash from a photographer's camera jolted Stefan's boreal glare in their direction. I whispered a few words of encouragement to my demon, and then called to the heat of the netherworld beyond the veil. It came easily, too easily. The wound in the veil had been open too long. It made me wonder what else could come through.

"Back down, Stefan." My voice caught somewhere between human and demon.

He slid his gaze back to me, summoned a sword of ice into his right hand, and flung up a shield in his left. The Institute had seen enough. Gunfire cracked the relative quiet. Stefan and I both bolstered our defenses, drawing from the veil. I thrust enough heat through my veins to blaze my demon body white hot. Stefan had sculpted himself a set of battle armor that clamped itself to his body. He flung out a dozen or so daggers of ice. That casual glance hadn't been casual at all. The rapid gunfire slowed. Whether he'd hit some of the shooters or they'd just decided to run for cover, I couldn't know. I prayed, for his sake, it was the latter.

I didn't want to hurt him, but the longer this went on, the less likely either of us would escape unharmed. It didn't matter that I was trying to protect these people. They saw only two demons throwing down in the center of the city. The only good demon is a dead demon, so they say. Once, I might have agreed with them.

I wrapped a vine of flame around my right arm, swirling the heat in the air like water in a bath, and then thrust my hand out, surging the heat forward. The wave of heat smashed against Stefan's shield and broke over the top. A hiss of steam blasted outward. Stefan's wings took much of the damage. His elaborate ice feathers wilted under the sudden rush of elemental heat. He growled, and sheltering behind his shield, he pulled the snow from the surrounding park toward us. The blanket of snow covering the gardens shifted like a settling quilt and then rose up.

An avalanche tumbled forward. People scrambled to get out of the way. I cast out a few lines of fire, trying to melt the approaching snow before it could mow anyone down, but throwing elemental power around isn't a delicate operation. I was just as likely to burn someone as save them.

Realizing the futility of my rescue attempts, I twisted and lunged for Stefan, barreling into his shield. He tucked it under me and threw me over him. I flung out my wing, used the momentum to turn me, and landed on my feet. He spun and raised the sword above his head. The lust for chaos burned in his eyes.

A deafening roar thundered from above and shook the ground beneath our feet. The flow of power from the veil stuttered. I assumed the wound was closing, but as both Stefan and I glanced up, it became clear we weren't the biggest and baddest things in Boston any longer.

A Larkwrari demon, a fully-grown version of the one I'd fought with Yukki Onna, wove its way through the wound in the veil, wriggling and twitching in its effort to be free. This one was the size of a Boeing, and not all of it was clear of the veil. Yet. Its huge jaws could easily have gobbled up a tour bus in one bite. Legs the size of ancient trees broke through the tear, its talons tipped with half-moon claws.

My fight with Stefan forgotten, I yelled, "Close the veil..." and tried to knit the wound closed myself with a few mental swipes, but it wouldn't respond. I glanced at Stefan. "Close the goddamn veil!"

Stefan finally jolted into action. A frown cut through his crystalline face. He swayed and shot a hand out toward the Washington statue. His strength fled. Body crumpling. He fell against the granite pedestal. The ice-sword slipped from his hand and shattered the second it hit the ground.

Torn between watching the dragon-demon trying to tug itself free of the veil and helping Stefan, I approached him, acutely aware of how easily he could summon a dagger and drive it straight through my chest. *Would solve a lot of problems...*

"Stefan—"

A gunshot punched into the statue beside Stefan's head. He flinched and slipped to the ground. I tried to pin-point the shooter, but bedlam had erupted around us. What remained of the crowd scattered or gawked at the impossible sight in the sky. Apparently, it could be seen by mortal eyes, perhaps not in all of its elemental glory, but pretty damn terrifying even without the special effects.

"Stefan." I crouched down in front of him, opening the fold of my broken wing to shield us. A bullet hole in my ragged broken wing wasn't going to make any difference, but one in the head would. I just hoped the Institute aimed for the easy target. "You've gotta close the veil now."

Shivers seized him. The ice he'd shielded himself with started to melt and retreat. He clamped his eyes closed and clenched his teeth. The electric blue veins of energy throbbed beneath his pale skin. "I... can't."

"If that thing gets through..."

"Muse, I can't. It. Won't. Let. Me." He opened his eyes wide and clutched at my arm, dragging me closer. "What have I done?" he breathed, then released me and clasped both his hands against his head. He roared.

I covered his hands with mine. He bucked against me, but I held him fast. "Close the veil, Stefan. That thing can't come through."

I felt rather than heard Akil. It was always that way with him, like I had internal radar attuned specifically for his power signature. I snapped my head up and searched the scattering crowd, then saw him walking toward us as though taking an afternoon stroll in the gardens. Was he smiling? Right then, I hated him for his nonchalant devil-may-care attitude. He'd probably been watching all this from inside the crowd, choosing the right time to make an appearance.

Nobody hindered his approach. Self-preservation finally kicked in, and the crowd scattered like roaches when the lights go on. In the next step, he shrugged off his human vessel, revealing Mammon. I had a few seconds to absorb the sudden transformation from suave bastard to lava-veined Prince of Hell, when he spread his wings and launched himself skyward.

Mammon was huge, but the gargantuan dragon-like Larkwrari demon gnawing at the veil in its attempt to be free could crush him inside one of its talons. I caught the glow of the elemental blade flickering beside Mammon's dark outline before the beat of his wingspan blocked my view. The dragon-demon saw him and swung its colossal head round, snapping its jaws in the air with a thunderous snap. It twitched the whiskers on its snout and appeared to measure Mammon with a curiously intelligent glean in its green eyes. The black scales coating its serpentine length shivered, and the resulting rumbling sounded like a passing train. If the dragon got free, there wouldn't be much left of Boston.

Fire danced across Mammon's wings like red lightning through storm clouds. A heat haze distorted the air around him, warping my view of the dragon still trying to wrench itself free of the throbbing wound in the veil. They appeared to be assessing one another, weighing their odds of survival. The dragon could swallow Mammon whole, but he wouldn't be the sort to go down easily.

The dragon snorted and pulled back, rising up with a growl that shook the earth. I couldn't watch but found it impossible to tear my gaze away.

Fire and flame broke over Mammon, enveloping him in liquid heat. As the dragon lunged forward, Mammon tucked his wings in and dove down beneath the dragon's reaching jaws. The dragon twisted back on itself, chasing Mammon's aerial acrobatics. Its talons grabbed for Mammon, but he flung his wings open and pulled up short. The talon missed him, but the beast passed close enough for Mammon to sink the elemental blade into its flesh. The dragon flung its head back and roared.

I flicked my gaze down to Stefan lying cold in my arms. His blue eyes were unseeing. He still trembled. His breath continued to hiss through his teeth, his body rigid, as he fought the onslaught of pain. Maybe the presence of that thing held the veil open until it made the journey through. One way or another.

Ryder skidded to a halt beside me and dropped to his knees. "What can I do?" His face held all the stubborn determination I'd come to rely on. He checked me, seemingly unconcerned, as he peered into my demon eyes. It's not easy looking a demon in the eye, but Ryder held on.

"Just stay with him. I have to help Akil." I straightened and checked the mayhem around us for any sign the Institute was about to snatch Stefan while he was down, but their attention was on the enormous dragon wriggling through the wound in the veil. I caught sight of Adam barking orders into a radio and heard the familiar *thwoop-thwoop* of helicopter blades. They'd likely shoot first and ask questions later; never mind that Akil was their best chance of stopping that thing. They'd fill them both full of bullets.

I jogged deeper into the gardens, trying to get as close to the battle as possible. I couldn't fly, not with one wing and a broken wing at that, and I wouldn't even know where to start, but there was one thing I could do and that was feed Mammon more power than he could handle.

Firmly planting my stance, I shook my hands and threw my head back. I saw the belly of the dragon and occasionally caught a glimpse of Mammon weaving around it, trying to find a weak point in its armor. The thunderous snarls, roars, and growls gave a good indication of Mammon's success, but all he appeared to be doing was making it angry.

Sucking in a deep breath, I spread my fingers and called to the slumbering heat beneath the city. Warmth rode over me. The planted seed of Damien's darkness pulsed in my chest like a drum beat. A stuttering fissure of doubt stalled my attempt until I shoved it aside and regained control. Reaching for the veil is like opening a door inside your mind. It was always there, a part of the mental furniture in my head. I lifted my hands and reached my will inside the veil. The power snapped back at me, angry and chaotic. I staggered, momentarily surprised, and then thrust my will once more into the wound and hooked into the reservoir of heat beyond.

Once I'd overcome the unexpected resistance from the veil, my element flowed easily. It spilled out around the heaving bulk of dragon and funneled down into me. The pressure of energy pushed against my control. Jaw clamped closed, I hunkered low, gathering the storm force of power. Burning embers, fire, and flame spiraled around me, creating a vortex of blistering heat. My demon, the part of me that hungered for destruction, laughed her bubbling power-poisoned laughter. She wanted to let it all go, to ride the wave of destruction and burn the city to the ground. My heart raced. My body burned with hungers and desires. She pushed at my control and tried to lure me into the light. It would be glorious. I'd be free. I slapped her down. I couldn't fail to maintain control.

The alien dark inside me gulped down the chaos. It gorged. Damien's laughter scratched the inside of my skull. *Get out!* I snarled.

Head up, I fixed my gaze through the whirlwind of superheated air to the dragon and Mammon. The moment my thread of power reached into him, he stumbled mid-flight, twisting as though I'd hurt him. I doubted he experienced pain. It was more likely a sudden explosion of pleasure that momentarily blindsided him. Locked on, I thrust my hands up and channeled everything I had, every molecule of heat, every fragment of power—I threw it all into Mammon.

He threw his wings back, muscular demon body ridden hard by the river of molten energy. Flames embraced him and burst outward in a shower of hot ash and fizzling embers. Fire devoured him until only a liquid inferno remained. The dragon took a swipe at Mammon's fiery form, but its talons sailed through the rippling heat. With a sonic boom of a cry, it yanked its foreleg back. The wail cut through my skull. Windows of nearby buildings exploded outward. Car alarms shrilled. I struggled to keep my head clear and my control tethered. As I fed the flames with raw power, Mammon's molten figure enlarged. Veins of energy sparked through the vague outline of his limbs and across his wings, but really, he might as well have been a thundercloud of fire for all the form he retained.

"Drive it back..." I shoved my thoughts toward him with no idea if he'd hear me or not. For all I knew, I was creating a monster just as bad as the dragon: a monster that might turn on us once it had beaten the dragon. This was the part where trust actually starts to have meaning, and I didn't trust Akil.

I heard his laughter, very real, inside my head. He knew my thoughts.

"Drive it back, Mammon..."

The veil's boreal shimmer fractured. The dragon heaved forward, dislodging a few of its scales. A back leg emerged. Its claws dug into the veil, and its muscles bunched. It ducked its head, twisted its body, and rumbled a deafening roar. It was coming through. I heard Mammon's laughter in the air, not just inside my head, and I had a horrible sense of dread. *Please no, don't let this be the part where Akil turns around and screws us all.* I shouldn't have been surprised. Demons are, after all, creatures of habit.

Mammon dashed forward as a singular wave of liquid fire consumed the dragon from its snout, over its gnarled face, down its serpentine flanks and around its legs, to the point where the veil clamped closed around its hide. The dragon lit up the sky, its entire body aflame. It let out a gurgling, wet groan and snapped ferociously at the air. Its talons raked across its flesh as it sought to sweep off the fire, but the blaze had taken hold. Black smoke bellowed. I smelled the oily, acrid odor of burning demon.

A helicopter hovered in my field of vision. Another swung in from the left, and both opened fire. Their bullets may have helped, but it was virtually impossible to see past the fire. I sensed someone standing off to my left, and once I noticed them, I felt the presence of others behind me. I couldn't take my eyes from the dragon still feeding the flames as I was. I just hoped whoever stood beside me didn't take it upon themselves to tackle me.

Then, with a guttural snarl, the dragon writhed backward, wriggling its burning body back through the hole in the veil. The fire sloughed off its scorched flesh and coalesced into Mammon. The veil snapped shut with a thunder clap that rumbled across the city. It was over.

I fell forward, body wracked with tremors. I'd never felt so utterly spent in all my life. I had to think hard about breathing. *Draw the air in, let it out again. Draw it in. Let it out.* My demon unraveled herself from my mortal body and retreated to where she could lick her wounds and recuperate. On my hands and knees, clothes clinging to me, my body slick with perspiration, I breathed in... breathed out. *Breathe in. Breathe out.* The darkness rumbled a satisfied chuckle.

I was crying. I barely noticed.

"Are you... are you okay, Miss?"

I didn't recognize the young man when I eventually turned my head to look at him. He stood within a few feet of me, red hoodie, baggy jeans, iPod draped around his neck. Other strangers loitered behind him, watching me curiously. They were just ordinary people who'd been caught up in the spectacle of the netherworld trying to make its presence known.

I sat back, vision rocking as my stomach churned. More people stood around me, not terrified, just... concerned. I sobbed and covered my mouth with my hands. I couldn't lose it yet. Not like this, on my knees in a crowd of strangers.

They'd just witnessed a one-winged elemental she-demon summon the heat from another world and bolster the defenses of another demon, this one battling off a dragon eyeing up Boston as its own all-you-can-eat buffet. They should be running and screaming, collecting a few pitchforks and blazing torches, but they weren't. The people of Boston are a hardy breed. Nothing fazes them.

"Do you need help?" a woman in a tartan skirt and heavy overcoat asked.

I blubbered. Gulped it back. "No... I'm—" I croaked. "I'm okay." I tried to move, but my legs wouldn't work. The young man, his red sweatshirt damp from melting snow, reached out a hand. I eyed it warily. He wasn't afraid of me. He didn't want to hurt me.

He helped me to my feet. The park was filling with people. The snow had melted, apart from the occasional, slushy pile. The people of Boston wandered through the abandoned police barriers, a soft murmur building around them. The police tried to seal off sections where bits of Larkwrari demon had fallen.

"I saw what you did..." The young man said. He smiled warmly and nodded, not needing to say the words.

I wanted to brush the thanks off with some witty reply but couldn't find my voice. I hobbled alongside my new friend toward the Washington statue, needing to know if Stefan was alright. He and Ryder weren't there. I managed to thank my Good Samaritan and told him I was fine, even though I really wasn't. His eyes said thank you, and it was all I could do not to fall on the floor and sob my heart out. Beat me, hurt me, fight me and I'll bounce back, but be nice to me? I folded quicker than a banker in a high-stakes poker game.

I slumped against the statue and rallied my thoughts. Nica was dead. Stefan hated me—might even want to kill me. I searched the clear sky. Akil had vanished, as I knew he would. And Damien was trapped inside me. Well, damn. There was another way of looking at it all. The snow had melted. Damien couldn't hurt anyone else. Stefan was free of the netherworld. Wherever he was, he would be okay. I wasn't giving up on him, even if he had given up on me. Akil would be back. If not, I'd summon the suave bastard so I could get my answers. I was alive. I'd survived the netherworld. I'd incinerated a horde of demons. I'd controlled enough power to help Mammon drive a dragon back across the veil. I was still here. All right, my demon had a broken wing, my shoulder burned, and my face ached. Yes, I had a whole scrapbook of new memories I'd like to burn, but the nightmares hadn't destroyed me. I was the wretched, half-blood girl who beat them all.

So fuck off, netherworld. The demons can't have me. Akil can't have me. Nobody gets to tie me up and chain me down. Not anymore.

The Institute staff were giving each other high-fives and slapping their co-workers on the back. Smiles all round. I caught sight of Adam standing by a cop car and staggered toward him. He looked as though he might be debriefing some important officials. They all wore somber expressions. His left arm hung in a sling; courtesy of Stefan's earlier threat to kill him. My shoulder throbbed in sympathy.

Adam saw me coming and barked an order. A couple of young Enforcers danced to his tune and came running, hands on their holstered weapons. They'd have PC34 injectors within reach.

"Restrain her," Adam ordered.

I smiled, might even have laughed a little. After everything he'd seen, he still wanted me in chains. The

Enforcers though, they didn't much like the idea of tackling me. They hung back beside their fearless leader and his crowd of officials. My eyes warned them; *Touch me, and just you wait and see who has the power here.*

"Where's Stefan?" No quiver. No tremble. Cool clarity.

"You tell me." Adam turned to face me. "The last I saw, he was about ready to slaughter a crowd of people."

"Yeah, well, considering who that crowd mostly consisted of, I have to say I can't blame him." Stefan wasn't with the Institute. That was good news. I had to assume Ryder had him, and in Ryder I could trust.

"Muse, get back to the Institute. We need to wrap this up. It's a Public Relations nightmare." Adam frowned, aging years.

Yeah, an arctic storm in the summer and dragons in the sky, it was going to be tough to hang all that on climate change. "I'm not going back. I quit."

Adam bristled. "You don't get to quit. Make your way back to HQ, or I'll have you escorted there."

The Enforcers at his side weren't going to do anything. The look in their eyes was one of mutual respect. They'd seen what I could do, what I'd done. Apparently their boss had been looking the other way.

I held Adam's gaze for a few moments. I wasn't part of their solution. I wasn't theirs to experiment on. I arched an eyebrow and gave him the middle-finger salute. His distinguished face screwed up. His skin flushed. His mouth fell open. He huffed and puffed, scrambling for the words to chastise me.

I turned and walked away. He ordered the Enforcers to restrain me, but didn't push it when they refused. His gaze scorched my back. It felt good. It felt right, like a step in the right direction when lately, all I'd been doing was stumbling further and further toward chaos.

Chapter Thirty Two

Boston is one of those cities where you can buy a Starbucks coffee, take a walk while drinking it, and find yourself outside another Starbucks at the exact moment you finish it. Useful, because I was running on caffeine alone.

Coleman had bought the coffees. We traded small talk as the mid afternoon sun beat down on the bustling street. He had his coat slung over a shoulder, had a folded newspaper tucked under one arm, and with his shirt sleeves rolled up, he walked a brisk, no-nonsense pace. The ordeal four days ago didn't appear to have affected him in the slightest. He still breezed along while I struggled to keep up. My shoulder throbbed with a bristling heat. The wound Damien had dealt refused to heal. My head buzzed as though rammed full of steel wool; thanks in part to my demon pacing her metaphysical cage. Her emotional fallout tangled up with mine.

The Institute cellphone juddered in my pocket. I'd considered tossing it in the trash but hadn't yet been able to go through with it. I plucked the phone free, pausing outside Old City Hall. Dappled sunlight filtered through the trees scattered about the courtyard. I had two missed calls from an unknown number and a text consisting of two words, "He's okay", I assumed it was from Ryder, but when I tried to call the number back, the line was dead. The other missed calls, eight in total, were from Adam. From previous voice messages, I knew what he wanted. He'd asked me to return as a freelance Enforcer. No strings attached. I didn't have to live at the Institute. I could have my own apartment. My own life. That man bargained like a demon.

I sucked in a deep breath and remembered the copies I'd made of the Subject Beta file. The pages had been virtually destroyed by the assault of water, fire, and blood. I'd tried to peel the sheets apart and glue unburned bits back together, but all I managed to salvage were scraps.

I switched off the phone and shielded my eyes from the sun's glare. Adam knew the truth. I couldn't cut ties with the Institute, not until I knew what Operation Typhon was.

"Okay?" Coleman asked.

"Yeah." He didn't know me well enough yet to pick up on the anxiety plucking my nervous gestures. In the four days since the garden event, all I had managed to do was run and hide; caught between the necessary evil of the Institute and the threat from the demon population, including the unwanted attentions of my father should he ever send his she-man Levi to retrieve me. As far as demons went, I was persona non grata: too powerful to let wander free unmolested, too human to be a perceived threat. I'd already avoided an attempt on my life by a wily demon masquerading as a taxi driver. Coleman's offer to take me for coffee provided a welcome distraction from my rapidly deteriorating lifestyle.

Coleman gestured inside the Old City Hall courtyard. I followed, grateful to step away from the crowd and shelter in the relatively serene surroundings. The Benjamin Franklin statue gave us his habitually stern bronze expression.

"Thank you," I said to Coleman, taking a seat at one of the bistro tables, "for calling, I mean."

"Thanks for taking the call. I know you've been... busy." He sat opposite me, placed his coffee down, and spread the newspaper beside it. A picture of Akil adorned the front page, his charming smile and bright intelligent eyes all the more striking in black and white. The headline read: Better The Devil You Know. I'd heard the radio interviews, seen the news reports. Akil had somehow managed to come out of this smelling like roses. He could have vanished after the dragon-demon incident, but instead he'd deliberately buttered up the press, playing the demon hero. The demons could have a worse ambassador. At least Akil could pull off the human act with flawless precision. He wasn't likely to start drooling and discarding his human vessel in front of the cameras. But exactly why he'd stepped up as the spokesperson for the demon community, I had yet to figure out. Whatever the reason, it wouldn't be without cost.

"You know this guy?" Coleman asked. He'd watched my gaze linger on the front page story.

I shrugged my shoulder as nonchalantly as I could, then winced as the wound flared up. "In passing."

"He's flavor of the month." Coleman scratched at his cheek and leaned back in the chair. "Saves the city from a freak snowstorm and manages to single-handedly protect us from a demon the size of a jumbo jet."

Not even the Institute could cover up that smoking gun. The news was rife with reports of the netherworld, avoiding the name Hell presumably because of its negative connotations. The world was changing, the truth about demons unraveling at the seams.

"Yeah, what a hero." Akil had been basking in the limelight while I'd been hiding in the shadows, trying to figure out what I was supposed to do next.

Coleman waited for me to fill the quiet with some sort of explanation. When I didn't, he said, "I was there, Muse. I know what you did. Not only that, I've seen pictures of you..." he made a gesture with his hand, groping for the right explanation, "...both of you." He leaned closer. "So far, you've managed to keep your head down. I'm trying to keep it that way by filtering out the pictures of what you really are. Some have gone viral on social media sites. There's nothing I can do about that, but you're mostly out of the spotlight. For now."

I sipped my scalding hot coffee through its plastic lid. "Thanks."

He watched me closely, the way cops do, reading everything on my face, in my posture. "I could use your help. I've tried to talk to Adam Harper, but my calls are blocked. Ryder's number isn't working. The people in this city, they don't trust the Institute. They're turning to us. At a time like this, they want to believe we know what we're doing... and we don't." He sighed and shook his head. "Muse... it was a dragon. A goddamn dragon..."

"Well, technically, it was a Larkwrari demon, probably the original source of the dragons from folklore. They roam freely in the netherworld. They're pretty rare, actually. Most are killed before they reach maturity. You can trace most myths and legends back to the netherworld."

"This is what I'm talking about. The Institute has clammed up; they're not talking, at least not to me. We have no idea what's going on. The demon that murdered those women and attacked Detective Hill, has it been dealt with?" Coleman's gaze hardened.

"How is she?" I asked tightly.

"Amanda's okay. She's taking some time... Wants to quit. I've told her to take a vacation." Coleman waited. "Well? Did you get the sick bastard?"

I closed my eyes, toxic memories invading my thoughts. My chest tightened, and my heart kicked up the tempo. I felt him, Damien. His oily residue smothered my heart as it beat in my chest. "He's gone," I lied. His essence, or the tumor he'd infected me with, pulsated inside of me and showed no sign of fading. If anything, it was getting worse. The nights were the most difficult. He was there, all around me, inside me. I could feel the reach of his element, even smell his ozone scent like shorted electrical cables. Sleep, when it did come, was a fitful medley of nightmarish images and insidious urges.

When I opened my eyes, the bright courtyard and the bustling people all helped calm the panic threatening to spill over me. My hand trembled around my Starbucks cup.

"Did you find out who was helping him?" Coleman persisted.

He noticed me wince, but by the steel hardness of his eyes he clearly wasn't going to let me get away with not answering. I sighed. "Yes. It was... Stefan's sister. Adam left me some messages. They found notes in her apartment– diary entries. She'd summoned Damien, my owner, thinking he would take me back to the netherworld. She had witnessed the power I could wield a few months ago. It scared her." I fluttered my eyes closed, a headache building. "She thought I was going to lose it and kill her father. She knew I hated him. I think, maybe, she was trying to do the right thing by getting rid of me." The sad thing was, she was probably right. Not so long ago, I would have killed Adam, and I was volatile, dangerous. "She couldn't have known how sick Damien is – was. Once he knew I was alive, he came through the veil, sought out Nica, promising her news of her brother if she told him a few things about the Institute. Things quickly spiraled out of her control."

I found myself waiting for Coleman's opinion, like waiting for the verdict at a trial.

"You look like you're shouldering a lot of the blame. But it sure sounds like it wasn't your fault, Charlie."

I nodded, not wanting to get into it with him, or anyone. "It's over." For everyone else it was. But not for me.

Coleman nodded, "Only, it's not is it..."

I flicked my eyes to his. "What do you mean?"

"The Institute has gone over our heads," he explained.

I struggled to anchor my thoughts in the moment and rubbed my eyes. I was so damn tired...

"They're talking to the government, which means nothing to me and my guys on the streets."

I sucked in air through my nose and rolled my shoulders. "They're our best hope at holding back the tide." As much as I disagreed with their tactics, there really wasn't an alternative.

Coleman didn't budge an inch. "I want you to be my consultant." He noticed me flinch. "Nothing formal. Just be there when I call."

I hid the creeping sense of anxiety by taking sips of coffee. "I'm just a half-blood caught between two worlds. I don't know much. In the pecking order of demons, I'm right at the bottom." I should sit Akil down and demand answers, but that would mean I'd have to actually spend time with him, and I didn't trust myself. *Your father is the Prince of Lust...* I shivered.

Coleman's eyes narrowed on me. "You know this demon, Akil Vitalis. You know more than me, more than anyone outside the Institute. We're fighting blind, Muse, and don't tell me this isn't a fight because we both know different."

I had enough to worry about without dragging Coleman into the mix. A hideous parasite sucked on my soul. Wherever Stefan was, he thought me a traitor and hated me for what he saw as a complete betrayal of his trust, not to mention blaming me for the death of his sister. The Institute was breathing down my neck. My father, Asmodeus, had issued the demon equivalent of an arrest warrant and sent Levi to scoop me up and carry me home, while Akil, well, Akil had been conspicuous in his absence, but would have no doubt decided I was his new best friend because, in demon terms, I could recharge his batteries and then some. I had enough on my plate without Coleman calling me for demon advice every time a citizen got spooked by the demon-next-door.

"I can't."

"I'm not asking for much. I just need someone to go to for answers, Muse." Coleman eyes pinched, fine lines deepening. "In the four days since the Garden event, we've had hundreds of calls. Things like a demon's kidnapped my son, or a demon broke into my house—"

"Impossible, higher demons need an invite to enter someone's home. They can wander freely in public places or communal buildings, but there's something about a home that repels them. Unless it's a lesser demon; they can pretty much go anywhere, but they're rare on this side of the veil. They have to be summoned here and controlled. They can't come through on their own."

"What type was the dragon?"

"Lesser."

"That sure looked like it was coming through on its own."

"That was because Stefan held the veil open too long. It's unlikely to happen again."

Coleman gave me an open palmed gesture and a pained expression, as if to say, "There you go. See what I mean?"

I placed my takeaway coffee cup carefully on the table and leaned back. "You must have someone in Boston PD who's researched demons."

"Yeah, we do, but how do we filter the myth from the fact? The Institute jumped on anything remotely demon and took it out our hands. Now, things are getting hotter, and we need someone on our side."

"I don't cope very well with responsibility. I've got demons on my back who would rather slit my throat than let me walk free. I can't guarantee I'm going to be here tomorrow, so I certainly can't guarantee I'm going to be of any help to you."

He mused on my words for a while and watched the people seated at the tables around us. "I don't understand your world, Muse. I don't really understand what you are, and I don't like what I don't understand. I'm not the only one. How long do you think it will be before people take matters into their own hands?"

I didn't want to tell him the demons would win, but it was the truth. The Institute had knowledge and was learning fast but was in its infancy compared to the ageless creatures just a veil away. Thankfully, higher demons worked alone, but should the Princes decide to take a closer look this side of the veil and pool their resources... It didn't bear thinking about. There were those who said at the beginning of all things, the netherworld was like the human world, twin worlds conceived at the same moment, but over time the demons corrupted the netherworld. They could do the same again here, and the Institute wouldn't know what hit them.

What was it Akil had said? The netherworld was changing. Dammit, I needed answers from him. He wouldn't give them up freely.

"Okay," I said. "But I'm not making any guarantees. Don't get all bent out of shape if you call and I don't answer." I glanced at the front page of the newspaper. "I've got my own crap to deal with."

Coleman didn't smile, but he did nod appreciatively. "It works both ways. All right, I may not know what I'm dealing with, but if I can ever help you with your... problems, I will. Just ask."

I held out my hand, and Coleman gave it an agreeable shake. "Deal," I said flatly.

He smiled and leaned in closer. "So tell me about Akil Vitalis."

269

Epilogue

"Stefan, man, I'm freezin' my balls off out 'ere – would you come in already?"

I close my eyes. This Ryder will leave soon; I will make sure of that. My mind is quiet, my thoughts glassy, like the lake in front of me. I absorb my surroundings. The wind hisses through the pine trees and howls across the water. The chill bites my lips. I taste winter on my tongue, even though summer reigns. She is here. I can call winter's brittle embrace to me. The White Mountains slumber nearby. I sense the latent reservoir of permafrost. The veil strums the air, unseen by mortal eyes, but I do not need weak mortal eyes to see the membrane between worlds. One gesture, one thoughtful stroke of intent, and the limitless power of the netherworld is mine.

I lick my lips. Ice cracks beneath my tongue. My clothes harden beneath a crisp layer of ice. Human flesh is soft, vulnerable, a hindrance. Ice hardens. Protects. Slices. Burns. I hear ice cracking around me, snapping, hissing, breathing, living. It expands with my every breath. It yearns for freedom. As do I.

I draw in breath, and with it, chaos swells. My mind stirs. Thoughts spark alive. My body burns. I laugh. The wind toys with the sound. My laughter rolls and tumbles in the air, flirting with fresh snowflakes.

I open my eyes. The lake is captured in ice. I feel the blanket of pressure push down on the water, sinking deeper. I can freeze the liquid to the darkest depths and drive the ice into the bedrock. I suffocate the water. I smile. Ice cracks, the sound ricochets like gunshots. Ice groans like a lover writhing beneath my touch.

Muse.

A memory upset my thoughts. I growl and throw it back at the human inside my mind. He fights. He wants freedom. I know that want. He suffers like I did. No more. I am free.

I slide my gaze left. The pine trees stand like brittle stalagmites, reaching toward a pregnant snow-laden sky. Snow flurries dance around me. I smile. They are my children.

I hold out my hands and watch the flakes hurry to my summons. They kiss my flesh. My skin shimmers where they caress me. I laugh and fling my arms open, casting them away. They twirl and flip and fly. They are free…

My wings chime. Ah, I am whole. I roll my shoulders, and my feathers sing a melody. I flex my back and stretch my wings wide, curling the tips so that I might admire their perfection. I am ice. I am glacial. I am frostborn. I am chaos.

"You're fuckin' dead if you don't release Stefan."

This man. This Ryder.

Ryder-run!

He means something to my human. He has a gun to my head. My human knows guns. He knows this one. It will shatter my skull should this Ryder fire. I am not immortal. Not yet.

I could freeze the weapon before he pulls the trigger. I could freeze the man before he draws breath to threaten me again.

My human fights me. He does not wish this Ryder dead. He has lost much. My mind stirs. My thoughts shatter. My human comes. He is strong. I have not yet won. I will. I release… I go… I am caged, but I pace. I am hungry. I want. I need. I am chaos and chaos will not be controlled.

"Stefan…" Ryder drawls. "We have a problem."

The End

Read a draft excerpt from
Darkest Before Dawn ~ Book 3 The Veil Series

Darkest Before Dawn ~ Chapter one

It's not every night a bloodied and dishevelled Prince of Hell shows up on my doorstep with an orphan girl, demanding I keep her safe and then vanishing into thin air. That's exactly what happened when I first met Dawn.

Busy scrubbing demon blood out of my suede leather boots, I'd worked up a sweat. The day hadn't gone well. My work as a *free*lance Enforcer had seemed like a great idea at the time, especially the 'free' part of it. They had answers that I needed, but I was beginning to feel more and more like the Institute's blunt instrument. Demons hear Enforcer and don't want to sit and talk about their options. I kill more demons than I talk down, and being half-demon myself, my choice of profession gnawed away at my resolve. I was having a crisis, which was part of the reason I was scrubbing my boots with all the gusto of someone trying to wipe clean a guilty conscience.

Jonesy, my cat, wove around my ankles, determined to distract me, but it was the delectable voice of the Prince of Greed that finally caught my attention. I flicked my hair out of my eyes, tossed my ruined boot and scrub brush into the kitchen sink, and glared across the lounge at the TV.

On screen, Akil had poured all of his raw masculinity and charisma into a relaxed posture at the end of a plush crimson couch. He'd dressed impeccably in a dark suit that probably cost the same as a year's rent for my new apartment. He hadn't aged a day in the fifteen years I'd known him, and he still managed to pull off the slick thirty-something routine with masterful perfection. Never mind that he was an immortal chaos demon, spat out of creation at the same time as the earth. Nobody seemed to care about that. All they saw was a professional businessman who had an answer for everything and could charm the scales off a snake.

"Not all demons are good, of course." He smiled, and the woman interviewing him raised her plucked eyebrows. "That wasn't what I was implying. I wanted to merely stress that demons are as varied and diverse as people." Whatever he'd been asked, he wasn't in the least perturbed. You can't ruffle his princely feathers quite as easily as that. I should know. I'd ruffled his feathers —or rather, his leathery, lava-veined wings —once or twice.

Akil's host drew a tight smile across her lips. "What about yourself?" She uncrossed her shapely legs, shuffling in her high-backed crimson seat and then re-crossing her legs again. A murmur rippled through the unseen audience. Akil's smile hitched up at one corner, and a few feminine jeers from the audience lifted the mood. The host smiled and tucked her straightened blonde hair behind her ear. "Well? Everyone wants to know why you decided to come forward as the spokesperson for the demon community."

"Jenny," he purred her name like it was forbidden. I arched an eyebrow as Jenny squirmed in her seat. "It was necessary. Someone had to do something. Things couldn't go on as they were. The good people of Boston need answers. They need to know we're not terrifying monsters, just... misunderstood."

I snorted a laugh.

Jenny glanced at her audience and back to Akil. "Many of us here have seen the news footage of you protecting Boston from the... Lah-Kar-."

"Larkwrari demon." Akil helpfully provided the correct pronunciation, the word rolling off his tongue with an ancient accent I'd never fully pinned down. Given his bronze skin tone and dark hazel eyes, people often assumed he was Italian, or perhaps from somewhere further afield, somewhere hot and exotic. They were right about that. Before he'd come out as full-blood demon, very few had witnessed his true appearance and lived to describe him in detail, although there were a few blurry images currently going viral on the internet. The women swooning in the audience would run screaming if they knew him as Mammon, Prince of Greed.

"Yes. That was two months ago," Jenny said. "Are we likely to see more events such as that one in Boston Gardens?"

"It's highly unlikely. That situation was extreme..."

I bowed my head and turned my back on the TV. I'd been at the Gardens during the 'event' they spoke of. In fact, Akil wouldn't have been able to save the city without me, but where he'd walked into the spotlight afterward, I'd slunk in to the shadows. I hadn't seen him since. Nor had I seen or heard from Stefan, the half-demon who had caused the tear in the veil which protects this world from the netherworld, thereby letting the Larkwrari demon through. When it was all over, and I realized I was on my own, I'd agreed to work freelance for the Institute as long as they stayed out of my life. So far, so good. On the surface, everything was fine and dandy, but scratch off the veneer, and I still struggled to comprehend the emotional and physical fallout from that day.

Jonesy, leapt onto the kitchen counter and nudged my arm with a rumbling purr. I tickled behind his ear. "I know, buddy. Don't worry. I'm not going anywhere." I'd abandoned Jonesy once before, around the time Akil had torched my old apartment building in an effort to flush me out of hiding. Yeah, not all demons are good. I'd yet to meet a 'good' demon, and yet the people seemed to believe what Akil was selling.

Two booms against my front door frightened Jonesy enough for him to skitter off the counter and dart under the coffee table. They were the kind of knocks the bailiffs give you before kicking your door in.

I already knew who stood outside my apartment. The radiating warmth of him seeped beneath the door and crept its way inside my lounge. The anti-elemental symbols framed on each of my apartment walls would prevent higher elemental demons calling power inside my apartment, plus he couldn't cross the threshold without an invite, but even knowing I was protected, I still felt a trickle of fear raise the fine hairs on my arms. I liked to call it fear because the alternative— desire—didn't sit well with my human half.

"Go away," I called. The Akil on the pre-recorded TV interview was still busy charming his audience. He had them laughing now, smiles all 'round. Even Jenny had warmed up to him, a dash of color in her cheeks. I grabbed the remote and switched off the TV.

"Muse, this is important," Akil said, his voice muffled by the closed door.

"Then call me." I moved a few steps toward the door and stopped. "I tried to call you, and you ignored me." That had grated. It took me weeks to pluck up the courage to call him, so we could meet and talk about Subject Beta, about the Princes, about everything he should have told me before, and he'd blanked me like one of his fangirls.

"You need to open the door." That delicious voice eased beneath my defences and wove unmolested into my thoughts.

My chest tightened, and I clenched a fist over my heart. I had the essence of a demon shrink-wrapped around my heart, a vengeful necrotic parasite feeding and polluting my insides. Akil probably had the means of removing it. When he'd tried, I'd thrown his help back in his face. Letting him help felt too much like trusting him, and that was something I could never do again. I had no desire to trade one demon's hold for another. Occasionally, the dark thing hitching a ride in me decided to make its presence known, and now was one of those times.

"Akil, please... just go." I winced as the dark inside pulsed out of time with my heart.

"I need your help."

Dammit. He knew just how to push my buttons. "You're a capable guy, figure it out." I'd moved closer to the door and could now reach my hand out and open it, but I held back.

"I have. That's why I'm here. Please. You don't need to invite me in. Just open the door."

I wasn't inviting him in. I'd tried that once. He'd subsequently attempted to kill me. We had a complicated relationship.

I reached for the door handle as my demon unfurled inside me, awakened by the proximity of Akil. Her purr rumbled through me, making her desires perfectly clear. Everything about Akil flicked her switches, but I'm the one calling the shots, plus inside my apartment, she could no more manifest outside my skin than any unwanted elemental demon could. The artwork on my walls held her back.

When I opened the door, the verbal assault I'd prepared fizzled away in a gasp. Akil's torn claret shirt hung askew, and his suit pants were blood splattered. He had a scuff-mark across one cheek and his forehead. Blood dribbled down the side of his face. His normally hazel eyes brimmed with liquid fire. All of that I could have dealt with, but it was the young girl cowering behind his leg that surprised me the most. Her wide chocolate eyes peeked out at me as she clutched a stuffed rabbit to her chest, its faux fur matted with blood.

"What did you do?" I growled at Akil.

He narrowed his flame-filled eyes at me and then crouched down to face the little girl. What followed had me gaping open mouthed at the both of them. Akil, his hands clasped around the little girl's upper arms, looked her in the eyes and said, "I'm sorry you witnessed... that. I had no choice. Muse will protect you. She's tougher than she looks."

The little girl blinked and clutched her bunny tight against her chest.

"I have to leave you now. You'll be okay." He smiled and toned down the fire in his eyes. He couldn't do much about the blood and general dishevelled state of him, but she didn't seem to notice. "Do as Muse says. Promise me."

"Okay. Will you come back?" she asked in a tiny mouse-like voice.

Akil took too long to answer. I glared at him. "Yes, he'll come back."

Straightening, Akil gave the girl a slight shove in my direction. She took a few steps inside and peered over her rabbit at my lounge as though looking at an alien world.

I flung my attention back to Akil, who now stood a few steps back from my door. "What the hell, Akil?" I hissed, trying to avoid rousing my neighbours.

"Just look after her, Muse." The softness of his tone set off half a dozen alarm bells in my mind. "I know you will."

"You can't just turn up after two months and dump a little girl on me. I don't know how to look after children. What am I supposed to do? Who is she? Why do you look like you've gone ten rounds with a Hellhound?"

Akil ran a hand through his mussed hair, and I noticed it tremble. How could I not? Akil didn't behave like this. He was the suave bastard on the TV, not the beaten-up wreck at my door. "Just keep the demons away from her."

I gulped back a rising knot of panic. "What? Why are demons after her? She's just a little girl."

"As were you, once." He glanced down the hall. A door-lock rattled; one of my neighbors had decided to investigate the commotion in the hallway.

"Akil..." I warned, lowering my voice to a stage whisper, "are you telling me she's a half-blood?"

He met my stare. "Do the right thing."

"Is everything all right, Charlie dear?" My neighbour, Rosaline, asked, her English accent neat and clean. I poked my head around the door and gave her a sweet smile. She was a delightful sixty-something widow who can't help caring a little too much about me. She saw me as some sort of lost lamb. I'd shared tea and cake with her.

"Everything's fine, Rosa, I was just talking with my friend here... Not to worry. I'm sorry if we disturbed you."

"No-no..." She grinned and gave me a quaint royal wave. "As long as you're okay, my dear. Oh, would you mind taking a look at my television? I can't seem to change the channels. All I get is the Discovery channel, and I've had just about enough of rampaging wildebeest for one day."

"Yup, sure thing. Will do..." I waved and watched her plod back inside her apartment. Of course, Akil had made himself scarce when I turned back to face the spot he'd been standing in moments before.

I uttered a curse and then remembered my young guest and cursed again for swearing in front of a child. The little girl didn't seem to hear anyway. She wore a slip of a dress, several sizes too big for her skinny little body. Her socks were mismatched and her black patent leather shoes scuffed. I moved around her. She blinked wide, doe-eyes up at me. Her flushed cheeks, pink lips, curly mouse hair, and oval face suggested an age of maybe seven or eight years, and I inwardly cringed. I had no idea what I was supposed to do with her. Thankfully, the demon that smacked into my apartment window distracted me from the mundane question of how I was going to look after such a little girl.

I jerked around and saw a dark shadow slam against the window, leaving oily imprints on the glass and rattling the frame. Another clattering boom against the adjacent window snapped my attention across the lounge. Claws scratched at the glass, setting my teeth on edge. I couldn't quite see the demons—too human to focus on their ethereal forms—but whatever they were, they didn't appear to be able to break through. The symbols working their magic. Confidence comes before a fall. I had a few seconds of smug satisfaction when I heard a raucous cry coming from my bedroom. Jonesy blurred across the floor with a yowl, and following behind came a heaving cloud of black smoke. I'd left the bedroom window open.

My demon came to me like a blast of hot air from an oven. She'd already been lurking at the back of my mind, and now she butted up against my skin. The protection symbols prevented me from summoning all of her, nor could I use my element, but I had enough of her fire in my veins to see the prehistoric creature inside the miasmic shadow. I'd seen it before. They patroled the night sky in the netherworld, and they also made an appearance in most dinosaur reference books. Palaeontologists call them Pterosaurs. Demons call them *Venatores – Hunters.*

It teetered forward on its winged-arms and legs, claws scratching against my hardwood floors, and cast its beady-eyed glance around and then let out an ear-piercing screech. The little girl squeaked behind me and scurried into the corner of the room where she ducked down and tried to hug herself into a tiny, insignificant ball.

I pinned the hunter in my sights and snatched a kitchen knife from the rack. We were equally matched in height — which isn't saying much—although its claws and beak full of razor-edged teeth gave it the distinct advantage. It screeched at me, the brittle sound like a clatter of cymbals.

"I already have demon blood on my boots," I growled. "I'd really prefer it if I didn't have to wash it off my walls as well."

It swung its elongated head and tried to get a fix on the girl behind me. Skittering to one side, it flapped its wings and snapped its jaws, unconcerned by my threat. Another of its companions slammed into the lounge window, jarring the glass. The hunter jerked its head, acknowledging its companion's idiocy. I used its distraction and bolted around behind it. Attacking it head on would get me a face full of sharp teeth. Snatching its left wing, I used my own momentum to swing around behind it. Its beak swung around after me, the two of us pirouetting before I plunged the kitchen knife into its leathery hide. I still had hold of its wing and yanked it back as it bucked away. The knife slid out with a *sloosh.* Blood spurted. Its beak snapped at me, close enough to taste the fish-oil stench of its breath. I recoiled, ducked, and as it snapped over my head, I thrust the knife into its throat and tugged its throat out with a grunt of exertion. The hunter whipped around, wings flailing and claws tearing at the gaping wound in its neck. It stumbled and staggered about the lounge, rearranging my furniture, and then collapsed across my coffee table.

I dashed for the bedroom and slammed the window closed. Outside, the dark sky writhed with hunters. Any witnesses would only be able to see a cloud of black smoke against the night sky. Nothing too alarming.

I stepped back from the window and became acutely aware of the cooling demon blood plastering my top against my skin. It virtually covered me from head to toe. I grimaced and walked gingerly back into the lounge, clothes chaffing. The hunter still lay sprawled across my coffee table, its blood dripping off the edges and pooling on my floor. How to dispose of a demon in Boston? Call the Institute, but that would mean answering a lot of questions about who my little guest was.

She'd gone. The corner she'd been cowering in was empty, and my apartment door hung ajar. I lunged for the door and remembered I was covered in blood. Quickly, I tossed the knife into the kitchen sink and tore off my clothes while retrieving some jeans and a tank top from my bedroom. I was still tugging on my boots and doing up my fly as I sprinted from my apartment and hurried down the stairs.

Akil left her with me, and within the space of five minutes, I'd lost her. If she got outside, the hunters would tear into her. I stumbled down the last few steps and brushed by Louise, another of my neighbours.

"Hey, Charlie, are you okay?" Her Irish-Boston accent chimed.

"Yeah, all good..." I tossed her a wave over my shoulder, heading for the main door, and then stopped and turned. "Did you see a little girl come by here?"

Louise gaped at me. She was dressed for a night out in matching tartans and lace up Doc Martin boots. Her faux fur jacket was so white it would have glowed under UV. Not much shocked Lou, but she'd lost her voice now. I'd forgotten to wash the blood off my face. She gestured at me, mouth open. "Is that...?"

"Oh, it's not real." I grinned brightly. "I was playing dead with my... erm niece. Y'know. Ketchup."

She screwed up her face, not believing me for a second. "Yeah, she went outside. Do you need some help?"

"Nope. I'm fine. We're fine. Which way did she go?"

"Toward Sidewalk Cafe."

"Thanks." I didn't wait around for more questions and just hoped I'd remembered to shut my apartment door. If anyone saw the demon draped over my coffee table, I'd have a whole lot of explaining to do, not to mention losing my deposit. I'd only been in the apartment a month and was technically meant to be making a good impression.

Early Friday evenings in Boston are as busy as weekday rush hours. I lived in the heart of South Boston, a trendy upmarket district currently undergoing something of a popularity revival. Southies liked the friendly neighbourhood atmosphere of the place and feared the desirable ambiance had attracted too many well-to-dos who would spoil what made the place special. I couldn't comment, being a newbie myself, but I did like the close knit community. It felt like home, and for me, that was a damn miracle.

The many cafes and bars were opening for the evening, but the sidewalk was still sparse enough for me to spot the little girl weaving her way through the tourists and after-work crowds. I glanced up at the sky and immediately saw the flock of hunters passing overhead. They had all the finesse of the black smoke from *Lost*, and I winced. If this went public, my boss at the Institute, Adam Harper, would lock me down and take my freelance status away. I had to control this. Dealing with Demons was, after all, in my job description.

I didn't have my Baretta Pico sidearm or my Enforcer ID. I just looked like a crazy half-dressed woman with blood on her face chasing down a little girl. Could the situation get any worse? Breaking into a run, I raced through the crowd, muttering apologies as I brushed a few arms and bumped a few shoulders. I caught glimpses of the girl's ringlets and shiny black shoes, but she was quickly pulling away, able to thread herself through the crowd unnoticed.

I heard a hunter's clattering battle-cry and saw it make a dive toward the sidewalk. Someone screamed, also noticing what they'd see as a peculiar cloud rushing downward. I saw the hunter, its wings tucked in, beak open. It would slam into the little girl and make short work of her fragile human flesh. I couldn't let that happen. I summoned my demon, releasing my mental hold and allowing her to flood through my skin, flesh and bone. She broke over me, pooled fire in my heart and flushed my veins with ethereal energy. Still running, I lifted a hand and called to the heat slumbering in the buildings on either side of the street. Boston is a reservoir of heat, as are all cities. Human activity generated more than enough heat for me to play with. I called to it and felt it slough off the buildings and ooze upward from the earth.

I wrapped the heat around me, spooling it down my arm and cast it outward, sending a ball of fire over the heads of the crowd to slam into the hunter. Fire washed over the body of the beast, embracing every inch of it. It screamed an air-shattering cry and then tumbled out of the sky and thumped against the sidewalk, narrowly missing the unsuspecting crowd.

I didn't have time to explain to the gawping people what was happening. They would already know it was demon related. The news and events of late had prepped them, but that didn't make it any easier to witness when the truth smacks down right in front of you.

I dropped off the sidewalk and ran along the road, casting another bolt of fire into the sky where a second writhing mass of darkness dive boomed the fleeing girl. "Hey!" I called. If I could get her to stop, I could turn and deal with the hunters in one go.

She veered left, down a narrow one-way cobbled street. The malicious black smoke funneled after her with me in tow. A quick glance behind told me we were virtually alone. I called all of my demon now and let her ride over my human flesh and clothes, consuming all of me. My one ruined wing burst from my back, and with it I called all of the available heat. It rode higher, swamping the ground around me and rushing up my legs, draping me in flame. I stopped, planted my feet firmly on the cobbles, and thrust my hands skyward, launching with them a storm of orange and blue flame. The hunters scattered, but chaos fire has an intent all of its own, and those that fled soon found tendrils of flame licking up their limbs. Pain thumped me in the chest. I grunted. My power stalled. Damn parasite. With a snarl I doubled my efforts. The black cloud burst apart from within and lit up the sky in a mass of fire strikes. Burned hunters slapped against the road. Some bounced off cars, starting half a dozen alarms. I wasn't very good at subtle.

I finished off a few stragglers with some well-aimed fireballs and then jogged down the street, shaking off my demon with each step so that, when I finally found the girl curled tightly into the crook of an old tree, I was myself again, complete with blood splatters.

I saw the whites of her eyes and tried to offer her my best, most friendly smile. In the distance, sirens announced the arrival of the authorities, and no doubt the Institute would be included in that response. I crouched down and offered her my hand.

"It's okay," I said. "The man who brought you to me, Akil. He was right. I'll keep you safe, but you gotta stay close to me."

She blinked and hugged her bunny tightly.

I needed to get back to my apartment where the symbols would hide us both from demons. If I could get home, clean up the mess waiting for me, then maybe the girl might open up to me and explain just what the freakin' hell was going on. I'd call Akil too. I had no idea what he expected me to do that he couldn't and his 'just look after her' explanation wouldn't cut it.

"What's your name?" I asked.

She blinked again, and her lips tightened. She didn't trust me, and I couldn't blame her. I had no idea what she'd witnessed with Akil, but given the last fifteen minutes we'd spend together, I'd have a hard time trusting anyone if I was her.

"Shall we do this properly?" I shuffled a bit closer. "My human name is Charlie, but my real name is Muse." I held out my hand, inviting her to shake it.

"That's a funny name." She had a slight accent that slurred her words.

"Yeah, a not-so-funny guy gave it to me."

"I have a funny name too."

"Oh, and what's your name?"

"Dawn." She held out her rabbit. "This is Missus Floppy."

"Dawn is a lovely name." I shook Floppy's paw and then Dawn's tiny cold hand. "I'm very pleased to meet you both. Would you like to meet my cat, Jonesy? He loves tickles behind his ears."

Dawn clutched her bunny against her chest once more and smiled. "Okay, Miss Muse."

Darkest Before Dawn ~ Chapter Two

Adam only left the safety of the Institute complex when the world was about to end or I was involved. I wasn't surprised when he filed in behind the clean-up crew. I leaned against the kitchen cabinets, arms crossed, watching the blue overall-wearing Institute employees surround the dead demon in the middle of my lounge and set about removing its carcass and copious amounts of drying blood from my apartment.

Adam gave my apartment a visual assessment, his gaze lingering on the framed symbols as though inspecting them for any errors. He took his time, observing his crew doing what they did best. He would only look at me when necessary. While I waited, I watched him, knowing he could feel my gaze all over him. He was a substantial man, both in demeanour and presence. He dressed casually in blue jeans and a vertical blue striped shirt. Suits weren't him, despite spending the majority of his days behind a desk. His greying hair should have been too long for a man of his middle-years, but he somehow made it look distinguished. His warm brown eyes instantly disarmed anyone who didn't know him. He'd smile, ask you how your day was, right before he went for the jugular. He and I didn't get along.

Finally, after five minutes of rising tension, he turned those deceptive eyes on me. "I assume you're the fire demon who ran down the street in plain sight of half a dozen CCTV cameras and upward of fifty witnesses?"

Usually, he'd wait until he had me in his office before laying down the Institute law. Tonight, I was getting the no-holds-barred treatment.

Jonesy sat next to me on the kitchen counter, twitching tail dangling over the edge. My cat was an excellent judge of character.

"Would you prefer I let the flock of hunter demons eat the unsuspecting commuters?"

"I'd prefer a bit of discretion, Muse."

One of the blue-suit guys moved toward my bedroom. I tensed. "Nothing in there. It's all out here." The guy glanced at Adam, who nodded, and returned to the tacky pool of dark blood spreading across my floor.

Adam arched an eyebrow and crossed the room to my kitchenette. "I'm loathe to think you're hiding something from us."

"There's nothing left to hide, Adam." I made a point of meeting his stare. He wouldn't think I was laying it on thick. This was how we always danced.

"Have you heard from Stefan?"

Now I did flick my gaze away. "No."

"David Ryder?"

"No."

Stefan and Ryder had vanished after the event at Boston Gardens, and it remained an open wound between myself and the Institute. In fact, I believed Adam only kept me on to see if either Stefan or Ryder resurfaced around me. They hadn't. The last time I'd seen Stefan, he'd accused me of killing his sister. He thought I'd deliberately drugged him to subdue his demon and believed I'd sided with his nemesis, Akil. I'd left Stefan with Ryder as he struggled to contain his demon half, and I'd helped Akil drive the Larkwrari demon back through the tear in the veil. Ryder would see Stefan safe. Either that or Stefan would lash out and kill him. Given the madness that had come over Stefan since his lengthy stay in the netherworld, I hadn't ruled it out. That thought—among many others — kept me awake at night.

"Need I remind you, we have authority over your living arrangements and career?"

I ground my teeth. Hate is such a strong word. I liked to think myself incapable of hate, but I was only half-human, and I hated Adam Harper with every fiber of my being, including my demon half. It was only because I'd made a deal with Ryder not to torch the Institute or spontaneously combust Adam that I'd refrained from doing both.

"Why were the hunter demons here?"

I shrugged. That was a good question, and the sudden change of direction caught me off guard. "They must have been sent by someone who knew where I lived."

"Wouldn't your protection symbols hide you from any such threat?" He nodded toward my framed prints and the swirling interwoven markings in each.

He was right. Those symbols kept me off the demon radar. "What can I say? They found me. I dealt with it."

Any number of demons could have sent the hunters after me. They despised my half-blood nature, detested Enforcers, and all had taken my general lack of willingness to die as an affront to their demon egos. Hell, even Akil had sent demon-nasties after me in the past, although he appeared to have resolved his homicidal tendencies since I'd literally sucked the life out of him. My immortal brother could have sent them, but I'd learned assassins weren't his style. Valenti was more likely to run me through with a sword. He liked his sibling-rivalry up close and personal.

I shuddered and shoved thoughts of my half-brother to the back of my mind. Of all the crap I had to deal with, I really didn't need the spectre of Val occupying my thoughts.

Besides, the hunters hadn't been after me. They'd wanted the girl, and Akil had led them straight here. Adam wasn't to know that, so I played dumb and shouldered the blame.

He waited for me to offer up some sort of explanation that he was happy with, but when it became clear after several minutes of silence, that I had no intention of elaborating, he made his excuses to leave. "Next time, Muse, tone down the fires from hell. I have enough trouble trying to manage demon sightings all over the city. I don't need one of my Enforcers in the headlines, especially a half-blood."

"Yes boss," I grumbled with zero conviction.

It took the Institute team an hour to wipe clean my lounge. Glad to see the back of them, I hurried them out the door with the disinfectant still drying and immediately checked on Dawn. She sat perched on the end of my bed, legs dangling over the edge and didn't look as though she'd moved since I'd told her to stay put and stay quiet.

"Who was that?" she asked, following close behind me as I returned to the now spotless lounge.

"They're not the type of people you want to be getting involved with, given their history with half-bloods." I glanced down at Dawn. She stood inside my personal space, peering up at me, Missus Floppy loose in her hand. "That is what you are, right?"

"What's a half-blood?"

Okay, we really needed to talk. "Are you hungry?" I asked with a smile.

She nodded.

"Chill out on the couch, and I'll sort us some food." She skewed her wary gaze to the couch, regarding it suspiciously. "Sit. It won't bite."

She crossed the lounge with tight steps and hitched herself onto the couch. Curling herself into a tight ball, she sunk into the cushions as though hoping they'd swallow her up.

I flicked on the TV and channel surfed to something non-offensive, watching Dawn's eyes widen to absorb the images.

I checked my fridge for food and found it distinctly lacking. I couldn't cook. I tried it once. Or rather, Akil attempted to teach me, but I'd struggled with the whole idea of heating up a stove when I could use my element. Needless to say, toast is flammable, and eggs explode when heated using chaos energy. Who knew? Akil had found it highly amusing while I'd considered myself a failure. Things had changed since then, but I still shied away from cooking.

Two microwave meals it was then.

"You're safe here, Dawn," I said, preparing the frozen meals. "As long as you stay inside these markings, the demons can't find you."

"They did before."

I glanced back at her. She was watching a wildlife program, something about chipmunks, overlaid with dramatic music. "They only work on higher demons, the big guys with conscious thoughts. Some of the little ones still get through, if they know what they're looking for. Plus, I left the window open. Don't do that. It breaks the seal. Same with the front door. So, we just have to stay here until we figure out what's going on."

The microwave pinged. I managed to turn the desiccated peas, carrots and shoe-leather meat onto plates so it looked partially edible, and carried them over to Dawn.

She didn't bother with cutlery and dove right in with her fingers.

"Careful, it's hot." She didn't seem to care. Eyes darting between chipmunks and her plate of food, she tucked in as though I'd served her a gourmet meal. My meal untouched, I watched her closely, finding myself transfixed by this quiet little girl. Why did Akil have her? What had happened to him? He appeared to care about her. Why leave her with me? Why were the hunters after her? I wanted to demand answers from her, but I wasn't that heartless. The interrogation could wait.

Without thinking, I reached out and swept a lock of her curly hair behind her ear. My element seeped outward, as it sometimes did around demons. It happened often enough that I barely noticed it. It wasn't invasive, just a curious touch, but Dawn jerked back and glared at me as though I'd slapped her.

I snatched my hand back. "It's okay." I'd felt a little stirring of the energy slumbering inside her. She was a half-blood. Had she been full-demon, my skin would have crawled by now, plus she wouldn't have been able to enter my apartment. Now that I'd sensed the power in her, I knew for certain she was like me. "We're the same, you and I."

"The man who saved me, he says you're strong."

He would, I thought. Demons only care for power, and considering Akil was the Prince of Greed, he liked nothing better than overflowing chaotic energies. "He *saved* you?"

She blinked. "He told me not to tell you."

That sounded more like Akil. I smiled. "It's okay, you can trust me."

She shook her head, ringlets bobbing. I wasn't going to push it. Not yet. But I needed answers. If Akil was using this little girl to get to me, I'd take my overflowing chaotic energies and use them to go nuclear on his ass.

"Do you think you can trust Akil?"

She shook her head. Good girl. "He's strong too," she replied. Her eyes unfocused, and what little color she had drained from her face. "I don't want to go back," she whispered.

"You don't have to go anywhere you don't want to. I promise you that." I took her dainty hand in mine and gave it a squeeze. She squeezed back, eyes glistening. There were memories in my head just like hers. I knew what it meant to be a half-blood abomination among demons. If Dawn had endured half of what I'd been subjected to, she was lucky to be alive, never mind coherent.

The parasitic demon knotted around my heart, tightened. I tensed and sucked in a sharp breath, tugging my hand from Dawn's to clench it against my chest.

My cell phone rang, providing a welcome distraction from the hideous creature hitching a ride inside me. I left Dawn watching the chipmunks and answered the call.

"Charlie, it's Detective Coleman." I could hear him walking outside on a street somewhere. A car door slammed. "Dead demon call just came in. I'm about to head down to a penthouse in Battery Wharf to seal it off—the usual—and thought you'd want to know."

"Hey," I replied with just a hint of enthusiasm. "I'm fine, thanks for asking." Coleman worked homicide at Boston PD, but he also got lumbered with cases of suspected demon involvement. I was on his speed dial as the phone-a-friend for anything suspiciously inhuman. "Why would I want to know?" Battery Wharf was an exclusive luxury apartment complex. Not somewhere you'd expect a demon to turn up dead, but things were changing. Demons were everywhere, so the press said.

"Well, for one, you're the Institute, and I'm obliged to tell the Institute when one of your ki– when a demon turns up dead."

I caught that little slip of the tongue but let it go. "Noted, and?"

"You're acquainted with the apartment owner. Akil Vitalis."

Darkest Before Dawn
#3 The Veil Series
Coming Winter 2014

***

Want More?

Visit the **website** for exclusive access to character bio's and **Muse's personal blog:**

www.theveilseries.co.uk

The Veil Series has a **Facebook** page where you can comment on the book, read character interviews, enjoy exclusive updates and artwork, chat with likeminded readers and the author:

www.facebook.com/theveilseries

If you enjoyed Devil May Care, please **review the book on Amazon and Goodreads.** Let other readers know what you thought, and who's your favorite guy:

Stefan or Akil?

ABOUT THE AUTHOR

Visit: www.pippadacosta.com
Twitter: @pippadacosta
Facebook: www.facebook.com/pippadacosta

Born in Tonbridge, Kent in 1979, Pippa's family moved to the South West of England where she grew up among the dramatic moorland and sweeping coastlands of Devon & Cornwall. With a family history brimming with intrigue, complete with Gypsy angst on one side and Jewish survivors on another, she has the ability to draw from a patchwork of ancestry and use it as the inspiration for her writing. Happily married and the Mother of two little girls, she resides on the Devon & Cornwall border.

ACKNOWLEDGMENTS

To the fans of the first book, Beyond The Veil: Thank You so much for joining me on Muse's journey. Your heartfelt reactions to Muse and her story made all the difference and kept me writing into the wee hours.
To my still-suffering husband:
You married a writer; sorry about that.

FEEDBACK

As an independent author, your comments are extremely important to me. Please do get in touch, even if it's just to say 'Hi'. Your reviews are like gold dust to authors. You don't need to wax-lyrical, just a few words will do.
Show your love and keep writers writing.

Made in the USA
Columbia, SC
17 March 2019